METHUEN · ENGLISH · TEXTS
GENERAL EDITOR · JOHN DRAKAKIS

JOSEPH CONRAD

Selected Literary Criticism
and
The Shadow-Line

METHUEN · ENGLISH · TEXTS
GENERAL EDITOR · JOHN DRAKAKIS

JOSEPH CONRAD

*Selected Literary Criticism
and
The Shadow-Line*

Edited by Allan Ingram

METHUEN · LONDON AND NEW YORK

First published in 1986 by
Methuen & Co. Ltd
11 New Fetter Lane
London EC4P 4EE

Published in the USA by
Methuen & Co.
in association with Methuen, Inc.
29 West 35th Street
New York NY 10001

Introduction, Critical commentary and
Notes © 1986 Allan Ingram

Typeset in Great Britain by
Scarborough Typesetting Services
and printed by
Richard Clay, The Chaucer Press
Bungay, Suffolk

British Library Cataloguing in
Publication Data

Conrad, Joseph
Joseph Conrad: selected literary criticism:
The shadow-line. – (Methuen English
texts)
1. Literature, Modern – 19th century –
History and criticism   2. Literature,
Modern – 20th century – History and
criticism
I. Title   II. Ingram, Allan
823'.912 [F]   PR6005.04

ISBN 0 416 39350 0

Library of Congress Cataloging in
Publication Data

Conrad, Joseph, 1857–1924.
Selected literary criticism.
(Methuen English texts)
1. Criticism.   I. Ingram, Allan.
II. Title.   III. Series.
PR6005.04A6   1986b
823'.912   86–12582

ISBN 0 416 39350 0

*To Lena Gledhill
and in memory of Bill*

Contents

Acknowledgements

I am grateful to Cambridge University Press and to Duke University Press for permission to reproduce copyright material as detailed in the Introduction (p. 19). My thanks, too, to my wife and daughters for their patient support, to John Cox, Shelagh Frawley, Jan Hewitt and Richard Prior for their help and advice, and to Duncan Graham, who imparted to me some of his own love for the works of Conrad. My debt to the researches of Norman Sherry will be apparent in the pages that follow: it is one shared by all those who write about Conrad. I am indebted, too, to John Drakakis for his encouragement and for suggestions that were crucial to the shaping of the material in this volume.

A.S.I.

Introduction

On 22 January 1910, after two years' work on what he had intended as a break from *Chance*, Conrad finally finished the manuscript of *Under Western Eyes*. It had been begun, like many of his novels, as a short story, to be called simply 'Razumov', in which he would try 'to capture the very soul of things Russian' (Jean-Aubry, 1927, II, p. 64). Some 130,000 words later, Conrad was physically, mentally and emotionally exhausted. His wife, Jessie, wrote to their friend David Meldrum:

> The novel is finished, but the penalaty [*sic*] has to be paid. Months of nervous strain have ended in a complete nervous breakdown. Poor Conrad is very ill and Dr Hackney says it will be a long time before he is fit for anything requiring mental exertion. I know both you and dear Mrs Meldrum will feel every sympathy with him. There is the M.S. complete but uncorrected and his fierce refusal to let even I touch it. It lays on a table at the foot of his bed and he lives mixed up in the scenes and holds converse with the characters.
>
> I have been up with him night and day since Sunday week and he, who is usually so depressed by illness, maintains he is not ill, and accuses the Dr and I of trying to put him into an asylum.
>
> (Blackburn, 1958, p. 192)

Quite clearly, Conrad's collapse was much more serious than either his frequent bouts of ill health and depression or the exhaustion

1

attending the conclusion of a long period of intense application. Conrad, in fact, seemed to be close to death, alarming Jessie by the irregularity of his breathing, by his cold, heavy sweats, and by 'faintly murmuring the words of the burial service'. He would talk to himself in Polish, and would often be found 'tottering' around the room 'in search of something he had dreamed of' (Conrad, Jessie, 1935, pp. 143 – 4).

Some of Conrad's own correspondence at the end of the previous year gives hints of the breakdown to come, and of some of the pressures under which he was working. To William Rothenstein ('Dear Old Will'), he wrote in November:

> The last year and a half has been like hell, from which I have just emerged thanks to a good volunteer doctor who took me in hand, I believe, only just in time. But twenty months have gone already over a novel and now I *must* finish it – or I am totally undone. I daren't budge from the desk. (Jean-Aubry, 1927, II, p. 103)

And he went on to add, 'The fourteenth year of my writing life draws to and end, and when I look at the result I am appalled. I speak from a worldly point of view. . . . And there are just 14 published volumes. Not a great tale (ibid., pp. 103 – 4). To John Galsworthy, too, he had written in description of his working day:

> I walk a couple of hours and sit for no more than 10 to 11 hours. I think that's strain enough for a man who knows that when this bout is over, there can be no lying back (unless in illness) and that this sort of thing must be kept up, and moreover that even if kept up, it won't be good enough anyhow. (ibid., pp. 105 – 6)

Hard labour, then (as he wrote to Norman Douglas, 'I envy the serene fate and the comparative honesty of the gentlemen in gray who live in Dartmoor' (ibid., p. 105)), together with abiding financial hardship, were the twin evils of Conrad's existence. His fourteen years had already produced most of his masterpieces – *The Nigger of the 'Narcissus'*, *Heart of Darkness*, *Lord Jim*, *Youth*, *Typhoon*, *Nostromo*, *The Secret Agent* – among the '14 published volumes', yet reviews, while including high and intelligent praise, had been consistently uneven, and in material terms he was so much the failure that he had been reduced to borrowing from friends – Galsworthy, for example – and to building up huge debts to his agent, J. B. Pinker, on account of future copy. And he could, as he observed to Galsworthy, see nothing in the future other than a repetition of this same pattern of effort and failure.

There are other features, though, of Conrad's breakdown which seem more to do with the novel *Under Western Eyes* itself, and with the issues he found it necessary to meet in the writing, issues that went right to the heart of his own past and of what he had made of himself. In a second letter to Rothenstein he had written:

> Here I've been 2 years writing a novel which is not finished. Two years! Of which surely one half has been illness, complicated by a terrible moral stress. Imagine yourself painting with the Devil jogging your elbow *all the time*. But you, who are one of the most intelligent men I know, or know of, and a stylist also . . . will know what a torture that sort of thing is when the effort and hindrance are mental.   (Jean-Aubry, 1927, II, p. 104)

For Conrad, capturing 'the very soul of things Russian' was coming very close to home. In 1857, when he was born Józef Teodor Konrad Korzeniowski, in Berdyczów, Poland was (and was still, in 1910) partitioned between Austria, Prussia and Russia, of which by far the most aggressive occupier and the most hated by the Polish people was Russia. Conrad's parentage was Polish nobility on both sides, with a strong tradition of patriotism. When Apollo Korzeniowski was exiled for his anti-Russian literary activities to Vologda, 250 miles northwest of Moscow, both Conrad's mother Ewa and Conrad himself, then aged 4, went with him. It was to be the end of the family. Conrad fell seriously ill on the journey. His recovery, however, was followed in 1865 by the death of Ewa and, four years later, of Apollo. Conrad, alone at the head of the cortège, walked behind his father's coffin through the streets of Kracòw. For the next five years, under the care of his maternal uncle, Tadeusz Bobrowski, the salutary lessons of his father's shortcomings and failure and of his mother's wasted life were rehearsed for him. When he left, in 1874, to his uncle's surprise and against his wishes, for Marseilles and the life of a seaman, Conrad took his first step towards the making of himself, a foreigner living and speaking and working, quite literally, under western eyes.

Conrad's sea career, while remarkable (though not as remarkable as what he was later to make of it), was not, however, a life of complete independence, for his uncle Tadeusz had constantly to supplement his earnings, and felt obliged, too, to offer stern warnings and advice over his fecklessness, and to point out Conrad's proximity to his family's pattern of failure. And yet it was, in a most important way, the great gamble that paid off, for the 'Devil' of family and national failure, as Conrad rose to qualify as third mate, second, first, and finally in 1886 as master in the British Merchant Navy, could be lost sight of beneath the steady roll of achievement in the service of the sea. (Significantly, in later accounts Conrad overlooks his initial failure in more than one of his merchant service examinations.)

The sea, apparently, was the making of Conrad, giving him a sense of self and a security that was lacking in his Polish childhood, just as the sea also gives 'generously' to Tom Lingard in *An Outcast of the Islands*, but gives him, too, what is described as 'his absurd faith in himself' (1896, p. 13). One aspect of the sea life is particularly emphasized among the reminiscences and recreated episodes of *The Mirror of the Sea* and *A Personal Record*, the two volumes Conrad wrote dealing with his life and 'the somewhat exceptional psychology of my sea-going' (1912a, p. 119), and that is the achievement of sailing and of the mastery of the sea. A ship, he says in *Mirror of the Sea*, 'is a creature which we have brought into the world, as it were on purpose to keep us up to the mark' (1906, p. 28), and

> the attainment of proficiency, the pushing of your skill with attention to the most delicate shades of excellence, is a matter of vital concern. Efficiency of a practically flawless kind may be reached naturally in the struggle for bread. But there is something beyond – a higher point, a subtle and unmistakable touch of love and pride beyond mere skill; almost an inspiration which gives to all work that finish which is almost art – which *is* art.
>
> (ibid., p. 24)

Moreover, 'To forget one's self, to surrender all personal feeling in the service of that fine art, is the only way for a seaman to the faithful discharge of his trust' (ibid., p. 30). Conrad found, in the life of the seaman, conditions in which he could, if not 'forget', then at least 'surrender' his legacy of frustration, failure and loneliness.

Conrad's sea years, of course, provided him, either directly or indirectly through the tales he picked up, with a significant proportion of his later literary output. But there are other aspects of his being able to forget himself 'in the service of that fine art' that are equally influential on Conrad the novelist, for whom, like the Charlie Marlow of *Heart of Darkness* and *Lord Jim*, fidelity, work and craftsmanship are among the cardinal virtues, literary as much as nautical. Not the least of these features is the sailor's precision in the use of language. Early in *Mirror of the Sea* Conrad criticizes the journalist, who 'almost invariably "casts" his anchor'. An anchor, says Conrad, 'is not cast, and to take a liberty with technical language is a crime against the clearness, precision, and beauty of perfected speech'. Such technical language, for Conrad, seems to bear in itself many of the virtues of tradition and application he associates with the sea life, for it is 'an instrument wrought into perfection by ages of experience, a flawless thing for its purpose' (1906, p. 13). It has been 'created by simple men with keen eyes for the real aspect of the things they see in their trade', and it therefore 'achieves the just expression seizing upon the essential, which is the ambition of the artist in words' (ibid., p. 21). Conrad, we must remember, is writing here with the benefit of hindsight: he *is* an artist in words and has been for over ten years. Yet he was also a seaman, and would not have been the writer he became had it not been for the influence of his sea years; for the sea was the element in which the Polish refugee immersed himself to emerge with not only a new sense of achievement, but a new awareness of values and a new language. If the achievement enabled him to take the new gamble of giving up the sea for a life of literature, the values and the language were to shape the character itself of his new career.

This is one side of the man who, by the time of his breakdown, had produced several of the twentieth century's most significant literary achievements. But there is another side. It was Conrad who described himself as 'homo duplex', and the idea of the double man has been picked up by later critics (Karl, 1979; Said, 1966; Watts, 1982).

The English novelist of 52, married to an Englishwoman, with two English sons and a wide circle of English literary friends, the English ex-master-mariner, jabbering in Polish during his breakdown gives some idea of his deep-seated doubleness, of how the devil at his elbow had never really been forgotten, but only evaded. Again, Marlow's insistence in *Heart of Darkness* on finding oneself in work (1902, p. 85) is matched by Conrad's remarking of Charles Gould in *Nostromo* that action 'is consolatory. It is the enemy of thought and the friend of flattering illusion' (1904, p. 66). Even the sea itself, where Conrad's own early work was done, can become, in the epigraph to *The Shadow-Line*, the '*grand miroir/De mon désespoir*'. A significant number of his protagonists do go through periods of deepest despair – Kurtz, Jim, the Captain in *The Shadow-Line* – and several actually commit suicide, which Conrad himself attempted in Marseilles in 1878, a time when gambling debts and his inability to secure permanent employment made his new venture seem doomed to failure. In literature, too, Conrad's doubleness frequently takes away as much as he appears to give. It is Ford Madox Ford (with whom Conrad had finally broken in 1909 after a close friendship and collaboration) who observes of Conrad that 'few men in self-revelations and prefaces have ever so contrived under an aspect of lucidity to throw over themselves veils of confusion' (Ford, 1924, p. 232). And of the very act of writing, we find Conrad caught between the toil of permanent labour and the agony of not working, what he describes to Galsworthy as 'losing my footing in deep waters' (Jean-Aubry, 1927, I, p. 322), an image which itself suggests that writing, far from being a pleasure to him, is rather a matter of keeping afloat, of trying, as he says in the same letter, 'to keep despair under'. Even when his writing is progressing well, he can refer to it in very ambiguous phrasing, as to *Heart of Darkness*, which is growing 'like the geni out of the bottle' (cited by Karl, 1979, p. 473).

Ford's comment on Conrad's evasive lucidity is picked up in Edward Said's book *Joseph Conrad and the Fiction of Autobiography*. He speaks of Conrad 'hiding himself within rhetoric' in his fiction, and he finds the reason for this in Conrad's 'immense struggle with himself'. His prose, when it is 'extravagant or chatty', is so because it is 'the easiest way to conceal the embarrassments and the difficulties

6

of an overwhelmingly untidy existence as a French-speaking, self-exiled, extremely articulate Pole, who had been a sailor and was now . . . a writer of so-called adventure stories' (Said, 1966, p. 4). If Conrad's life at sea, shipping where he could with crews of mixed nationalities, was carried out self-consciously under western eyes, then his life as a writer, often drawing on those sea experiences, and conducted in one of his acquired languages, was equally self-conscious, equally the object of critical observation. Losing oneself, whether in the craft of ships or of fiction, was equally the evasion of a deep-seated uncertainty, and keeping afloat, whether on a surface of water or one of words, equally a matter of avoiding the despair beneath.

And yet, as Frederick Karl in his biography of Conrad observes, 'personal weakness could feed aesthetic needs, in that very reversal of elements which is so essential to artistic transmutation' (1979, p. 324). One significant area in which we see this is in the 'so-called adventure stories'. William Blackwood, the Edinburgh publisher and owner of *Blackwood's Magazine* (familiarly known as *Maga*), continued to publish Conrad's early work because he expected him to become, with maturity, a writer of the patriotic adventure stories, like Stevenson's and Kipling's, of which Blackwood could wholeheartedly approve. Like many contemporaries, he was expecting something that Conrad could not and would not give. It is Leggatt in 'The secret sharer' who says 'we are not living in a boy's adventure tale' (1912b, p. 131), and here, if anywhere, he speaks for Conrad. More than any other modern English novelist, Conrad's own early years resembled the material of an adventure story, and yet he was, fortunately, one of the least suited, temperamentally, to use them as such. He quotes in approval to Blackwood the remark of a reviewer of *Youth* (elsewhere identified as Sir Arthur Quiller-Couch) that it is 'after all . . . a story for boys yet – ' and, picking up the 'yet' he goes on to stress what he has made out of 'the material of a boys' story', just as in *Heart of Darkness* he has made 'of that story something quite on another plane than an anecdote of a man who went mad in the Centre of Africa' (Blackburn,1958, p. 154; see also p. 138, n.4). Frederick Karl points out:

While we must recognize how Conrad depended on certain conventions of the adventure story, we must stress his departure from

7

melodrama and a debased romanticism. His reliance on passivity, inertness, immobility is one of his major achievements in reshaping the romantic sense of adventure. (1979, p. 452n.)

That Conrad was able to achieve this – the rendering of the material of adventure in a way that brings out quite other features than the adventurous – is in large part due to the temperament which sent him in 1874 to a self-exile of uncertainty and activity. When the arena for adventure is also the 'element' for evasion, when the carrying out of heroic actions is also the hiding of a deeply feared sense of failure, then the account of those actions will not be the conventionally melodramatic one of deeds done for their own glory or the romanticized indulgence of creating a spotlessly ideal hero – the man that Kurtz or Jim might have been. Instead, we find, as Karl says, passivity, inertness, forced upon us both by the kind of stories Conrad writes – long periods of delay between the few scenes of action, of frequently tortured self-examination by protagonists (both of which are features of *The Shadow-Line*) – and by the way he writes them – layers of narrative, as in *Heart of Darkness*, to hold the reader back from the experience, dislocation of plot so that (and *Nostromo* is the supreme example here) the focus of the tale is never where the reader expects it to be. Action, in fact, is always undermined by Conrad's way of telling it, so far that the action comes to seem almost incidental to the true point of the story, which is something, or somewhere, between the self-consciousness of the protagonist, and the self-consciousness of the narrator, and the self-consciousness of Conrad himself, hiding behind walls of narration, behind the dislocation of time, denying, almost, that he has anything to do with the creation at all – losing himself, in other words, in the exercise of his craft.

For some critics, most notably E. M. Forster, this means that Conrad 'is misty in the middle as well as at the edges, that the secret casket of his genius contains a vapour rather than a jewel' (1936, p. 152). For others, and Conrad was always laying stress on the point, what Forster mistakes as 'vapour' is the single most important distinction between Conrad's work and the fiction of his more conventional contemporaries – the adventurous Stevenson, who had died in 1894, Anthony Hope, Rider Haggard, Kipling, and the 'plagiarizing' Buchan whom Conrad so scorned (see especially item 22 below). His refusal to offer easy solutions to the problems posed by the incomprehensible universe, a universe he has nevertheless brought by his created fictions 'into the ken of human understanding' (Schwarz, 1982, p. 89), is the refusal of a man who knew by experience the deceptiveness of action, with its impression of easy answers, and knew too the fundamental dishonesty of the conventional fictions he saw being produced by popular contemporaries. Such works – and he refers to several of them in the letter to Mme Zagórska included later as item 18 – are dishonest because things are not like that. The world and the people they deal with are make-believes in which straightforward action is possible and if there are no answers provided it is only because there are no questions either. Conrad's own work, on the contrary, as he writes to Blackwood – and again it is 'action' that is the focus for the argument – is rooted in the real, a real world, real sensations. His work, he says,

> is not an endless analysis of affected sentiments but in its essence it is action (strange as this affirmation may sound at the present time) nothing but action – action observed, felt and interpreted with an absolute truth to my sensations (which are the basis of art in literature) – action of human beings that will bleed to a prick, and are moving in a visible world. (item 25)

If we look at this assertion alongside a passage from *A Personal Record*, we see how far Conrad's 'action observed, felt and interpreted with an absolute truth to my sensations' means a reliance in his work upon memory, upon the life he has lived and also upon the temperament that has lived it and been shaped by it. This kind of man with this kind of past, these memories, will produce in his creative work this kind of imaginative rendering of what has been lived and remembered. That is Conrad's brand of authenticity, his guarantee of fictional truth.

> Only in men's imagination does every truth find an effective and undeniable existence. Imagination, not invention, is the supreme

master of art as of life. An imaginative and exact rendering of authentic memories may serve worthily that spirit of piety towards all things human which sanctions the conceptions of a writer of tales, and the emotions of the man reviewing his own experience.

(1912a, p. 25)

Fiction, for Conrad, deals with the real, but to apprehend the real entails the performance of an imaginative act towards 'all things human', rather than the mere surveying of unsorted facts. It is the task of the novelist to bring about the imaginative act through his rendering of the 'authentic'. 'And what is a novel', he asks, 'if not a conviction of our fellow-men's existence strong enough to take upon itself a form of imagined life clearer than reality and whose accumulated verisimilitude of selected episodes puts to shame the pride of documentary history?' (1912a, p. 15).

One consequence of this insistence on authentic imaginative rendering is, as Cedric Watts says, that we come closer to the real Conrad in his fiction, for all its complexities and personal evasiveness, than we do in any of his other apparently more conversational or confessional work.

This rendering of complexities shows that Conrad's nature is most fully present in his best works of fiction: there we come closer to the true Conrad than in letters or non-fictional writing – closer even than we would come if we were to interview him in person. The disciplines of good fiction are truth-seeking disciplines; and at its best Conrad's preoccupation with ambiguity and paradox is a sign neither of uncertainty nor of a fence-sitting attitude, but, on the contrary, of an uncompromising commitment to the true complexities of human experience.   (Watts, 1982, p. 58)

That there are dangers, mental and emotional, to such an uncompromising commitment, is apparent. In 1891, when he was still in the early stages of *Almayer's Folly*, and still a seaman, Conrad had written to his Polish relation in Paris, Marguerite Poradowska (who would later help him to his Congo post, as Marlow is helped in *Heart of Darkness*):

As for myself, I shall never need to be consoled for any act of my life, and this because I am strong enough to judge my own conscience rather than be its slave, as the orthodox would like to persuade us to be.

(Gee and Sturm, 1940, p. 36; original in French)

For nearly twenty years Conrad made good this assertion (which is picked up again, of course, in Captain Giles's remarks at the end of *The Shadow-Line*), performing, in Bernard Meyer's words, 'introspective journeys into the self that constitute the greatness of the impressionistic art he created during [those] years' (1967, p. 243). The significance of the *Under Western Eyes* breakdown (and this is part of Meyer's argument) is that Conrad was no longer 'strong enough'. The difficulties he expressed while writing the work, the 'mental' hindrances, the devil jogging his elbow, and the features of his breakdown – the talking in Polish to himself, the conversations with those authentically imagined characters – are the signs of a mind that has journeyed further than ever before, further even than the second-hand 'horror' of *Heart of Darkness*, right back to an emotionally insecure childhood, to 'the very soul of things Russian', to the root causes of why he left, or deserted, his homeland to remake himself on the lonely seas of the globe. He has journeyed, in fact, to the line between life and created fiction, that is to the very borders of sanity. Everything that had made Conrad what he was, including the fourteen years' hard labour, was collapsing around him. The achievements, apparently, were built on sand, or written in water, while the problems were as real as ever. As he wrote to Norman Douglas in December 1909, he envied 'the life convict' who at least could 'consider the account with his conscience closed' (Jean-Aubry, 1927, II, p. 105). Conrad's 'conscience' would apparently remain perpetually troubled and troubling, not judged once and for all, but coming always closer to making a 'slave of its owner'. To Galsworthy he wrote of his fear of 'the temptation to throw away the oar' (ibid., p. 106). Instead he became ill, showed signs of approaching – and perhaps even of wishing for, if we remember the muttered burial service – death, and, after a slow convalescence (even by May 1910 he can write to

Galsworthy only 'in 10 minute snatches' (ibid., p. 108)), returned to the inevitable writing.

Success, ironically, in popular terms was at this time already in his hands. *Chance*, which he had suspended for 'Razumov', was a market success in 1914, bringing a significant measure of financial ease. But it is with *Chance*, too, again ironically, given Conrad's frequent castigations of public taste (for example item 18 below), that most critics agree to place the beginning of Conrad's decline, as if the effort on *Under Western Eyes* had proved the last straw. This is not strictly accurate, for there are exceptions – notably *Victory* and *The Shadow-Line*. But it is quite true that the work produced after 1910 – *Chance* itself, *The Arrow of Gold*, *The Rescue*, finished after twenty-two years, and *The Rover* – is rarely of the power and controlled complexity of his greatest years. By then, though, Conrad has established himself as a 'modern', and had done so long before he became a popular success. Early reviews frequently lay stress on how different his work is from that of his contemporaries. *Almayer's Folly* 'departs altogether from the conventional happy ending, as well as from many other conventions of the novelist's art' (Sherry, 1973, p. 55); *An Outcast of the Islands* 'is unquestionably one of the strongest and most original novels of the year' (ibid., p. 79); *Lord Jim* is a work of 'remarkable originality and merit' (ibid., p. 111). It was something Conrad himself insisted upon and valued. His remarks to Blackwood are typical of the attitudes expressed over and over again in the earlier part of his writing career.

> I am *modern*, and I would rather recall Wagner the musician and Rodin the Sculptor who both had to starve a little in their day – and Whistler the painter who made Ruskin the critic foam at the mouth with scorn and indignation. They too have arrived. They had to suffer for being 'new'. And I too hope to find my place in the rear of my betters. But still – my place. (item 25)

Conrad's modesty, writing in 1902, before *Nostromo* and *The Secret Agent*, is perhaps understandable. T. S. Eliot, himself even more identified with the *'modern'* in literature and criticism than Conrad was, had no such qualms. He concludes his essay on 'Swinburne as poet' in *The Sacred Wood* with the declaration that 'the language which is . . . important to us is that which is struggling to digest and express new objects, new groups of objects, new feelings, new aspects, as, for instance, the prose of Mr. James Joyce or the earlier Conrad' (Eliot, 1920, p. 150).

'Modernism' is usually taken to refer to those developments in the arts which took place between the turn of this century and around 1930, and which produced radical changes both in the subject matter and in the techniques of literature, music and the fine arts across the whole of western Europe. What Eliot identifies here is one significant feature of literary modernism: the language developed by modern writers was required to be new to the extent that new 'objects', 'feelings' and 'aspects' were felt to demand suitable expression. That writers as different as Conrad and Joyce could be associated by Eliot in this way was partly due to their shared experimentation with style and form. But what validated such experimentation was the realization that the subject matter of art, what had been 'seen' by the artist, to adopt Conrad's own term (item 7 below), was important *only* because of the way he had seen it. New 'objects', 'feelings' and 'aspects' were in themselves no more memorable than the old. What stylistic and formal innovation could achieve was to make the reader see, as if for himself, different assumptions about reality than those of his everyday seeing, or those fostered by more conventional modes of narration. Here is the force of Meyer's term, 'impressionistic art' (1967, p. 243). Literary form and literary language, in the hands of Conrad or Joyce, can embody the seeing as much as the seen. If the world is seen by the artist as fragmentary, or in the light of one particular obsession, or as evidence of a hostile or meaningless universe, then that should be reflected in the form and style of the literary work. The coherence of such a work will differ markedly from, say, the traditional Victorian novel, living on, in Conrad's eyes, in the undemanding productions of Rider Haggard and Anthony Hope. Chronology, for example, is frequently distorted or ignored altogether; the single, stable narrator disappears. Instead a more complex coherence emerges, demanding from the reader patience and attentiveness: an intricate pattern of motifs, as in *Ulysses*; the multiple viewpoints of *Nostromo*; or what Cedric Watts calls the 'delayed decoding' (1982, p. 172) of, for instance, *The Secret Agent*. Modernism, in short, had profound implications, for the developing relation between the writer and what he saw meant not only new demands upon form and language, but a redefining of the whole relationship between writer and reader.

Watts speaks of Conrad as an 'intermediary between Romantic and Victorian traditions and the innovations of Modernism' (1982, p. 171). Certainly, during the period of Conrad's most innovative writing, the major figures of English literary modernism, Joyce, Lawrence and Woolf in the novel, Yeats, Eliot and Pound in poetry, were yet to produce their most original and challenging work. And it is with this background in mind that we should approach Conrad's criticism as much as his fiction. When he writes of his practice as a novelist, or offers detailed advice to beginners like Edward Noble and Helen Sanderson (items 3, 4 and 36 below) or to established literary friends like Galsworthy (item 24 below, for example), or when he castigates public taste and popular literature, he is writing as a man who measures himself against the influential 'modern' writers of his early youth, against Mallarmé, who died in 1898, Flaubert and Turgenev, who died in 1881 and 1883 respectively, and, outside literature, against Wagner, who also died in 1883, and Rodin, who was to die in 1917 at the age of 77, predeceasing Conrad himself by only seven years. When we read him, however, it is with the knowledge of those major texts of literary modernism, *Ulysses*, for example, and Eliot's *The Waste Land*, that followed Conrad's most challenging period, and which, especially in the case of Eliot's work, were shaped by his vision and his practice.

We should keep in mind too, though, the kind of criticism Conrad writes – not series of articles, and rarely set pieces, but moments in letters, and the occasional invited essay or book review. The disadvantage of this is that we have no large-scale critical working through of principles or of artistic practice such as we find in the critical work of Henry James or D. H. Lawrence, Yeats or Eliot. The advantage, however, is that when Conrad is seen as critic it is frequently when he is at his most personal, writing to close friends or to close professional associates, when he can be sure of an intelligent and usually affectionate response. Even in his essays and author's notes (the single series in his critical work) the tone Conrad adopts is the personal, the chatty, though interspersed, as indeed are some of his letters, with patches of a more stylized rhetoric. Not that we should be hoodwinked by the personal: in the prefaces especially his often rather throwaway style of reminiscence disguises the fact that Conrad, writing in 1917–20, is quite deliberately trying to reshape public opinion of his earlier work in order to make himself more acceptable, less the difficult, unconventional writer of 'so-called' adventure stories. Of the writing of The Secret Agent, for example, he remarks, 'All this sounds a very old story now! And yet it is not such a long time ago. I must conclude that I had still preserved much of my pristine innocence in the year 1907' (item 50). The notes were written for the first collected edition of his works, and Conrad was interested in sales. After a lifetime of financial hardship he was determined (not unreasonably) to make the most of his late popularity. The author's notes are part of the publicity campaign.

And yet we should not mistrust the personal as inevitably a disguise. Conrad's intimacy with Garnett, Galsworthy and Cunninghame Graham was lifelong and genuine, a long way from the kind of half-manipulative half-petulant friendship he enjoyed with later admirers such as Richard Curle. From the bulk of Conrad's correspondence we are left with the impression not only of a man in the fortunate possession of a number of reliable and intimate friends, but of a mind that was always ready to throw out comments and ideas on literary and artistic questions, on his own work and state of mind, and on the work of others. The insights we can gain are invaluable for the appreciation of Conrad's fiction and of the temperament that could produce it.

Conrad was upset, as Frederick Karl explains, by contemporary reaction to the serialization of The Shadow-Line. As it appeared in the English Review from September 1916, its division, into seven instalments, made it seem 'unduly harsh' and 'morbid' (Karl, 1979, p. 792). For the book version Conrad replaced his chapter designations by numerals and did away with his original separation of the story into two parts, the intention now being 'to encourage a read-through at a single sitting' (ibid., p. 793). The modifications obviously had the desired effect, for not only were the 5000 copies of the first edition in March 1917 sold out within four days, but the reviews following its publication presented a chorus of praise. Norman Sherry summarizes the reception, quoting, among others, the *Nation*: 'one of the great ones, not of the present, but of the world'; the *Spectator*: 'The genius of Mr. Conrad disarms criticism'; and the *Sphere*: 'it is a great and never-to-be-forgotten book' (Sherry, 1973, pp. 32–3). Later critical opinion has moderated a little, but *The Shadow-Line* has never wanted its share of admirers. F. R. Leavis agrees with the 'common recognition' that it is 'one of Conrad's masterpieces', superior, he believes, 'to *Heart of Darkness* and even to *Typhoon*'. It is 'a supremely sinister and beautiful evocation of enchantment in tropic seas' (Leavis, 1948, p. 206). For Albert Guerard, *The Shadow-Line* and 'The secret sharer' are 'perhaps his two great triumphs of a style plain and pure'. They 'maintain exquisite control over their materials' and, with *Heart of Darkness* 'they are among the first and best – one is tempted to say only – symbolist masterpieces in English fiction' (1958, pp. 14–15). And the roll of approval goes on: the story is 'an outstandingly well-told tale in crisp, vivid prose' (Baines, 1960, p. 405); it displays 'triumphant art' (Thorburn, 1974, p. 20); it is one of the 'most memorable of his tales and a work that neatly summarizes the qualities of his finest short fiction' (Graver, 1969, p. 179); it is 'one of his finest novels' (Watts, 1982, p. 27).

When Conrad began writing *The Shadow-Line* in January 1915 (he was to finish it by the end of the year – the 1916 of the Author's note seems to be an innocent mistake), he was looking back almost thirty years, to January 1888 when, for no better reason, apparently, than boredom, he had given up his berth as mate on the *Vidar*, a steamship making trading journeys between Singapore, Borneo and Celebes, with the intention of returning to England. Instead, he had suddenly been appointed captain of the barque *Otago* with instructions to bring her from Bangkok, where the mate Charles Born had taken her following the death at sea of the previous master, Captain John Snadden, to Singapore. This accomplished, Conrad was confirmed in his post as captain (the only period during his sea career when he was actually master of a ship – unlike Marlow in *Heart of Darkness*, Conrad was not captain of the river boat *Roi des Belges*, although he was originally appointed to the post and did assume command for a short period while Koch, the captain, was ill). He then spent a little over a year trading with the *Otago* between Sydney and Mauritius until finally resigning his command in March 1889 and embarking as a passenger bound for England. It is, however, with the events of the *Otago*'s first voyage under Conrad, from Bangkok to Singapore, that *The Shadow-Line* is concerned and, in terms of the 'exact autobiography' (Jean-Aubry, 1927, II, p. 181) claimed by Conrad, the events actually taken from life are, as Norman Sherry has shown (1966, pp. 211–49), those of the appointment and the taking up of the command, rather than the precise details of the voyage itself. Captain Snadden, for example, was not the monster he is made out to be in *The Shadow-Line* and, while Conrad was not on good terms with the mate for the early part of their time together, nevertheless, as *The Mirror of the Sea* makes clear (1906, pp. 18–19), he and Charles Born came to a sufficiently good understanding for Conrad to recommend Born as his successor when he left the *Otago* – unsuccessfully, as Brierley's recommendation in *Lord Jim* that his first mate Jones should succeed him on the *Ossa* is unsuccessful, after Brierley's mysterious suicide. This is Sherry's concluding paragraph:

> One would not wish to deny that Conrad's experiences in taking up his first command were in many ways nightmarish. He certainly struggled against sickness, lack of crew, and calms in the Gulf of Siam. The memory of these trials was strong enough to inspire *The Shadow-Line* as a tale of trial in extreme circumstances. But it is not 'exact autobiography' in the sense Conrad claims. The creative instinct in Conrad was too strong to allow him to set down unvarnished facts. (1966, p. 249)

The 'creative instinct', though, moves in mysterious ways, and while we rightly expect to find in *The Shadow-Line* some reflection of Conrad's own concerns as a young man – his attitudes towards command and responsibility, towards the sea, and his proximity to a state of personal despair and madness, everything, in fact, that makes up the test that this protagonist faces in common with many other young heroes of Conrad's fiction, especially the fiction of the eastern seas – we should not be surprised by the preoccupations of the later

17

writer which inevitably add a colouring of their own to the raw experience of youth. So, most obviously, the teller–protagonist of the tale is himself now past the 'region of early youth', is reflecting upon his own experience as he narrates it – experience which he did not necessarily understand at the time – and has to draw in places upon his own diary of the events in order to authenticate, as it were, not so much the events themselves but the accompanying state of mind and especially the despair he was then feeling. This kind of hiding is something we are used to in Conrad the writer, a hiding which means that the 'exact autobiography' within the story is attained only at one or two places where the diary is quoted, like a piece of evidence framed by the layers of its telling. And then there is the dedication to Conrad's son Borys, and its reference to those 'who like himself have crossed in early youth the shadow-line of their generation', which specifies the time of the story's composition and that most appalling test undergone by the millions who fought in the Great War. However 'nightmarish' Conrad's original experiences, his state of mind would have needed very careful rendering – or varnishing – to make disease and a ship becalmed equivalent to shells and trench warfare. Finally, of course, Conrad's long years as a professional writer and the experience of the breakdown of 1910 make for a far more thorough understanding of despair and madness than would have been available to him at 30. Indeed, if the crisis of 1910 was the price to be paid for what Conrad had made of himself, he had, in writing *The Shadow-Line*, to cast himself back to a more innocent time when a test passed was a permanent gain, and despair and self-doubt were passing hardships rather than the enduring features of existence they had become by 1910. That *The Shadow-Line* does not end with the ambiguity of, say, *Heart of Darkness* is a measure both of Conrad's success in recapturing that spiritual innocence and of how little he was now prepared or able to confront the ambiguity of his own experience during 'his introspective journeys into the self'. If, in this respect, there is an appealing innocence about the characters who, like this captain and the captain in 'The secret sharer', come through their test, there is also a poignancy in the innocence of Captain Giles who, picking up the terms of the young Conrad's letter of 1891, ends *The Shadow-Line* with the remark that 'a man should stand up to his bad luck, to his mistakes, to his conscience, and all that sort of thing. Why – what else would you have to fight against?' Or rather, the poignancy is in Conrad's finding for this piece of advice such an amiable old innocent, for by this time it was something that Conrad was himself no longer able to do.

TEXTS

All prefaces, essays and reviews are taken from the Dent *Collected Edition of the Works of Joseph Conrad*, London, 1946–55. Original publication details of essays and reviews are provided in the Notes. Extracts from letters are taken from the following sources:

Blackburn, William, *Joseph Conrad: Letters to William Blackwood and David S. Meldrum*, pp. 9–10, 36–7, 71–3, 154–6, copyright © 1958 Duke University Press, items 9, 19, 22, 25.

Curle, Richard, *Conrad to a Friend: 150 Selected Letters from Joseph Conrad to Richard Curle*, London, Sampson Low, Marston & Co., 1928, items 53, 56.

Garnett, Edward, *Letters from Conrad, 1895–1924*, London, Nonesuch, 1928, items 2, 5, 6, 10, 11, 12, 23, 35, 37, 38, 39, 40.

Jean-Aubry, G., *Joseph Conrad: Life and Letters* (2 vols), London, Heinemann, 1927, items 3, 4, 14, 17 ,18, 20, 21, 24, 26, 33, 34, 36, 41, 42, 45, 46, 47, 49, 54, 55, 57.

Watts, C. T., *Joseph Conrad's Letters to R. B. Cunninghame Graham*, pp. 45, 56–7, 70–1, 157, copyright © 1969 Cambridge University Press, items, 8, 13, 15, 30.

Omissions in extracts are indicated by ellipses within square brackets. All others are in the originals.

The Shadow-Line was first published serially in the *Metropolitan Magazine* in New York between September and October 1916, and in the *English Review* between September 1916 and March 1917. It was published as a book in London in March 1917 by J. M. Dent & Sons and in New York in April by Doubleday, Page. The manuscript, which is dated 15 December 1915 on the final page, is now at the Yale University Library (Beinecke Rare Book and Manuscript Library). Conrad's corrected page proofs for the Heinemann edition of 1921 (in their limited edition of *The Works of Joseph Conrad*, London, 1921–7) are at the Rosenbach Museum and Library, Philadelphia. The present text is taken from Dent's *Collected Edition of the Works of Joseph Conrad*, London, 1950. Most of the textual variations between the Dent *Collected* and Heinemann editions are minor matters of punctuation or capitalization, and are listed in Hawthorn (1985, pp. xxviii–xxxi). Like Hawthorn, I prefer the Heinemann reading of 'this of' on p. 181, l. 5, to the Dent *Collected* 'of this', and 'exorcising' on p. 208, l. 13, as in the Dent first edition and Heinemann, to 'exercising', an obvious mistake in the Dent *Collected*. On p. 120, l. 6, I emend 'residental' to 'residential'. There are many changes between Conrad's manuscript and the published texts, some of them quite substantial – especially the deletions – but which are beyond the scope of the present volume. Some can be found in Hawthorn, but full annotation can be expected only from the kind of scholarly edition planned by Cambridge University Press of the whole Conrad canon.

CHRONOLOGY

1857	Birth of Conrad, 3 December, in Russian-occupied Poland.
1862	Exile of Conrad's father, Apollo Korzeniowski, for political activities, to Russia. Conrad and his mother accompany him.
1865	Death of Conrad's mother, Ewa.
1869	Death of Apollo. Conrad lives with his maternal uncle, Tadeusz Bobrowski.
1874	Leaves Poland for Marseilles, intending to become a merchant seaman.
1878	Attempted suicide in Marseilles after building up large gambling debts. Finds a berth aboard his first British ship.
1880	Qualifies as second mate in British Merchant Service.
1884	Qualifies as first mate.
1886	Becomes a British subject. Qualifies as master, although unable to find an appointment as captain.

1887	Position as first mate aboard the *Highland Forest*, from where a back injury puts him into hospital in Singapore. Secures post of first mate on the *Vidar*.
1888	Leaves the *Vidar* and is unexpectedly appointed to command the *Otago*, his only period of command.
1889	Leaves the *Otago*, and ships for London. Begins writing *Almayer's Folly*.
1890	Journey to the Belgian Congo.
1891	As first mate of the *Torrens* meets John Galsworthy, a passenger.
1894	*Almayer's Folly* completed and accepted for publication by Unwin. Meets Edward Garnett, Unwin's reader.
1895	Publication of *Almayer's Folly*.
1896	Publication of *An Outcast of the Islands*. Marriage to Jessie George. Begins writing 'The rescuer'.
1897	Publication of *The Nigger of the 'Narcissus'*. Meets R. B. Cunninghame Graham.
1898	Publication of *Tales of Unrest* ('Karain', 'The idiots', 'An outpost of progress', 'The return', 'The lagoon'). Meets Ford Madox Ford (Hueffer). Serialization of *Youth*. Borys Conrad born.
1899	Serialization of *Heart of Darkness*. Agrees with J. B. Pinker that he should become Conrad's literary agent.
1899–1900	Serialization of *Lord Jim*.
1900	Book publication of *Lord Jim*.
1901	Publication of *The Inheritors* (with Ford).
1902	Serialization of *Typhoon*. Publication of *Youth: A Narrative and Two Other Stories* ('Youth', 'Heart of darkness', 'The end of the tether').
1903	Publication of *Typhoon and Other Stories* ('Typhoon', 'Amy Foster', 'Falk', 'Tomorrow') and *Romance* (with Ford).
1904	Serialization and book publication of *Nostromo*.
1905–6	Serialization of *The Mirror of the Sea*.
1906	Book publication of *The Mirror of the Sea*. John Conrad born. Serialization of *The Secret Agent*.
1907	Book publication of *The Secret Agent*.

1908	Publication of *A Set of Six* ('Gasper Ruiz', 'The informer', 'The brute', 'An anarchist', 'The duel', 'Il Conde').
1908–9	Serialization of *Some Reminiscences* (later entitled *A Personal Record*).
1909	Serialization of *The Nature of a Crime* (with Ford). Falls out with Ford.
1910	Serialization of 'The secret sharer'. Conrad's breakdown.
1910–11	Serialization of *Under Western Eyes*.
1911	Book publication of *Under Western Eyes*.
1912	Publication of *A Personal Record* and *'Twixt Land and Sea* ('A smile of fortune', 'The secret sharer', 'Freya of the Seven Isles'). Serialization of *Chance*.
1913	Book publication of *Chance*.
1914	Large sales of *Chance*. The Conrads visit Poland.
1915	Publication of *Within the Tides* ('The planter of Malata', 'The partner', 'The Inn of the Two Witches', 'Because of the dollars'). Serialization and book publication of *Victory*.
1916–17	Serialization of *The Shadow-Line*.
1917	Book publication of *The Shadow-Line*.
1917–20	Conrad writing author's notes for his collected works.
1918–20	Serialization of *The Arrow of Gold*.
1919	Book publication of *The Arrow of Gold*. Serialization of *The Rescue* (formerly 'The rescuer').
1920	Book publication of *The Rescue*.
1921	Publication of *Notes on Life and Letters*.
1922	Dramatization of *The Secret Agent* staged. Death of Pinker.
1923	Serialization and book publication of *The Rover*. Visit by Conrad to America a great success.
1924	Conrad declines a knighthood in May, and on 3 August dies of a heart attack at his home near Canterbury. Book publication of *The Nature of a Crime* (with Ford).
1925	Publication of *Tales of Hearsay* ('The warrior's soul',

'Prince Roman', 'The tale', 'The black mate'). Serialization and book publication of the unfinished *Suspense*.
1926   Publication of *Last Essays*.
1928   Publication of the fragment, *The Sisters*.

JOSEPH CONRAD
Selected Literary Criticism

1   Author's note to *Almayer's Folly* (1895). This, Conrad's first
    novel, was completed by 22 May 1894, having been begun in 1889
    during a lull in his full-time career as a seaman.

I am informed that in criticizing that literature which preys on
strange people and prowls in far-off countries, under the shade of
palms, in the unsheltered glare of sunbeaten beaches, amongst honest
cannibals and the more sophisticated pioneers of our glorious virtues,
a lady – distinguished in the world of letters – summed up her dis-
approval of it by saying that the tales it produced were 'decivilized'.
And in that sentence not only the tales but, I apprehend, the strange
people and the far-off countries also, are finally condemned in a
verdict of contemptuous dislike.

  A woman's judgement: intuitive, clever, expressed with felicitous
charm – infallible. A judgement that has nothing to do with justice.
The critic and the judge seems to think that in those distant lands all
joy is a yell and a war dance, all pathos is a howl and a ghastly grin of
filed teeth, and that the solution of all problems is found in the barrel
of a revolver or on the point of an assegai. And yet it is not so. But
the erring magistrate may plead in excuse the misleading nature of
the evidence.

  The picture of life, there as here, is drawn with the same
elaboration of detail, coloured with the same tints. Only in the cruel
serenity of the sky, under the merciless brilliance of the sun, the
dazzled eye misses the delicate detail, sees only the strong outlines,
while the colours, in the steady light, seem crude and without
shadow. Nevertherless it is the same picture.

  And there is a bond between us and that humanity so far away. I
am speaking here of men and women – not of the charming and
graceful phantoms that move about in our mud and smoke and are
softly luminous with the radiance of all our virtues; that are possessed
of all refinements, of all sensibilities, of all widsom – but, being only
phantoms, possess no heart.

  The sympathies of those are (probably) with the immortals: with the
angels above or the devils below. I am content to sympathize with
common mortals, no matter where they live; in houses or in tents, in
the streets under a fog, or in the forests behind the dark line of dismal

mangroves that fringe the vast solitude of the sea. For, their land – like ours – lies under the inscrutable eyes of the Most High. Their hearts – like ours – must endure the load of the gifts from Heaven: the curse of facts and the blessing of illusions, the bitterness of our wisdom and the deceptive consolation of our folly.

2 From a letter to Edward Garnett, 24 September 1895. Garnett was the reader who had recommended publication of *Almayer's Folly* and became a lifelong friend. Conrad is replying to his comments on the manuscript of *An Outcast of the Islands* (1896), and especially to his criticisms of what was then chapter 14.

Nothing now can unmake my mistake. I shall try – but I shall try without faith, because all my work is produced unconsciously (so to speak) and I cannot meddle to any purpose with what is within myself. – I am sure you understand what I mean. – It isn't in me to improve what has got itself written.

Still with your help I may try. All the paragraphs marked by you to that effect shall be cut out. For Willems to want to escape from *both* women *is* the very idea. Only – don't you see – I did not feel it so. Shame! The filiation of feelings in Willems on the evening when Aissa speaks to him arises from my view of that man – of the effect produced upon him by the loss of things precious to him coming (the loss) after his passion is appeased. Consequently – his deliberate effort to recall the passion as a last resort, as the last refuge from his regrets, from the obsession of his longing to return whence he came. It's an impulse of thought not of the senses. The senses are done with. Nothing lasts! So with Aissa. Her passion is burnt out too. There is in her that desire to be something for him – to be in his mind, in his heart – to shelter him in her affection – her woman's affection which is simply the ambition to be an important factor in another's life. They both long to have a significance in the order of nature or of society. To me they are typical of mankind where every individual wishes to assert his power, woman by sentiment, man by achievement of some sort – mostly base. I myself – as you see from this – have been ambitious to make it clear and have failed in that as Willems fails in his effort to throw off the trammels of earth and of heaven.

So much in defence of my view of the case. For the execution I have no word to say. It is very feeble and all the strokes fall beside the mark. Why? – If I knew that – if I knew the causes of my weakness I would destroy them and then produce nothing but colossal master-pieces – which 'no fellow could understand'. As it is I am too lazy to change my thoughts, my words, my images, and my dreams. Laziness is a sacred thing. It's the sign of our limitations beyond which there is nothing worth having. Nobody is lazy to accomplish things without any effort – and things that can only be attained by effort are not worth having.

In the treatment of the last scenes I wanted to convey the kind of placidity that is caused by extreme surprise. You must not forget that they are all immensely amazed. That's why they are so quiet – (At least I wanted them to be quiet and only managed to make them colourless). That's why I put in the quiet morning – the immobility of surrounding matter emphasized only by the flutter of small birds. Then the sense of their position penetrates the hearts – stirs them. They wake up to the reality. Then comes violence: Joanna's slap in Aissa's face, Aissa's shot – and the end just as he sees the joy of sunshine and of life.

3 From a letter to Edward Noble, 28 October 1895. Noble, himself a seaman with hopes of turning writer, had approached Conrad earlier in the year. Noble went on to become a moderately success-ful novelist.

Only, my dear Noble, do not throw yourself away in fables. Talk about the river, – the people, – the events, as seen through your temperament. You have a remarkable gift of expression, the outcome of an artistic feeling for the world around you, and you must not waste that gift in (if I may say so) illegitimate sensation. You remember perhaps what I said about the vampire story. A capital thing, – wonderfully well put, as far as the impression of the thing went, – only, – only to me all the charm, all the truth of it are thrown away by the construction, – by the mechanism (so to speak) of the story which makes it appear false.

Do not be angry with me. I have thought your letter over many times during the day and now I put down here my exact thoughts, – right or wrong.

You have any amount of stuff in you, but you (I think) have not found your way yet. Remember that death is not the most pathetic, – the most poignant thing, – and you must treat events only as illustrative of human sensation, – as the outward sign of inward feelings, – of live feelings, – which alone are truly pathetic and interesting. You have much imagination: much more than I ever will have if I live to be a hundred years old. That much is clear to me. Well, that imagination (I wish I had it) should be used to create human souls: to disclose human hearts, – and not to create events that are properly speaking *accidents* only. To accomplish it you must cultivate your poetic faculty, – you must give yourself up to emotions (no easy task). You must squeeze out of yourself every sensation, every thought, every image, – mercilessly, without reserve and without remorse: you must search the darkest corners of your heart, the most remote recesses of your brain, – you must search them for the image, for the glamour, for the right expression. And you must do it sincerely, at any cost: you must do it so that at the end of your day's work you should feel exhausted, emptied of every sensation and every thought, with a blank mind and an aching heart, with the notion that there is nothing, – nothing left in you. To me it seems that this is the only way to achieve true distinction – or even to go some way towards it.

It took me 3 years to finish the *Folly*.[1] There was not a day I did not think of it. Not a day. And after all I consider it honestly a miserable failure. Every critic (but two or three) overrated the book. It took me a year to tear the *Outcast* out of myself and upon my word of honour, – I look on it (now it's finished) with bitter disappointment. Judge from that whether my opinion is worth having.

4 From a letter to Noble, 2 November 1895.

When I speak about writing from an inward point of view, – I mean from the depth of our own inwardness. I do not want you to drag out for public inspection the very entrails of your characters. Lay bare your own heart, and people will listen to you for that, – and only that is interesting.

Everyone must walk in the light of his own heart's gospel. No man's light is good to any of his fellows. That's my creed from beginning to end. That's my view of life, – a view that rejects all formulas, dogmas and principles of other people's making. These are only a web of illusions. We are too varied. Another man's truth is only a dismal lie to me. I am telling you things that I would never dream of telling anybody, but I don't want to speak to you from the shelter of false pretences.

5 From a letter to Garnett, 29 November 1896. Conrad encloses several manuscript pages of *The Nigger*.

Of course nothing can alter the course of the *Nigger*. Let it be unpopularity; it *must* be. But it seems to me that the thing – precious as it is to me – is trivial enough on the surface to have some charm for the man in the street. As to lack of incident well – it's life. The incomplete joy, the incomplete sorrow, the incomplete rascality or heroism – the incomplete suffering. Events crowd and push and nothing happens. You know what I mean. The opportunities do not last long enough. Unless in a boy's book of adventures. Mine were never finished. They fizzled out before I had a chance to do more than another man would.

6 From a letter to Garnett, 13 February 1897. Conrad had sent *An Outcast* to Henry James.

I had this morning a charming surprise in the shape of the *Spoils of Poynton* sent me by H. James with a very characteristic and friendly inscription on the fly leaf.[2] I need not tell you how pleased I am. I have already read the book. It is as good as anything of his – almost – a story of love and wrongheadedness revolving around a houseful of artistic furniture. It's Henry James and nothing but Henry James. The delicacy and tenuity of the thing are amazing. It is like a great sheet of plate glass – you don't know it's there till you run against it. Of course I do not mean to say it is anything as gross as plate glass.

It's only as *pellucid* as clean plate glass. The only fault I find is its length. It's just a trifle too long. Personally I don't complain as you may imagine, but I imagine with pain the man in the street trying to read it! And my common humanity revolts at the evoked image of his suffering. One could almost see the globular lobes of his brain painfully revolving and crushing, mangling the delicate thing. As to his exasperation it is a thing impossible to imagine and too horrid to contemplate.

7 Preface to *The Nigger of the 'Narcissus'* (1897). This is Conrad's earliest and fullest statement of his artistic principles, and stands as a touchstone for much of his writing career.

A work that aspires, however humbly, to the condition of art should carry its justification in every line. And art itself may be defined as a single-minded attempt to render the highest kind of justice to the visible universe, by bringing to light the truth, manifold and one, underlying its every aspect. It is an attempt to find in its forms, in its colours, in its light, in its shadows, in the aspects of matter, and in the facts of life what of each is fundamental, what is enduring and essential – their one illuminating and convincing quality – the very truth of their existence. The artist, then, like the thinker or the scientist, seeks the truth and makes his appeal. Impressed by the aspect of the world the thinker plunges into ideas, the scientists into facts – whence, presently, emerging they make their appeal to those qualities of our being that fit us best for the hazardous enterprise of living. They speak authoritatively to our common sense, to our intelligence, to our desire of peace, or to our desire of unrest; not seldom to our prejudices, sometimes to our fears, often to our egoism – but always to our credulity. And their words are heard with reverence, for their concern is with weighty matters: with the cultivation of our minds and the proper care of our bodies, with the attainment of our ambitions, with the perfection of the means and the glorification of our precious aims.

It is otherwise with the artist.

Confronted by the same enigmatical spectacle the artist descends within himself, and in that lonely region of stress and strife, if he be deserving and fortunate, he finds the terms of his appeal. His appeal is made to our less obvious capacities: to that part of our nature which, because of the warlike conditions of existence, is necessarily kept out of sight within the more resisting and hard qualities – like the vulnerable body within a steel armour. His appeal is less loud, more profound, less distinct, more stirring – and sooner forgotten. Yet its effect endures for ever. The changing wisdom of successive generations discards ideas, questions facts, demolishes theories. But the artist appeals to that part of our being which is not dependent on wisdom; to that in us which is a gift and not an acquisition – and, therefore, more permanently enduring. He speaks to our capacity for delight and wonder, to the sense of mystery surrounding our lives; to our sense of pity, and beauty, and pain; to the latent feeling of fellowship with all creation – and to the subtle but invincible conviction of solidarity that knits together the loneliness of innumerable hearts, to the solidarity in dreams, in joy, in sorrow, in aspirations, in illusions, in hope, in fear, which binds men to each other, which binds together all humanity – the dead to the living and the living to the unborn.

It is only some such train of thought, or rather of feeling, that can in a measure explain the aim of the attempt, made in the tale which follows, to present an unrestful episode in the obscure lives of a few individuals out of all the disregarded multitude of the bewildered, the simple, and the voiceless. For, if any part of truth dwells in the belief confessed above, it becomes evident that there is not a place of splendour or a dark corner of the earth that does not deserve, if only a passing glance of wonder and pity. The motive then, may be held to justify the matter of the work; but this preface, which is simply an avowal of endeavour, cannot end here – for the avowal is not yet complete.

Fiction – if it at all aspire to be art – appeals to temperament. And in truth it must be, like painting, like music, like all art, the appeal of one temperament to all the other innumerable temperaments whose subtle and resistless power endows passing events with their true meaning, and creates the moral, the emotional atmosphere of the place and time. Such an appeal to be effective must be an impression conveyed through the senses; and, in fact, it cannot be made in any other way, because temperament, whether individual or collective, is not amenable to persuasion. All art, therefore, appeals primarily to the senses, and the artistic aim when expressing itself in written words must also make its appeal through the senses, if its high desire is to reach the secret spring of responsive emotions. It must strenuously aspire to the plasticity of sculpture, to the colour of painting, and to the magic suggestiveness of music – which is the art of arts. And it is only through complete, unswerving devotion to the perfect blending of form and substance; it is only through an un-remitting never-discouraged care for the shape and ring of sentences that an approach can be made to plasticity, to colour, and that the light of magic suggestiveness may be brought to play for an evane-scent instant over the commonplace surface of words: of the old, old words, worn thin, defaced by ages of careless usage.

The sincere endeavour to accomplish that creative task, to go as far on that road as his strength will carry him, to go undeterred by faltering, weariness, or reproach, is the only valid justification for the worker in prose. And if his conscience is clear, his answer to those who in the fulness of a wisdom which looks for immediate profit, demand specifically to be edified, consoled, amused; who demand to be promptly improved, or encouraged, or frightened, or shocked, or charmed, must run thus: My task which I am trying to achieve is, by the power of the written word to make you hear, to make you feel – it is, before all, to make you *see*. That – and no more, and it is every-thing. If I succeed, you shall find there according to your deserts: encouragement, consolation, fear, charm – all you demand – and, perhaps, also that glimpse of truth for which you have forgotten to ask.

To snatch in a moment of courage, from the remorseless rush of time, a passing phase of life, is only the beginning of the task. The task approached in tenderness and faith is to hold up unquestionably, without choice and without fear, the rescued fragment before all eyes in the light of a sincere mood. It is to show its vibrations, its colour, its form; and through its movement, its form, and its colour, reveal the substance of its truth – disclose its inspiring secret: the stress and passion within the core of each convincing moment. In a single-minded attempt of that kind, if one be deserving and fortunate, one may perchance attain to such clearness of sincerity that at last the presented vision of regret or pity, of terror or mirth, shall awaken in the hearts of the beholders that feeling of unavoidable solidarity; of the solidarity in mysterious origin, in toil, in joy, in hope, in uncertain fate, which binds men to each other and all mankind to the visible world.

It is evident that he who, rightly or wrongly, holds by the convictions expressed above cannot be faithful to any one of the temporary formulas of his craft. The enduring part of them – the truth which each only imperfectly veils – should abide with him as the most precious of his possessions, but they all: Realism, Romanticism, Naturalism, even the unofficial sentimentalism (which like the poor, is exceedingly difficult to get rid of), all these gods must, after a short period of fellowship, abandon him – even on the very threshold of the temple – to the stammerings of his conscience and to the outspoken consciousness of the difficulties of his work. In that uneasy solitude the supreme cry of Art for Art itself loses the exciting ring of its apparent immorality. It sounds far off. It has ceased to be a cry, and is heard only as a whisper, often incomprehensible, but at times faintly encouraging.

Sometimes, stretched at ease in the shade of a roadside tree, we watch the motions of a labourer in a distant field, and after a time, begin to wonder languidly as to what the fellow may be at. We watch the movements of his body, the waving of his arms, we see him bend down, stand up, hesitate, begin again. It may add to the charm of an idle hour to be told the purpose of his exertions. If we know he is trying to lift a stone, to dig a ditch, to uproot a stump, we look with a more real interest at his efforts; we are disposed to condone the jar of his agitation upon the restfulness of the landscape; and even, if in a brotherly frame of mind, we may bring ourselves to forgive his failure. We understood his object, and, after all, the fellow has tried, and perhaps he had not the strength – and perhaps he had not the knowledge. We forgive, go on our way – and forget.

And so it is with the workman of art. Art is long and life is short, and success is very far off. And thus, doubtful of strength to travel so far, we talk a little about the aim – the aim of art, which, like life itself, is inspiring, difficult – obscured by mists. It is not in the clear logic of a triumphant conclusion; it is not in the unveiling of one of those heartless secrets which are called the Laws of Nature. It is not less great, but only more difficult.

To arrest, for the space of a breath, the hands busy about the work of the earth, and compel men entranced by the sight of distant goals to glance for a moment at the surrounding vision of form and colour, of sunshine and shadows; to make them pause for a look, for a sigh, for a smile – such is the aim, difficult and evanescent, and reserved only for a very few to achieve. But sometimes, by the deserving and the fortunate, even that task is accomplished. And when it is accomplished – behold! – all the truth of life is there: a moment of vision, a sigh, a smile – and the return to an eternal rest.

8 From a letter to R. B. Cunninghame Graham, 5 August 1897. Conrad's letter, the first of many, is in reply to an approach by Graham who had written comparing 'An outpost of progress' (1897) to Kipling's 'Slaves of the lamp'.[3]

Mr Kipling has the wisdom of the passing generations – and holds it in perfect sincerity. Some of his work is of impeccable form and because of that little thing he shall sojourn in Hell only a very short while. He squints with the rest of his excellent sort. It is a beautiful squint; it is an useful squint. And – after all – perhaps he sees round the corner? And suppose Truth is just round the corner like the elusive and useless loafer it is? I can't tell. No one can tell. It is impossible to know. It is impossible to know anything tho' it is possible to believe a thing or two.

9 From a letter to William Blackwood, 6 September 1897. Conrad is outlining the scheme for his novel *The Rescue*, on which he was to work intermittently for over twenty years. It was finally published in 1920.

The situation 'per se' is not new. Consequently all the effect must be produced in the working out – in the manner of telling. This necessity from my point of view is fascinating. I am sure you will understand my feeling though you may differ with me in the view.

On the other hand the situation is not prosaic. It is suitable for a romance. The human interest of the tale is in the contact of Lingard the simple, masterful, imaginative adventurer with a type of civilized woman – a complex type. He is a man tenacious of purpose, enthusiastic in undertaking, faithful in friendship. He jeopardizes the success of his plans first to assure her safety and then absolutely sacrifices them to what he believes the necessary conditions of her happiness. He is throughout mistrusted by the whites whom he wishes to save; he is unwillingly forced into a contest with his Malay friends. Then when the rescue, for which he had sacrificed all the interests of his life, is accomplished, he has to face his reward – an inevitable separation. This episode of his life lifts him out of himself; I want to convey in the action of the story the stress and exaltation of the man under the influence of a sentiment which he hardly understands and yet which is real enough to make him as he goes on reckless of consequences. It is only at the very last that he is perfectly enlightened when the work of rescue and destruction is ended and nothing is left to him but to try and pick up as best he may the broken thread of his life. Lingard – not the woman – is the principal personage. That's why all the first part is given up to the presentation of his personality. It illustrates the method I intend to follow. I aim at stimulating vision in the reader. If after reading the *part 1st* you don't *see* my man then I've absolutely failed and must begin again – or leave the thing alone. Of course the paraphernalia of the story are hackneyed. The yacht, the shipwreck, the pirates, the coast – all this has been used times out of number; whether it has been done, that's another question. Be it as it may I think rightly or wrongly I can present it in a fresh way. At any rate as I wish to obtain the effect of reality in my story and also wanted the woman – that kind of woman – there was no other way to bring her there but in the time-honoured yacht. Nothing impossible shall happen. I shall tell of some events I've seen, and also relate things I've heard.

10 From a letter to Garnett, 29 September 1897. Conrad refers to Alvan Hervey, the central character in 'The return'. The story was finished only a few days earlier, and was included in *Tales of Unrest* (1898).

I am hoist with my own petard. My dear fellow what I aimed at was just to produce the effect of cold water in every one of my man's speeches. I swear to you that was my intention. I wanted to produce the effect of insincerity, of artificiality. Yes! I wanted the reader to *see him think* and then to hear him speak – and shudder. The whole point of the joke is there. I wanted the truth to be first dimly seen through the fabulous untruth of that man's convictions – of his idea of life – and then to make its way out with a rush at the end. But if I have to explain that to you – to you! – then I've egregiously failed. I've tried with all my might to avoid just these trivialities of rage and distraction which you judge necessary to the truth of the picture. I counted it a virtue, and lo and behold! You say it is a sin. Well! Never more! It is evident that my fate is to be descriptive and descriptive only. There are things I *must* leave alone.

11 From a letter to Garnett, 11 October 1897. The subject is again 'The return'.

I wrote that you have the knowledge of artistic effect because I believe you have. You do know. I wish to goodness you didn't. But the more I think of the story the more I feel (I don't see yet) the justice of your pronouncement as to the unreality of the dialogue. Where we differ is there: you say: it is too logical – I say: It is too crude; but I admit that the crudeness (proceeding from want of skill) produces that effect of logic – which is offensive. You see I wanted to give out the gospel of the beastly bourgeois – and wasn't clever enough to do it in a more natural way. Hence the logic which resembles the logic of a melodrama. The childishness of mind coming to the surface. All this I feel. I don't see; because if I did see it I would also see the other way, the mature way – the way of art. I would work from conviction to conviction – through inevitable moments to the final situation. Instead of which I went on creating the moments for the illustration of the idea. Am I right in that view? If so the story is bad art. It is built on the same falsehood as a melodrama.

12 From a letter to Garnett, 5 December 1897. Conrad had met Stephen Crane that autumn and the two saw each other frequently until Crane's early death in 1900.[4]

I had Crane here last Sunday. We talked and smoked half the night. He is strangely hopeless about himself. I like him. The two stories are excellent. Of course *A Man and Some Others* is the best of the two but the boat thing interested me more. His eye is very individual and his expression satisfies me artistically. He certainly is *the* impressionist and his temperament is curiously unique. His thought is concise, connected, never very deep – yet often startling. He is *the only* impressionist and *only* an impressionist. Why is he not immensely popular? With his strength, with his rapidity of action, with that amazing faculty of vision – why is he not? He has outline, he has colour, he has movement, with that he ought to go very far. But – will he? I sometimes think he won't. It is not an opinion – it is a feeling. I could not explain why he disappoints me – why my enthusiasm withers as soon as I close the book. While one reads, of course he is not to be questioned. He is the master of his reader to the very last line – then – apparently for no reason at all – he seems to let go his hold. It is as if he had gripped you with greased fingers. His grip is strong but while you feel the pressure on your flesh you slip our from his hand – much to your own surprise. That is my stupid impression and I give it to you in confidence. It just occurs to me that it is perhaps my own self that is slippery. I don't know. *You* would know. No matter.

13 From a letter to Cunninghame Graham, 20 December 1897. Graham was an active socialist, while Conrad might best be described as a political agnostic, though with important reservations, especially concerning Russia and Poland.

You are a most hopeless idealist – your aspirations are irrealizable. You want from men faith, honour, fidelity to truth in themselves and others. You want them to have all this, to show it every day, to make out of these words their rule of life. The respectable classses which suspect you of such pernicious longings lock you up and would just as soon have you shot – because your personality counts and you can not deny that you are a dangerous man. What makes you dangerous is your unwarrantable belief that your desire may be realized. This is the only point of difference between us. I do not believe. And if I desire the very same things no one cares. Consequently I am not likely to be locked up or shot. Therein is another difference – this time to your manifest advantage.

There is a – let us say – a machine. It evolved itself (I am severely scientific) out of a chaos of scraps of iron and behold! – it knits. I am horrified at the horrible work and stand appalled. I feel it ought to embroider – but it goes on knitting. You come and say: 'this is all right: it's only a question of the right kind of oil. Let us use this – for instance – celestial oil and the machine shall embroider a most beautiful design in purple and gold.' Will it? Alas no. You cannot by any special lubrication make embroidery with a knitting machine. And the most withering thought is that the infamous thing has made itself; made itself without thought, without conscience, without foresight, without eyes, without heart. It is a tragic accident – and it has happened. You can't interfere with it. The last drop of bitterness is in the suspicion that you can't even smash it. In virtue of that truth one and immortal which lurks in the force that made it spring into existence it is what it is – and it is indestructible!

It knits us in and it knits us out. It has knitted time, space, pain, death, corruption, despair and all the illusions – and nothing matters. I'll admit however that to look at the remorseless process is sometimes amusing.

14 From a letter to John Galsworthy, 16 January 1898. Galsworthy's *From the Four Winds* is the book referred to.

The good lady in the North judges from a remote standpoint. It never probably occurred to her to ask herself what you intended doing, how near you've come to that intention. Now I contend that (if I understood your attitude of mind) you have absolutely done what you set out to do. I contend that the people you take being what they are, the book is *their* psychology. This is my opinion. And the merit of the book (apart from distinguished literary expression), is just in this: You have given the exact measure of your characters in a language of great felicity, with measure, with poetical appropriateness to characters, tragic indeed but within the bounds of their nature. That's what makes the book valuable, apart from its many qualities as a piece of literary work. [. . .]

P.S. In fact the force of the book is in the fidelity to the surface of life, to the surface of events, – to the surface of things and ideas. Now this is not being shallow. If the episode of life you describe strikes your critic as without profundity, it is not because the treatment is not deep. To me you have absolutely touched the bottom, and the achievement is as praiseworthy as though you had plumbed the very ocean. It is not your business to invent depths, – to invent depths is not art either. Most things and most natures have nothing but a surface. A fairly prosperous man in the state of modern society is without depth, – but he is complicated, – just in the way you show him. I don't suppose you admire such beings any more than I do. Your book is a dispassionate analysis of high-minded and contempt-ible types, and you awaken sympathy, interest, feeling in an im-partial, artistic way. It is an achievement. I am rather angry with your critic for so wholly missing the value and the *fundamental* art of the book. As to the executive beauty of the work she could not very well have said less. The book is desperately convincing. She quarrels with you for not making it inspiring! Just like a clever woman. You and I know that there is very little inspiration in such as phase of life, but women won't have it so. Prepare yourself to be misunderstood right and left. The work is good. And *as work*, it *is* inspiring. Even so!

15 From a letter to Cunninghame Graham, 31 January 1898. *Santa Teresa: Being Some Account of Her Life and Times* was by Graham's wife Gabriela, in political life a socialist like himself.

Now the first sensation of oppression has worn off a little what remains with one after reading the Life of St Theresa is the impression of a wonderful richness; a world peopled thickly – with the breath of mysticism over all – the landscapes, the walls, the men, the woman. Of course I am quite incompetent to criticize such a work; but I can appreciate it. It is vast and suggestive; it is a distinct acquisition to the reader – or at least to me; it makes one *see* and reflect. It is absorbing like a dream and as difficult to keep hold of. And it is – to me – profoundly saddening. It is indeed old life re-vived. And old life is like new life after all – an uninterrupted agony of effort. Yes. Egoism is good, and altruism is good, and fidelity to nature would be the best of all, and systems could be built, and rules could be made – if we could only get rid of consciousness. What makes mankind tragic is not that they are the victims of nature, it is that they are conscious of it. To be part of the animal kingdom under the conditions of this earth is very well – but as soon as you know of your slavery the pain, the anger, the strife – the tragedy begins. We can't return to nature, since we can't change our place in it. Our refuge is in stupidity, in drunkenness of all kinds, in lies, in beliefs, in murder, thieving, reforming – in negation, in contempt – each man according to the promptings of his particular devil. There is no morality, no knowledge and no hope; there is only the consciousness of ourselves which drives us about a world that whether seen in a convex or a concave mirror is always but a vain and fleeting appearance.

16 'Tales of the sea' (1898).[5]

It is by his irresistible power to reach the adventurous side in the character, not only of his own but of all nations, that Marryat is largely human. He is the enslaver of youth, not by the literary artifices of presentation, but by the natural glamour of his own temperament. To his young heroes the beginning of life is a splendid and warlike lark, ending at last in inheritance and marriage. His novels are not the outcome of his art, but of his character, like the deeds that make up his record of naval service. To the artist his work is interesting as a completely successful expression of an unartistic nature. It is absolutely amazing to us, as the disclosure of the spirit animating the stirring time when the nineteenth century was young. There is an air of fable about it. Its loss would be irreparable, like the curtailment of national story or the loss of a historical document. It is the beginning and the embodiment of an inspiring tradition.

To this writer of the sea the sea was not an element. It was a stage, where was displayed an exhibition of valour, and of such achievement as the world had never seen before. The greatness of that achievement cannot be pronounced imaginary, since its reality has affected the destinies of nations; nevertheless, in its grandeur it has all the remoteness of an ideal. History preserves the skeleton of facts and, here and there, a figure or a name; but it is in Marryat's novels that we find the mass of the nameless, that we see them in the flesh, that we obtain a glimpse of the everyday life and an insight into the spirit animating the crowd of obscure men who knew how to build for their country such a shining monument of memories.

Marryat is really a writer of the Service. What sets him apart is his fidelity. His pen serves his country as well as did his professional skill and his renowned courage. His figures move about between water and sky, and the water and the sky are there only to frame the deeds of the Service. His novels, like amphibious creatures, live on the sea and frequent the shore, where they flounder deplorably. The loves and the hates of his boys are as primitive as their virtues and their vices. His women, from the beautiful Agnes to the witch-like mother of Lieutenant Vanslyperken, are, with the exception of the sailors' wives, like the shadows of what has never been. His Silvas, his Ribieras, his Shriftens, his Delmars remind us of people we have heard of somewhere, many times, without ever believing in their existence. His morality is honourable and conventional. There is cruelty in his fun and he can invent puns in the midst of carnage. His naiveties are perpetrated in a lurid light. There is an endless variety of types, all surface, with hard edges, with memorable eccentricities of outline, with a childish and heroic effect in the drawing. They do not belong to life; they belong exclusively to the Service. And yet they live; there is a truth in them, the truth of their time; a headlong, reckless audacity, an intimacy with violence, an unthinking fearlessness, and an exuberance of vitality which only years of war and victories can give. His adventures are enthralling; the rapidity of his action fascinates; his method is crude, his sentimentality, obviously incidental, is often factitious. His greatness is undeniable.

It is undeniable. To a multitude of readers the navy of today is Marryat's navy still. He has created a priceless legend. If he be not immortal, yet he will last long enough for the highest ambition, because he has dealt manfully with an inspiring phase in the history of that Service on which the life of his country depends. The tradition of the great past he has fixed in his pages will be cherished for ever as the guarantee of the future. He loved his country first, the Service next, the sea perhaps not at all. But the sea loved him without reserve. It gave him his professional distinction and his author's fame – a fame such as not often falls to the lot of a true artist.

At the same time, on the other side of the Atlantic, another man wrote of the sea with true artistic instinct. He is not invincibly young and heroic; he is mature and human, though for him also the stress of adventure and endeavour must end fatally in inheritance and marriage. For James Fenimore Cooper nature was not the framework, it was an essential part of existence. He could hear its voice, he could understand its silence, and he could interpret both for us in his prose with all that felicity and sureness of effect that belong to a poetical conception alone. His fame, as wide but less brilliant than that of his contemporary, rests mostly on a novel which is not of the sea. But he loved the sea and looked at it with consummate understanding. In his sea tales the sea inter-penetrates with life; it is in a subtle way a factor in the problem of existence, and, for all its greatness, it is always in touch with the men, who, bound on errands of war or gain, traverse its immense solitudes. His descriptions have the magistral ampleness of a gesture indicating the sweep of a vast horizon. They embrace the colours of sunset, the peace of starlight, the aspects of calm and storm, the great loneliness of the waters, the stillness of watchful coasts, and the alert readiness which marks men who live face to face with the promise and the menace of the sea.

He knows the men and he knows the sea. His method may be often faulty, but his art is genuine. The truth is within him. The road to legitimate realism is through poetical feeling, and he possesses that – only it is expressed in the leisurely manner of his time. He has the knowledge of simple hearts. Long Tom Coffin is a monumental seaman with the individuality of life and the significance of a type. It is hard to believe that Manual and Borroughcliffe, Mr Marble of Marble-Head, Captain Tuck of the packet-ship *Montauk*, or Daggett, the tenacious commander of the *Sea Lion* of Martha's Vineyard, must pass away some day and be utterly forgotten. His sympathy is large, and his humour is as genuine – and as perfectly unaffected – as is his art. In certain passages he reaches, very simply, the heights of inspired vision.

He wrote before the great American language was born, and he wrote as well as any novelist of his time. If he pitches upon episodes redounding to the glory of the young republic, surely England has glory enough to forgive him, for the sake of his excellence, the patriotic bias at her expense. The interest of his tales is convincing and unflagging; and there runs through his work a steady vein of friendliness for the old country which the succeeding generations of his compatriots have replaced by a less definite sentiment.

Perhaps no two authors of fiction influenced so many lives and gave to so many the initial impulse towards a glorious or a useful career. Through the distances of space and time those two men of another race have shaped also the life of the writer of this appreciation. Life is life, and art is art – and truth is hard to find in either. Yet in testimony to the achievement of both these authors it may be said that, in the case of the writer at least, the youthful glamour, the headlong vitality of the one and the profound sympathy, the artistic insight of the other – to which he had surrendered – have withstood the brutal shock of facts and the wear of laborious years. He has never regretted his surrender.

17 From a letter to H. G. Wells, 4 December 1898. Wells wrote a complimentary review of Conrad's first novels, which led to a lifelong friendship despite periods of disagreement.

Thanks ever so much for the *Invisible Man*. I shall keep him a few days longer.

Frankly – it is uncommonly fine. One can always *see* a lot in your work – there is always a 'beyond' to your books – but into this (with due regard to theme and length) you've managed to put an amazing quantity of effects. If it just misses being tremendous, it is because you didn't make it so – and if you didn't, there isn't a man in England who could. As to b____ furriners they ain't in it at all.

I suppose you'll have the common decency to believe me when I tell you I am always powerfully impressed by your work. Impressed is *the* word, O Realist of the Fantastic! whether you like it or not. And if you want to know what impresses me it is to see how you contrive to give over humanity into the clutches of the Impossible and yet manage to keep it down (or up) to its humanity, to its flesh, blood, sorrow, folly. *That* is the achievement! In this little book you do it with an appalling completeness. I'll not insist on the felicity of incident. This must be obvious even to yourself. Three of us have been reading the book (I had two men staying here after Pugh left) and we have been tracking with delight the cunning method of your logic. It is masterly – it is ironic – it is very relentless – and it is very true. We all three (the two others are no fools) place the *I.M.* above the *War of the Worlds*. Whether we are right – and if so why – I am not sure, and cannot tell. I fancy the book is more strictly human, and thus your diabolical psychology plants its points right into a man's bowels. To me the *W. of the W.* has less of that sinister air of truth that arrests the reader in reflexion at the turn of the page so often in the *I.M.* In reading this last, one is touched by the anguish of it as by something that any day may happen to oneself. It is a great triumph for you.

18 From a letter to Mme Angèle Zagórska, Christmas 1898. Mme Zagórska was a distant relation to Conrad. Her daughter, Aniela, later translated some of Conrad's works into Polish.[6]

With regard to Grant Allen's *Woman Who Did*, *c'est un livre mort*. The *Woman Who Did* had a kind of success, of curiosity mostly and that only amongst the philistines – the sort of people who read Marie Corelli and Hall Caine. All three are very popular with the public – and they are also puffed in the press. There are no lasting qualities in their work. The thought is commonplace and the style without any distinction. They are popular because they express the common thought, and the common man is delighted to find himself in accord with people he supposes distinguished. This is the secret of many popularities. (You can develop this idea as an explanation of the enthusiasm of the public for books which are of no value.) As to Allen, he is considered a man of letters among scholars and a scholar among men of letters. He writes popular scientific manuals equally well. Marie Corelli is *not* noticed critically by the serious reviews. She is simply ignored. Her books sell largely. Hall Caine is a kind of male Marie Corelli.

Among the people in literature who deserve attention the first is Rudyard Kipling (his last book *The Day's Work,* novel), J. M. Barrie – a Scotsman. His last book *Sentimental Tommy* (last year). George Meredith did not bring out anything this year. The last volumes of the charming translation of Turgeniev came out a fortnight ago. The translation is by Mrs Constance Garnett. George Moore has published the novel *Evelyn Innes* – *un succès d'estime*. He is supposed to belong to the naturalist school and Zola is his prophet. *Tout ca, c'est très vieux jeu*. A certain Mr T. Watts-Dunton published the novel *Aylwin*, a curiosity success, as this Watts-Dunton (who is a barrister) is supposed to be the friend of different celebrities in the world of Fine Arts (especially in the pre-Raphaelite School). He has crammed them all into his book. H. G. Wells published this year *The War of the Worlds* and *The Invisible Man*. He is a very original writer with a very individualistic judgement in all things and an astonishing imagination.

But, my dearest, really I read nothing and I never look at the papers, so I know nothing of politics or literature.

19 From a letter to William Blackwood, 31 December 1898. Blackwood had written asking for something for the thousandth number of *Blackwood's*.

Your proposal delights me. As it happens I am (and have been for the last 10 days) working for *Maga*. The thing is far advanced and would have been finished by this only our little boy fell ill, I was disturbed and upset and the work suffered. I expect to be ready in a very few days. It is a narrative after the manner of *youth* told by the same man dealing with his experience on a river in Central Africa. The *idea* in it is not as obvious as in *youth* – or at least not so obviously presented. I tell you all this, for tho' I have no doubts as to the *workmanship* I do not know whether the *subject* will commend itself to you for that particular number. Of course I should be very glad to appear in it and shall try to hurry up the copy for that express purpose, but I wish you to understand that I am prepared to leave the ultimate decision as to the date of appearance to your decision after perusal.

The title I am thinking of is '*The Heart of Darkness*' but the narrative is not gloomy. The criminality of inefficiency and pure

47

selfishness when tackling the civilizing work in Africa is a justifiable idea. The subject is of our time distinctly – though not topically treated. It is a story as much as my *Outpost of Progress* was but, so to speak 'takes in' more – is a little wider – is less concentrated upon individuals.

20 From a letter to Galsworthy, 11 February 1899.[7]

I think that to say Henry James does not write from the heart is maybe hasty. He is cosmopolitan, civilized, very much *homme du monde* and the acquired (educated if you like) side of his temperament, – that is, – restraints, the instinctive, the nurtured, fostered, cherished side is always presented to the reader first. To me even the R. T. seems to flow from the heart because and only because the work, approaching so near perfection, yet does not strike cold. Technical perfection, unless there is some real glow to illumine and warm it from within, must necessarily be cold. I argue that in H. J. there is such a glow and not a dim one either, but to us used, absolutely accustomed, to unartistic expression of fine, headlong, honest (or dishonest) sentiments the art of H. J. does appear heartless. The outlines are so clear, the figures so finished, chiselled, carved and brought out that we exclaim, – we, used to the shades of the contemporary fiction, to the more or less malformed shades, – we exclaim, – stone! Not at all. I say flesh and blood, – very perfectly presented, – perhaps with too much perfection of *method*.

The volume of short stories entitled, I think, *The Lesson of the Master* contains a tale called 'The Pupil', if I remember rightly, where the underlying feeling of the man, – his really wide sympathy, – is seen nearer the surface. Of course he does not deal in primitive emotions. I maintain he is the most civilized of modern writers. He is also an idealizer. His heart shows itself in the delicacy of his handling. Things like 'The Middle Years' and 'The Altar of the Dead' in the vol. entitled *Terminations* would illustrate my meaning. Moreover, your cousin admits the element of pathos. Mere technique won't give the elements of pathos. I admit he is not *forcible*, – or let us say, the only forcible thing in his work is his technique. Now a literary intelligence would be naturally struck by the wonderful technique, and that is so wonderful in its way that it dominates the bare expression. The more so that the expression is only of delicate shades. He is never in deep gloom or in violent sunshine. But he feels deeply and vividly every delicate shade. We cannot ask for more. Not everyone is a Turgeniev. Moreover Turgeniev is not civilized (therein much of his charm for us) in the sense H. J. is civilized.

21 From a letter to Sir Hugh Clifford, 9 October 1899. Conrad had received Clifford's book, *In a Corner of Asia*, 'three hours ago' and had 'read it twice' before writing. He had reviewed Clifford's *Studies in Brown Humanity* in 1898, which led to a lifelong friendship.

You do not leave enough to the imagination. I do not mean as to facts – the facts cannot be too explicitly stated;. I am alluding simply to the phrasing. True, a man who knows so much (without taking into account the manner in which his knowledge was acquired) may well spare himself the trouble of meditating over the words, only that words, groups of words, words standing alone, are symbols of life, have the power in their sound or their aspect to present the very thing you wish to hold up before the mental vision of your readers. The things 'as they are' exist in words; therefore words should be handled with care lest the picture, the image of truth abiding in facts, should become distorted – or blurred.

These are the considerations for a mere craftsman – you may say; and you may also conceivably say that I have nothing else to trouble my head about. However, the *whole* of the truth lies in the presentation; therefore the expression should be studied in the interest of veracity. This is the only morality of *art* apart from *subject*.

I have travelled a good way from my original remark – not enough left to the imagination in the phrasing. I beg leave to illustrate my meaning from extracts on p. 261 – not that I pose for an accomplished craftsman or fondly think I am free from that very fault and others much worse. No; it is only to explain what I mean.

. . . 'When the whole horror of his position forced itself with an agony of realization upon his frightened mind, Pa' Tûa for a space lost his reason.' . . . In this sentence the reader is borne down by the full expression. The words: *with an agony of realization* completely destroy the effect – therefore interfere with the truth of the statement. The word *frightened* is fatal. It seems as if it had been written without any thought at all. It takes away all sense of reality – for if you read the sentence *in its place on the page* you will see that the word 'frightened' (or indeed any word of the sort) is inadequate to express the true state of that man's mind. No word is adequate. The imagination of the reader should be left free to arouse his feeling.

'. . . When the whole horror of his position forced itself upon his mind, Pa' Tûa for a space lost his reason. . . .' This is truth; this it is which, thus stated, carries conviction because it is a *picture* of a mental state. And look how finely it goes on with a perfectly legitimate effect.

. . . 'He screamed aloud, and the hollow of the rocks took up his cries' . . . It is magnificent! It is suggestive. It is truth effectively stated. But '*and hurled them back to him mockingly*' is nothing at all. It is a phrase anybody can write to fit any sort of situation; it is the sort of thing that writes itself; it is the sort of thing I write twenty times a day and (with the fear of overtaking fate behind me) spend half my nights in taking out of my work – upon which depends the daily bread of the house (literally – from day to day); not to mention (I dare hardly think of it) the future of my child, of those nearest and dearest to me, between whom and the bleakest want there is only my pen – as long as life lasts. And I can sell all I write – as much as I can write!

This is said to make it manifest that I practise the faith which I take the liberty to preach – if you allow me to say so – in a brotherly spirit. To return.

Please observe how strikingly the effect is carried on.

'When the whole horror of his position forced itself upon his mind, Pa' Tûa for a space lost his reason. He screamed aloud, and the hollow of the rocks took up his cries; the bats awoke in thousands and joined the band that rustled and squeaked above the man,' etc., etc. In the last two lines the words hurrying – motiveless – already – defenceless – are not essential and therefore not true to the fact. The impression of *hurrying motiveless* has been given already in lines 2,

50

3, 4, at the top of the page. If they *joined*, it is because the others were *already* flying. *Already* is repetition. *Defenceless* is inadequate for a man held in the merciless grip of a rock.

And pray believe me that if I have selected this passage, it is because I am alive to its qualities and not because I have looked consciously for its defects.

For the same reason I do not apologize for my remarks. They are not an impertinence, they are a tribute to the work, that appeals so strongly to me by its subject, partly – but most by its humanity, its comprehension, by its spirit and by its expression too – which I have made a subject of critical analysis. If I have everlastingly bored you, you must forgive me. I trust you will find no other cause of offence.

22 From a letter to William Blackwood, 8 November 1899. John Buchan's 'The far islands' had just appeared in *Blackwood's*.[8]

Criticism is poor work, and to expose the weaknesses of humanity as exhibited in literary work is a thankless and futile task. I've always thought that Macaulay's smashing of R. Montgomery's poems (!) was a pathetic example of mighty truth powerless before the falsehood of pretences, like the great sea before a very small rock. To point out to the crowd beauties not manifest to the common eye, to flash the light of one's sympathetic perception upon great, if not obvious, qualities, and even upon generous failings that hold the promise of better things this is indeed a toil worthy of a man's pen, a task that would repay for the time given up, for the strength expended for that sadness that comes of thinking over the sincere endeavour of a soul – for ever debarred from attaining perfection. But the blind distribution of praise or blame, done with a light heart and an empty mind, which is of the very essence of 'periodical' criticism seems to me to be a work less useful than skirt-dancing and not quite as honourable as pocket-picking.

There is too a sort of curse upon the critical exercise of human thought. Should one attempt honestly an analysis of another man's production it is ten to one, that one will get the credit for all sorts of motives except for that of sincere conviction; this is the taint of the literary life; and though writing to you I would not expose myself to the risk of being misunderstood I prefer to say nothing critical about John Buchan's story. I am willing to admit it is grammatically written – (I know nothing of grammar myself as he who runs may see) – if anybody desires to make that assertion. I do happen however to know one or two things that might conceivably be found to have a bearing upon the story and on these I shall hold my peace.

There is one thing (though hardly pertaining to criticism proper) which ought to be said of that – production. It is this: its idea, its feeling, its suggestion *and even the most subtly significant incidents* have been wrenched alive out of Kipling's tale *The finest Story in the World*. What became of the idea, of the feeling, of the suggestion and of the incidents, in the process of that wrenching I leave it for the pronouncement not of posterity but of any contemporary mind that would be brought (for less than ten minutes) to the consideration of Mr Buchan's story. The thing is patent – it is the only impression that remains after reading the last words – it argues naiveness of an appalling kind or else a most serene impudence. I write strongly – because I feel strongly.

One does not expect style, construction, or even common intelligence in the fabrication of story; but one has the right to demand some sort of sincerity and to expect common honesty. When that fails – what remains?

23 From a letter to Garnett, 12 November 1900. Conrad is referring to *Lord Jim* (1900).

Yes! you've put your finger on the plague spot. The division of the book into two parts which is the basis of your criticism demonstrates to me once more your amazing insight; and your analysis of the effect of the book puts into words precisely and suggestively the dumb thoughts of every reader – and my own.

Such is indeed the effect of the book; the effect which you can name and others can only feel. I admit I stood for a great triumph and I have only succeeded in giving myself utterly away. Nobody'll see it, but you have detected me falling back into my lump of clay I had been lugging up from the bottom of the pit, with the idea of breathing big life into it. And all I have done was to let it fall with a silly crash.

For what is fundamentally wrong with the book – the cause and the effect – is want of power. I do not mean the 'power' of reviewers' jargon. I mean the want of illuminating imagination. I wanted to obtain a sort of lurid light out of the very events. You know what I have done – alas! I haven't been strong enough to breathe the right sort of life into my clay – the *revealing* life.

I've been satanically ambitious, but there's nothing of a devil in me, worse luck. The *Outcast* is a heap of sand, the *Nigger* a splash of water, *Jim* a lump of clay. A stone, I suppose will be my next gift to the impatient mankind – before I get drowned in mud to which even my supreme struggles won't give a simulacrum of life. Poor mankind! Drop a tear for it – but look how infinitely more pathetic I am! This pathos is a kind of triumph no criticism can touch. Like the philosopher who crowed at the Universe I shall know when I am utterly squashed. This time I am only very bruised, very sore, very humiliated.

24 From a letter to Galsworthy, 11 November 1901. Conrad refers to Galsworthy's *The Man of Devon and Other Stories*, which he has read 'twice – watching the effect of it impersonally during the second reading', and also to his *Villa Rubein*.

There is a certain caution of touch which will militate against popularity. After all, to please the public (if one isn't a sugary imbecile or an inflated fraud) one must handle one's subject intimately. Mere intimacy with the subject won't do. And conviction is found for others, – not for the author, only in certain contradictions and irrelevancies to the general conception of character (or characters) and of the subject. Say what you like, man lives in his eccentricities (so called) alone. They give a vigour to his personality which mere consistency can never do. One must explore deep and believe the incredible to find the few particles of truth floating in an ocean of insignificance. And before all one must divest oneself of every particle of respect for one's character. You are really most profound and attain the greatest art in handling the people you do not respect. For instance the minor characters in *V. R.* And in this volume I am bound to recognize that Forsyte is the best. I recognize this with a certain reluctance because indubitably there is more beauty (and more felicity of style too) in the *M. of D.* The story of the mine shows best your strength and your weakness. There is hardly a word I would have changed; there are things in it that I would give a pound of my flesh to have written. Honestly, – there are. And your mine-manager remains unconvincing because he is too confoundedly perfect in his very imperfections. The fact is you want more scepticism at the very foundation of your work. Scepticism, the tonic of minds, the tonic of life, the agent of truth, – the way of art and salvation. In a book you should love the idea and be scrupulously faithful to your conception of life. There lies the honour of the writer, not in the fidelity to his personages. You must never allow them to decoy you out of yourself. As against your people you must preserve an attitude of perfect indifference, the part of creative power. A creator must be indifferent; because directly the 'Fiat!' has issued from his lips, there are the creatures made in his image that'll try to drag him down from his eminence, – and belittle him by their worship. Your attitude to them should be purely intellectual, more independent, freer, less rigorous than it is. You seem, for their sake, to hug your conceptions of right and wrong too closely. There is exquisite atmosphere in your tales. What they want now is more air.

25 From a letter to William Blackwood, 31 May 1902. The story referred to is 'The end of the tether', later included in *Youth: A Narrative and Two Other Stories* (1902).

I know exactly what I am doing. Mr George Blackwood's incidental remark in his last letter that the story is not fairly begun yet is in a measure correct but, on a large view, beside the point. For, the writing is as good as I can make it (first duty), and in the light of the final incident, the whole story in all its descriptive detail shall fall into its place – acquire its value and its significance. This is my method based on deliberate conviction. I've never departed from it. I call your own kind self to witness and I beg to instance Karain – Lord Jim (where the method is fully developed) – the last pages of Heart of Darkness where the interview of the man and the girl locks in – as it were – the whole 30,000 words of narrative description into one suggestive view of a whole phase of life, and makes of that story something quite on another plane than an anecdote of a man who went mad in the Centre of Africa. And *Youth* itself (which I delight to know you like so well) exists only in virtue of my fidelity to the idea and the method. The favourable critics of that story, Q amongst others remarked with a sort of surprise 'This after all is a story for boys yet ____'

Exactly. Out of the material of a boys' story I've made *Youth* by the force of the idea expressed in accordance with a strict conception of my method. And however unfavourably it may affect the business in hand I must confess that I shall not depart from my method. I am at need prepared to explain on what grounds I think it a true method. All my endeavours shall be directed to understand it better, to develop its great possibilities, to acquire greater skill in the handling – to mastery in short. [. . .]

I am long in my development. What of that? Is not Thackeray's penny worth of mediocre fact drowned in an ocean of twaddle? And yet he lives. And Sir Walter, himself, was not the writer of concise anecdotes I fancy. And G. Eliot – is she as swift as the present public (incapable of fixing its attention for five consecutive minutes) requires us to be at the cost of all honesty, of all truth, and even the most elementary conception of art? But these are great names. I don't compare myself with them. I am *modern*, and I would rather recall Wagner the musician and Rodin the Sculptor who both had to starve a little in their day – and Whistler the painter who made Ruskin the critic foam at the mouth with scorn and indignation. They too have arrived. They had to suffer for being 'new'. And I too hope to find my place in the rear of my betters. But still – my place. My work shall not be an utter failure because it has the solid basis of a definite intention – first: and next because it is not an endless analysis of affected sentiments but in its essence it is action (strange as this affirmation may sound at the present time) nothing but action – action observed, felt and interpreted with an absolute truth to my sensations (which are the basis of art in literature) – action of human beings that will bleed to a prick, and are moving in a visible world.

This is my creed. Time will show.

26 From a letter to Arnold Bennett, 6 November 1902. Bennett's *Anna of the Five Towns* is the book referred to. Bennett was another in the group of writers with whom Conrad frequently exchanged works.

But if I could not write to you, I had found time to read your book. I read it once, twice, and then kept it upstairs for dipping into when I came up to bed, jaded with my unavailing efforts to express myself in the absence of any sort of mood; and your firm grip, the firm grip of style and the mastery of the subject, have more than once refreshed my weariness.

I doubt if hitherto my mind had been fresh enough to appreciate your work – intellectually as it deserves to be. Its appeal had been to me emotional, a matter of art purely as apart from underlying thought. Of course, you understand that my emotion is awakened by the *skill* of your work first – and I may almost say: first and last – this word in my mind embracing everything; from the first coordination of your inspiration, through the effective processes of your thought, down to the last small touches of expression, delightful to trace along the pages and which resume to me the whole extent of the remarkable gifts which you display in the freshness and the cadence of your sentences.

It is indeed a thing *done*: good to see and friendly to live with for a space. This is the final impression.

27 From 'A glance at two books' (1904).[9]

The national English novelist seldom regards his work – the exercise of his Art – as an achievement of active life by which he will produce certain definite effects upon the emotions of his readers, but simply as an instinctive, often unreasoned, outpouring of his own emotions. He does not go about building up his book with a precise intention and a steady mind. It never occurs to him that a book is a deed, that the writing of it is an enterprise as much as the conquest of a colony. He has no such clear conception of his craft. Writing from a full heart, he liberates his soul for the satisfaction of his own sentiment; and when he has finished the scene he is at liberty to strike his forehead and exclaim: 'This is genius!'

Thackeray is reported to have done this, and there is no reason why any novelist of his type should not. He is, as a matter of fact, writing lyrically (a lyric is the expression of a mood); he is expressing his own moods: I take what the gods give me – he says in all humility, and when the godhead inspires him with what seems good to his heart, to his imagination, to his tenderness or to his indignation, he may say, and use the words literally, 'This is genius!'

It is. And it is probably the reason why the distinctively English novelist is always at his best in denunciations of institutions, of types or of conventionalized society.

It is comparatively easy for us, when we are really moved by the clearness of our vision, to convince an audience that Messrs A., B. and C. are callous, ferocious or cowardly. We should have to use much more conscious art to give a permanent impression of those gentlemen as purely altruist.

Thus Mr Osborne, the hard merchant, father of Captain Osborne, is more definite and flawless than many of Thackeray's so-called good characters; and thus Mr Pecksniff is, through scorn and dislike, rendered more memorable than the brothers Cheeryble. It is not perhaps so much that these distinguished writers were completely incapable of loving their fellow men simply as men, exposed to suffering, temptation and affliction, as that, neglecting the one indispensable thing, neglecting to use their powers of selection and observation, they emotionally excelled in rendering the disagreeable. And that is easy. To find beauty, grace, charm in the bitterness of truth is a graver task.

Thackeray, we imagine, did not love his gentle heroines. He did not love them. He was in love with the sentiments they represented. He was, in fact, in love with what does not exist – and that is why Amelia Osborne does not exist, either in colour, in shape, in grace, in goodness. Turgeniev probably did not love his Lisa, a most pathetic, pure, charming and profound creation, for what she was, in her creator's mind. He loved her disinterestedly, as it were, out of pure warmth of heart, as a human being in the tumult and hazard of life. And that is why we must feel, suffer and live with that wonderful creation. That is why she is as real to us as her stupid mother, as the men of the story, as the sombre Varvard, and all the others that may be called the unpleasant characters in 'The House of Gentle-folk'.

28 'Guy de Maupassant' (1904).[10]

To introduce Maupassant to English readers with apologetic explanations as though his art were recondite and the tendency of his work immoral would be a gratuitous impertinence.

Maupassant's conception of his art is such as one would expect from a practical and resolute mind; but in the consummate simplicity of his technique it ceases to be perceptible. This is one of its greatest qualities, and like all the great virtues it is based primarily on self-denial.

To pronounce a judgement upon the general tendency of an author is a difficult task. One could not depend upon reason alone, nor yet trust solely to one's emotions. Used together, they would in many cases traverse each other, because emotions have their own unanswerable logic. Our capacity for emotion is limited, and the field of our intelligence is restricted. Responsiveness to every feeling, combined with the penetration of every intellectual subterfuge, would end, not in judgement, but in universal absolution. *Tout comprendre c'est tout pardonner*. And in this benevolent neutrality towards the warring errors of human nature all light would go out from art and from life.

We are at liberty then to quarrel with Maupassant's attitude towards our world in which, like the rest of us, he has that share which his senses are able to give him. But we need not quarrel with him violently. If our feelings (which are tender) happen to be hurt because his talent is not exercised for the praise and consolation of mankind, our intelligence (which is great) should let us see that he is a very splendid sinner, like all those who in this valley of compromises err by over-devotion to the truth that is in them. His determinism, barren of praise, blame and consolation, has all the merit of his conscientious art. The worth of every conviction consists precisely in all the steadfastness with which it is held.

Except for his philosophy, which in the case of so consummate an artist does not matter (unless to the solemn and naive mind)

Maupassant of all writers of fiction demands least forgiveness from his readers. He does not require forgiveness because he is never dull.

The interest of a reader in a work of imagination is either ethical or that of simple curiosity. Both are perfectly legitimate, since there is both a moral and an excitement to be found in a faithful rendering of life. And in Maupassant's work there is the interest of curiosity and the moral of a point of view consistently preserved and never obtruded for the end of personal gratification. The spectacle of this immense talent served by exceptional faculties and triumphing over the most thankless subjects by an unswerving singleness of purpose is in itself an admirable lesson in the power of artistic honesty, one may say of artistic virtue. The inherent greatness of the man consists in this, that he will let none of the fascinations that beset a writer working in loneliness turn him away from the straight path, from the vouchsafed vision of excellence. He will not be led into perdition by the seductions of sentiment, of eloquence, of humour, of pathos; of all that splendid pageant of faults that pass between the writer and his probity on the blank sheet of paper, like the glittering cortège of deadly sins before the austere anchorite in the desert air of Thebaïde. This is not to say that Maupassant's austerity has never faltered; but the fact remains that no tempting demon has ever succeeded in hurling him down from his high, if narrow, pedestal.

It is the austerity of his talent, of course, that is in question. Let the discriminating reader, who at times may well spare a moment or two to the consideration and enjoyment of artistic excellence, be asked to reflect a little upon the texture of two stories included in this volume: 'A Piece of String', and 'A Sale'. How many openings the last offers for the gratuitous display of the author's wit or clever buffoonery, the first for an unmeasured display of sentiment! And both sentiment and buffoonery could have been made very good too, in a way accessible to the meanest intelligence, at the cost of truth and honesty. Here it is where Maupassant's austerity comes in. He refrains from setting his cleverness against the eloquence of the facts. There is humour and pathos in these stories; but such is the greatness of his talent, the refinement of his artistic conscience, that all his high qualities appear inherent in the very things of which he speaks, as if they had been altogether independent of his presentation. Facts, and again facts are his unique concern. That is why he is not always properly understood. His facts are so perfectly rendered that, like the actualities of life itself, they demand from the reader the faculty of observation which is rare, the power of appreciation which is generally wanting in most of us who are guided mainly by empty phrases requiring no effort, demanding from us no qualities except a vague susceptibility to emotion. Nobody has ever gained the vast applause of a crowd by the simple and clear exposition of vital facts. Words alone strung upon a convention have fascinated us as worthless glass beads strung on a thread have charmed at all times our brothers the unsophisticated savages of the islands. Now, Maupassant, of whom it has been said that he is the master of the *mot juste*, has never been a dealer in words. His wares have been, not glass beads, but polished gems: not the most rare and precious, perhaps, but of the very first water of their kind.

That he took trouble with his gems, taking them up in the rough and polishing each facet patiently, the publication of the two posthumous volumes of short stories proves abundantly. I think it proves also the assertion made here that he was by no means a dealer in words. On looking at the first feeble drafts from which so many perfect stories have been fashioned, one discovers that what has been matured, improved, brought to perfection by unwearied endeavour is not the diction of the tale, but the vision of its true shape and detail. Those first attempts are not faltering or uncertain in expression. It is the conception which is at fault. The subjects have not yet been adequately seen. His proceeding was not to group expressive words, that mean nothing, around misty and mysterious shapes dear to muddled intellects and belonging neither to earth nor to heaven. His vision by a more scrupulous, prolonged and devoted attention to the aspects of the visible world discovered at last the right words as if miraculously impressed for him upon the face of things and events. This was the particular shape taken by his inspiration; it came to him directly, honestly in the light of his day, not on the tortuous, dark roads of meditation. His realities came to him from a genuine source, from this universe of vain appearances wherein we men have found everything to make us proud, sorry, exalted, and humble.

Maupassant's renown is universal, but his popularity is restricted. It is not difficult to perceive why. Maupassant is an intensely national writer. He is so intensely national in his logic, in his clearness, in his aesthetic and moral conceptions, that he has been accepted by his countrymen without having had to pay the tribute of flattery either to the nation as a whole, or to any class, sphere or division of the nation. The truth of his art tells with an irresistible force; and he stands excused from the duty of patriotic posturing. He is a Frenchman of Frenchmen beyond question or cavil, and with that he is simple enough to be universally comprehensible. What is wanting to his universal success is the mediocrity of an obvious and appealing tenderness. He neglects to qualify his truth with the drop of facile sweetness; he forgets to strew paper roses over the tombs. The disregard of these common decencies lays him open to the charges of cruelty, cynicism, hardness. And yet it can be safely affirmed that this man wrote from the fulness of a compassionate heart. He is merciless and yet gentle with his mankind; he does not rail at their prudent fears and their small artifices; he does not despise their labours. It seems to me that he looks with an eye of profound pity upon their troubles, deceptions and misery. But he looks at them all. He sees – and does not turn away his head. As a matter of fact he is courageous.

Courage and justice are not popular virtues. The practice of strict justice is shocking to the multitude who always (perhaps from an obscure sense of guilt) attach to it the meaning of mercy. In the majority of us, who want to be left alone with our illusions, courage inspires a vague alarm. This is what is felt about Maupassant. His qualities, to use the charming and popular phrase, are not lovable. Courage being a force will not masquerade in the robes of affected delicacy and restraint. But if his courage is not of a chivalrous stamp, it cannot be denied that it is never brutal for the sake of effect. The writer of these few reflections, inspired by a long and intimate acquaintance with the work of the man, has been struck by the appreciation of Maupassant manifested by many women gifted with tenderness and intelligence. Their more delicate and audacious souls are good judges of courage. Their finer penetration has discovered his genuine masculinity without display, his virility without a pose.

They have discerned in his faithful dealings with the world that enterprising and fearless temperament, poor in ideas but rich in power, which appeals most to the feminine mind.

It cannot be denied that he thinks very little. In him extreme energy of perception achieves great results, as in men of action the energy of force and desire. His view of intellectual problems is perhaps more simple than their nature warrants; still a man who has written 'Yvette' cannot be accused of want of subtlety. But one cannot insist enough upon this, that his subtlety, his humour, his grimness, though no doubt they are his own, are never presented otherwise but as belonging to our life, as found in nature, whose beauties and cruelties alike breathe the spirit of serene unconsciousness.

Maupassant's philosophy of life is more temperamental than rational. He expects nothing from gods or men. He trusts his senses for information and his instinct for deductions. It may seem that he has made but little use of his mind. But let me be clearly understood. His sensibility is really very great; and it is impossible to be sensible, unless one thinks vividly, unless one thinks correctly, starting from intelligible premises to an unsophisticated conclusion.

This is literary honesty. It may be remarked that it does not differ very greatly from the ideal honesty of the respectable majority, from the honesty of law-givers, of warriors, of kings, of bricklayers, of all those who express their fundamental sentiment in the ordinary course of their activities, by the work of their hands.

The work of Maupassant's hands is honest. He thinks sufficiently to concrete his fearless conclusions in illuminative instances. He renders them with that exact knowledge of the means and that absolute devotion to the aim of creating a true effect – which is art. He is the most accomplished of narrators.

It is evident that Maupassant looked upon his mankind in another spirit than those writers who make haste to submerge the difficulties of our holding-place in the universe under a flood of false and sentimental assumptions. Maupassant was a true and dutiful lover of our earth. He says himself in one of his descriptive passages: '*Nous autres que séduit la terre. . .*' It was true. The earth had for him a compelling charm. He looks upon her august and furrowed face with the fierce insight of real passion. His is the power of detecting the one immutable quality that matters in the changing aspects of nature and under the ever-shifting surface of life. To say that he could not embrace in his glance all its magnificance and all its misery is only to say that he was human. He lays claim to nothing that his matchless vision has not made his own. This creative artist has the true imagination; he never condescends to invent anything; he sets up no empty pretences. And he stoops to no littleness in his art – least of all to the miserable vanity of a catching phrase.

29 From 'Henry James: an appreciation' (1904).[11]

All creative art is magic, is evocation of the unseen in forms persuasive, enlightening, familiar and surprising, for the edification of mankind, pinned down by the conditions of its existence to the earnest consideration of the most insignificant tides of reality.

Action in its essence, the creative art of a writer of fiction may be compared to rescue work carried out in darkness against cross gusts of wind swaying the action of a great multitude. It is rescue work, this snatching of vanishing phases of turbulence, disguised in fair words, out of the native obscurity into a light where the struggling forms may be seen, seized upon, endowed with the only possible form of permanence in this world of relative values – the permanence of memory. And the multitude feels it obscurely too; since the demand of the individual to the artist is, in effect, the cry 'Take me out of myself!' meaning really, out of my perishable activity into the light of imperishable consciousness. But everything is relative, and the light of consciousness is only enduring, merely the most enduring of the things of this earth, imperishable only as against the short-lived work of our industrious hands.

When the last aqueduct shall have crumbled to pieces, the last airship fallen to the ground, the last blade of grass have died upon a dying earth, man, indomitable by his training in resistance to misery and pain, shall set this undiminished light of his eyes against the feeble glow of the sun. The artistic faculty, of which each of us has a minute grain, may find its voice in some individual of that last group, gifted with a power of expression and courageous enough to interpret the ultimate experience of mankind in terms of his temperament, in terms of art. I do not mean to say that he would attempt to beguile the last moments of humanity by an ingenious tale. It would be too much to expect – from humanity. I doubt the heroism of the hearers. As to the heroism of the artist, no doubt is necessary. There would be on his part no heroism. The artist in his calling of interpreter creates (the clearest form of demonstration) because he must. He is so much of a voice that, for him, silence is like death; and the postulate was, that there is a group alive, clustered on his threshold to watch the last flicker of light on a black sky, to hear the last word uttered in the stilled workshop of the earth. It is safe to affirm that, if anybody, it will be the imaginative man who would be moved to speak on the eve of that day without to-morrow – whether in austere exhortation or in a phrase of sardonic comment, who can guess?

For my own part, from a short and cursory acquaintance with my kind, I am inclined to think that the last utterance will formulate, strange as it may appear, some hope now to us utterly inconceivable. For mankind is delightful in its pride, its assurance, and its indomitable tenacity. It will sleep on the battlefield among its own dead, in the manner of an army having won a barren victory. It will not know when it is beaten. And perhaps it is right in that quality. The victories are not, perhaps, so barren as it may appear from a purely strategical, utilitarian point of view. Mr Henry James seems to hold that belief. Nobody has rendered better, perhaps, the tenacity of temper, or known how to drape the robe of spiritual honour about the drooping form of a victor in a barren strife. And the honour is always well won; for the struggles Mr Henry James chronicles with such subtle and direct insight are, though only personal contests, desperate in their silence, none the less heroic (in the modern sense) for the absence of shouted watchwords, clash of arms and sound of trumpets. Those are adventures in which only choice souls are ever involved. And Mr Henry James records them with a fearless and insistent fidelity to the *péripéties* of the contest, and the feeling of the combatants. [. . .]

In one of his critical studies, published some fifteen years ago, Mr Henry James claims for the novelist the standing of the historian as the only adequate one, as for himself and before his audience. I think that the claim cannot be contested, and that the position is unassailable. Fiction is history, human history, or it is nothing. But it is also more than that; it stands on firmer ground, being based on the reality of forms and the observation of social phenomena, whereas history is based on documents, and the reading of print and handwriting – on second-hand impression. Thus fiction is nearer truth. But let that pass. A historian may be an artist too, and a novelist is a historian, the preserver, the keeper, the expounder, of human experience. As is meet for a man of his descent and tradition, Mr Henry James is the historian of fine consciences.

Of course, this is a general statement; but I don't think its truth will be, or can be questioned. Its fault is that it leaves so much out; and, besides, Mr Henry James is much too considerable to be put into the nutshell of a phrase. The fact remains that he has made his choice, and that his choice is justified up to the hilt by the success of his art. He has taken for himself the greater part. The range of a fine conscience covers more good and evil than the range of conscience which may be called, roughly, not fine; a conscience, less troubled by the nice discrimination of shades of conduct. A fine conscience is more concerned with essentials; its triumphs are more perfect, if less profitable, in a wordly sense. There is, in short, more truth in its working for a historian to detect and to show. It is a thing of infinite complication and suggestion. None of these escapes the art of Mr Henry James. He has mastered the country, his domain, not wild indeed, but full of romantic glimpses, of deep shadows and sunny places. There are no secrets left within his range. He has disclosed them as they should be disclosed – that is, beautifully. And, indeed, ugliness has but little place in this world of his creation. Yet it is always felt in the truthfulness of his art; it is there, it surrounds, the scene, it presses close upon it. It is made visible, tangible, in the struggles, in the contacts of the fine consciences, in their perplexities, in the sophism of their mistakes. For a fine conscience is naturally a virtuous one. What is natural about it is just its fineness, and abiding sense of the intangible, ever-present, right. It is most visible in their ultimate triumph, in their emergence from miracle, through an energetic act of renunciation. Energetic, not violent;

the distinction is wide, enormous, like that between substance and shadow.

Through it all Mr Henry James keeps a firm hold of the substance, of what is worth having, of what is worth holding. The contrary opinion has been, if not absolutely affirmed, then at least implied, with some frequency. To most of us, living willingly in a sort of intellectual moonlight, in the faintly reflected light of truth, the shadows so firmly renounced by Mr Henry James's men and women, stand out endowed with extraordinary value, with a value so extraordinary that their rejection offends, by its uncalled-for scrupulousness, those business-like instincts which a careful Providence has implanted in our breasts. And, apart from that just cause of discontent, it is obvious that a solution by rejection must always present a certain lack of finality, especially startling when contrasted with the usual methods of solution by rewards and punishments, by crowned love, by fortune, by a broken leg or a sudden death. Why the reading public which, as a body, has never laid upon a story-teller the command to be an artist, should demand from him this sham of Divine Omnipotence, is utterly incomprehensible. But so it is; and these solutions are legitimate inasmuch as they satisfy the desire for finality, for which our hearts yearn, with a longing greater than the longing for the loaves and fishes of this earth. Perhaps the only true desire of mankind, coming thus to light in its hours of leisure, is to be set at rest. One is never set at rest by Mr Henry James's novels. His books end as an episode in life ends. You remain with the sense of the life still going on; and even the subtle presence of the dead is felt in that silence that comes upon the artist-creation when the last word has been read. It is eminently satisfying, but it is not final. Mr Henry James, great artist and faithful historian, never attempts the impossible.

30 From a letter to Cunninghame Graham, 31 October 1904. The writing of *Nostromo* (1904) owed much, directly and indirectly, to Graham's knowledge of South American affairs.

Your letter was indeed worth having and I blush deeply as I re-read it both with pleasure and shame. For in regard to that book I feel a great fraud.

What is done cannot be mended. I know that you have made the most of my audacious effort; but still it is to me a comfort and a delight that you have found so much to say in commendation. Your friendship and good nature, great as they are where my person and scribbling are concerned, would not have induced you to accept anything utterly contemptible – that I know. It is a great load off my chest. Now as to an explanation or two.

I don't defend Nostromo himself. Fact is he does not take *my* fancy either. As to his conduct generally and with women in particular I only wish to say that he is not a Spaniard or S. American. I tried to differentiate him even to the point of mounting him upon a mare which I believe is not or *was not* the proper thing to do in Argentina; though in Chile there was never much of that nonsense. But truly N is nothing at all – a fiction-embodied vanity of the sailor kind – a romantic mouthpiece of 'the people' which (I mean 'the people') frequently experience the very feelings to which he gives utterance. I do not defend him as a creation.

31 'Books' (1905).[12]

1

'I have not read this author's books, and if I have read them I have forgotten what they were about.'

These words are reported as having been uttered in our midst not a hundred years ago, publicly, from the seat of justice, by a civic magistrate. The words of our municipal rulers have a solemnity and importance far above the words of other mortals, because our municipal rulers more than any other variety of our governors and masters represent the average wisdom, temperament, sense, and virtue of the community. This generalization, it ought to be promptly said in the interests of eternal justice (and recent friendship), does not apply to the United States of America. There, if one may believe the long and helpless indignations of their daily and weekly Press, the majority of municipal rulers appear to be thieves of a particularly irrepressible sort. But this by the way. My concern is with a statement issuing from the average temperament and the average wisdom of a great and wealthy community, and uttered by a civic magistrate obviously without fear and without reproach.

I confess I am pleased with his temper, which is that of prudence. 'I have not read the books,' he says, and immediately he adds, 'and if I have read them I have forgotten.' This is excellent caution. And I like his style: it is unartificial and bears the stamp of manly sincerity. As a reported piece of prose this declaration is easy to read and not difficult to believe. Many books have not been read; still more have been forgotten. As a piece of civic oratory this declaration is strikingly effective. Calculated to fall in with the bent of the popular mind, so familiar with all forms of forgetfulness, it has also the power to stir up a subtle emotion while it starts a train of thought – and what greater force can be expected from human speech? But it is in naturalness that the declaration is perfectly delightful, for there is nothing more natural than for a grave City Father to forget what the books he has read once – long ago – in his giddy youth maybe – were about.

And the books in question are novels, or, at any rate, were written as novels. I proceed thus cautiously (following my illustrious example) because being without fear and desiring to remain as far as possible without reproach, I confess at once that I have not read them.

I have not; and of the million persons or more who are said to have read them, I never met one yet with the talent of lucid exposition sufficiently developed to give me a connected account of what they are about. But they are books, part and parcel of humanity, and as such, in their ever-increasing, jostling multitude, they are worthy of regard, admiration, and compassion.

Especially of compassion. It has been said a long time ago that books have their fate. They have, and it is very much like the destiny of man. They share with us the great incertitude of ignominy or glory – of severe justice and senseless persecution – of calumny and misunderstanding – the shame of undeserved success. Of all the inanimate objects, of all men's creations, books are the nearest to us, for they contain our very thought, our ambitions, our indignations, our illusions, our fidelity to truth, and our persistent leaning towards error. But most of all they resemble us in their precarious hold on life.

A bridge constructed according to the rules of the art of bridge-building is certain of a long, honourable, and useful career. But a book as good in its way as the bridge may perish obscurely on the very day of its birth. The art of their creators is not sufficient to give them more than a moment of life. Of the books born from the restlessness, the inspiration, and the vanity of human minds those that the Muses would love best lie more than all others under the menace of an early death. Sometimes their defects will save them. Sometimes a book fair to see may – to use a lofty expression – have no individual soul. Obviously a book of that sort cannot die. It can only crumble into dust. But the best of books drawing sustenance from the sympathy and memory of men have lived on the brink of destruction, for men's memories are short, and their sympathy is, we must admit, a very fluctuating, unprincipled emotion.

No secret of eternal life for our books can be found amongst the formulas of art, any more than for our bodies in a prescribed combination of drugs. This is not because some books are not worthy of enduring life, but because the formulas of art are dependent on things variable, unstable, and untrustworthy; on human sympathies, on prejudices, on likes and dislikes, on the sense of virtue and the sense of propriety, on beliefs and theories that, indestructible in themselves, always change their form – often in the lifetime of one fleeting generation.

2

Of all books, novels, which the Muses should love, make a serious claim on our compassion. The art of the novelist is simple. At the same time it is the most elusive of all creative arts, the most liable to be obscured by the scruples of its servants and votaries, the one pre-eminently destined to bring trouble to the mind and the heart of the artist. After all, the creation of a world is not a small undertaking except perhaps to the divinely gifted. In truth every novelist must begin by creating for himself a world, great or little, in which he can honestly believe. This world cannot be made otherwise than in his own image: it is fated to remain individual and a little mysterious, and yet it must resemble something already familiar to the experience, the thoughts, and the sensations of his readers. At the heart of fiction, even the least worthy of the name, some sort of truth can be found – if only the truth of a childish theatrical ardour in the game of life, as in the novels of Dumas the father. But the fair truth of human delicacy can be found in Mr Henry James's novels; and the comical, appalling truth of human rapacity let loose amongst the spoils of existence lives in the monstrous world created by Balzac. The pursuit of happiness by means lawful and unlawful, through resignation or revolt, by the clever manipulation of conventions or by solemn hanging on to the skirts of the latest scientific theory, is the only theme that can be legitimately developed by the novelist who is the chronicler of the kingdom of the earth. And the kingdom of this earth itself, the ground upon which his individualities stand, stumble, or die, must enter into his scheme of faithful record. To encompass all this in one harmonious conception is a great feat; and even to attempt it deliberately with serious intention, not from the senseless prompting of an ignorant heart, is an honourable ambition. For it requires some courage to step in calmly where fools may be eager to rush. As a distinguished and successful French novelist once observed of fiction, 'C'est un art *trop* difficile.'

It is natural that the novelist should doubt his ability to cope with his task. He imagines it more gigantic than it is. And yet literary creation being only one of the legitimate forms of human activity has no value but on the condition of not excluding the fullest recognition of all the more distinct forms of action. This condition is sometimes forgotten by the man of letters, who often, especially in his youth, is inclined to lay a claim of exclusive superiority for his own amongst all the other tasks of the human mind. The mass of verse and prose may glimmer here and there with the glow of a divine spark, but in the sum of human effort it has no special importance. There is no justificative formula for its existence any more than for any other artistic achievement. With the rest of them it is destined to be forgotten, without, perhaps, leaving the faintest trace. Where a novelist has an advantage over the workers in other fields of thought is in his privilege of freedom – the freedom of expression and the freedom of confessing his innermost beliefs – which should console him for the hard slavery of the pen.

Liberty of imagination should be the most precious possession of a novelist. To try voluntarily to discover the fettering dogmas of some romantic, realistic, or naturalistic creed in the free work of its own inspiration, is a trick worthy of human perverseness which, after inventing an absurdity, endeavours to find for it a pedigree of distinguished ancestors. It is a weakness of inferior minds when it is not the cunning device of those who, uncertain of their talent, would seek to add lustre to it by the authority of a school. Such, for instance, are the high priests who have proclaimed Stendhal for a prophet of Naturalism. But Stendhal himself would have accepted no limitation of his freedom. Stendhal's mind was of the first order. His spirit above must be raging with a peculiarly Stendhalesque scorn and indignation. For the truth is that more than one kind of intellectual cowardice hides behind the literary formulas. And Stendhal was pre-eminently courageous. He wrote his two great novels, which so few people have read, in a spirit of fearless liberty.

It must not be supposed that I claim for the artist in fiction the freedom of moral Nihilism. I would require from him many acts of faith of which the first would be the cherishing of an undying hope; and hope, it will not be contested, implies all the piety of effort and renunciation. It is the God-sent form of trust in the magic force and inspiration belonging to the life of this earth. We are inclined to forget that the way of excellence is in the intellectual, as distinguished from emotional, humility. What one feels so hopelessly barren in declared pessimism is just its arrogance. It seems as if the discovery made by many men at various times that there is much evil in the world were a source of proud and unholy joy unto some of the modern writers. That frame of mind is not the proper one in which to approach seriously the art of fiction. It gives an author – goodness only knows why – an elated sense of his own superiority. And there is nothing more dangerous than such an elation to that absolute loyalty towards his feelings and sensations an author should keep hold of in his most exalted moments of creation.

To be hopeful in an artistic sense it is not necessary to think that the world is good. It is enough to believe that there is no impossibility of its being made so. If the flight of imaginative thought may be allowed to rise superior to many moralities current amongst mankind, a novelist who would think himself of a superior essence to other men would miss the first condition of his calling. To have the gift of words is no such great matter. A man furnished with a long-range weapon does not become a hunter or a warrior by the mere possession of a fire-arm; many other qualities of character and temperament are necessary to make him either one or the other. Of him from whose armoury of phrases one in a hundred thousand may perhaps hit the far-distant and elusive mark of art I would ask that in his dealings with mankind he should be capable of giving a tender recognition to their obscure virtues. I would not have him impatient with their small failings and scornful of their errors. I would not have him expect too much gratitude from that humanity whose fate, as illustrated in individuals, it is open to him to depict as ridiculous or terrible. I would wish him to look with a large forgiveness at men's ideas and prejudices, which are by no means the outcome of malevolence, but depend on their education, their social status, even their professions. The good artist should expect no recognition of his toil and no admiration of his genius, because his toil can with difficulty be appraised and his genius cannot possibly mean anything to the illiterate who, even from the dreadful wisdom of their evoked dead, have, so far, culled nothing but inanities and platitudes. I would wish him to enlarge his sympathies by patient and loving observation while he grows in mental power. It is in the impartial practice of life, if anywhere, that the promise of perfection for his art can be found, rather than in the absurd formulas trying to prescribe this or that particular method of technique or conception. Let him mature the strength of his imagination amongst the things of this earth, which it is his business to cherish and know, and refrain from calling down his inspiration ready-made from some heaven of perfections of which he knows nothing. And I would not grudge him the proud illusion that will come sometimes to a writer: the illusion that his achievement has almost equalled the greatness of his dream. For what else could give him the serenity and the force to hug to his breast as a thing delightful and human, the virtue, the rectitude and sagacity of his own City, declaring with simple eloquence through the mouth of a Conscript Father: 'I have not read this author's books, and if I have read them I have forgotten. . . .'

32 'John Galsworthy' (1906).[13]

When in the family's assembly at Timothy Forsyte's house there arose a discussion of Francie Forsyte's verses, Aunt Hester expressed her preference for the poetry of Shelley, Byron and Wordsworth, on the ground that, after reading the works of these poets, 'one felt that one had read a book'. And the reader of Mr Galsworthy's latest volume of fiction, whether in accord or in difference with the author's view of his subject, would feel that he had read a book.

Beyond that impression one perceives how difficult it is to get critical hold of Mr Galsworthy's work. He gives you no opening. Defending no obvious thesis, setting up no theory, offering no cheap panacea, appealing to no naked sentiment, the author of 'The Man of Property' disdains also the effective device of attacking insidiously the actors of his own drama, or rather of his dramatic comedy. This is because he does not write for effect, though his writing will be found effective enough for all that. This book is of a disconcerting honesty, backed by a discouraging skill. There is not a single phrase in it written for the sake of its cleverness. Not one. Light of touch, though weighty in feeling, it gives the impression of verbal austerity, of a *willed* moderation of thought. The passages of high literary merit, so uniformly sustained as to escape the notice of the reader, expose the natural and logical development of the story with a purposeful progression which is primarily satisfying to the intelligence, and ends by stirring the emotions. In the essentials of matter and treatment it is a book of to-day. Its critical spirit and its impartial method are meant for a humanity which has outgrown the stage of fairy tales, realistic, romantic or even epic.

For the fairy tale, be it not ungratefully said, has walked the earth in many unchallenged disguises, and lingers amongst us to this day wearing, sometimes, amazingly heavy clothes. It lingers; and even it lingers with some assurance. Mankind has come of age, but the successive generations still demand artlessly to be amazed, moved and amused. Certain forms of innocent fun will never grow old, I suppose.

73

But the secret of the long life of the fairy tale consists mainly in this, I suspect: that it is amusing to the writer thereof. Whatever public wants it supplies, it ministers first of all to his vanity in an intimate and delightful way. The pride of fanciful invention; the pride of that invention which soars (on goose's wings) into the empty blue is like the intoxication of an elixir sent by the gods above. And whether it is that the gods are unduly generous, or simply because the sight of human folly amuses their idle malice, that sort of felicity is easier attained pen in hand than the sober pride, always mingled with misgivings, of a single-minded observer and conscientious interpreter of reality. This is why the fairy tale, in its various disguises of optimism, pessimism, romanticism, naturalism and what not, will always be with us. And, indeed, that is very comprehensible; the seduction of irresponsible freedom is very great; and to be tied to the earth (even as the hewers of wood and drawers of water are tied to the earth) in the exercise of one's imagination, by every scruple of conscience and honour, may be considered a lot hard enough not to be lightly embraced. This is why novelists are comparatively rare. But we must not exaggerate. This world, even if one is tied fast to its earthy foundations by the subtle and tyrannical bonds of artistic conviction, is not such a bad place to write fiction in. At any rate, we can know of no other; an excellent reason for us to try to think as well as possible of the world we do know.

In this world, whose realities are discovered, interpreted, commented on, criticized and exposed in works of fiction, Mr Galsworthy selects for the subject-matter of his book the Family, an institution which has been with us as long, I should think, as the oldest and the least venerable pattern of fairy tale. As Mr Galsworthy, however, is no theorist but an observer, it is a definite kind of family that falls under his observation. It is the middle-class family; and even with more precision, as we are warned in the subtitle, an upper middle-class family anywhere at large in space and time, but a family; if not exactly of to-day, then of only last evening, so to say. Thus at the outset we are far removed from the vagueness of the traditional 'once upon a time in a far country there was a king', which somehow always manages to peep through the solemn disguises of fairy tales masquerading as novels with and without purpose. The Forsytes walk the pavement of London and own some of London's houses. They wish to own more; they wish to own them all. And maybe they will. Time is on their side. The Forsytes never die – so Mr Galsworthy tells us, while we watch them assembling in old Jolyon Forsyte's drawing room on the occasion of June Forsyte's engagement to Mr Bosinney, incidentally an architect and an artist, but, by the only definition that matters, a man of no property whatever.

A family is not at first sight an alarming phenomenon. But Mr Galsworthy looks at the Forsytes with the individual vision of a novelist seeking his inspiration amongst the realities of this earth. He points out to us this family's formidable character as a unit of society, as a reproduction in miniature of society itself. It is made formidable, he says, by the cohesion of its members (between whom there need not exist either affection or even sympathy) upon a concrete point, the possession of property.

The solidity of the foundation laid by Mr Galsworthy for his fine piece of imaginative work becomes at once apparent. For whichever came first, family or property, in the beginnings of social organization, or whether they came together and were indeed at first scarcely distinguishable from each other, it is clear that in the close alliance of these two institutions society has found the way of its development and nurses the hope of its security. In their sense of property the Forsytes establish the consciousness of their right and the promise of their duration. It is an instinct, a primitive instinct. The practical faculty of the Forsytes has erected it into a principle; their idealism has expanded it into a sort of religion which has shaped their notions of happiness and decency, their prejudices, their piety, such thoughts as they happen to have and the very course of their passions. Life as a whole has come to be perceptible to them exclusively in terms of property. Preservation, acquisition – acquisition, preservation. Their laws, their morality, their art and their science appear to them, justifiably enough, consecrated to that double and unique end. It is the formula of their virtue.

In this world of Forsytes (who never die) organized in view of acquiring and preserving property, Mr Galsworthy (who is no inventor of didactic fairy tales) places with the sure instinct of a novelist a man and a woman who are no Forsytes, it is true, but whom he presents as in no sense the declared adversaries of the great principle of property. They only happen to disregard it. And this is a crime. They are simply two people to whom life speaks imperatively in terms of love. And this is enough to establish their irreconcilable antagonism and to precipitate their unavoidable fate. Deprived naturally and suddenly of the support of laws and morality, of all human countenance, and even, in a manner of speaking, of the consolations of religion, they find themselves miserably crushed, both the woman and the man. And the principle of property is vindicated. The woman being the weaker, it is in her case vindicated with consummate cruelty. For a peculiar cowardice is one of the characteristics of this great and living principle. Strong in the worship of so many thousands and in the possession of so many millions, it starts with affright at the slightest challenge, it trembles before mere indifference, it directs its heaviest blows at the disinherited who should appear weakest in its sight. Irene's fate is made unspeakably atrocious, no less – but nothing more. Mr Galsworthy's instinct and observation serve him well here. In Soames Forsyte's town house, whose front door stands wide open for half an hour or so on a certain foggy night, there is no room for tragedy. It is one of the temples of property, of a sort of unholy religion whose fundamental dogma, public ceremonies and awful secret rites, forming the subject matter of this remarkable novel, take no account of human dignity. Irene, as last seen crushed and alive within the hopeless portals, remains for us a poignantly pitiful figure and nothing more.

This then, roughly and summarily, is the book in its general suggestion. Going on to particulars, which make up the intrinsic value of a work of art, it rests upon the subtle and interdependent relation of Mr Galsworthy's intellect and feelings which form his temperament, and reveals Mr Galsworthy's very considerable talent as a writer – a talent so considerable that it commands at once our respectful attention. The foundation of this talent, it seems to me, lies in a remarkable power of ironic insight combined with an extremely keen and faithful eye for all the phenomena on the surface of the life he observes. These are the purveyors of his imagination, whose servant is a style clear, direct, sane, illumined by a perfectly unaffected sincerity. It is the style of a man whose sympathy with mankind is too genuine to allow him the smallest gratification of his vanity at the cost of his fellow creatures. In its moderation it is a style sufficiently pointed to carry deep his remorseless irony and grave enough to be the dignified vehicle of his profound compassion. Its sustained harmony is never interrupted by those bursts of cymbals and fifes which some deaf people acclaim for brilliance. Before all, it is a style well under control, and therefore it never betrays this tender and ironic writer into an odious cynicism of laughter or tears. For there are two kinds of cynicism, the cynicism of the hyena and the cynicism of the crocodile, which last, by the way, commands all sorts of respects from the inhabitants of these Isles. Mr Galsworthy remains always a man, whether he is amused or moved.

I am afraid that my unavowed intention in writing about this book (of which I have talked to much and said so little) has been discovered by now. Therfore I confess. Confession – public, I mean – is good for one's conscience. Such is my intention. And it would be easier to carry out if I only knew exactly the motives which prompt people to read novels. But I do not know them all. Some of us, I understand, take up a novel to gratify a natural malevolence, the author being supposed to hold the mirror up to the odiously ridiculous nature of our next-door neighbour. From laboriously collected information I am, however, led to believe that most people read novels for amusement. This is as it should be. But, whatever be their motives, I entertain towards all novel-readers (for reasons which must remain concealed from the readers of this paper) the feelings of warm and respectful affection. I would not try to deceive them for worlds. Never! This being understood, I go on to declare, in the peace of my heart and the serenity of my conscience, that if they want amusement they will find it between the covers of this book. They will find plenty of it in this episode in the history of the Forsytes, where the reconciliation of a father and son, the dramatic and poignant comedy of Soames Forsyte's marital relations, and the tragedy of Bosinney's failure are exposed to our gaze with the remorseless yet sympathetic irony of Mr Galsworthy's art, in the light of the unquenchable fire burning on the altar of property. They will find amusement, and perhaps also something more lasting – if they care for it. I say this with all the reserves and qualifications which strict truth requires around every statement of opinion. Mr Galsworthy may possibly be found disappointing by some, but he will never be found futile by any one, and never uninteresting by the most exacting. I myself, for instance, am not so sure of Bosinney's tragedy. But this hesitation of my mind, for which the author may not be wholly responsible after all, need only be mentioned and no more, in the face of his considerable achievement.

33 From a letter to Messrs Methuen & Co., 30 May 1906. Methuen was one of the many publishers with whom Conrad signed contracts early in his career. The work referred to is *The Mirror of the Sea* (1906).

You ask me for something very difficult. Any definition of one's work must be either very intimate or very superficial. There is only one man to whom I could open my confidence on that extremely elusive matter without the fear of being misunderstood. The intention of temperamental writing is infinitely complex, and to talk about my work is repugnant to me – beyond anything. And what could I say that would be of use to you? I may say that the book is an imaginative rendering of a reminiscent mood. This is a sort of definition and it is true enough in a way. But the book is also a record of a phase, now nearly vanished, of a certain kind of activity, sympathetic to the inhabitants of this Island. It is likewise an attempt to set down graphically certain genuine feelings and emotions born from the experience of a respectable and useful calling, which, at the same time, happens to be of national importance. It may be defined as a discourse (with a personal note) on ships, seamen, and the sea.

34 From a letter to Galsworthy, 12 September 1906. Conrad is responding to Galsworthy's comments on the manuscript of *The Secret Agent* (1907).

The point of treatment you raise I have already considered. In such a tale one is likely to be misunderstood. After all, you must not take it too seriously. The whole thing is superficial and it is but a tale. I had no idea to consider Anarchism politically, or to treat it seriously in its philosophical aspect; as a manifestation of human nature in its discontent and imbecility. The general reflections whether right or wrong are not meant as bolts. You can't say I hurl them in any sense. They come in by the way and are not applicable to particular instances, – Russian or Latin. They are, if anything, mere digs at the people in the tale. As to attacking Anarchism as a form of humanitarian enthusiasm or intellectual despair or social atheism, that – if it were worth doing – would be the work for a more vigorous hand and for a mind more robust, and perhaps more honest than mine. [. . .]

As to the beastly trick of style, I have fallen into it through worry and hurry. I abominate it myself. It isn't even French really. It is Zola jargon simply. Why it should have fastened on me I don't know. But anything may happen to a man writing in a state of distraction. We shall see to that with great care when the tale is finished.

35 From a letter to Garnett, 1 October 1907. Garnett had reviewed *The Secret Agent* in the *Nation* magazine.[14]

It makes a fine reading for an author and no mistake. I am no end proud to see you've spotted my poor old woman. You've got a fiendishly penetrating eye for one's most secret intentions. She *is* the heroine. And you are appallingly quick in jumping upon a fellow. Yes O! yes my dear Edward – that's what's the matter with the estimable Verloc and his wife: 'the hidden weakness in the springs of impulse'. I was so convinced that something was wrong there that to read your definition has been an immense relief – great enough to be akin to joy. The defect is so profoundly temperamental that to this moment I can't tell *how* I went wrong. Of going wrong I was aware even at the time of writing – all the time. You may imagine what a horrible grind it was to keep on going with this suspicion at the back of the head.

36 From a letter to Helen Sanderson, September 1910. Conrad and the Sandersons were old friends. Helen's prose sketches were currently being published in magazines.

All these sketches have the quality without which neither beauty nor, I am afraid, truth are effective; that is they are interesting in themselves. Thus one may say safely that you have the root of the matter. Yes. It is there. I've spent all yesterday with your pages and so the impression being made and even assimilated, I've slept on it. *La nuit porte conseil*, – as you know.

As to what sort of *conseil*, that's another matter. I am not very fit to give advice. That is an especial talent. The few remarks that I offer are not valuable in themselves: they can be only worth something in the way of stimulus for self-examination. You have an individuality which *can* express itself. There's no doubt of that. So a seed in the ground expresses itself, manifests itself, in plant and flower. What is necessary is cultivation.

I understand now perfectly what you meant when you said that your subjects presented themselves to you in a very short form. You must let your gift of expression expand freely, so as to touch what may seem irrelevant to the matter in hand. The apparently irrelevant is often the illuminative. You must never be afraid of remote connections: you must let your mind range widely about your subject. This is the more necessary because your vision is very direct, very clear. Your expression too is very direct and certainly not obscure: but it is not always sufficiently precise.

You must try to say things fully: but do not imagine that I would lead you into verbosity. It is not mere words that I recommend but, – alas! – more toil.

I find it rather difficult to explain what is in my mind. Generally I would say that your prose, full of merits as it is, wants 'stringing up'. If we could have an hour together with the pages before us, I could make my meaning clear enough. I say this with confidence, because as a matter of fact our ways of thinking and of looking at things are not dissimilar. However I have taken the liberty to take the last page of the 'Spirit of the Land' and make use of it to illustrate what I would be at in my dumb way. But for goodness' sake don't suspect me of setting up a model for your writing. You have and you must keep your own way of saying what you have got to say.

The extract from the diary interested me very much as being a short story. And it is good. The general effect, however, is too harsh.

I have asked myself, why? I think that the fault lies in the want of atmosphere. We see these people in the flesh and, as it were, in vacuo. It needs a little more detail. For instance, we don't know how the poor little woman came to marry Owen. His attitude towards his wife is indicated, but you don't say anything of her attitude towards him. A little of that sort of detail is necessary to humanize the story. As it is, it seems written only to show up Miss Anstruther: and that's all right. I am with you there. But a short story should, before all, be a human episode.

37   From a letter to Garnett, 20 October 1911. Garnett had reviewed *Under Western Eyes* (1911) in the *Nation*, touching upon one of Conrad's lifelong prejudices, his feelings about Russia.[15]

I don't understand your picturesque allusions to packing spinach into the saucepan and the hell broth that's supposed to be the result of that culinary operation. There's just about as much or as little hatred in this book as in the *Outcast of the Islands* for instance. Subjects lay about for anybody to pick up. I have picked up this one. And that's all there is to it. I don't expect you will believe me. You are so russianized, my dear, that you don't know the truth when you see it – unless it smells of cabbage-soup when it at once secures your profoundest respect. I suppose one must make allowances for your position of Russian Embassador to the Republic of Letters. Official pronouncements ought to be taken with a grain of salt and that is how I shall take your article in the Nation which I hope to see tomorrow evening when the carrier comes back from Ashford. But it is hard after lavishing a 'wealth of tenderness' on Tekla and Sophia, to be charged with the rather low trick of putting one's hate into a novel. If you seriously think that I have done that then my dear fellow let me tell you that you don't know what the accent of hate is. Is it possible that you haven't seen that in this book I am concerned with nothing but ideas, to the exclusion of everything else, with no arrière pensée of any kind. Or are you like the Italians (and most women) incapable of conceiving that anybody ever should speak with perfect detachment, without some subtle hidden purpose, for the sake of what is said, with no desire of gratifying some small personal spite – or vanity. [. . .]

And anyhow if hatred there were it would be too big a thing to be put into a 6/– novel. This too might have occurred to you, if you had condescended to look beyond the literary horizon where all things sacred and profane are turned into copy.

38 From a letter to Miss O. R. Garnett, 20 October 1911. Dated the same day as the previous item, Conrad shows a remarkable change of mood concerning the same work, though some of his points clearly underline those made to Edward.

You are a good critic. That girl does not move. No excuse can be offered for such a defect but there is an explanation. I wanted a pivot for the action to turn on. And I had to be very careful because if I had allowed myself to make more of her she would have killed the artistic purpose of the book: the development of a single mood. It isn't that I was afraid or ignorant of her possibilities. Indeed they were very tempting. But it had to be a performance on one string. It had to be. You may think such self-imposed limitation a very stupid thing. But something of the kind must be done or else novel-writing becomes a mere debauch of the imagination. No doubt if I had taken another line the book would have been richer. But what I aimed at this time was an effect of virtuosity before anything else. Still I need not have made Miss Haldin a mere peg as I am sorry to admit she is. Result of over caution.

Your kind appreciation of the book gives me great pleasure and I am glad you think it is true – as far as it goes. I am quite aware it does not go very far. But the fact is that I know extremely little of Russians. Practically nothing. In Poland we have nothing to do with them. One knows they are there. And that's disagreeable enough. In exile the contact is even slighter if possible if more unavoidable. I crossed the Russian frontier at the age of ten. Not having been to school then I never knew Russian. I could not tell a Little Russian from a Great Russian to save my life. In the book as you must have seen I am exclusively concerned with ideas.

39 From a letter to Garnett, 5 November 1912. *'Twixt Land and Sea* (1912) contains 'A smile of fortune', 'The secret sharer' and 'Freya of the Seven Isles'.

Thanks for your letter of the 3 tales – very much of sorts. I daresay *Freya* is pretty rotten. On the other hand the *Secret Sharer*, between you and me, is *it*. Eh? No damned tricks with girls there. Eh? Every word fits and there's not a single uncertain note. Luck my boy. Pure luck. I knew you would spot the thing at sight. But I repeat: mere luck.

40 From a letter to Garnett, 23 February 1914. Garnett had just published his *Tolstoy: A Study*.

Dislike as definition of my attitude to Tols. is but a rough and approximate term. I judge him not – for this reason. That his anti-sensualism is suspect to me. In that matter (which is not worth the fuss which is made about it) the pros and the antis seem to be tarred with the same brush. Moreover the base from which he starts – Christianity – is distasteful to me. I am not blind to its services but the absurd oriental fable from which it starts irritates me. Great, improving, softening, compassionate it may be but it has lent itself with amazing facility to cruel distortion and is the only religion which, with its impossible standards, has brought an infinity of anguish to innumerable souls – on this earth.

41 From a letter to Sir Sidney Colvin, 27 February 1917. Colvin, a close friend of Conrad's, had been requested to write a review of *The Shadow-Line* (1917) for the *Observer*. The review was written, and appeared in March.[16]

Very dear of you to write so appreciatively about the little book. But I don't agree that a local-knowledge man would be the right reviewer for it. The locality doesn't matter; and if it is the Gulf of Siam it's simply because the whole thing is exact autobiography. I always meant to do it, and on our return from Austria, when I had to write something, I discovered that this was what I could write in my then moral and intellectual condition; tho' even *that* cost me an effort which I remember with a shudder. To sit down and invent fairy tales was impossible then. It isn't very possible even now. I was writing that thing in Dec., 1914, and Jan. to March, 1915. The very speeches are (I won't say authentic – they are that absolutely) I believe, verbally accurate. And all this happened in March–April, 1887. Giles is a Capt. Patterson, a very well known person there. It's the only name I've changed. Mr Burn's craziness being the pivot is perhaps a little accentuated. My last scene with Ransome is only indicated. There are things, moments, that are not to be tossed to the public's incomprehension, for journalists to gloat over. No. It was not an experience to be exhibited 'in the street'. – I am sorry you have received an impression of horror. I tried to keep the mere horror out. It would have been easy to pile it on. You may believe me, *J'ai vécu tout cela*. However, I will tell you a little more about that when we meet. Here I'll only say that experience is transposed into spiritual terms – in art a perfectly legitimate thing to do, as long as one preserves the exact truth enshrined therein. That's why I consented to this piece being published by itself. I did not like the idea of its being associated with fiction in a vol. of stories. And this is also the reason I've inscribed it to Borys – and the Others.

Our love to your house.

P.S. Re-reading your letter and going over the story I see that both places, Bangkok and Singapore, are distinctly named – but obviously they are not named in the right way or in proper context, since the mind of an 'experienced reader' like yourself is left in doubt. And I must confess that the matter seemed to me of such slight importance compared with the subject treated that I really did not consider it at all while writing. *Don't* refuse Garvin's request if your heart is at all that way inclined.

42 From a letter to Sir Sidney Colvin, 18 March 1917.

In answer to your card, I write at once – first to tell you how glad I am to hear you have consented to Garvin's request, next to say that there can be no possible objection to your recognizing the autobio- graphical character of that piece of writing – let us call it. It is so much so that I shrink from calling it a Tale. If you will notice I call it *A Confession* on the title page. For, from a certain point of view, it is that – and essentially as sincere as any confession can be. The more perfectly so, perhaps, because its object is not the usual one of self-revelation. My object was to show all the others and the situation through the medium of my own emotions. The most heavily tried (because the most self-conscious), the least 'worthy' perhaps, there was no other way in which I could render justice to all these souls 'worthy of my undying regard'.

Perhaps you won't find it presumption if, after 22 years of work, I may say that I have not been very well understood. I have been called a writer of the sea, of the tropics, a descriptive writer, a romantic writer – and also a realist. But as a matter of fact all my concern has been with the 'ideal' value of things, events and people. That and nothing else. The humorous, the pathetic, the passionate, the sentimental *aspects* came in of themselves – *mais en vérité c'est les valeurs idéales des faits et gestes humains qui se sont imposés à mon activité artistique.*

Whatever dramatic and narrative gifts I may have are always, instinctively, used with that object – to get at, to bring forth *les valeurs idéales*.

Of course this is a very general statement – but roughly I believe it is true.

43 'Turgenev' (1917).[17]

Dear Edward:

I am glad to hear that you are about to publish a study of Turgenev, that fortunate artist who has found so much in life for us and no doubt for himself, with the exception of bare justice. Perhaps that will come to him, too, in time. Your study may help the consummation. For his luck persists after his death. What greater luck an artist like Turgenev could wish for than to find in the English-speaking world a translator who has missed none of the most delicate, most simple beauties of his work, and a critic who has known how to analyse and point out its high qualities with perfect sympathy and insight.

After twenty odd years of friendship (and my first literary friendship too) I may well permit myself to make that statement, while thinking of your wonderful Prefaces as they appeared from time to time in the volumes of Turgenev's complete edition, the last of which came into the light of public indifference in the ninety-ninth year of the nineteenth century.

With that year one may say, with some justice, that the age of Turgenev had come to an end too; yet work so simple and human, so independent of the transitory formulas and theories of art, belongs as you point out in the Preface to 'Smoke' 'to all time'.

Turgenev's creative activity covers about thirty years. Since it came to an end the social and political events in Russia have moved at an accelerated pace, but the deep origins of them, in the moral and intellectual unrest of the souls, are recorded in the whole body of his work with the unerring lucidity of a great national writer. The first stirrings, the first gleams of the great forces can be seen almost in every page of the novels, of the short stories and of 'A Sportsman's Sketches' – those marvellous landscapes peopled by unforgettable figures.

Those will never grow old. Fashions in monsters do change, but the truth of humanity goes on for ever, unchangeable and inexhaustible in the variety of its disclosures. Whether Turgenev's art, which has captured it with such mastery and such gentleness, is for 'all time' it is hard to say. Since, as you say yourself, he brings all his problems and characters to the test of love we may hope that it will endure at least till the infinite emotions of love are replaced by the exact simplicity of perfected Eugenics. But even by then, I think, women would not have changed much; and the women of Turgenev who understood them so tenderly, so reverently and so passionately – they, at least, are certainly for all time.

Women are, one may say, the foundation of his art. They are Russian of course. Never was a writer so profoundly, so whole-souledly national. But for non-Russian readers, Turgenev's Russia is but a canvas on which the incomparable artist of humanity lays his colours and his forms in the great light and the free air of the world. Had he invented them all and also every stick and stone, brook and hill and field in which they move, his personages would have been just as true and as poignant in their perplexed lives. They are his own and also universal. Any one can accept them with no more question than one accepts the Italians of Shakespeare.

In the larger, non-Russian view, what should make Turgenev sympathetic and welcome to the English-speaking world, is his essential humanity. All his creations, fortunate and unfortunate, oppressed and oppressors are human beings, not strange beasts in a menagerie or damned souls knocking themselves to pieces in the stuffy darkness of mystical contradictions. They are human beings, fit to live, fit to suffer, fit to struggle, fit to win, fit to lose, in the endless and inspiring game of pursuing from day to day the ever-receding future.

I began by calling him lucky, and he was, in a sense. But one ends by having some doubts. To be so great without the slightest parade and so fine without any tricks of 'cleverness' must be fatal to any man's influence with his contemporaries.

Frankly, I don't want to appear as qualified to judge of things Russian. It wouldn't be true. I know nothing of them. But I am aware of a few general truths, such as, for instance, that no man, whatever may be the loftiness of his character, the purity of his motives and the peace of his conscience – no man, I say, likes to be beaten with sticks during the greater part of his existence. From what one knows of his history it appears clearly that in Russia almost any stick was good enough to beat Turgenev with in his latter years. When he died the characteristically chicken-hearted Autocracy hastened to stuff his mortal envelope into the tomb it refused to honour, while the sensitive Revolutionists went on for a time flinging after his shade those jeers and curses from which that impartial lover of *all* his countrymen had suffered so much in his lifetime. For he, too, was sensitive. Every page of his writing bears his testimony to the fatal absence of callousness in the man.

And now he suffers a little from other things. In truth it is not the convulsed terror-haunted Dostoevski but the serene Turgenev who is under a curse. For only think! Every gift has been heaped on his cradle: absolute sanity and the deepest sensibility, the clearest vision and the quickest responsiveness, penetrating insight and unfailing generosity of judgement, an exquisite perception of the visible world and an unerring instinct for the significant, for the essential in the life of men and women, the clearest mind, the warmest heart, the largest sympathy – and all that in perfect measure. There's enough there to ruin the prospects of any writer. For you know very well, my dear Edward, that if you had Antinous himself in a booth of the world's fair, and killed yourself in protesting that his soul was as perfect as his body, you wouldn't get one per cent of the crowd struggling next door for a sight of the Double-headed Nightingale or of some weak-kneed giant grinning through a horse collar.

44 From the Author's note to *Youth* (written 1917).

'Youth' is a feat of memory. It is a record of experience; but that experience, in its facts, in its inwardness and in its outward colouring, begins and ends in myself. 'Heart of Darkness' is experience, too; but it is experience pushed a little (and only very little) beyond the actual facts of the case for the perfectly legitimate, I believe, purpose of bringing it home to the minds and bosoms of the readers. There it was no longer a matter of sincere colouring. It was like another art altogether. That sombre theme had to be given a sinister resonance, a tonality of its own, a continued vibration that, I hoped, would hang in the air and dwell on the ear after the last note had been struck.

45 From a letter to Barrett H. Clark, 4 May 1918. Clark had written to Conrad inquiring about his aesthetic principles. Conrad chose to give a full and reasoned reply.

You are right in thinking that I would be gratified by the appreciation of a mind younger than my own. But in truth I don't consider myself an Ancient. My writing life extends but only over twenty-three years, and I need not point out to an intelligence as alert as yours that all that time has been a time of evolution, in which some critics have detected three marked periods – and that the process is still going on. Some critics have found fault with me for not being constantly myself. But they are wrong. I am always myself. I am a man of formed character. Certain conclusions remain immovably fixed in my mind, but I am no slave to prejudices and formulas, and I shall never be. My attitude to subjects and expressions, the angles of vision, my methods of composition will, within limits, be always changing – not because I am unstable or un-principled but because I am free. Or perhaps it may be more exact to say, because I am always trying for freedom – within my limits.

Coming now to the subject of your inquiry, I wish at first to put before you a general proposition: that a work of art is very seldom limited to one exclusive meaning and not necessarily tending to a definite conclusion. And this for the reason that the nearer it approaches art, the more it acquires a symbolic character. This state-ment may surprise you, who may imagine that I am alluding to the Symbolist School of poets or prose writers. Theirs, however, is only a literary proceeding against which I have nothing to say. I am concerned here with something much larger. But no doubt you have meditated on this and kindred questions yourself.

So I will only call your attention to the fact that the symbolic conception of a work of art has this advantage, that it makes a triple appeal covering the whole field of life. All the great creations of liter-ature have been symbolic, and in that way have gained in complexity, in power, in depth and in beauty.

I don't think you will quarrel with me on the ground of lack of precision; for as to precision of images and analysis my artistic conscience is at rest. I have given there all the truth that is in me; and all that the critics may say can make my honesty neither more nor less. But as to 'final effect' my conscience has nothing to do with that. It is the critic's affair to bring to its contemplation his own honesty, his sensibility and intelligence. The matter for his conscience is just his judgement. If his conscience is busy with petty scruples and trammelled by superficial formulas then his judgement will be superficial and petty. But an artist has no right to quarrel with the inspirations, either lofty or base, of another soul.

Of course, your interpretation of *Victory*'s final aim, of its artistic secret as it were, is correct; and indeed I must say that I did not wrap it up in very mysterious processes of art. I made my appeal to feelings in as clear a language as I can command; and I don't think there is a critic in England or France who was in any doubt about it. In one or two instances the book was attacked on grounds which I simply cannot understand. Other criticisms struck me by their acuteness in the analysis of method and language. Some readers frankly did not like the book; but not on the ground of irony. And yet irony is not altogether absent from those pages, which, I am glad to think, have not failed to move your feelings and imagination.

46 From a letter to Hugh Walpole, 7 June 1918. The book referred to is Walpole's *Joseph Conrad*.

I want to thank you at once for the little book and to tell you that I am profoundly touched by many things you have found it possible in your heart and conscience to say about my work. The only thing that grieves me and makes me dance with rage is the cropping up of the legend set afloat by Hugh Clifford about my hesitation between English and French as a writing language. For it is absurd. When I wrote the first words of *Almayer's Folly*, I had been already for years and years *thinking* in English. I began to think in English long before I mastered, I won't say the style (I haven't done that yet), but the mere uttered speech. Is it thinkable that anybody possessed of some effective inspiration should contemplate for a moment such a frantic thing as translating it into another tongue? And there are also other considerations: such as the sheer appeal of the language, my quickly awakened love for its prose cadences, a subtle and unforeseen accord of my emotional nature with its genius. To that last, my dear Walpole, you bear witness yourself in your critical sketch or I have misunderstood you completely! You may take it from me that if I had not known English I wouldn't have written a line for print, in my life. C. and I were discussing the nature of the two languages and what I said was: that if I had been offered the alternative I would have been afraid to grapple with French, which is crystallized in the form of its sentence and therefore more exacting and less appealing. But there was never any alternative offered or even dreamed of. Somehow C. transformed a general remark into a personal statement.

Another matter of fact.

You say that I have been under the formative influence of *Madame*

Bovary. In fact, I read it only after finishing *A.F.*, as I did all the other works of Flaubert, [18] and anyhow, my Flaubert is the Flaubert of *St. Antoine* and *Ed[ucation]: Sent[imentale]*: and that only from the point of view of the rendering of concrete things and visual impressions. I thought him marvellous in that respect. I don't think I learned anything from him. What he did for me was to open my eyes and arouse my emulation. One can learn something from Balzac, but what could one learn from Flaubert? He compels admiration, – about the greatest service one artist can render another.

47 From a letter to F. N. Doubleday, 21 December 1918. Conrad was trying to persuade Doubleday to agree to an American serialization of *The Arrow of Gold* (1919).

I am sufficient of a democrat to detest the idea of being a writer of any 'coterie' of some small self-appointed aristocracy in the vast domain of art or letters. As a matter of feeling – not as a matter of business – I want to be read by many eyes and by all kinds of them, at that. I pride myself that there is no sentence of my writing, either thought or image, that is not accessible, I won't say to the meanest intelligence (meaness is a matter of temperament rather) but to the simplest intelligence that is aware at all of the world in which we live. Therefore I will confess without shame that the failure in serializing the *Arrow of Gold* has affected me to a certain extent. The question of what is or is not fit for publication reduces itself, when all is said and done, to the single point of 'suspended interest'. That, I judge, is the 'master-quality' of a serial; and it is not always to be obtained by the mere multiplicity of episodes. One single episode out of a life, one single feeling combined with a certain form of action (you'll notice I say *action* not analysis) may give the quality of 'suspended interest' to the tale of one single adventure in which the deepest sensations (and not only the bodies) of the actors are involved.

48 From the Author's note to *Typhoon and Other Stories* (written 1919).

The main characteristic of this volume consists in this, that all the stories composing it belong not only to the same period but have been written one after another in the order in which they appear in the book.

The period is that which follows on my connexion with *Blackwood's Magazine*. I had just finished writing *The End of the Tether* and was casting about for some subject which could be developed in a shorter form than the tales in the volume of *Youth* when the instance of a steamship full of returning coolies from Singapore to some port in northern China occurred to my recollection. Years before I had heard it being talked about in the East as a recent occurrence. It was for us merely one subject of conversation amongst many others of the kind. Men earning their bread in any very specialized occupation will talk shop, not only because it is the most vital interest of their lives but also because they have not much knowledge of other subjects. They have never had the time to get acquainted with them. Life, for most of us, is not so much a hard as an exacting taskmaster.

I never met anybody personally concerned in this affair, the interest of which for us was, of course, not the bad weather but the extraordinary complication brought into the ship's life at a moment of exceptional stress by the human element below her deck. Neither was the story itself ever enlarged upon in my hearing. In that company each of us could imagine easily what the whole thing was like. The financial difficulty of it, presenting also a human problem, was solved by a mind much too simple to be perplexed by anything in the world except men's idle talk for which it was not adapted.

From the first the mere anecdote, the mere statement I might say, that such a thing had happened on the high seas, appeared to me a sufficient subject for meditation. Yet it was but a bit of a sea yarn after all. I felt that to bring out its deeper significance which was quite apparent to me, something other, something more was required; a leading motive that would harmonize all these violent noises, and a point of view that would put all that elemental fury into its proper place.

What was needed of course was Captain MacWhirr. Directly I perceived him I could see that he was the man for the situation. I don't mean to say that I ever saw Captain MacWhirr in the flesh, or had ever come in contact with his literal mind and his dauntless temperament. MacWhirr is not an acquaintance of a few hours, or a few weeks, or a few months. He is the product of twenty years of life. My own life. Conscious invention had little to do with him. If it is true that Captain MacWhirr never walked and breathed on this earth (which I find for my part extremely difficult to believe) I can also assure my readers that he is perfectly authentic. I may venture to assert the same of every aspect of the story, while I confess that the particular typhoon of the tale was not a typhoon of my actual experience.

At its first appearance *Typhoon*, the story, was classed by some critics as a deliberately invented stormpiece. Others picked out MacWhirr, in whom they perceived a definite symbolic intention. Neither was exclusively my intention. Both the typhoon and Captain MacWhirr presented themselves to me as the necessities of the deep conviction with which I approached the subject of the story. It was their opportunity. It was also my opportunity; and it would be vain to discourse about what I made of it in a handful of pages, since the pages themselves are here, between the covers of this volume, to speak for themselves.

This is a belated reflection. If it had occurred to me before it would have perhaps done away with the existence of this Author's Note; for, indeed, the same remark applies to every story in this volume. None of them are stories of experience in the absolute sense of the word. Experience in them is but the canvas of the attempted picture. Each of them has its more than one intention. With each the question is what the writer had done with his opportunity; and each answers the question for itself in words which, if I may say so without undue solemnity, were written with a conscientious regard for the truth of my own sensations. And each of those stories, to mean something, must justify itself in its own way to the conscience of each successive reader.

Falk – the second story in the volume – offended the delicacy of one critic at least by certain peculiarities of its subject. But what is the subject of *Falk*? I personally do not feel so very certain about it. He who reads must find out for himself. My intention in writing

Falk was not to shock anybody. As in most of my writings I insist not on the events but on their effect upon the persons in the tale. But in everything I have written there is always one invariable intention, and that is to capture the reader's attention, by securing his interest and enlisting his sympathies for the matter in hand, whatever it may be, within the limits of the visible world and within the boundaries of human emotions.

49 From a letter to J. B. Pinker, 11 November 1919. James Pinker was Conrad's agent from 1899 and a main source of financial support, especially during the early and middle years of his career. *Typhoon* (1903) was the first of Conrad's works to be handled by him. He died suddenly in 1922. Conrad is referring to his own dramatization of *The Secret Agent* (performed November 1922).

As I go on in my adaptation, stripping off the garment of artistic expression and consistent irony which clothes the story in the book, I perceive more clearly how it is bound to appear to the collective mind of the audience a merely horrible and sordid tale, giving a most unfavourable impression of both the writer himself and of his attitude to the moral aspect of the subject. In the book the tale, whatever its character, was at any rate not treated sordidly; neither in tone, nor in diction, nor yet in the suggested images. The peculiar light of my mental insight and of my humane feeling (for I have *that* too) gave to the narrative a sort of grim dignity. But on the stage all this falls off. Every rag of the drapery drops to the ground. It is a terribly searching thing – I mean the stage.

I will confess that I myself had no idea of what the story was till I came to grips with it in this process of dramatization. Of course I can't stop now. Neither can I tamper with the truth of my conception by introducing into it any extraneous sentiment. It must remain what it is. Having arrived at that conclusion (which, at any rate, is honest) I have resolved that since the story is horrible I shall make it as horrible as I possible can. If there is any salvation for it, it may possibly be found just in *that*. But I have not many illusions on that score. There is very little chance of salvation. There will be very little glory or profit in this production. In fact, I have a feeling that it will be to me rather damaging than otherwise.

50 From the Author's note to *The Secret Agent* (written 1920).

The origin of *The Secret Agent*: subject, treatment, artistic purpose, and every other motive that may induce an author to take up his pen, can, I believe, be traced to a period of mental and emotional reaction.

The actual facts are that I began this book impulsively and wrote it continuously. When in due course it was bound and delivered to the public gaze I found myself reproved for having produced it at all. Some of the admonitions were severe, others had a sorrowful note. I have not got them textually before me but I remember perfectly the general argument, which was very simple; and also my surprise at its nature. All this sounds a very old story now! And yet it is not such a long time ago. I must conclude that I had still preserved much of my pristine innocence in the year 1907. It seems to me now that even an artless person might have foreseen that some criticisms would be based on the ground of sordid surroundings and the moral squalor of the tale. [. . .]

The inception of *The Secret Agent* followed immediately on a two years' period of intense absorption in the task of writing that remote novel, *Nostromo*, with its far-off Latin-American atmosphere; and the profoundly personal *Mirror of the Sea*. The first an intense creative effort on what I suppose will always remain my largest canvas, the second an unreserved attempt to unveil for a moment the profounder intimacies of the sea and the formative influences of nearly half my lifetime. It was a period, too, in which my sense of the truth of things was attended by a very intense imaginative and emotional readiness which, all genuine and faithful to facts as it was, yet made me feel (the task once done) as if I were left behind, aimless amongst mere husks of sensations and lost in a world of other, of inferior, values.

I don't know whether I really felt that I wanted a change, change in my imagination, in my vision, and in my mental attitude. I rather think that a change in the fundamental mood had already stolen over me unawares. I don't remember anything definite happening. With

The Mirror of the Sea finished in the full consciousness that I had dealt honestly with myself and my readers in every line of that book, I gave myself up to a not unhappy pause. Then, while I was yet standing still, as it were, and certainly not thinking of going out of my way to look for anything ugly, the subject of *The Secret Agent* – I mean the tale – came to me in the shape of a few words uttered by a friend in a casual conversation about anarchists or rather anarchist activities; how brought about I don't remember now. [. . .]

It was at first for me a mental change, disturbing a quieted-down imagination, in which strange forms, sharp in outline but imperfectly apprehended, appeared and claimed attention as crystals will do by their bizarre and unexpected shapes. One fell to musing before the phenomenon – even of the past: of South America, a continent of crude sunshine and brutal revolutions, of the sea, the vast expanse of salt waters, the mirror of heaven's frowns and smiles, the reflector of the world's light. Then the vision of an enormous town presented itself, of a monstrous town more populous than some continents and in its man-made might as if indifferent to heaven's frowns and smiles; a cruel devourer of the world's light. There was room enough there to place any story, depth enough for any passion, variety enough there for any setting, darkness enough to bury five millions of lives.

Irresistibly the town became the background for the ensuing period of deep and tentative meditations. Endless vistas opened before me in various directions. It would take years to find the right way! It seemed to take years! . . . Slowly the dawning conviction of Mrs Verloc's maternal passion grew up to a flame between me and that background, tingeing it with its secret ardour and receiving from it in exchange some of its own sombre colouring. At last the story of Winnie Verloc stood out complete from the days of her childhood to the end, unproportioned as yet, with everything still on the first plan, as it were; but ready now to be dealt with. It was a matter of about three days.

This book is *that* story, reduced to manageable proportions, its whole course suggested and centred round the absurd cruelty of the Greenwich Park explosion. I had there a task I will not say arduous but of the most absorbing difficulty. But it had to be done. It was a necessity. The figures grouped about Mrs Verloc and related directly or indirectly to her tragic suspicion that 'life doesn't stand much looking into', are the outcome of that very necessity. Personally I have never had any doubt of the reality of Mrs Verloc's story; but it had to be disengaged from its obscurity in that immense town, it had to be made credible, I don't mean so much as to her soul but as to her surroundings, not so much as to her psychology but as to her humanity. For the surroundings hints were not lacking. I had to fight hard to keep at arm's length the memories of my solitary and nocturnal walks all over London in my early days, lest they should rush in and overwhelm each page of the story as these emerged one after another from a mood as serious in feeling and thought as any in which I ever wrote a line. In that respect I really think that *The Secret Agent* is a perfectly genuine piece of work. Even the purely artistic purpose, that of applying an ironic method to a subject of that kind, was formulated with deliberation and in the earnest belief that ironic treatment alone would enable me to say all I felt I would have to say in scorn as well as in pity. It is one of the minor satisfactions of my writing life that having taken that resolve I did manage, it seems to me, to carry it right through to the end. As to the personages whom the absolute necessity of the case – Mrs Verloc's case – brings out in front of the London background, from them, too, I obtained those little satisfactions which really count for so much against the mass of oppressive doubts that haunt so persistently every attempt at creative work. [. . .]

The twelve years that have elapsed since the publication of the book have not changed my attitude. I do not regret having written it. Lately, circumstances, which have nothing to do with the general tenor of this preface, have compelled me to strip this tale of the literary robe of indignant scorn it has cost me so much to fit on it decently, years ago. I have been forced, so to speak, to look upon its bare bones. I confess that it makes a grisly skeleton. But still I will submit that telling Winnie Verloc's story to its anarchistic end of utter desolation, madness, and despair, and telling it as I have told it here, I have not intended to commit a gratuitous outrage on the feelings of mankind.

51 From the Author's note to *Under Western Eyes* (written 1920).[19]

It must be admitted that by the mere force of circumstances *Under Western Eyes* has become already a sort of historical novel dealing with the past.

This reflection bears entirely upon the events of the tale; but being as a whole an attempt to render not so much the political state as the psychology of Russia itself, I venture to hope that it has not lost all its interest. I am encouraged in this flattering belief by noticing that in many articles on Russian affairs of the present day reference is made to certain sayings and opinions uttered in the pages that follow, in a manner testifying to the clearness of my vision and the correctness of my judgement. I need not say that in writing this novel I had no other object in view than to express imaginatively the general truth which underlies its action, together with my honest convictions as to the moral complexion of certain facts more or less known to the whole world.

As to the actual creation I may say that when I began to write I had a distinct conception of the first part only, with the three figures of Haldin, Razumov, and Councillor Mikulin defined exactly in my mind. It was only after I had finished writing the first part that the whole story revealed itself to me in its tragic character and in the march of its events as unavoidable and sufficiently ample in its outline to give free play to my creative instinct and to the dramatic possibilities of the subject.

The course of action need not be explained. It has suggested itself more as a matter of feeling than a matter of thinking. It is the result not of a special experience but of general knowledge, fortified by earnest meditation. My greatest anxiety was in being able to strike and sustain the note of scrupulous impartiality. The obligation of absolute fairness was imposed on me historically and hereditarily, by the peculiar experience of race and family, in addition to my primary conviction that truth alone is the justification of any fiction which makes the least claim to the quality of art or may hope to take its place in the culture of men and women of its time. I had never been called before to a greater effort of detachment: detachment from all passions, prejudices, and even from personal memories. *Under*

Western Eyes, on its first appearance in England, was a failure with the public, perhaps because of that very detachment. I obtained my reward some six years later when I first heard that the book had found universal recognition in Russia and had been re-published there in many editions.

The various figures playing their part in the story also owe their existence to no special experience but to the general knowledge of the condition of Russia and of the moral and emotional reactions of the Russian temperament to the pressure of tyrannical lawlessness, which, in general human terms, could be reduced to the formula of senseless desperation provoked by senseless tyranny. What I was concerned with mainly was the aspect, the character, and the fate of the individuals as they appeared to the Western Eyes of the old teacher of languages. [. . .]

The most terrifying reflection (I am speaking now for myself) is that all these people are not the product of the exceptional but of the general – of the normality of their place, and time, and race. The ferocity and imbecility of an autocratic rule rejecting all legality and in fact basing itself upon complete moral anarchism provokes the no less imbecile and atrocious answer of a purely Utopian revolutionism encompasssing destruction by the first means to hand, in the strange conviction that a fundamental change of hearts must follow the downfall of any given human institutions. These people are unable to see that all they can effect is merely a change of names. The oppressors and the oppressed are all Russians together; and the world is brought once more face to face with the truth of the saying that the tiger cannot change his stripes nor the leopard his spots.

52 From the Author's note to *Within the Tides* (written 1920).[20]

The tales collected in this book have elicited on their appearance two utterances in the shape of comment and one distinctly critical charge. A reviewer observed that I liked to write of men who go to sea or live on lonely islands untrammelled by the pressure of worldly circumstances, because such characters allowed freer play to my imagination which in their case was only bounded by natural laws and the universal human conventions. There is a certain truth in this remark no doubt. It is only the suggestion of deliberate choice that misses its mark. I have not sought for special imaginative freedom or a larger play of fancy in my choice of characters and subjects. The nature of the knowledge, suggestions or hints used in my imaginative work has depended directly on the conditions of my active life. It depended more on contacts, and very slight contacts at that, than on actual experience; because my life as a matter of fact was far from being adventurous in itself. Even now when I look back on it with a certain regret (who would not regret his youth?) and positive affection, its colouring wears the sober hue of hard work and exacting calls of duty, things which in themselves are not much charged with a feeling of romance. If these things appeal strongly to me even in retrospect it is, I suppose, because the romantic feeling of reality was in me an inborn faculty. This in itself may be a curse but when disciplined by a sense of personal responsibility and a recognition of the hard facts of existence shared with the rest of mankind becomes but a point of view from which the very shadows of life appear endowed with an internal glow. And such romanticism is not a sin. It is none the worse for the knowledge of truth. It only tries hard to make the best of it, hard as it may be; and in this hardness discovers a certain aspect of beauty.

I am speaking here of romanticism in relation to life, not of romanticism in relation to imaginative literature, which, in its early days, was associated simply with mediæval subjects, or, at any rate, with subjects sought for in a remote past. My subjects are not mediæval and I have a natural right to them because my past is very much my own. If their course lie out of the beaten past of organized social life, it is, perhaps, because I myself did in a sort break away from it early in obedience to an impulse which must have been very genuine since it has sustained me through all the dangers of disillusion. But that origin of my literary work was very far from giving a larger scope to my imagination. On the contrary, the mere fact of dealing with matters outside the general run of everyday experience laid me under the obligation of a more scrupulous fidelity to the truth of my own sensations. The problem was to make unfamiliar things credible. To do that I had to create for them, to reproduce for them, to envelop them in their proper atmosphere of actuality. This was the hardest task of all and the most important, in view of that conscientious rendering of truth in thought and fact which has been always my aim.

53 From a letter to Richard Curle, 24 April 1922. Curle was one of the new generation of writers and critics who idolized Conrad during the last years of his life. Curle made his acquaintance in 1912 and produced dozens of pieces about Conrad until his own death in 1968. The article, 'Joseph Conrad in the East', was issued as a pamphlet in July 1922.

I have this morning received the article for the *Blue Peter*. I think I have given you already to understand the nature of my feelings. Indeed, I spoke to you very openly, expressing my fundamental objection to the character you wished to give to it. I do not for a moment expect that what I am going to say here will convince you or influence you in the least. And, indeed, I have neither the wish nor the right to assert my position. I will only point out to you that my feelings in that matter are at least as legitimate as your own. It is a strange fate that everything that I have, of set artistic purpose, laboured to leave indefinite, suggestive, in the penumbra of initial inspiration, should have that light turned on to it and its insignificance (as compared with, I might say without megalomania, the ampleness of my conceptions) exposed for any fool to comment upon or even for average minds to be disappointed with. Didn't it ever occur to you, my dear Curle, that I knew what I was doing in leaving the facts of my life and even of my tales in the background? Explicitness, my dear fellow, is fatal to the glamour of all artistic work, robbing it of all suggestiveness, destroying all illusion. You seem to believe in literalness and explicitness, in facts and also in expression. Yet nothing is more clear than the utter insignificance of explicit statement and also its power to call attention away from things that matter in the region of art. [. . .]

However, those are all private feelings. I think too that the impression of gloom, oppression, and tragedy, is too much emphasized. You know, my dear, I have suffered from such judgements in the early days; but now the point of view, even in America, has swung in another direction; and truly I don't believe myself that my tales are gloomy, or even very tragic, that is, not with a pessimistic intention. Anyway, that reputation, whether justified or not, has deprived me of innumerable readers and I can only regret that you have found it necessary to make it, as it were, the ground-tone of your laudatory article.

One more suggestion. Perhaps you may find it possible to shorten to a certain extent the quotations, which are, of course, admirably selected. I think that for *Blue Peter* there would be too much text; in America it would, of course, not matter.

54 From a letter to C. K. Scott Moncrieff, 17 December 1922. Scott Moncrieff had translated Proust's *Du Côté de chez Swann*. He was attempting to compile a commemorative volume of tributes following Proust's death on 18 November. Conrad's contribution, 'Proust as creator', contained part of this letter when the book, *Marcel Proust, an English Tribute*, was published in 1923.

In the volumes you sent me I was much more interested and fascinated by your rendering than by Proust's creation. One has revealed to me something and there is no revelation in the other. I am speaking now of the sheer *maîtrise de langue*; I mean how far it can be pushed – in your case of two languages – by a supreme faculty akin to genius. For to think that such a result could be obtained by mere study and industry would be too depressing. And that is the revelation. As far as the *maîtrise de langue* is concerned there is no revelation in Proust.

Of course this is for you. It isn't a statement for a propaganda booklet.

Now as to Marcel Proust, *créateur*, I don't think he has been written about much in English, and what I have seen of it was rather superficial. I have seen him praised for his 'wonderful' pictures of Paris life and provincial life. But that has been done admirably before, for us, either in love, or in hatred, or in mere irony. One critic goes so far as to say that P.'s great art reaches the universal and that in depicting his own past he reproduces for us the general experience of mankind. But I doubt it. I admire him rather for disclosing a past like nobody else's, for enlarging, as it were, the general experience of mankind by bringing to it something that has not been recorded before. However, all that is not of much importance. The important thing is that whereas before we had analysis allied to creative art, great in poetic conception, in observation, or in style, his is a creative art absolutely based on analysis. It is really more than that. He is a writer who has pushed analysis to the point when it became creative. All that crowd of personages in their infinite variety through all the gradations of the social scale are made to stand up, to live, and are rendered visible to us by the force of analysis alone. I don't say P. has got no gift of description or characterization; but to take an example from each end of the scale: Françoise, the devoted servant, and le baron de Charlus – a consummate portrait – how many descriptive lines have they got to themselves in the whole body of that immense work? Perhaps, counting the lines, half a page each. And yet no intelligent person can doubt for a moment their plastic and coloured existence. One would think that method (and P. has no other, because his method is the expression of his temperament) may be pushed too far, but as a matter of fact it is never wearisome. There may be here and there among those thousands of pages a paragraph that one might think over subtle, a bit of analysis pushed so far as to vanish into nothingness. But those are very few, and all minor instances. The intense interest never flags because one has got the feeling that the last word is being said upon a subject much studied, much written about and of undying interest – the last word of its time. Those that have found beauty in Proust's work are perfectly right. It is there. What amazes one is its inexplicable character. In that prose so full of life there is no reverie, no emotion, no marked irony, no warmth of conviction, not even a marked rhythm to charm our fancy. It appeals to our sense of wonder and gains our assent by its veiled greatness. I don't think there ever has been in the whole of literature such an example of the power of analysis and I feel pretty safe in saying that there will never be another.

This is more or less what I think, or imagine that I think. It is not really half of what I imagine I think. If it is any good to you, you may alter, cut down, expand, twist, turn over and do anything you like with the above lines to make them suitable. It's indubitable that you know much more about Proust than I do, so please strike out (as a friendly service to me) whatever may appear to you absurd in this thing without a name. I mean it!

55 Letter to Ernst Bendz, 7 March 1923. Dr Bendz, a Swedish academic, published his *Joseph Conrad: An Appreciation* in English in 1923.

Thank you very much for the copy of the pamphlet on myself and my work. I need not tell you that I have perused it with great attention and no small appreciation.

I have the more reason to be grateful to you for this remarkable, and in so many ways generous, recognition of my work because I have heard, from a friend who visited Sweden last year, that I am regarded in that country as literarily a sort of Jack London.[21] I don't mean to depreciate in the least the talent of the late Jack London, who wrote to me in a most friendly way many years ago at the very beginning, I think, of his literary career, and with whom I used to exchange messages through friends afterwards; but the fact remains that temperamentally, mentally, and as a prose writer, I am a different person. I sympathized much with the warmth and direct talent of Jack London, and was sorry to hear of his death – but, after all, one doesn't like to be taken for what one is not. For one thing, for instance, I am much less of a good humanitarian than Jack London; but I think that I am not taking too much on myself in saying that I am a good European, not exactly in the superficial cosmopolitan sense, but in the blood and bones as it were, and as the result of a long heredity.

Apart from the natural gratification one finds in meeting with such admirably expressed sympathy, I followed your analysis with no little curiosity. It is interesting to learn about one's self from a judge for whose attainments one cannot but have a sincere respect. I will confess to you frankly that I do not know much about my own work. I cannot defend myself from the suspicion that you make perhaps too much of its merits, while I see with profound satisfaction

104

that you never question its absolute sincerity, both in its qualities and in its defects.

I will take the liberty to point out that *Nostromo* has never been intended for the hero of the Tale of the Seaboard. Silver is the pivot of the moral and material events, affecting the lives of everybody in the tale. That this was my deliberate purpose there can be no doubt. I struck the first note of my intention in the unusual form which I gave to the title of the First Part, by calling it 'The Silver of the Mine', and by telling the story of the enchanted treasure on Azuera, which, strictly speaking, has nothing to do with the rest of the novel. The word 'silver' occurs almost at the very beginning of the story proper, and I took care to introduce it in the very last paragraph, which would perhaps have been better without the phrase which contains that key-word. Some of my critics have perceived my intention; the last of them being Miss Ruth Stauffer in her little study of my Romantic Realism, published in Boston in 1922.

I am only too acutely aware of my lapses of style, but, in one or two instances which you give, the construction of the speech is shaped on purpose to characterize the person; as for instance when Therese speaks, all through *The Arrow of Gold*.

It is very obvious that I don't possess the English language in any exceptional way; but that is no reason to doubt my sincerity when I say that is has possessed and even shaped my thoughts. Idiomatically I am never at fault, and it is absolutely true that if I had not written in English I would not have written at all.

56 From a letter to Curle, 14 July 1923. The article is Curle's review for the *Times Literary Supplement* of Conrad's collected works in Dent's Uniform Edition. It has the title 'The history of Mr. Conrad's books', and appeared in August, despite Conrad's objection to the idea in an earlier letter to Curle.

I am returning you the article with two corrections as to matters of fact and one of style.

As it stands I can have nothing against it. As to my feelings that is a different matter; and I think that, looking at the intimate character of our friendship and trusting to the indulgence of your affection, I may disclose them to you without reserve.

My point of view is that this is an opportunity, if not unique then not likely to occur again in my lifetime. I was in hopes that on a general survey it could also be made an opportunity for me to get freed from that infernal tail of ships, and that obsession of my sea life which has about as much bearing on my literary existence, on my quality as a writer, as the numeration of drawing-rooms which Thackeray frequented could have had on his gift as a great novelist. After all, I may have been a seaman, but I am a writer of prose. Indeed, the nature of my writing runs the risk of being obscured by the nature of my material. I admit it is natural; but only the appreciation of a special personal intelligence can counteract the superficial appreciation of the inferior intelligence of the mass of readers and critics. Even Doubleday was considerably disturbed by that characteristic as evidenced in press notices in America, where such headings as 'Spinner of sea-yarns – master-mariner – seaman writer' and so forth predominated. I must admit that the letter-press had less emphasis than the headings; but that was simply because they didn't know the facts. That the connection of my ships with my writing stands, with my concurrence I admit, recorded in your book is, of course, a fact. But that was biographical matter not literary. And where it stands it can do no harm. Undue prominence has been given to it since, and yet you know yourself very well that in the body of my work barely one-tenth is what may be called sea stuff, and even of that, the bulk, that is *Nigger* and *Mirror*, has a very special purpose, which I emphasize myself in my Prefaces.

Of course, there are seamen in a good many of my books. That doesn't make them sea stories, any more than the existence of de Barral in *Chance* (and he occupies there as much space as Captain Anthony) makes that novel a story about the financial world. I do wish that all those ships of mine were given a rest, but I am afraid that when the Americans get hold of them they will never, never, never get a rest.

The summarizing of Prefaces, though you do it extremely well, has got this disadvantage that it doesn't give their atmosphere, and indeed it can not give their atmosphere, simply because those pages are an intensely personal expression, much more so than all the rest of my writing, with the exception of the *Personal Record* perhaps. A question of policy arises there: whether it is a good thing to give people the bones, as it were. It may destroy their curiosity for the dish. I am aware, my dear Richard, that while talking over with you the forthcoming article, I used the word historical in connection with my fiction, or with my method, or something of the sort. I expressed myself badly, for I certainly had not in my mind the history of the books. What I was thinking at the time was a phrase in a long article in the *Seccolo*. The critic remarked that there was no difference in method or character between my fiction and my professedly autobiographical matter, as evidenced in the *Personal Record*. He concluded that my fiction was not historical, of course, but had an authentic quality of development and style, which in its ultimate effect resembled historical perspective.

My own impression is that what he really meant was that my manner of telling, perfectly devoid of familiarity as between author and reader, aimed essentially at the intimacy of a personal communication, without any thought for other effects. As a matter of fact, the thought for effects is there all the same (often at the cost of mere directness of narrative) and can be detected in my unconventional grouping and perspective, which are purely temperamental and wherein almost all my 'art' consists. That, I suspect, has been the difficulty the critics felt in classifying it as romantic or realistic. Whereas, as a matter of fact, it is fluid, depending on grouping (sequence) which shifts, and on the changing lights giving varied effects of perspective.

It is in those matters gradually, but never completely, mastered that the history of my books really consists. Of course the plastic matter of this grouping and of those lights has its importance, since without it the actuality of that grouping and that lighting could not be made evident any more than Marconi's electric waves could be made evident without the sending-out and receiving instruments. In other words, without mankind, my art, an infinitesimal thing, could not exist.

57 From a letter to Henry S. Canby, 7 April 1924. Canby, an
   American academic, was part of the growing Conrad industry.

It seems to me that people imagine I sit here and brood over sea stuff.
That is quite a mistake. I brood certainly, but. . . .

'Youth' has been called a fine sea-story. Is it? Well, I won't bore
you with a discussion of fundamentals. But surely those stories of
mine where the sea enters can be looked at from another angle. In the
Nigger I give the psychology of a group of men and render certain
aspects of nature. But the problem that faces them is not a problem of
the sea, it is merely a problem that has arisen on board a ship where
the conditions of complete isolation from all land entanglements
make it stand out with a particular force and colouring. In other of
my tales the principal point is the study of a particular man, or a
particular event. My only sea-book, and the only tribute to a life
which I have lived in my own particular way, is *The Mirror of the Sea*.

JOSEPH CONRAD
The Shadow-Line

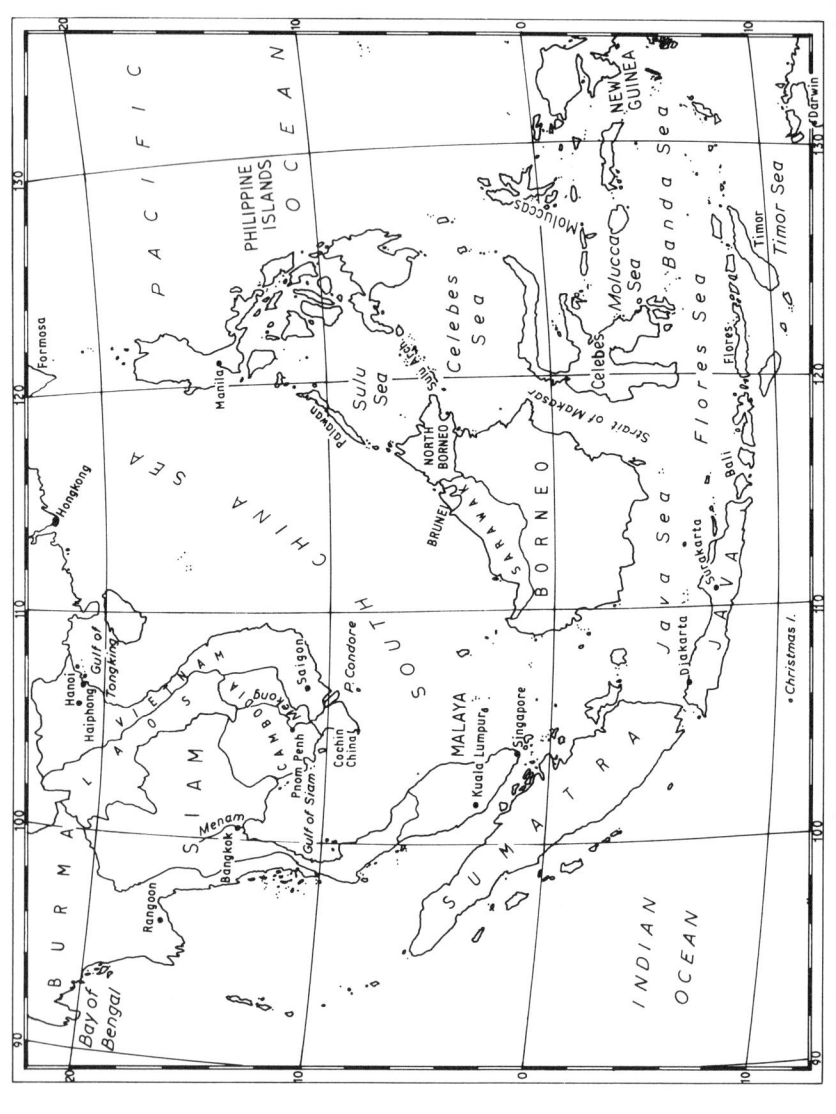

This story, which I admit to be in its brevity a fairly complex piece of work, was not intended to touch on the supernatural. Yet more than one critic has been inclined to take it in that way, seeing in it an attempt on my part to give the fullest scope to my imagination by taking it beyond the confines of the world of the living, suffering humanity. But as a matter of fact my imagination is not made of stuff so elastic as all that. I believe that if I attempted to put the strain of the supernatural on it it would fail deplorably and exhibit an unlovely gap. But I could never have attempted such a thing, because all my moral and intellectual being is penetrated by an invincible conviction that whatever falls under the dominion of our senses must be in nature and, however exceptional, cannot differ in its essence from all the other effects of the visible and tangible world of which we are a self-conscious part. The world of the living contains enough marvels and mysteries as it is; marvels and mysteries acting upon our emotions and intelligence in ways so inexplicable that it would almost justify the conception of life as an enchanted state. No, I am too firm in my consciousness of the marvellous to be ever fascinated by the mere supernatural, which (take it any way you like) is but a manufactured article, the fabrication of minds insensitive to the intimate delicacies of our relation to the dead and to the living, in their countless multitudes; a desecration of our tenderest memories; an outrage on our dignity.

Whatever my native modesty may be it will never condescend so low as to seek help for my imagination within those vain imaginings common to all ages and that in themselves are enough to fill all lovers of mankind with unutterable sadness. As to the effect of a mental or moral shock on a common mind that is quite a legitimate subject for study and description. Mr Burns' moral being receives a severe shock in his relations with his late captain, and this in his diseased state turns into a mere superstitious fancy compounded of fear and animosity. This fact is one of the elements of the story, but there is nothing supernatural in it, nothing so to speak from beyond the confines of this world, which in all conscience holds enough mystery and terror in itself.

Perhaps if I had published this tale, which I have had for a long time in my mind, under the title of 'First Command' no suggestion of the Supernatural would have been found in it by any impartial reader, critical or otherwise. I will not consider here the origins of the feeling in which its actual title, 'The Shadow Line', occurred to my mind. Primarily the aim of this piece of writing was the presentation of certain facts which certainly were associated with the change from youth, care-free and fervent, to the more self-conscious and more poignant period of maturer life. Nobody can doubt that before the supreme trial of a whole generation I had an acute consciousness of the minute and insignificant character of my own obscure experience. There could be no question here of any parallelism. That notion never entered my head. But there was a feeling of identity, though with an enormous difference of scale – as of one single drop measured against the bitter and stormy immensity of an ocean. And this was very natural too. For when we begin to meditate on the meaning of our own past it seems to fill all the world in its profundity and its magnitude. This book was written in the last three months of the year 1916. Of all the subjects of which a writer of tales is more or less conscious within himself this is the only one I found it possible to attempt at the time. The depth and the nature of the mood with which I approached it is best expressed perhaps in the dedication which strikes me now as a most disproportionate thing – as another instance of the overwhelming greatness of our own emotion to ourselves.

This much having been said I may pass on now to a few remarks about the mere material of the story. As to locality it belongs to that part of the Eastern Seas from which I have carried away into my writing life the greatest number of suggestions. From my statement that I thought of this story for a long time under the title of 'First Command' the reader may guess that it is concerned with my personal experience. And as a matter of fact it *is* personal experience seen in perspective with the eye of the mind and coloured by that affection one can't help feeling for such events of one's life as one has no reason to be ashamed of. And that affection is as intense (I appeal here to universal experience) as the shame, and almost the anguish with which one remembers some unfortunate occurrences, down to mere mistakes in speech, that have been perpetrated by one in the past. The effect of perspective in memory is to make things loom large because the essentials stand out isolated from their surroundings of insignificant daily facts which have naturally faded out of one's mind. I remember that period of my sea-life with pleasure because begun inauspiciously it turned out in the end a success from a personal point of view, leaving a tangible proof in the terms of the letter the owners of the ship wrote to me two years afterwards when I resigned my command in order to come home.[1] This resignation marked the beginning of another phase of my seaman's life, its terminal phase, if I may say so, which in its own way has coloured another portion of my writings. I didn't know then how near its end my sea-life was, and therefore I felt no sorrow except at parting with the ship. I was sorry also to break my connection with the firm which owned her and who were pleased to receive with friendly kindness and give their confidence to a man who had entered their service in an accidental manner and in very adverse circumstances. Without disparaging the earnestness of my purpose I suspect now that luck had no small part in the success of the trust reposed in me. And one cannot help remembering with pleasure the time when one's best efforts were seconded by a run of luck.

The words '*Worthy of my undying regard*' selected by me for the motto on the title page are quoted from the text of the book itself; and, though one of my critics surmised that they applied to the ship, it is evident from the place where they stand that they refer to the men of that ship's company: complete strangers to their new captain and yet who stood by him so well during those twenty days that seemed to have been passed on the brink of a slow and agonizing destruction. And *that* is the greatest memory of all! For surely it is a great thing to have commanded a handful of men worthy of one's undying regard.

1920   J.C.

113

The Shadow-Line[2]

A Confession

'Worthy of my undying regard'

TO
BORYS AND ALL OTHERS
who like himself have crossed
in early youth the shadow-line
of their generation
WITH LOVE[3]

– D'autres fois, calme plat, grand miroir
De mon désespoir.
BAUDELAIRE[4]

1

Only the young have such moments. I don't mean the very young.
No. The very young have, properly speaking, no moments. It is the
privilege of early youth to live in advance of its days in all the

beautiful continuity of hope which knows no pauses and no intro-spection.

One closes behind one the little gate of mere boyishness – and enters an enchanted garden. Its very shades glow with promise. Every turn of the path has its seduction. And it isn't because it is an undiscovered country.[5] One knows well enough that all mankind had streamed that way. It is the charm of universal experience from which one expects an uncommon or personal sensation – a bit of one's own.

One goes on recognizing the landmarks of the predecessors, excited, amused, taking the hard luck and the good luck together – the kicks and the halfpence, as the saying is – the picturesque common lot that holds so many possibilities for the deserving or perhaps for the lucky. Yes. One goes on. And the time, too, goes on – till one perceives ahead a shadow-line warning one that the region of early youth, too, must be left behind.

This is the period of life in which such moments of which I have spoken are likely to come. What moments? Why, the moments of boredom, of weariness, of dissatisfaction. Rash moments. I mean moments when the still young are inclined to commit rash actions, such as getting married suddenly or else throwing up a job for no reason.

This is not a marriage story. It wasn't so bad as that with me. My action, rash as it was, had more the character of divorce – almost of desertion. For no reason on which a sensible person could put a finger I threw up my job – chucked my berth – left the ship of which the worst that could be said was that she was a steamship and therefore, perhaps, not entitled to that blind loyalty which.[6] . . . However, it's no use trying to put a gloss on what even at the time I myself half suspected to be a caprice.

It was in an Eastern port. She was an Eastern ship, inasmuch as then she belonged to that port. She traded among dark islands on a blue reef-scarred sea, with the Red Ensign over the taffrail and at her mast-head a house-flag, also red, but with a green border and with a white crescent in it. For an Arab owned her, and a Syed at that. Hence the green border on the flag. He was the head of a great House of Straits Arabs, but as loyal a subject of the complex British Empire[7]

116

as you could find east of the Suez Canal.[8] World politics did not trouble him at all, but he had a great occult power amongst his own people.

It was all one to us who owned the ship. He had to employ white men in the shipping part of his business, and many of those he so employed had never set eyes on him from the first to the last day. I myself saw him but once, quite accidentally on a wharf – an old, dark little man blind in one eye, in a snowy robe and yellow slippers. He was having his hand severely kissed by a crowd of Malay pilgrims to whom he had done some favour, in the way of food and money. His alms-giving, I have heard, was most extensive, covering almost the whole Archipelago. For isn't it said that 'The charitable man is the friend of Allah'?[9]

Excellent (and picturesque) Arab owner, about whom one needed not to trouble one's head, a most excellent Scottish ship – for she was that from the keel up – excellent sea-boat, easy to keep clean, most handy in every way, and if it had not been for her internal propulsion, worthy of any man's love, I cherish to this day a profound respect for her memory. As to the kind of trade she was engaged in and the character of my shipmates, I could not have been happier if I had had the life and the men made to my order by a benevolent Enchanter.

And suddenly I left all this. I left it in that, to us, inconsequential manner in which a bird flies away from a comfortable branch. It was as though all unknowing I had heard a whisper or seen something. Well – perhaps! One day I was perfectly right and the next everything was gone – glamour, flavour, interest, contentment – everything. It was one of these moments, you know. The green sickness of late youth descended on me and carried me off. Carried me off that ship, I mean.

We were only four white men on board, with a large crew of Kalashes and two Malay petty officers. The Captain[10] stared hard as if wondering what ailed me. But he was a sailor, and he too, had been young at one time. Presently a smile came to lurk under his thick iron-grey moustache, and he observed that, of course, if I felt I must go he couldn't keep me by main force. And it was arranged that I should be paid off the next morning. As I was going out of the chart-room he added suddenly, in a peculiar, wistful tone, that he hoped I would find what I was so anxious to go and look for. A soft, cryptic utterance which seemed to reach deeper than any diamond-hard tool could have done. I do believe he understood my case.

But the second engineer attacked me differently. He was a sturdy young Scot, with a smooth face and light eyes. His honest red countenance emerged out of the engine-room companion and then the whole robust man, with shirt sleeves turned up, wiping slowly the massive fore-arms with a lump of cotton-waste. And his light eyes expressed bitter distaste, as though our friendship had turned to ashes. He said weightily: 'Oh! Aye! I've been thinking it was about time for you to run away home and get married to some silly girl.'

It was tacitly understood in the port that John Nieven was a fierce mysogynist;[11] and the absurd character of the sally convinced me that he meant to be nasty – very nasty – had meant to say the most crushing thing he could think of. My laugh sounded deprecatory. Nobody but a friend could be so angry as that. I became a little crestfallen. Our chief engineer also took a characteristic view of my action, but in a kindlier spirit.

He was young, too, but very thin, and with a mist of fluffy brown beard all round his haggard face. All day long, at sea or in harbour, he could be seen walking hastily up and down the after-deck, wearing an intense, spiritually rapt expression, which was caused by a perpetual consciousness of unpleasant physical sensations in his internal economy. For he was a confirmed dyspeptic. His view of my case was very simple. He said it was nothing but deranged liver. Of course! He suggested I should stay for another trip and meantime dose myself with a certain patent medicine in which his own belief was absolute.[12] 'I'll tell you what I'll do. I'll buy you two bottles, out of my own pocket. There. I can't say fairer than that, can I?'

I believe he would have perpetrated the atrocity (or generosity) at the merest sign of weakening on my part. By that time, however, I was more discontented, disgusted, and dogged than ever. The past eighteen months, so full of new and varied experience, appeared a dreary, prosaic waste of days. I felt – how shall I express it? – that there was no truth to be got out of them.[13]

What truth? I should have been hard put to it to explain.

Probably, if pressed, I would have burst into tears simply. I was young enough for that.

Next day the Captain and I transacted our business in the Harbour Office. It was a lofty, big, cool, white room, where the screened light of day glowed serenely. Everybody in it – the officials, the public – were in white. Only the heavy polished desks gleamed darkly in a central avenue, and some papers lying on them were blue. Enormous punkahs sent from on high a gentle draught through that immaculate interior and upon our perspiring heads.

The official behind the desk we approached grinned amiably and kept it up till, in answer to his perfunctory question, 'Sign off and on again?' my Captain answered, 'No! Signing off for good.' And then his grin vanished in sudden solemnity. He did not look at me again till he handed me my papers with a sorrowful expression, as if they had been my passports for Hades.[14]

While I was putting them away he murmured some question to the Captain, and I heard the latter answer good-humouredly:

'No. He leaves us to go home.'

'Oh!' the other exclaimed, nodding mournfully over my sad condition.

I didn't know him outside the official building, but he leaned forward over the desk to shake hands with me, compassionately, as one would with some poor devil going out to be hanged; and I am afraid I performed my part ungraciously, in the hardened manner of an impenitent criminal.

No homeward-bound mail-boat was due for three or four days. Being now a man without a ship, and having for a time broken my connection with the sea – become, in fact, a mere potential passenger – it would have been more appropriate perhaps if I had gone to stay at an hotel. There it was, too, within a stone's throw of the Harbour Office, low, but somehow palatial, displaying its white, pillared pavilions surrounded by trim grass plots. I would have felt a passenger indeed in there! I gave it a hostile glance and directed my steps towards the Officers' Sailors' Home.[15]

I walked in the sunshine, disregarding it, and in the shade of the big trees on the Esplanade without enjoying it. The heat of the tropical East descended through the leafy boughs, enveloping my thinly clad body, clinging to my rebellious discontent, as if to rob it of its freedom.

The Officers' Home was a large bungalow with a wide verandah and a curiously suburban-looking little garden of bushes and a few trees between it and the street. That institution partook somewhat of the character of a residential club, but with a slightly Governmental flavour about it, because it was administered by the Harbour Office. Its manager was officially styled Chief Steward. He was an unhappy, wizened little man, who if put into a jockey's rig would have looked the part to perfection. But it was obvious that at some time or other in his life, in some capacity or other, he had been connected with the sea. Possibly in the comprehensive capacity of a failure.[16]

I should have thought his employment a very easy one, but he used to affirm for some reason or other that his job would be the death of him some day. It was rather mysterious. Perhaps everything naturally was too much trouble for him. He certainly seemed to hate having people in the house.

On entering it I thought he must be feeling pleased. It was as still as a tomb. I could see no one in the living rooms; and the verandah, too, was empty, except for a man at the far end dozing prone in a long chair. At the noise of my footsteps he opened one horribly fish-like eye. He was a stranger to me. I retreated from there, and, crossing the dining-room – a very bare apartment with a motionless punkah hanging over the centre table – I knocked at a door labelled in black letters: 'Chief Steward.'

The answer to my knock being a vexed and doleful plaint: 'Oh, dear! Oh, dear! What is it now?' I went in at once.

It was a strange room to find in the tropics. Twilight and stuffiness reigned in there. The fellow had hung enormously ample, dusty, cheap lace curtains over his windows, which were shut. Piles of cardboard boxes, such as milliners and dressmakers use in Europe, cumbered the corners; and by some means he had procured for himself the sort of furniture that might have come out of a respectable parlour in the East End of London – a horsehair sofa, arm-chairs of the same. I glimpsed grimy antimacassars scattered over that horrid upholstery, which was awe-inspiring, insomuch that one could not guess what mysterious accident, need, or fancy had collected it there. Its owner had taken off his tunic, and in white trousers and a thin short-sleeved singlet prowled behind the chair-backs nursing his meagre elbows.

An exclamation of dismay escaped him when he heard that I had come for a stay; but he could not deny that there were plenty of vacant rooms.

'Very well. Can you give me the one I had before?'

He emitted a faint moan from behind a pile of cardboard boxes on the table, which might have contained gloves or handkerchiefs or neckties. I wonder what the fellow did keep in them? There was a smell of decaying coral, or Oriental dust, of zoological specimens in that den of his. I could only see the top of his head and his unhappy eyes levelled at me over the barrier.

'It's only for a couple of days,' I said, intending to cheer him up.

'Perhaps you would like to pay in advance?' he suggested eagerly.

'Certainly not!' I burst out directly I could speak. 'Never heard of such a thing! This is the most infernal cheek. . . .'

He had seized his head in both hands – a gesture of despair which checked my indignation.

'Oh, dear! Oh, dear! Don't fly out like this. I am asking every-body.'

'I don't believe it,' I said bluntly.

'Well, I am going to. And if you gentlemen all agreed to pay in advance I could make Hamilton pay up too. He's always turning up ashore dead broke, and even when he has some money he won't settle his bills. I don't know what to do with him. He swears at me and tells me I can't chuck a white man out into the street here. So if you only would. . . .'

I was amazed. Incredulous too. I suspected the fellow of gratuitous impertinence. I told him with marked emphasis that I would see him and Hamilton hanged first, and requested him to conduct me to my room with no more of his nonsense. He produced then a key from somewhere and led the way out of his lair, giving me a vicious sidelong look in passing.

'Any one I know staying here?' I asked him before he left my room.

He had recovered his usual pained impatient tone, and said that Captain Giles was there, back from a Solo Sea trip.[17] Two other guests were staying also. He paused. And, of course, Hamilton, he added.

'Oh, yes! Hamilton,' I said, and the miserable creature took himself off with a final groan.

His impudence still rankled when I came into the dining-room at tiffin time.[18] He was there on duty overlooking the Chinamen servants. The tiffin was laid on one end only of the long table, and the punkah was stirring the hot air lazily – mostly above a barren waste of polished wood.

We were four around the cloth. The dozing stranger from the chair was one. Both his eyes were partly opened now, but they did not seem to see anything. He was supine. The dignified person next him, with short side whiskers and a carefully scraped chin, was, of course, Hamilton. I have never seen any one so full of dignity for the station in life Providence had been pleased to place him in.[19] I had been told that he regarded me as a rank outsider. He raised not only his eyes, but his eyebrows as well, at the sound I made pulling back my chair.

Captain Giles was at the head of the table. I exchanged a few words of greeting with him and sat down on his left. Stout and pale, with a great shiny dome of a bald forehead and prominent brown eyes, he might have been anything but a seaman. You would not have been surprised to learn that he was an architect. To me (I know how absurd it is) he looked like a church-warden. He had the appearance of a man from whom you would expect sound advice, moral sentiments, with perhaps a platitude or two thrown in on occasion, not from a desire to dazzle, but from honest conviction.

Though very well known and appreciated in the shipping world, he had no regular employment. He did not want it. He had his own peculiar position. He was an expert. An expert in – how shall I say it? – in intricate navigation. He was supposed to know more about remote and imperfectly charted parts of the Archipelago than any man living. His brain must have been a perfect warehouse of reefs, positions, bearings, images of headlands, shapes of obscure coasts, aspects of innumerable islands, desert and otherwise.[20] Any ship, for instance, bound on a trip to Palawan[21] or somewhere that way would have Captain Giles on board, either in temporary command or 'to assist the master'. It was said that he had a retaining fee from a wealthy firm of Chinese steamship owners, in view of such services. Besides, he was always ready to relieve any man who wished to take a spell ashore for a time. No owner was ever known to object to an arrangement of that sort. For it seemed to be the established opinion at the port that Captain Giles was as good as the best, if not a little better. But in Hamilton's view he was an 'outsider'. I believe that for Hamilton the generalization 'outsider' covered the whole lot of us; though I suppose that he made some distinctions in his mind.

I didn't try to make conversation with Captain Giles, whom I had not seen more than twice in my life. But, of course, he knew who I was. After a while, inclining his big shiny head my way, he addressed me first in his friendly fashion. He presumed from seeing me there, he said, that I had come ashore for a couple of days' leave.

He was a low-voiced man. I spoke a little louder, saying that: No – I had left the ship for good.

'A free man for a bit,' was his comment.

'I suppose I may call myself that – since eleven o'clock,' I said.

Hamilton had stopped eating at the sound of our voices. He laid down his knife and fork gently, got up, and muttering something about 'this infernal heat cutting one's appetite', went out of the room. Almost immediately we heard him leave the house down the verandah steps.

On this Captain Giles remarked easily that the fellow had no doubt gone off to look after my old job. The Chief Steward, who had been leaning against the wall, brought his face of an unhappy goat nearer to the table and addressed us dolefully. His object was to unburden himself of his eternal grievance against Hamilton. The man kept him in hot water with the Harbour Office as to the state of his accounts. He wished to goodness he would get my job, though in truth what would it be? Temporary relief at best.

I said: 'You needn't worry. He won't get my job. My successor is on board already.'

He was surprised, and I believe his face fell a little at the news. Captain Giles gave a soft laugh. We got up and went out on the

123

verandah, leaving the supine stranger to be dealt with by the Chinamen. The last thing I saw they had put a plate with a slice of pineapple on it before him and stood back to watch what would happen. But the experiment seemed a failure. He sat insensible.

It was imparted to me in a low voice by Captain Giles that this was an officer of some Rajah's yacht which had come into our port to be dry-docked. Must have been 'seeing life' last night, he added, wrinkling his nose in an intimate, confidential way which pleased me vastly. For Captain Giles had prestige. He was credited with wonderful adventures and with some mysterious tragedy in his life. And no man had a word to say against him. He continued:

'I remember him first coming ashore here some years ago. Seems only the other day. He was a nice boy. Oh! these nice boys!'

I could not help laughing aloud. He looked startled, then joined in the laugh. 'No! No! I didn't mean that,' he cried. 'What I meant is that some of them do go soft mighty quick out here.'

Jocularly I suggested the beastly heat as the first cause. But Captain Giles disclosed himself possessed of a deeper philosophy. Things out East were made easy for white men. That was all right. The difficulty was to go on keeping white, and some of these nice boys did not know how. He gave me a searching look, and in a benevolent, heavy-uncle manner asked point blank:

'Why did you throw up your berth?'

I became angry all of a sudden; for you can understand how exasperating such a question was to a man who didn't know. I said to myself that I ought to shut up that moralist; and to him aloud I said with challenging politeness:

'Why. . . ? Do you disapprove?'

He was too disconcerted to do more than mutter confusedly: 'I! . . . In a general way. . .' and then gave me up. But he retired in good order, under the cover of a heavily humorous remark that he, too, was getting soft, and that this was his time for taking his little siesta – when he was on shore. 'Very bad habit. Very bad habit.'

The simplicity of the man would have disarmed a touchiness even more youthful than mine. So when next day at tiffin he bent his head towards me and said that he had met my late Captain last evening, adding in an undertone: 'He's very sorry you left. He had never had a mate that suited him so well,' I answered him earnestly, without any affectation, that I certainly hadn't been so comfortable in any ship or with any commander in all my sea-going days.

'Well – then,' he murmured.

'Haven't you heard, Captain Giles, that I intend to go home?'

'Yes,' he said benevolently. 'I have heard that sort of thing so often before.'

'What of that?' I cried. I thought he was the most dull, unimaginative man I had ever met. I don't know what more I would have said, but the much-belated Hamilton came in just then and took his usual seat. So I dropped into a mumble.

'Anyhow, you shall see it done this time.'

Hamilton, beautifully shaved, gave Captain Giles a curt nod, but didn't even condescend to raise his eyebrows at me; and when he spoke it was only to tell the Chief Steward that the food on his plate wasn't fit to be set before a gentleman. The individual addressed seemed much too unhappy to groan. He only cast his eyes up to the punkah and that was all.

Captain Giles and I got up from the table, and the stranger next to Hamilton followed our example, manœuvring himself to his feet with difficulty. He, poor fellow, not because he was hungry but I verily believe only to recover his self-respect, had tried to put some of that unworthy food into his mouth. But after dropping his fork twice and generally making a failure of it, he had sat still with an air of intense mortification combined with a ghastly glazed stare. Both Giles and I avoided looking his way at table.

On the verandah he stopped short on purpose to address to us anxiously a long remark which I failed to understand completely. It sounded like some horrible unknown language. But when Captain Giles, after only an instant for reflection, answered him with homely friendliness, 'Aye, to be sure. You are right there,' he appeared very much gratified indeed, and went away (pretty straight too) to seek a distant long chair.

'What was he trying to say?' I asked with disgust.

'I don't know. Mustn't be down too much on a fellow. He's feeling pretty wretched, you may be sure; and to-morrow he'll feel worse yet.'

125

Judging by the man's appearance it seemed impossible. I wondered what sort of complicated debauch had reduced him to that unspeakable condition. Captain Giles' benevolence was spoiled by a curious air of complacency which I disliked. I said with a little laugh:

'Well, he will have you to look after him.'

He made a deprecatory gesture, sat down, and took up a paper. I did the same. The papers were old and uninteresting, filled up mostly with dreary stereotyped descriptions of Queen Victoria's first jubilee celebrations.[22] Probably we should have quickly fallen into a tropical afternoon doze if it had not been for Hamilton's voice raised in the dining-room. He was finishing his tiffin there. The big double doors stood wide open permanently, and he could not have had any idea how near to the doorway our chairs were placed. He was heard in a loud, supercilious tone answering some statement ventured by the Chief Steward.

'I am not going to be rushed into anything. They will be glad enough to get a gentleman I imagine. There is no hurry.'

A loud whispering from the steward succeeded and then again Hamilton was heard with even intenser scorn.

'What? That young ass who fancies himself for having been chief mate with Kent so long? . . . Preposterous.'

Giles and I looked at each other. Kent being the name of my late commander, Captain Giles' whisper, 'He's talking of you,' seemed to me sheer waste of breath. The Chief Steward must have stuck to his point whatever it was, because Hamilton was heard again more supercilious, if possible, and also very emphatic:

'Rubbish, my good man! One doesn't *compete* with a rank outsider like that. There's plenty of time.'

Then there was pushing of chairs, footsteps in the next room, and plaintive expostulations from the Steward, who was pursuing Hamilton, even out of doors through the main entrance.

'That's a very insulting sort of man,' remarked Captain Giles – superfluously, I thought. 'Very insulting. You haven't offended him in some way, have you?'

'Never spoke to him in my life,' I said grumpily. 'Can't imagine what he means by competing. He has been trying for my job after I left – and didn't get it. But that isn't exactly competition.'

126

Captain Giles balanced his big benevolent head thoughtfully. 'He didn't get it,' he repeated very slowly. 'No, not likely either, with Kent. Kent is no end sorry you left him. He gives you the name of a good seaman too.'

I flung away the paper I was still holding. I sat up, I slapped the table with my open palm. I wanted to know why he would keep harping on that, my absolutely private affair. It was exasperating, really.

Captain Giles silenced me by the perfect equanimity of his gaze. 'Nothing to be annoyed about,' he murmured reasonably, with an evident desire to soothe the childish irritation he had aroused. And he was really a man of an appearance so inoffensive that I tried to explain myself as much as I could. I told him that I did not want to hear any more about what was past and gone. It had been very nice while it lasted, but now it was done with I preferred not to talk about it or even think about it. I had made up my mind to go home.

He listened to the whole tirade in a particular, lending-the-ear attitude, as if trying to detect a false note in it somewhere; then straightened himself up and appeared to ponder sagaciously over the matter.

'Yes. You told me you meant to go home. Anything in view there?'

Instead of telling him that it was none of his business I said sullenly: 'Nothing that I know of.'

I had indeed considered that rather blank side of the situation I had created for myself by leaving suddenly my very satisfactory employment. And I was not very pleased with it. I had it on the tip of my tongue to say that common sense had nothing to do with my action, and that therefore it didn't deserve the interest Captain Giles seemed to be taking in it. But he was puffing at a short wooden pipe now, and looked so guileless, dense, and commonplace, that it seemed hardly worth while to puzzle him either with truth or sarcasm.

He blew a cloud of smoke, then surprised me by a very abrupt: 'Paid your passage money yet?'

Overcome by the shameless pertinacity of a man to whom it was rather difficult to be rude, I replied with exaggerated meekness that I had not done so yet. I thought there would be plenty of time to do that to-morrow.

And I was about to turn away, withdrawing my privacy from his fatuous, objectless attempts to test what sort of stuff it was made of, when he laid down his pipe in an extremely significant manner, you know, as if a critical moment had come, and leaned sideways over the table between us.

'Oh! You haven't yet!' He dropped his voice mysteriously. 'Well, then I think you ought to know that there's something going on here.'

I had never in my life felt more detached from all earthly goings on. Freed from the sea for a time, I preserved the sailor's consciousness of complete independence from all land affairs. How could they concern me? I gazed at Captain Giles' animation with scorn rather than with curiosity.

To his obviously preparatory question whether our steward had spoken to me that day I said he hadn't. And what's more he would have had precious little encouragement if he had tried to. I didn't want the fellow to speak to me at all.

Unrebuked by my petulance, Captain Giles, with an air of immense sagacity, began to tell me a minute tale about a Harbour Office peon. It was absolutely pointless. A peon was seen walking that morning on the verandah with a letter in his hand. It was in an official envelope. As the habit of these fellows is, he had shown it to the first white man he came across. That man was our friend in the arm-chair. He, as I knew, was not in a state to interest himself in any sublunary matters. He could only wave the peon away. The peon then wandered on along the verandah and came upon Captain Giles, who was there by an extraordinary chance. . . .

At this point he stopped with a profound look. The letter, he continued, was addressed to the Chief Steward. Now what could Captain Ellis, the Master Attendant,[23] want to write to the Steward for? The fellow went every morning, anyhow, to the Harbour Office with his report, for orders or what not. He hadn't been back more than an hour before there was an office peon chasing him with a note. Now what was that for?

And he began to speculate. It was not for this – and it could not be for that. As to that other thing it was unthinkable.

The fatuousness of all this made me stare. If the man had not been somehow a sympathetic personality I would have resented it like an insult. As it was, I felt only sorry for him. Something remarkably earnest in his gaze prevented me from laughing in his face. Neither did I yawn at him. I just stared.

His tone became a shade more mysterious. Directly the fellow (meaning the Steward) got that note he rushed for his hat and bolted out of the house. But it wasn't because the note called him to the Harbour Office. He didn't go there. He was not absent long enough for that. He came darting back in no time, flung his hat away, and raced about the dining-room moaning and slapping his forehead. All these exciting facts and manifestations had been observed by Captain Giles. He had, it seems, been meditating upon them ever since.

I began to pity him profoundly. And in a tone which I tried to make as little sarcastic as possible I said that I was glad he had found something to occupy his morning hours.

With his disarming simplicity he made me observe, as if it were a matter of some consequence, how strange it was that he should have spent the morning indoors at all. He generally was out before tiffin, visiting various offices, seeing his friends in the harbour, and so on. He had felt out of sorts somewhat on rising. Nothing much. Just enough to make him feel lazy.

All this with a sustained, holding stare which, in conjunction with the general inanity of the discourse, conveyed the impression of mild, dreary lunacy. And when he hitched his chair a little and dropped his voice to the low note of mystery, it flashed upon me that high professional reputation was not necessarily a guarantee of sound mind.

It never occurred to me then that I didn't know in what soundness of mind exactly consisted and what a delicate and, upon the whole, unimportant matter it was. With some idea of not hurting his feelings I blinked at him in an interested manner. But when he proceeded to ask me mysteriously whether I remembered what had passed just now between that Steward of ours and 'that man Hamilton', I only grunted sour assent and turned away my head.

'Aye. But do you remember every word?' he insisted tactfully.

'I don't know. It's none of my business,' I snapped out, consigning, moreover, the Steward and Hamilton aloud to eternal perdition.

I meant to be very energetic and final, but Captain Giles continued to gaze at me thoughtfully. Nothing could stop him. He went on to point out that my personality was involved in that conversation. When I tried to preserve the semblance of unconcern he became positively cruel. I heard what the man had said? Yes? What did I think of it then? – he wanted to know.

Captain Giles' appearance excluding the suspicion of mere sly malice, I came to the conclusion that he was simply the most tactless idiot on earth. I almost despised myself for the weakness of attempting to enlighten his common understanding. I started to explain that I did not think anything whatever. Hamilton was not worth a thought. What such an offensive loafer . . . – 'Aye! that he is,' interjected Captain Giles – . . . thought or said was below any decent man's contempt, and I did not propose to take the slightest notice of it.

This attitude seemed to me so simple and obvious that I was really astonished at Giles giving no sign of assent. Such perfect stupidity was almost interesting.

'What would you like me to do?' I asked laughing. 'I can't start a row with him because of the opinion he has formed of me. Of course, I've heard of the contemptuous way he alludes to me. But he doesn't intrude his contempt on my notice. He has never expressed it in my hearing. For even just now he didn't know we could hear him. I should only make myself ridiculous.'

That hopeless Giles went on puffing at his pipe moodily. All at once his face cleared, and he spoke.

'You missed my point.'

'Have I? I am very glad to hear it,' I said.

With increasing animation he stated again that I had missed his point. Entirely. And in a tone of growing self-conscious complacency he told me that few things escaped his attention, and he was rather used to think them out, and generally from his experience of life and men arrived at the right conclusion.

This bit of self-praise, of course, fitted excellently the laborious inanity of the whole conversation. The whole thing strengthened in me that obscure feeling of life being but a waste of days, which, half-unconsciously, had driven me out of a comfortable berth, away from men I liked, to flee from the menace of emptiness . . . and to find inanity at the first turn. Here was a man of recognized character and achievement disclosed as an absurd and dreary chatterer. And it was probably like this everywhere – from east to west, from the bottom to the top of the social scale.

A great discouragement fell on me. A spiritual drowsiness. Giles' voice was going on complacently; the very voice of the universal hollow conceit. And I was no longer angry with it. There was nothing original, nothing new, startling, informing to expect from the world: no opportunities to find out something about oneself, no wisdom to acquire, no fun to enjoy. Everything was stupid and overrated, even as Captain Giles was. So be it.

The name of Hamilton suddenly caught my ear and roused me up.

'I thought we had done with him,' I said, with the greatest possible distaste.

'Yes. But considering what we happened to hear just now I think you ought to do it.'

'Ought to do it?' I sat up bewildered. 'Do what?'

Captain Giles confronted me very much surprised.

'Why! Do what I have been advising you to try. You go and ask the Steward what was there in that letter from the Harbour Office. Ask him straight out.'

I remained speechless for a time. Here was something unexpected and original enough to be altogether incomprehensible. I murmured, astounded:

'But I thought it was Hamilton that you. . . .'

'Exactly. Don't you let him. You do what I tell you. You tackle that Steward. You'll make him jump, I bet,' insisted Captain Giles, waving his smouldering pipe impressively at me. Then he took three rapid puffs at it.

His aspect of triumphant acuteness was indescribable. Yet the man remained a strangely sympathetic creature. Benevolence radiated from him ridiculously, mildly, impressively. It was irritating too. But I pointed out coldly, as one who deals with the incomprehensible, that I didn't see any reason to expose myself to a snub from the fellow. He was a very unsatisfactory steward and a miserable wretch besides, but I would just as soon think of tweaking his nose.

'Tweaking his nose,' said Captain Giles in a scandalized tone. 'Much use it would be to you.'

That remark was so irrelevant that one could make no answer to it. But the sense of the absurdity was beginning at last to exercise its well-known fascination. I felt I must not let the man talk to me any more. I got up, observing curtly that he was too much for me – that I couldn't make him out.

Before I had time to move away he spoke again in a changed tone of obstinacy and puffing nervously at his pipe.

'Well – he's a – no account cuss – anyhow. You just – ask him. That's all.'

That new manner impressed me – or rather made me pause. But sanity asserting its sway at once I left the verandah after giving him a mirthless smile. In a few strides I found myself in the dining-room, now cleared and empty. But during that short time various thoughts occurred to me, such as: that Giles had been making fun of me, expecting some amusement at my expense; that I probably looked silly and gullible; that I knew very little of life. . . .

The door facing me across the dining-room flew open to my extreme surprise. It was the door inscribed with the word 'Steward' and the man himself ran out of his stuffy Philistinish lair in his absurd hunted animal manner, making for the garden door.[24]

To this day I don't know what made me call after him: 'I say! Wait a minute.' Perhaps it was the sidelong glance he gave me; or possibly I was yet under the influence of Captain Giles' mysterious earnestness. Well, it was an impulse of some sort; an effect of that force somewhere within our lives which shapes them this way or that.[25] For if these words had not escaped from my lips (my will had nothing to do with that) my existence would, to be sure, have been still a seaman's existence, but directed on now to me utterly inconceivable lines.

No. My will had nothing to do with it. Indeed, no sooner had I made that fateful noise than I became extremely sorry for it. Had the man stopped and faced me I would have had to retire in disorder. For I had no notion to carry out Captain Giles' idiotic joke, either at my own expense or at the expense of the Steward.

But here the old human instinct of the chase came into play. He pretended to be deaf, and I, without thinking a second about it, dashed along my own side of the dining table and cut him off at the very door.

'Why can't you answer when you are spoken to?' I asked roughly.

He leaned against the side of the door. He looked extremely wretched. Human nature is, I fear, not very nice right through. There are ugly spots in it. I found myself growing angry, and that, I believe, only because my quarry looked so woe-begone. Miserable beggar!

I went for him without more ado. 'I understand there was an official communication to the Home from the Harbour Office this morning. Is that so?'

Instead of telling me to mind my own business, as he might have done, he began to whine with an undertone of impudence. He couldn't see me anywhere this morning. He couldn't be expected to run all over the town after me.

'Who wants you to?' I cried. And then my eyes became opened to the inwardness of things and speeches the triviality of which had been so baffling and tiresome.

I told him I wanted to know what was in that letter. My sternness of tone and behaviour was only half assumed. Curiosity can be a very fierce sentiment – at times.

He took refuge in a silly, muttering sulkiness. It was nothing to me, he mumbled. I had told him I was going home. And since I was going home he didn't see why he should. . . .

That was the line of his argument, and it was irrelevant enough to be almost insulting. Insulting to one's intelligence, I mean.

In that twilight region between youth and maturity, in which I had my being then, one is peculiarly sensitive to that kind of insult. I am afraid my behaviour to the Steward became very rough indeed. But it wasn't in him to face out anything or anybody. Drug habit or solitary tippling, perhaps. And when I forgot myself to far as to swear at him he broke down and began to shriek.

I don't mean to say that he made a great outcry. It was a cynical shrieking confession, only faint – piteously faint. It wasn't very coherent either, but sufficiently so to strike me dumb at first. I turned my eyes from him in righteous indignation, and perceived Captain Giles in the verandah doorway surveying quietly the scene, his own handiwork, if I may express it in that way.[26] His smouldering black pipe was very noticeable in his big, paternal fist. So, too, was the glitter of his heavy gold watch-chain across the breast of his white tunic. He exhaled an atmosphere of virtuous sagacity thick enough for any innocent soul to fly to confidently. I flew to him.

'You would never believe it,' I cried. 'It was a notification that a master is wanted for some ship. There's a command apparently going about and this fellow puts the thing in his pocket.'

The Steward screamed out in accents of loud despair, 'You will be the death of me!'

The mighty slap he gave his wretched forehead was very loud, too. But when I turned to look at him he was no longer there. He had rushed away somewhere out of sight. This sudden disappearance made me laugh.

This was the end of the incident – for me. Captain Giles, however, staring at the place where the Steward had been, began to haul at his gorgeous gold chain till at last the watch came up from the deep pocket like solid truth from a well. Solemnly he lowered it down again and only then said:

'Just three o'clock. You will be in time – if you don't lose any, that is.'

'In time for what?' I asked.

'Good Lord! For the Harbour Office. This must be looked into.'

Strictly speaking, he was right. But I've never had much taste for investigation, for showing people up and all that, no doubt, ethically meritorious kind of work. And my view of the episode was purely ethical. If any one had to be the death of the Steward I didn't see why it shouldn't be Captain Giles himself, a man of age and standing, and a permanent resident. Whereas I, in comparison, felt myself a mere bird of passage in that port. In fact, it might have been said that I had already broken off my connection. I muttered that I didn't think – it was nothing to me. . . .

'Nothing!' repeated Captain Giles, giving some signs of quiet, deliberate indignation. 'Kent warned me you were a peculiar young

fellow. You will tell me next that a command is nothing to you –
and after all the trouble I've taken, too!'

'The trouble!' I murmured, uncomprehending. What trouble? All
I could remember was being mystified and bored by his conversation
for a solid hour after tiffin. And he called that taking a lot of trouble.

He was looking at me with a self-complacency which would have
beed odious in any other man. All at once, as if a page of a book had
been turned over disclosing a word which made plain all that had
gone before, I perceived that this matter had also another than an
ethical aspect.

And still I did not move. Captain Giles lost his patience a little.
With an angry puff at his pipe he turned his back on my hesitation.

But it was not hesitation on my part. I had been, if I may express
myself so, put out of gear mentally. But as soon as I had convinced
myself that this stale, unprofitable world of my discontent contained
such a thing as a command to be seized, I recovered my powers of
locomotion.[27]

It's a good step from the Officers' Home to the Harbour Office;
but with the magic word 'Command' in my head I found myself
suddenly on the quay as if transported there in the twinkling of an
eye, before a portal of dressed white stone above a flight of shallow
white steps.[28]

All this seemed to glide towards me swiftly. The whole great
roadstead to the right was just a mere flicker of blue, and the dim
cool hall swallowed me up out of the heat and glare of which I had
not been aware till the very moment I passed in from it.

The broad inner staircase insinuated itself under my feet somehow.
Command is a strong magic. The first human beings I perceived
distinctly since I had parted with the indignant back of Captain Giles
was the crew of the harbour steam-launch lounging on the spacious
landing about the curtained archway of the shipping office.

It was there that my buoyancy abandoned me. The atmosphere of
officialdom would kill anything that breathes the air of human
endeavour, would extinguish hope and fear alike in the supremacy of
paper and ink. I passed heavily under the curtain which the Malay
coxswain of the harbour launch raised for me. There was nobody in
the office except the clerks, writing in two industrious rows. But the

head shipping-master hopped down from his elevation and hurried along on the thick mats to meet me in the broad central passage.

He had a Scottish name, but his complexion was of a rich olive hue, his short beard was jet black, and his eyes, also black, had a languishing expression.[29] He asked confidentially:

'You want to see Him?'

All lightness of spirit and body having departed from me at the touch of officialdom, I looked at the scribe without animation and asked in my turn wearily:

'What do you think? Is it any use?'

'My goodness! He has asked for you twice to-day.'

This emphatic He was the supreme authority, the Marine Superintendent, the Harbour-Master – a very great person in the eyes of every single quill-driver in the room. But that was nothing to the opinion he had of his own greatness.

Captain Ellis looked upon himself as a sort of divine (pagan) emanation, the deputy-Neptune[30] for the circumambient seas. If he did not actually rule the waves, he pretended to rule the fate of the mortals whose lives were cast upon the waters.

This uplifting illusion made him inquisitorial and peremptory. And as his temperament was choleric there were fellows who were actually afraid of him. He was redoubtable, not in virtue of his office, but because of his unwarrantable assumptions. I had never had anything to do with him before.

I said: 'Oh! He has asked for me twice. Then perhaps I had better go in.'

'You must! You must!'

The shipping-master led the way with a mincing gait round the whole system of desks to a tall and important-looking door, which he opened with a deferential action of the arm.

He stepped right in (but without letting go of the handle) and, after gazing reverently down the room for a while, beckoned me in by a silent jerk of the head. Then he slipped out at once and shut the door after me most delicately.

Three lofty windows gave on the harbour. There was nothing in them but the dark-blue sparkling sea and the paler luminous blue of the sky. My eye caught in the depths and distances of these blue tones the white speck of some big ship just arrived and about to anchor in the outer roadstead. A ship from home – after perhaps ninety days at sea. There is something touching about a ship coming from sea and folding her white wings for a rest.[31]

The next thing I saw was the top-knot of silver hair surmounting Captain Ellis' smooth red face, which would have been apoplectic if it hadn't had such a fresh appearance.

Our deputy-Neptune had no beard on his chin, and there was no trident to be seen standing in a corner anywhere, like an umbrella. But his hand was holding a pen – the official pen, far mightier than the sword in making or marring the fortune of simple toiling men. He was looking over his shoulder at my advance.

When I had come well within range he saluted me by a nerve-shattering: 'Where have you been all this time?'

As it was no concern of his I did not take the slightest notice of the shot. I said simply that I had heard there was a master needed for some vessel, and being a sailing-ship man I thought I would apply. . . .

He interrupted me. 'Why! Hang it! *You* are the right man for that job – if there had been twenty others after it. But no fear of that. They are all afraid to catch hold. That's what's the matter.'

He was very irritated. I said innocently: 'Are they sir? I wonder why?'

'Why!' he fumed. 'Afraid of the sails. Afraid of a white crew. Too much trouble. Too much work. Too long out here. Easy life and deck-chairs more their mark. Here I sit with the Consul-General's cable before me, and the only man fit for the job not to be found anywhere. I began to think you were funking it too. . . .'

'I haven't been long getting to the office,' I remarked calmly.

'You have a good name out here, though,' he growled savagely without looking at me.

'I am very glad to hear it from you, sir,' I said.

'Yes. But you are not on the spot when you are wanted. You know you weren't. That steward of yours wouldn't dare to neglect a message from this office. Where the devil did you hide yourself for the best part of the day?'

I only smiled kindly down on him, and he seemed to recollect himself, and asked me to take a seat. He explained that the master of a British ship having died in Bankok the Consul-General had cabled to him a request for a competent man to be sent out to take command.

Apparently, in his mind, I was the man from the first, though for the looks of the thing the notification addressed to the Sailors' Home was general. An agreement had already been prepared. He gave it to me to read, and when I handed it back to him with the remark that I accepted its terms, the deputy-Neptune signed it, stamped it with his own exalted hand, folded it in four (it was a sheet of blue foolscap), and presented it to me – a gift of extraordinary potency, for, as I put it in my pocket, my head swam a little.

'This is your appointment to the command,' he said with a certain gravity. 'An official appointment binding the owners to conditions which you have accepted. Now – when will you be ready to go?'

I said I would be ready that very day if necessary. He caught me at my word with great readiness. The steamer *Melita* was leaving for Bankok that evening about seven. He would request her captain officially to give me a passage and wait for me till ten o'clock.

Then he rose from his office chair, and I got up too. My head swam, there was no doubt about it, and I felt a heaviness of limbs as if they had grown bigger since I had sat down on that chair. I made my bow.

A subtle change in Captain Ellis' manner became perceptible as though he had laid aside the trident of deputy-Neptune. In reality, it was only his official pen that he had dropped on getting up.

2

He shook hands with me: 'Well, there you are, on your own, appointed officially under my responsibility.'

He was actually walking with me to the door. What a distance off it seemed! I moved like a man in bonds. But we reached it at last. I opened it with the sensation of dealing with mere dream-stuff, and then at the last moment the fellowship of seamen asserted itself, stronger than the difference of age and station. It asserted itself in Captain Ellis' voice.

'Good-bye – and good luck to you,' he said so heartily that I could only give him a grateful glance. Then I turned and went out, never to see him again in my life. I had not made three steps into the outer office when I heard behind my back a gruff, loud, authoritative voice, the voice of our deputy-Neptune.

It was addressing the head shipping-master, who, having let me in, had, apparently, remained hovering in the middle distance ever since.

'Mr R., let the harbour launch have steam up to take the captain here on board the *Melita* at half-past nine to-night.'

I was amazed at the startled assent of R.'s 'Yes, sir.' He ran before me out on the landing. My new dignity sat yet so lightly on me that I was not aware that it was I, the Captain, the object of this last graciousness. It seemed as if all of a sudden a pair of wings had grown on my shoulders. I merely skimmed along the polished floor.

But R. was impressed.

'I say!' he exclaimed on the landing, while the Malay crew of the steam-launch standing by looked stonily at the man for whom they were going to be kept on duty so late, away from their gambling, from their girls, or their pure domestic joys. 'I say! His own launch. What have you done to him?'

His stare was full of respectful curiosity. I was quite confounded.

'Was it for me? I hadn't the slightest notion,' I stammered out.

He nodded many times. 'Yes. And the last person who had it before you was a Duke. So, there!'

I think he expected me to faint on the spot. But I was in too much of a hurry for emotional displays. My feelings were already in such a whirl that this staggering information did not seem to make the slightest difference. It fell into the seething cauldron of my brain, and I carried it off with me after a short but effusive passage of leave-taking with R.

The favour of the great throws an aureole[32] round the fortunate object of its selection. That excellent man inquired whether he could do anything for me. He had known me only by sight, and he was well aware he would never see me again; I was, in common with the other seamen of the port, merely a subject for official writing, filling up of forms with all the artificial superiority of a man of pen and ink

139

to the men who grapple with realities outside the consecrated walls of official buildings. What ghosts we must have been to him! Mere symbols to juggle with in books and heavy registers, without brains and muscles and perplexities; something hardly useful and decidedly inferior.

And he – the office hours being over – wanted to know if he could be of any use to me!

I ought, properly speaking – I ought to have been moved to tears. But I did not even think of it. It was only another miraculous manifestation of that day of miracles. I parted from him as if he had been a mere symbol. I floated down the staircase. I floated out of the official and imposing portal. I went on floating along.

I use that word rather that the word 'flew', because I have a distinct impression that, though uplifted by my aroused youth, my movements were deliberate enough. To that mixed white, brown, and yellow portion of mankind, out abroad on their own affairs, I presented the appearance of a man walking rather sedately. And nothing in the way of abstraction could have equalled my deep detachment from the forms and colours of this world. It was, as it were, absolute.

And yet, suddenly, I recognized Hamilton. I recognized him without effort, without a shock, without a start. There he was, strolling towards the Harbour Office with his stiff, arrogant dignity. His red face made him noticeable at a distance. It flamed, over there, on the shady side of the street.

He had perceived me too. Something (unconscious exuberance of spirits perhaps) moved me to wave my hand to him elaborately. This lapse from good taste happened before I was aware that I was capable of it.

The impact of my impudence stopped him short, much as a bullet might have done. I verily believe he staggered, though as far as I could see he didn't actually fall. I had gone past in a moment and did not turn my head. I had forgotten his existence.

The next ten minutes might have been ten seconds or ten centuries for all my consciousness had to do with it. People might have been falling dead around me, houses crumbling, guns firing, I wouldn't have known. I was thinking: 'By Jove! I have got it.' *It* being the command. It had come about in a way utterly unforeseen in my modest day-dreams.

I perceived that my imagination had been running in conventional channels and that my hopes had always been drab stuff. I had envisaged a command as a result of a slow course of promotion in the employ of some highly respectable firm. The reward of faithful service. Well, faithful service was all right. One would naturally give that for one's own sake, for the sake of the ship, for the love of the life of one's choice; not for the sake of the reward.

There is something distasteful in the notion of a reward.

And now here I had my command, absolutely in my pocket, in a way undeniable indeed, but most unexpected; beyond my imaginings, outside all reasonable expectations, and even notwithstanding the existence of some sort of obscure intrigue to keep it away from me. It is true that the intrigue was feeble, but it helped the feeling of wonder – as if I had been specially destined for that ship I did not know, by some power higher than the prosaic agencies of the commercial world.

A strange sense of exultation began to creep into me. If I had worked for that command ten years or more there would have been nothing of the kind. I was a little frightened.

'Let us be calm,' I said to myself.

Outside the door of the Officers' Home the wretched Steward seemed to be waiting for me. There was a broad flight of a few steps, and he ran to and fro on the top of it as if chained there. A distressed cur. He looked as though his throat were too dry for him to bark.

I regret to say I stopped before going in. There had been a revolution in my moral nature. He waited open-mouthed, breathless, while I looked at him for half a minute.

'And you thought you could keep me out of it,' I said scathingly.

'You said you were going home,' he squeaked miserably. 'You said so. You said so.'

'I wonder what Captain Ellis will have to say to that excuse,' I uttered slowly with a sinister meaning.

His lower jaw had been trembling all the time and his voice was like the bleating of a sick goat. 'You have given me away? You have done for me?'

Neither his distress not yet the sheer absurdity of it was able to disarm me. It was the first instance of harm being attempted to be done to me – at any rate, the first I had ever found out. And I was still young enough, still too much on this side of the shadow-line, not to be surprised and indignant at such things.

I gazed at him inflexibly. Let the beggar suffer. He slapped his forehead and I passed in, pursued, into the dining-room, by his screech: 'I always said you'd be the death of me.'

This clamour not only overtook me, but went ahead as it were on to the verhandah and brought out Captain Giles.

He stood before me in the doorway in all the commonplace solidity of his wisdom. The gold chain glittered on his breast. He clutched a smouldering pipe.

I extended my hand to him warmly and he seemed surprised, but did respond heartily enough in the end, with a faint smile of superior knowledge which cut my thanks short as if with a knife. I don't think that more than one word came out. And even for that one, judging by the temperature of my face, I had blushed as if for a bad action. Assuming a detached tone, I wondered how on earth he had managed to spot the little underhand game that had been going on.

He murmured complacently that there were but few things done in the town that he could not see the inside of. And as to this house, he had been using it off and on for nearly ten years. Nothing that went on it it could escape his great experience. It had been no trouble to him. No trouble at all.

Then in his quiet thick tone he wanted to know if I had complained formally of the Steward's action.

I said that I hadn't – though, indeed, it was not for want of øpportunity. Captain Ellis had gone for me bald-headed in a most ridiculous fashion for being out of the way when wanted.

'Funny old gentleman,' interjected Captain Giles. 'What did you say to that?'

'I said simply that I came along the very moment I heard of his message. Nothing more. I didn't want to hurt the Steward. I would scorn to harm such an object. No. I made no complaint, but I believe he thinks I've done so. Let him think. He's got a fright that he won't forget in a hurry, for Captain Ellis would kick him out into the middle of Asia. . . .'

'Wait a moment,' said Captain Giles, leaving me suddenly. I sat down feeling very tired, mostly in my head. Before I could start a train of thought he stood again before me, murmuring the excuse that he had to go and put the fellow's mind at ease.

I looked up with surprise. But in reality I was indifferent. He explained that he had found the Steward lying face downwards on the horsehair sofa. He was all right now.

'He would not have died of fright,' I said contemptuously.

'No. But he might have taken an overdose out of one of those little bottles he keeps in his room,' Captain Giles argued seriously. 'The confounded fool has tried to poison himself once – a couple of years ago.'

'Really,' I said without emotion. 'He doesn't seem very fit to live, anyhow.'

'As to that, it may be said of a good many.'

'Don't exaggerate like this!' I protested, laughing irritably. 'But I wonder what this part of the world would do if you were to leave off looking after it, Captain Giles?[33] Here you have got me a command and saved the Steward's life in one afternoon. Though why you should have taken all that interest in either of us is more than I can understand.'

Captain Giles remained silent for a minute.

Then gravely:

'He's not a bad steward really. He can find a good cook, at any rate. And, what's more, he can keep him when found. I remember the cooks we had here before his time. . . .'

I must have made a movement of impatience, because he interrupted himself with a apology for keeping me yarning there, while no doubt I needed all my time to get ready.

What I really needed was to be alone for a bit. I seized this opening hastily. My bedroom was a quiet refuge in an apparently uninhabited wing of the building. Having absolutely nothing to do (for I had not unpacked my things), I sat down on the bed and abandoned myself to the influences of the hour. To the unexpected influences. . . .

And first I wondered at my state of mind. Why was I not more surprised? Why? Here I was, invested with a command in the twinkling of an eye, not in the common course of human affairs, but more as if by enchantment. I ought to have been lost in astonishment. But I wasn't. I was very much like people in fairy tales. Nothing ever astonishes them. When a fully appointed gala coach is produced out of a pumpkin to take her to a ball Cinderella does not exclaim. She gets in quietly and drives away to her high fortune.[34]

Captain Ellis (a fierce sort of fairy) had produced a command out of a drawer almost as unexpectedly as in a fairy tale. But a command is an abstract idea, and it seemed a sort of 'lesser marvel' till it flashed upon me that it involved the concrete existence of a ship.

A ship! My ship! She was mine, more absolutely mine for possession and care than anything in the world; an object of responsibility and devotion. She was there waiting for me, spellbound, unable to move, to live, to get out into the world (till I came), like an enchanted princess. Her call had come to me as if from the clouds. I had never suspected her existence. I didn't know how she looked, I had barely heard her name, and yet we were indissolubly united for a certain portion of our future, to sink or swim together!

A sudden passion of anxious impatience rushed through my veins and gave me such a sense of the intensity of existence as I have never felt before or since. I discovered how much of a seaman I was, in heart, in mind, and, as it were, physically – a man exclusively of sea and ships; the sea the only world that counted, and the ships the test of manliness, of temperament, of courage and fidelity – and of love.

I had an exquisite moment. It was unique also. Jumping up from my seat, I paced up and down my room for a long time. But when I came into the dining-room I behaved with sufficient composure. I only couldn't eat anything at dinner.

Having declared my intention not to drive but to walk down to the quay, I must render the wretched Steward justice that he bestirred himself to find me some coolies for the luggage. They departed, carrying all my worldly possessions (except a little money I had in my pocket) slung from a long pole. Captain Giles volunteered to walk down with me.

We followed the sombre, shaded alley across the Esplanade. It was moderately cool there under the trees. Captain Giles remarked, with a sudden laugh: 'I know who's jolly thankful at having seen the last of you.'

I guess that he meant the Steward. The fellow had borne himself to me in a sulkily frightened manner at the last. I expressed my wonder that he should have tried to do me a bad turn for no reason at all.

'Don't you see that what he wanted was to get rid of our friend Hamilton by dodging him in front of you for that job? That would have removed him for good, see?'[35]

'Heavens!' I exclaimed, feeling humiliated somehow. 'Can it be possible? What a fool he must be! That overbearing, impudent loafer! Why! He couldn't. . . . And yet he's nearly done it, I believe; for the Harbour Office was bound to send somebody.'

'Aye. A fool like our Steward can be dangerous sometimes,' declared Captain Giles sententiously. 'Just because he is a fool,' he added, imparting further instruction in his complacent low tones. 'For,' he continued in the manner of a set demonstration, 'no sensible person would risk being kicked out of the only berth between himself and starvation just to get rid of a simple annoyance – a small worry. Would he now?'

'Well, no,' I conceded, restraining a desire to laugh at that something mysteriously earnest in delivering the conclusions of his wisdom as though they were the product of prohibited operations. 'But that fellow looks as if he were rather crazy. He must be.'

'As to that, I believe everybody in the world is a little mad,' he announced quietly.

'You make no exceptions?' I inquired, just to hear his answer.

He kept silent for a little while, then got home in an effective manner.

'Why! Kent says that even of you.'[36]

'Does he?' I retorted, extremely embittered all at once against my former captain. 'There's nothing of that in the written character from him which I've got in my pocket. Has he given you any instances of my lunacy?'

Captain Giles explained in a conciliating tone that it had been only a friendly remark in reference to my abrupt leaving the ship for no apparent reason.

I muttered grumpily: 'Oh! leaving his ship,' and mended my pace. He kept up by my side in the deep gloom of the avenue as if it were his conscientious duty to see me out of the colony as an undesirable character. He panted a little, which was rather pathetic in a way. But I was not moved. On the contrary. His discomfort gave me a sort of malicious pleasure.

Presently I relented, slowed down, and said:

'What I really wanted was to get a fresh grip. I felt it was time. Is that so very mad?'

He made no answer. We were issuing from the avenue. On the bridge over the canal a dark, irresolute figure seemed to be awaiting something or somebody.

It was a Malay policeman, barefooted, in his blue uniform. The silver band on his little round cap shone dimly in the light of the street lamp. He peered in our direction timidly.

Before we could come up to him he turned about and walked in front of us in the direction of the jetty. The distance was some hundred yards; and then I found my coolies squatting on their heels. They had kept the pole on their shoulders, and all my worldly goods, still tied to the pole, were resting on the ground between them. As far as the eye could reach along the quay there was not another soul abroad except the police peon, who saluted us.

It seem he had detained the coolies as suspicious characters, and had forbidden them the jetty. But at a sign from me he took off the embargo with alacrity. The two patient fellows, rising together with a faint grunt, trotted off along the planks, and I prepared to take my leave of Captain Giles, who stood there with an air as though his mission were drawing to a close. It could not be denied that he had done it all. And while I hesitated about an appropriate sentence he made himself heard:

'I expect you'll have your hands pretty full of tangled up business.'

I asked him what made him think so; and he answered that it was his general experience of the world. Ship a long time away from her port, owners inaccessible by cable, and the only man who could explain matters dead and buried.

'And you yourself new to the business in a way,' he concluded in a sort of unanswerable tone.

'Don't insist,' I said. 'I know it only too well. I only wish you could impart to me some small portion of your experience before I go. As it can't be done in ten minutes I had better not begin to ask you. There's that harbour-launch waiting for me too. But I won't feel really at peace till I have that ship of mine out in the Indian Ocean.'

He remarked casually that from Bankok to the Indian Ocean was a pretty long step. And this murmur, like a dim flash from a dark lantern, showed me for a moment the broad belt of islands and reefs between that unknown ship, which was mine, and the freedom of the great waters of the globe.

But I felt no apprehension. I was familiar enough with the Archipelago by that time. Extreme patience and extreme care would see me through the region of broken land, of faint airs and of dead water to where I would feel at last my command swing on the great swell and list over to the great breath of regular winds, that would give her the feeling of a large, more intense life. The road would be long. All roads are long that lead towards one's heart's desire. But this road my mind's eye could see on a chart, professionally, with all its complications and difficulties, yet simple enough in a way. One is a seaman or one is not. And I had no doubt of being one.

The only part I was a stranger to was the Gulf of Siam. And I mentioned this to Captain Giles. Not that I was concerned very much. It belonged to the same region the nature of which I knew, into whose very soul I seemed to have looked during the last months of that existence with which I had broken now, suddenly, as one parts with some enchanting company.

'The Gulf. . . . Ay! A funny piece of water – that,' said Captain Giles.

Funny, in this connection, was a vague word. The whole thing sounded like an opinion uttered by a cautious person mindful of actions for slander.

I didn't inquire as to the nature of that funniness. There was really no time. But at the very last he volunteered a warning.

'Whatever you do keep to the east side of it. The west side is dangerous at this time of year. Don't let anything tempt you over. You'll find nothing but trouble there.'

Though I could hardly imagine what could tempt me to involve my ship amongst the currents and reefs of the Malay shore, I thanked him for his advice.

He gripped my extended arm warmly, and the end of our acquaintance came suddenly in the words: 'Good-night.'

That was all he said: 'Good-night.' Nothing more. I don't know what I intended to say, but surprise made me swallow it, whatever it was. I choked slightly, and then exclaimed with a sort of nervous haste: 'Oh! Good-night, Captain Giles, good-night.'

His movements were always deliberate, but his back had receded some distance along the deserted quay before I collected myself enough to follow his example and made a half turn in the direction of the jetty.

Only my movements were not deliberate. I hurried down to the steps and leaped into the launch. Before I had fairly landed in her stern-sheets the slim little craft darted away from the jetty with a sudden swirl of her propeller and the hard, rapid puffing of the exhaust in her vaguely gleaming brass funnel amidships.

The misty churning at her stern was the only sound in the world. The shore lay plunged in the silence of the deepest slumber. I watched the town recede still and soundless in the hot night, till the abrupt hail, 'Steam-launch, ahoy!' made me spin round face forward. We were close to a white, ghostly steamer. Lights shone on her decks, in her portholes. And the same voice shouted from her: 'Is that our passenger?'

'It is,' I yelled.

Her crew had been obviously on the jump. I could hear them running about. The modern spirit of haste was loudly vocal in the orders to 'Heave away on the cable' – to 'Lower the side-ladder,' and in urgent requests to me to 'Come along, sir! We have been delayed three hours for you. . . . Our time is seven o'clock, you know!'

I stepped on the deck. I said 'No! I don't know.' The spirit of modern hurry was embodied in a thin, long-armed, long-legged man, with a closely clipped grey beard. His meagre hand was hot and dry. He declared feverishly:

'I am hanged if I would have waited another five minutes – harbour-master or no harbour-master.'

'That's your own business,' I said. 'I didn't ask you to wait for me.'

'I hope you don't expect any supper,' he burst out. 'This isn't a boarding-house afloat. You are the first passenger I ever had in my life and I hope to goodness you will be the last.'

I made no answer to this hospitable communciation; and, indeed, he didn't wait for any, bolting away on to his bridge to get his ship under way.[37]

For the four days he had me on board he did not depart from that half-hostile attitude. His ship having been delayed three hours on my account he couldn't forgive me for not being a more distinguished person. He was not exactly outspoken about it, but that feeling of annoyed wonder was peeping out perpetually in his talk.

He was absurd.

He was also a man of much experience, which he liked to trot out; but no greater contrast with Captain Giles could have been imagined. He would have amused me if I had wanted to be amused. But I did not want to be amused. I was like a lover looking forward to a meeting. Human hostility was nothing to me. I thought of my unknown ship. It was amusement enough, torment enough, occupation enough.

He perceived my state, for his wits were sufficiently sharp for that, and he poked sly fun at my preoccupation in the manner some nasty, cynical old men assume towards the dreams and illusions of youth. I, on my side, refrained from questioning him as to the appearance of my ship, though I knew that being in Bankok every month or so he must have known her by sight. I was not going to expose the ship, my ship! to some slighting reference.

He was the first really unsympathetic man I had ever come in contact with. My education was far from being finished, though I didn't know it. No! I didn't know it.

All I knew was that he disliked me and had some contempt for my person. Why? Apparently because his ship had been delayed three hours on my account. Who was I to have such a thing done for me? Such a thing had never been done for him. It was a sort of jealous indignation.

My expectation, mingled with fear, was wrought to its highest pitch. How slow had been the days of the passage and how soon they were over. One morning early, we crossed the bar, and while the sun was rising splendidly over the flat spaces of the land we steamed up the innumerable bends, passed under the shadow of the great gilt pagoda, and reached the outskirts of the town.

There it was, spread largely on both banks, the Oriental capital which had as yet suffered no white conqueror; an expanse of brown houses of bamboo, of mats, of leaves, of a vegetable-matter style of architecture, sprung out of the brown soil on the banks of the muddy river.[38] It was amazing to think that in those miles of human habitations there was not probably half a dozen pounds of nails. Some of those houses of sticks and grass, like the nests of an aquatic race, clung to the low shores. Others seemed to grow out of the water; others again floated in long anchored rows in the very middle of the stream. Here and there in the distance, above the crowded mob of low, brown roof ridges, towered great piles of masonry, King's Palace, temples, gorgeous and dilapidated, crumbling under the vertical sunlight, tremendous, overpowering, almost palpable, which seemed to enter one's breast with the breath of one's nostrils and soak into one's limbs through every pore of one's skin.

The ridiculous victim of jealousy had for some reason or other to stop his engines just then. The steamer drifted slowly up with the tide. Oblivious of my new surroundings I walked the deck, in anxious, deadened abstraction, a commingling of romantic reverie with a very practical survey of my qualifications. For the time was approaching for me to behold my command and to prove my worth in the ultimate test of my profession.

Suddenly I heard myself called by that imbecile. He was beckoning me to come up on his bridge.

I didn't care very much for that, but as it seemed he had something particular to say I went up the ladder.

He laid his hand on my shoulder and gave me a slight turn, pointing with his other arm at the same time.

'There! That's your ship, Captain,' he said. I felt a thump in my breast – only one, as if my heart had ceased to beat. There were ten or more ships moored along the bank, and the one he meant was

150

partly hidden from my sight by her next astern. He said: 'We'll drift abreast her in a moment.'

What was his tone? Mocking? Threatening? Or only indifferent? I could not tell. I suspected some malice in this unexpected manifestation of interest.

He left me, and I leaned over the rail of the bridge looking over the side. I dared not raise my eyes. Yet it had to be done – and, indeed, I could not have helped myself. I believe I trembled.

But directly my eyes had rested on my ship all my fear vanished. It went off swiftly, like a bad dream. Only that a dream leaves no shame behind it, and that I felt a momentary shame at my unworthy suspicions.

Yes, there she was. Her hull, her rigging filled my eye with a great content. That feeling of life-emptiness which had made me so restless for the last few months lost its bitter plausibility, its evil influence, dissolved in a flow of joyous emotion.

At the first glance I saw that she was a high-class vessel, a harmonious creature in the lines of her fine body, in the proportioned tallness of her spars. Whatever her age and her history, she had preserved the stamp of her origin. She was one of those craft that in virtue of their design and complete finish will never look old. Amongst her companions moored to the bank, and all bigger than herself, she looked like a creature of high breed – an Arab steed in a string of cart-horses.[39]

A voice behind me said in a nasty equivocal tone: 'I hope you are satisfied with her, Captain.' I did not even turn my head. It was the master of the steamer, and whatever he meant, whatever he thought of her, I knew that, like some rare women, she was one of those creatures whose mere existence is enough to awaken an unselfish delight. One feels that it is good to be in the world in which she has her being.

That illusion of life and character which charms one in men's finest handiwork radiated from her. An enormous baulk of teak-wood timber swung over her hatchway; lifeless matter, looking heavier and bigger than anything aboard of her. When they started lowering it the surge of the tackle sent a quiver through her from water-line to the trucks up the fine nerves of her rigging, as though she had shuddered at the weight. It seemed cruel to load her so. . . .

Half-an-hour later, putting my foot on her deck for the first time, I received the feeling of deep physical satisfaction. Nothing could equal the fullness of that moment, the ideal completeness of that emotional experience which had come to me without the preliminary toil and disenchantments of an obscure career.

My rapid glance ran over her, enveloped, appropriated the form concreting the abstract sentiment of my command. A lot of details perceptible to a seaman struck my eye vividly in that instant. For the rest, I saw her disengaged from the material conditions of her being. The shore to which she was moored was as if it did not exist. What were to me all the countries of the globe? In all the parts of the world washed by navigable waters our relation to each other would be the same – and more intimate than there are words to express in the language. Apart from that, every scene and episode would be a mere passing show. The very gang of yellow coolies busy about the main hatch was less substantial than the stuff dreams are made of.[40] For who on earth would dream of Chinamen? . . .

I went aft, ascended the poop, where, under the awning, gleamed the brasses of the yacht-like fittings, the polished surfaces of the rails, the glass of the sky-lights. Right aft two seamen, busy cleaning the steering gear, with the reflected ripples of light running playfully up their bent backs, went on with their work, unaware of me and of the almost affectionate glance I threw at them in passing towards the companion-way of the cabin.

The doors stood wide open, the slide was pushed right back. The half-turn of the staircase cut off the view of the lobby. A low humming ascended from below, but it stopped abruptly at the sound of my descending footsteps.

3

The first thing I saw down there was the upper part of a man's body projecting backwards, as it were, from one of the doors at the foot of the stairs. His eyes looked at me very wide and still. In one hand he held a dinner plate, in the other a cloth.

'I am your new captain,' I said quietly.

In a moment, in the twinkling of an eye, he had got rid of the plate and the cloth and jumped to open the cabin door. As soon as I passed into the saloon he vanished, but only to reappear instantly, buttoning up a jacket he had put on with the swiftness of a 'quick-change' artist.

'Where's the chief mate?' I asked.

'In the hold, I think, sir. I saw him go down the after-hatch ten minutes ago.'

'Tell him I am on board.'

The mahogany table under the skylight shone in the twilight like a dark pool of water. The sideboard, surmounted by a wide looking-glass in an ormolu frame, had a marble top. It bore a pair of silver-plated lamps and some other pieces – obviously a harbour display. The saloon itself was panelled in two kinds of wood in the excellent, simple taste prevailing when the ship was built.

I sat down in the arm-chair at the head of the table – the captain's chair, with a small tell-tale compass swung above it – a mute reminder of unremitting vigilance.

A succession of men had sat in that chair. I became aware of that thought suddenly, vividly, as though each had left a little of himself between the four walls of these ornate bulkheads; as if a sort of composite soul, the soul of command, had whispered suddenly to mine of long days at sea and of anxious moments.[41]

'You, too!' it seemed to say, 'you, too, shall taste of that peace and that unrest in a searching intimacy with your own self – obscure as we were and as supreme in the face of all the winds and all the seas, in an immensity that receives no impress, preserves no memories, and keeps no reckoning of lives.'

Deep within the tarnished ormolu frame, in the hot half-light sifted through the awning, I saw my own face propped between my hands. And I stared back at myself with the perfect detachment of distance, rather with curiosity than with any other feeling, except of some sympathy for this latest representative of what for all intents and purposes was a dynasty;[42] continuous not in blood, indeed, but in its experience, in its training, in its conception of duty, and in the blessed simplicity of its traditional point of view on life.

It struck me that this quietly staring man whom I was watching, both as if he were myself and somebody else, was not exactly a lonely figure. He had his place in a line of men whom he did not know, of whom he had never heard; but who were fashioned by the same influences, whose souls in relation to their humble life's work had no secrets for him.

Suddenly I perceived that there was another man in the saloon, standing a little on one side and looking intently at me. The chief mate. His long, red moustache determined the character of his physiognomy, which struck me as pugnacious in (strange to say) a ghastly sort of way.[43]

How long had he been there looking at me, appraising me in my unguarded day-dreaming state? I would have been more disconcerted if, having the clock set in the top of the mirror-frame right in front of me, I had not noticed that its long hand had hardly moved at all.

I could not have been in that cabin more than two minutes altogether. Say three. . . . So he could not have been watching me more than a mere fraction of a minute, luckily. Still, I regretted the occurrence.

But I showed nothing of it as I rose leisurely (it had to be leisurely) and greeted him with perfect friendliness.

There was something reluctant and at the same time attentive in his bearing. His name was Burns. We left the cabin and went round the ship together. His face in the full light of day appeared very worn, meagre, even haggard. Somehow I had a delicacy as to looking too often at him; his eyes, on the contrary, remained fairly glued on my face. They were greenish and had an expectant expression.

He answered all my questions readily enough, but my ear seemed to catch a tone of unwillingness. The second officer, with three or four hands, was busy forward. The mate mentioned his name and I nodded to him in passing. He was very young. He struck me as rather a cub.

When we returned below I sat down on one end of a deep, semi-circular, or, rather, semi-oval settee, upholstered in red plush. It extended right acrosss the whole after-end of the cabin. Mr Burns, motioned to sit down, dropped into one of the swivel-chairs round the table, and kept his eyes on me as persistently as ever, and with that strange air as if all this were make-believe and he expected me to get up, burst into a laugh, slap him on the back, and vanish from the cabin.

There was an odd stress in the situation which began to make me feel uncomfortable. I tried to react against this vague feeling.

'It's only my inexperience,' I thought.

In the face of that man, several years, I judged, older than myself, I became aware of what I had left already behind me – my youth. And that was indeed poor comfort. Youth is a fine thing, a mighty power – as long as one does not think of it. I felt I was becoming self-conscious. Almost against my will I assumed a moody gravity. I said: 'I see you have kept her in very good order, Mr Burns.'

Directly I had uttered these words I asked myself angrily why the deuce did I want to say that? Mr Burns in answer had only blinked at me. What on earth did he mean?

I fell back on a question which had been in my thoughts for a long time – the most natural question on the lips of any seaman whatever joining a ship. I voiced it (confound this self-consciousness) in a *dégagé* cheerful tone: 'I suppose she can travel – what?'

Now a question like this might have been answered normally, either in accents of apologetic sorrow or with a visibly suppressed pride, in a 'I don't want to boast, but you shall see' sort of tone. There are sailors, too, who would have been roughly outspoken: 'Lazy brute,' or openly delighted: 'She's a flyer.' Two ways, if four manners.

But Mr Burns found another way, a way of his own which had, at all events, the merit of saving his breath, if no other.

Again he did not say anything. He only frowned. And it was an angry frown. I waited. Nothing more came.

'What's the matter? . . . Can't you tell after being nearly two years in the ship?' I addressed him sharply.

He looked as startled for a moment as though he had discovered my presence only that very moment. But this passed off almost at once. He put on an air of indifference. But I suppose he thought it better to say something. He said that a ship needed, just like a man, the chance to show the best she could do, and that this ship had never had a chance since he had been on board of her. Not that he could remember. The last captain. . . . He paused.[44]

'Has he been so very unlucky?' I asked with frank incredulity. Mr Burns turned his eyes away from me. No, the late captain was not an unlucky man. One couldn't say that. But he had not seemed to want to make use of his luck.

Mr Burns – man of enigmatic moods – made this statement with an inanimate face and staring wilfully at the rudder-casing. The statement itself was obscurely suggestive. I asked quietly:

'Where did he die?'

'In this saloon. Just where you are sitting now,' answered Mr Burns.

I repressed a silly impulse to jump up; but upon the whole I was relieved to hear that he had not died in the bed which was now to be mine. I pointed out to the chief mate that what I really wanted to know was where he had buried his late captain.

Mr Burns said that it was at the entrance to the Gulf. A roomy grave; a sufficient answer. But the mate, overcoming visibly something within him – something like a curious reluctance to believe in my advent (as an irrevocable fact, at any rate), did not stop at that – though, indeed, he may have wished to do so.

As a compromise with his feelings, I believe, he addressed himself persistently to the rudder-casing, so that to me he had the appearance of a man talking in solitude, a little unconsciously, however.

His tale was that at seven bells in the forenoon watch he had all hands mustered on the quarter-deck and told them that they had better go down to say good-bye to the captain.

Those words, as if grudged to an intruding personage, were enough for me to evoke vividly that strange ceremony: The bare-footed, bare-headed seamen crowding shyly into that cabin, a small mob pressed against that sideboard, uncomfortable rather than moved, shirts open on sunburnt chests, weather-beaten faces, and all staring at the dying man with the same grave and expectant expression.

'Was he conscious?' I asked.

'He didn't speak, but he moved his eyes to look at them,' said the mate.

After waiting a moment Mr Burns motioned the crew to leave the cabin, but he detained the two eldest men to stay with the captain while he went on deck with this sextant to 'take the sun'. It was getting towards noon and he was anxious to obtain a good observation for latitude. When he returned below to put his sextant away he found that the two men had retreated out into the lobby. Through the open door he had a view of the captain lying easy against the pillows. He had 'passed away' while Mr Burns was taking his observation. As near noon as possible. He had hardly changed his position.

Mr Burns sighed, glanced at me inquisitively, as much as to say, 'Aren't you going yet?' and then turned his thoughts from his new captain back to the old, who, being dead, had no authority, was not in anybody's way, and was much easier to deal with.

Mr Burns dealt with him at some length. He was a peculiar man – of about sixty-five – iron grey, hard-faced, obstinate, and uncommunicative. He used to keep the ship loafing at sea for inscrutable reasons. Would come on deck at night sometimes, take some sail off her, God only knows why or wherefore, then go below, shut himself up in his cabin, and play on the violin for hours – till daybreak perhaps. In fact, he spent most of his time day or night playing the violin. That was when the fit took him. Very loud, too.

It came to this, that Mr Burns mustered his courage one day and remonstrated earnestly with the captain. Neither he nor the second mate could get a wink of sleep in their watches below for the noise. . . . And how could they be expected to keep awake while on duty? he pleaded. The answer of that stern man was that if he and the second mate didn't like the noise, they were welcome to pack up their traps and walk over the side. When this alternative was offered the ship happened to be 600 miles from the nearest land.

Mr Burns at this point looked at me with an air of curiosity. I began to think that my predecessor was a remarkably peculiar old man.

But I had to hear stranger things yet. It came out that this stern, grim, wind-tanned, rough, sea-salted, taciturn sailor of sixty-five was not only an artist, but a lover as well. In Haiphong,[45] when they got there after a course of most unprofitable peregrinations (during which the ship was nearly lost twice), he got himself, in Mr Burns' own words, 'mixed up' with some woman. Mr Burns had had no personal knowledge of that affair, but positive evidence of it existed in the shape of a photograph taken in Haiphong. Mr Burns found it in one of the drawers in the captain's room.

In due course I, too, saw that amazing human document (I even threw it overboard later). There he sat with his hands reposing on his knees, bald, squat, grey, bristly, recalling a wild boar somehow; and by his side towered an awful, mature, white female with rapacious nostrils and a cheaply ill-omened stare in her enormous eyes. She was disguised in some semi-oriental, vulgar, fancy costume. She resembled a low-class medium or one of those women who tell fortunes by cards for half-a-crown. And yet she was striking. A professional sorceress from the slums.[46] It was incomprehensible. There was something awful in the thought that she was the last reflection of the world of passion for the fierce soul which seemed to look at one out of the sardonically savage face of that old seaman. However, I noticed that she was holding some musical instrument – guitar or mandoline – in her hand. Perhaps that was the secret of her sortilege.[47]

For Mr Burns that photograph explained why the unloaded ship was kept sweltering at anchor for three weeks in a pestilential hot harbour without air. They lay there and gasped. The captain, appearing now and then on short visits, mumbled to Mr Burns unlikely tales about some letters he was waiting for.

Suddenly, after vanishing for a week, he came on board in the middle of the night and took the ship out to sea with the first break of dawn. Daylight showed him looking wild and ill. The mere getting clear of the land took two days, and somehow or other they bumped slightly on a reef. However, no leak developed, and the captain, growling 'no matter', informed Mr Burns that he had made up his mind to take the ship to Hong-Kong and dry-dock her there.[48]

At this Mr Burns was plunged into despair. For indeed, to beat up to Hong-Kong against a fierce monsoon, with a ship not sufficiently ballasted and with her supply of water not completed, was an insane project.

But the captain growled peremptorily, 'Stick her at it,' and Mr Burns, dismayed and enraged, stuck her at it, and kept her at it, blowing away sails, straining the spars, exhausting the crew – nearly

maddened by the absolute conviction that the attempt was impossible and was bound to end in some catastrophe.

Meantime the captain, shut up in his cabin and wedged in a corner
of his settee against the crazy bounding of the ship, played the violin
– or, at any rate, made continuous noise on it.

When he appeared on deck he would not speak and not always
answer when spoken to. It was obvious that he was ill in some
mysterious manner, and beginning to break up.[49]

As the days went by the sounds of the violin became less and less
loud, till at last only a feeble scratching would meet Mr Burns' ear as
he stood in the saloon listening outside the door of the captain's
state-room.

One afternoon in perfect desperation he burst into that room and
made such a scene, tearing his hair and shouting such horrid impreca-
tions that he cowed the contemptuous spirit of the sick man. The
water-tanks were low, they had not gained 50 miles in a fortnight.
She would never reach Hong-Kong.

It was like fighting desperately towards destruction for the ship
and the men. This was evident without argument. Mr Burns, losing
all restraint, put his face close to his captain's and fairly yelled: 'You,
sir, are going out of the world. But I can't wait till you are dead
before I put the helm up. You must do it yourself. You must do it
now!'

The man on the couch snarled in contempt: 'So I am going out of
the world – am I?'

'Yes, sir – you haven't many days left in it,' said Mr Burns,
calming down. 'One can see it by your face.'

'My face, eh? . . . Well, put the helm up and be dammed to you.'

Burns flew on deck, got the ship before the wind, then came down
again, composed but resolute.

'I've shaped a course for Pulo Condor, sir,' he said.[50] 'When we
make it, if you are still with us, you'll tell me into what port you
wish me to take the ship and I'll do it.'

The old man gave him a look of savage spite, and said these
atrocious words in deadly, slow tones:

'If I had my wish, neither the ship nor any of you would ever reach
a port. And I hope you won't.'

Mr Burns was profoundly shocked. I believe he was positively frightened at the time. It seems, however, that he managed to produce such an effective laugh that it was the old man's turn to be frightened. He shrank within himself and turned his back on him.

'And his head was not gone then,' Mr Burns assured me excitedly. 'He meant every word of it.'

Such was practically the late captain's last speech. No connected sentence passed his lips afterwards. That night he used the last of his strength to throw his fiddle over the side. No one had actually seen him in the act, but after his death Mr Burns couldn't find the thing anywhere. The empty case was very much in evidence, but the fiddle was clearly not in the ship. And where else could it have gone to but overboard?

'Threw his violin overboard!' I exclaimed.

'He did,' cried Mr Burns excitedly. 'And it's my belief he would have tried to take the ship down with him if it had been in human power. He never meant her to see home again. He wouldn't write to his owners, he never wrote to his old wife either – he wasn't going to. He had made up his mind to cut adrift from everything. That's what it was. He didn't care for business, or freights, or for making a passage – or anything. He meant to have gone wandering about the world till he lost her with all hands.'[51]

Mr Burns looked like a man who had escaped great danger. For a little he would have exclaimed: 'If it hadn't been for me!' And the transparent innocence of his indignant eyes was underlined quaintly by the arrogant pair of moustaches which he proceeded to twist, and as if extend, horizontally.

I might have smiled if I had not been busy with my own sensations, which were not those of Mr Burns. I was already the man in command. My sensations could not be like those of any other man on board. In that community I stood, like a king in his country, in a class all by myself. I mean an hereditary king, not a mere elected head of a state.[52] I was brought there to rule by an agency as remote from the people and as inscrutable almost to them as the Grace of God.

And like a member of a dynasty, feeling a semi-mystical bond with the dead, I was profoundly shocked by my immediate predecessor.

That man had been in all essentials but his age just such another man as myself. Yet the end of his life was a complete act of treason, the betrayal of a tradition which seemed to me as imperative as any guide on earth could be. It appeared that even at sea a man could become the victim of evil spirits. I felt on my face the breath of unknown powers that shape our destinies.

Not to let the silence last too long I asked Mr Burns if he had written to his captain's wife. He shook his head. He had written to nobody.

In a moment he became sombre. He never thought of writing. It took him all his time to watch incessantly the loading of the ship by a rascally Chinese stevedore. In this Mr Burns gave me the first glimpse of the real chief mate's soul which dwelt uneasily in his body.

He mused, then hastened on with gloomy force.

'Yes! The captain died as near noon as possible. I looked through his papers in the afternoon. I read the service over him at sunset and then I stuck the ship's head north and brought her in here. I – brought – her – in.'

He struck the table with his fist.

'She would hardly have come in by herself,' I observed. 'But why didn't you make for Singapore instead?'

His eyes wavered. 'The nearest port,' he muttered sullenly.

I had framed the question in perfect innocence, but this answer (the difference in distance was insignificant) and his manner offered me a clue to the simple truth. He took the ship to a port where he expected to be confirmed in his temporary command from lack of a qualified master to put over his head. Whereas Singapore, he surmised justly, would be full of qualified men.

But his naïve reasoning forgot to take into account the telegraph cable reposing on the bottom of the very Gulf up which he had turned that ship which he imagined himself to have saved from destruction. Hence the bitter flavour of our interview. I tasted it more and more distinctly – and it was less and less to my taste.

'Look here, Mr Burns,' I began, very firmly. 'You may as well understand that I did not run after this command. It was pushed in my way. I've accepted it. I am here to take the ship home first of all, and you may be sure that I shall see to it that every one of you on board here does his duty to that end. This is all I have to say – for the present.'

161

He was on his feet by this time, but instead of taking his dismissal he remained with trembling, indignant lips, and looking at me hard as though, really, after this, there was nothing for me to do in common decency but to vanish from his outraged sight. Like all very simple emotional states this was moving. I felt sorry for him – almost sympathetic, till (seeing that I did not vanish) he spoke in a tone of forced restraint.

'If I hadn't a wife and a child at home you may be sure, sir, I would have asked you to let me go the very minute you came on board.'

I answered him with a matter-of-course calmness as though some remote third person were in question.

'And I, Mr Burns, would not have let you go. You have signed the ship's articles as chief officer, and till they are terminated at the final port of discharge I shall expect you to attend to your duty and give me the benefit of your experience to the best of your ability.'

Stony incredulity lingered in his eyes; but it broke down before my friendly attitude. With a slight upward toss of his arms (I got to know that gesture well afterwards) he bolted out of the cabin.

We might have saved ourselves that little passage of harmless sparring. Before many days had elapsed it was Mr Burns who was pleading with me anxiously not to leave him behind; while I could only return him but doubtful answers. The whole thing took on a somewhat tragic complexion.

And this horrible problem was only an extraneous episode, a mere complication in the general problem of how to get that ship – which was mine with her appurtenances and her men, with her body and her spirit now slumbering in that pestilential river – how to get her out to sea.

Mr Burns, while still acting captain, had hastened to sign a charter-party which in an ideal world without guile would have been an excellent document. Directly I ran my eye over it I foresaw trouble ahead unless the people of the other part were quite exceptionally fair-minded and open to argument.

Mr Burns, to whom I imparted my fears, chose to take great umbrage at them. He looked at me with that usual incredulous stare, and said bitterly:

'I suppose, sir, you want to make out I've acted like a fool?'

I told him, with my systematic kindliness which always seemed to augment his surprise, that I did not want to make out anything. I would leave that to the future.

And, sure enough, the future brought in a lot of trouble. There were days when I used to remember Captain Giles with nothing short of abhorrence. His confounded acuteness had let me in for this job; while his prophecy that I 'would have my hands full' coming true, made it appear as if done on purpose to play an evil joke on my young innocence.

Yes. I had my hands full of complications which were most valuable as 'experience'. People have a great opinion of the advantages of experience. But in that connection experience means always something disagreeable as opposed to the charm and innocence of illusions.

I must say I was losing mine rapidly. But on these instructive complications I must not enlarge more than to say that they could all be resumed in the one word: Delay.

A mankind which has invented the proverb, 'Time is money', will understand my vexation. The word 'Delay' entered the secret chamber of my brain, resounded there like a tolling bell which maddens the ear, affected all my senses, took on a black colouring, a bitter taste, a deadly meaning.

'I am really sorry to see you worried like this. Indeed, I am. . . .'

It was the only humane speech I used to hear at that time. And it came from a doctor, appropriately enough.

A doctor is humane by definition. But that man was so in reality. His speech was not professional. I was not ill. But other people were, and that was the reason of his visiting the ship.

He was the doctor of our Legation and, of course, of the Consulate too. He looked after the ship's health, which generally was poor, and trembling, as it were, on the verge of a break-up. Yes. The men ailed. And thus time was not only money, but life as well.

I had never seen such a steady ship's company. As the doctor remarked to me: 'You seem to have a most respectable lot of seamen.' Not only were they consistently sober, but they did not even want to go ashore. Care was taken to expose them as little as possible to the sun. They were employed on light work under the awnings. And the humane doctor commended me.

'Your arrangements appear to me to be very judicious, my dear Captain.'

It is difficult to express how much that pronouncement comforted me. The doctor's round full face framed in a light-coloured whisker was the perfection of a dignified amenity. He was the only human being in the world who seemed to take the slightest interest in me. He would generally sit in the cabin for half-an-hour or so at every visit.

I said to him one day:

'I suppose the only thing now is to take care of them as you are doing, till I can get the ship to sea?'

He inclined his head, shutting his eyes under the large specatacles, and murmured:

'The sea . . . undoubtedly.'

The first member of the crew fairly knocked over was the steward – the first man to whom I had spoken on board. He was taken ashore (with choleraic symptoms) and died there at the end of a week. Then, while I was still under the startling impression of this first home-thrust of the climate, Mr Burns gave up and went to bed in a raging fever without saying a word to anybody.[53]

I believe he had partly fretted himself into that illness; the climate did the rest with the swiftness of an invisible monster ambushed in the air, in the water, in the mud of the river bank. Mr Burns was a predestined victim.

I discovered him lying on his back, glaring sullenly and radiating heat on one like a small furnace. He would hardly answer my questions, and only grumbled: Couldn't a man take an afternoon off duty with a bad headache – for once?

That evening, as I sat in the saloon after dinner, I could hear him muttering continuously in his room. Ransome, who was clearing the table, said to me:

'I am afraid, sir, I won't be able to give the mate all the attention he's likely to need. I will have to be forward in the galley a great part of the time.'

Ransome was the cook.[54] The mate had pointed him out to me the first day, standing on the deck, his arms crossed on his broad chest, gazing on the river.

Even at a distance his well-proportioned figure, something thoroughly sailor-like in his poise, made him noticeable. On nearer view the intelligent, quiet eyes, a well-bred face, the disciplined independence of his manner made up an attractive personality. When, in addition, Mr Burns told me that he was the best seaman in the ship, I expressed my surprise that in his earliest prime and of such appearance he should sign on as cook on board a ship.

'It's his heart,' Mr Burns had said. 'There's something wrong with it. He mustn't exert himself too much or he may drop dead suddenly.'

And he was the only one the climate had not touched – perhaps because, carrying a deadly enemy in his breast, he had schooled himself into a systematic control of feelings and movements. When one was in the secret this was apparent in his manner. After the poor steward died, and as he could not be replaced by a white man in this Oriental port, Ransome had volunteered to do the double work.

'I can do it all right, sir, as long as I go about it quietly,' he had assured me.

But obviously he couldn't be expected to take up sick-nursing in addition. Moreover, the doctor peremptorily ordered Mr Burns ashore.

With a seaman on each side holding him up under the arms, the mate went over the gangway more sullen than ever. We built him up with pillows in the gharry, and he made an effort to say brokenly:

'Now – you've got – what you wanted – got me out of – the ship.'

'You were never more mistaken in your life, Mr Burns,' I said quietly, duly smiling at him; and the trap drove off to a sort of sanatorium, a pavilion of bricks which the doctor had in the grounds of his residence.

I visited Mr Burns regularly. After the first few days, when he didn't know anybody, he received me as if I had come either to gloat over a crushed enemy or else to curry favour with a deeply-wronged person. It was either one or the other, just as it happened according to his fantastic sick-room moods. Whichever it was, he managed to

165

convey it to me even during the period when he appeared almost too weak to talk. I treated him to my invariable kindliness.

Then one day, suddenly, a surge of downright panic burst through all this craziness.

If I left him behind in this deadly place he would die. He felt it, he was certain of it. But I wouldn't have the heart to leave him ashore. He had a wife and child in Sydney.

He produced his wasted fore-arms from under the sheet which covered him and clapsed his fleshless claws. He would die! He would die here. . . .

He absolutely managed to sit up, but only for a moment, and when he fell back I really thought that he would die there and then. I called to the Bengali dispenser, and hastened away from the room.

Next day he upset me thoroughly by renewing his entreaties. I returned an evasive answer, and left him the picture of ghastly despair. The day after I went in with reluctance, and he attacked me at once in a much stronger voice and with an abundance of argument which was quite startling. He presented his case with a sort of crazy vigour, and asked me finally how would I like to have a man's death on my conscience? He wanted me to promise that I would not sail without him.

I said that I really must consult the doctor first. He cried out at that. The doctor! Never! That would be a death sentence.

The effort had exhausted him. He closed his eyes, but went on rambling in a low voice. I had hated him from the start. The late captain had hated him too. Had wished him dead. Had wished all hands dead. . . .

'What do you want to stand in with that wicked corpse for, sir? He'll have you too,' he ended, blinking his glazed eyes vacantly.

'Mr Burns,' I cried, very much discomposed, 'what on earth are you talking about?'

He seemed to come to himself, though he was too weak to start.

'I don't know,' he said languidly. 'But don't ask that doctor, sir. You and I are sailors. Don't ask him, sir. Some day perhaps you will have a wife and child yourself.'

And again he pleaded for the promise that I would not leave him behind. I had the firmness of mind not to give it to him. Afterwards this sternness seemed criminal; for my mind was made up. That prostrated man, with hardly strength enough to breathe and ravaged by a passion of fear, was irresistible. And, besides, he had happened to hit on the right words. He and I were sailors. That was a claim, for I had no other family. As to the wife-and-child (some day) argument it had no force. It sounded merely bizarre.

I could imagine no claim that would be stronger and more absorbing than the claim of that ship, of these men snared in the river by silly commercial complications, as if in some poisonous trap.

However, I had nearly fought my way out. Out to sea. The sea – which was pure, safe, and friendly. Three days more.

That thought sustained and carried me on my way back to the ship. In the saloon the doctor's voice greeted me, and his large form followed his voice, issuing out of the starboard spare cabin where the ship's medicine chest was kept securely lashed in the bed-place.

Finding that I was not on board he had gone in there, he said, to inspect the supply of drugs, bandages, and so on. Everything was completed and in order.

I thanked him; I had just been thinking of asking him to do that very thing, as in a couple of days, as he knew, we were going to sea, where all our troubles of every sort would be over at last.

He listened gravely and made no answer. But when I opened to him my mind as to Mr Burns he sat down by my side, and, laying his hand on my knee amicably, begged me to think what it was I was exposing myself to.

The man was just strong enough to bear being moved and no more. But he couldn't stand a return of the fever. I had before me a passage of sixty days perhaps, beginning with intricate navigation and ending probably with a lot of bad weather. Could I run the risk of having to go through it single-handed, with no chief officer and with a second quite a youth? . . .

He might have added that it was my first command too. He did probably think of that fact, for he checked himself. It was very present to my mind.

He advised me earnestly to cable to Singapore for a chief officer, even if I had to delay my sailing for a week.

'Not a day,' I said. The very thought gave me the shivers. The hands seemed fairly fit, all of them, and this was the time to get them away. Once at sea I was not afraid of facing anything. The sea was now the only remedy for all my troubles.

The doctor's glasses were directed at me like two lamps searching the genuineness of my resolution. He opened his lips as if to argue further, but shut them again without saying anything. I had a vision of poor Burns so vivid in his exhaustion, helplessness, and anguish, that it moved me more than the reality I had come away from only an hour before. It was purged from the drawbacks of his personality, and I could not resist it.

'Look here,' I said. 'Unless you tell me officially that the man must not be moved I'll make arrangements to have him brought on board to-morrow, and shall take the ship out of the river next morning, even if I have to anchor outside the bar for a couple of days to get her ready for sea.'

'Oh! I'll make all the arrangements myself,' said the doctor at once. 'I spoke as I did only as a friend – as a well-wisher, and that sort of thing.'

He rose in his dignified simplicity and gave me a warm handshake, rather solemnly, I thought. But he was as good as his word. When Mr Burns appeared at the gangway carried on a stretcher, the doctor himself walked by its side. The programme had been altered in so far that this transportation had been left to the last moment, on the very morning of our departure.

It was barely an hour after sunrise. The doctor waved his big arm to me from the shore and walked back at once to his trap, which had followed him empty to the river-side. Mr Burns, carried across the quarter-deck, had the appearance of being absolutely lifeless. Ransome went down to settle him in his cabin. I had to remain on deck to look after the ship, for the tug had got hold of our tow-rope already.

The splash of our shore-fasts falling in the water produced a complete change of feeling in me. It was like the imperfect relief of awakening from a nightmare. But when the ship's head swung down the river away from that town, Oriental and squalid, I missed the expected elation of that striven-for-moment. What there was, undoubtedly, was a relaxation of tension which translated itself into a sense of weariness after an inglorious fight.

About mid-day we anchored a mile outside the bar. The afternoon was busy for all hands. Watching the work from the poop, where I remained all the time, I detected in it some of the languor of the six weeks spent in the steaming heat of the river. The first breeze would blow that away. Now the calm was complete. I judged that the second officer – a callow youth with an unpromising face – was not, to put it mildly, of that invaluable stuff from which a commander's right hand is made. But I was glad to catch along the main deck a few smiles on those seamen's faces at which I had hardly had time to have a good look as yet. Having thrown off the mortal coil of shore affairs, I felt myself familiar with them and yet a little strange, like a long-lost wanderer among his kin.[55]

Ransome flitted continually to and fro between the galley and the cabin. It was a pleasure to look at him. The man positively had grace. He alone of all the crew had not had a day's illness in port. But with the knowledge of that uneasy heart within his breast I could detect the restraint he put on the natural sailor-like agility of his movements. It was as though he had something very fragile or very explosive to carry about his person and was all the time aware of it.

I had occasion to address him once or twice. He answered me in his pleasant quiet voice and with a faint, slightly wistful smile. Mr Burns appeared to be resting. He seemed fairly comfortable.

After sunset I came out on deck again to meet only a still void. The thin, featureless crust of the coast could not be distinguished. The darkness had risen around the ship like a mysterious emanation from the dumb and lonely waters. I leaned on the rail and turned my ear to the shadows of the night. Not a sound. My command might have been a planet flying vertiginously on its appointed path in a space of infinite silence. I clung to the rail as if my sense of balance were leaving me for good. How absurd. I hailed nervously.

'On deck there!'

The immediate answer, 'Yes, sir,' broke the spell. The anchor-watch man ran up the poop ladder smartly. I told him to report at once the slightest sign of a breeze coming.

Going below I looked in on Mr Burns. In fact, I could not avoid seeing him, for his door stood open. The man was so wasted that, in that white cabin, under a white sheet, and with his diminished head sunk in the white pillow, his red moustaches captured one's eyes exclusively, like something artificial – a pair of moustaches from a shop exhibited there in the harsh light of the bulkhead-lamp without a shade.

While I stared with a sort of wonder he asserted himself by opening his eyes and even moving them in my direction. A minute stir.

'Dead calm, Mr Burns,' I said resignedly.

In an unexpectedly distinct voice Mr Burns began a rambling speech. Its tone was very strange, not as if affected by his illness, but as if of a different nature. It sounded unearthly. As to the matter, I seemed to make out that it was the fault of the 'old man' – the late captain – ambushed down there under the sea with some evil intention. It was a weird story.

I listened to the end; then stepping into the cabin I laid my hand on the mate's forehead. It was cool. He was light-headed only from extreme weakness. Suddenly he seemed to become aware of me, and in his own voice – of course, very feeble – he asked regretfully:

'Is there no chance at all to get under way, sir?'

'What's the good of letting go our hold of the ground only to drift, Mr Burns?' I answered.

He sighed, and I left him to his immobility. His hold on life was as slender as his hold on sanity. I was oppressed by my lonely responsibilities.[56] I went into my cabin to seek relief in a few hours' sleep, but almost before I closed my eyes the man on deck came down reporting a light breeze. Enough to get under way with, he said.

And it was no more that just enough. I ordered the windlass manned, the sails loosed, and the topsails set. But by the time I had cast the ship I could hardly feel any breath of wind. Nevertheless, I trimmed the yards and put everything on her. I was not going to give up the attempt.

4

With her anchor at the bow and clothed in canvas to her very trucks, my command seemed to stand as motionless as a model ship set on the gleams and shadows of polished marble. It was impossible to distinguish land from water in the enigmatical tranquillity of the immense forces of the world. A sudden impatience possessed me.

'Won't she answer the helm at all?' I said irritably to the man whose strong brown hands grasping the spokes of the wheel stood out lighted on the darkness; like a symbol of mankind's claim to the direction of its own fate.

He answered me:

'Yes, sir. She's coming-to slowly.'

'Let her head come up to south.'

'Aye, aye, sir.'

I paced the poop. There was not a sound but that of my footsteps, till the man spoke again.

'She is at south now, sir.'

I felt a slight tightness of the chest before I gave out the first course of my first command to the silent night, heavy with dew and sparkling with stars. There was a finality in the act committing me to the endless vigilance of my lonely task.

'Steady her head at that,' I said at last. 'The course is south.'

'South, sir,' echoed the man.

I sent below the second mate and his watch and remained in charge, walking the deck through the chill, somnolent hours that precede the dawn.

Slight puffs came and went, and whenever they were strong enough to wake up the black water the murmur alongside ran through my very heart in a delicate crescendo of delight and died away swiftly. I was bitterly tired. The very stars seemed weary of waiting for daybreak. It came at last with a mother-of-pearl sheen at the zenith, such as I had never seen before in the tropics, unglowing, almost grey, with a strange reminder of high latitudes.

The voice of the look-out man hailed from forward:

'Land on the port bow, sir.'

'All right.'

Leaning on the rail I never even raised my eyes. The motion of the ship was imperceptible. Presently Ransome brought me the cup of morning coffee. After I drunk it I looked ahead, and in the still streak of very bright pale orange light I saw the land profiled flatly as if cut out of black paper and seeming to float on the water as light as cork. But the rising sun turned it into mere dark vapour, a doubtful, massive shadow trembling in the hot glare.

The watch finished washing decks. I went below and stopped at Mr Burns' door (he could not bear to have it shut), but hesitated to speak to him till he moved his eyes. I gave him the news.

'Sighted Cape Liant at daylight. About fifteen miles.'[57]

He moved his lips then, but I heard no sound till I put my ear down, and caught the peevish comment: 'This is crawling. . . . No luck.'

'Better luck than standing still, anyhow,' I pointed out resignedly, and left him to whatever thoughts or fancies haunted his hopeless prostration.

Later that morning, when relieved by my second officer, I threw myself on my couch and for some three hours or so I really found oblivion. It was so perfect that on waking up I wondered where I was. Then came the immense relief of the thought: on board my ship! At sea! At sea!

Through the port-holes I beheld an unruffled, sun-smitten horizon. The horizon of a windless day. But its spaciousness alone was enough to give me a sense of a fortunate escape, a momentary exultation of freedom.

I stepped out into the saloon with my heart lighter than it had been for days. Ransome was at the sideboard preparing to lay the table for the first sea dinner of the passage. He turned his head, and something in his eyes checked my modest elation.

Instinctively I asked: 'What is it now?' not expecting in the least the answer I got. It was given with that sort of contained serenity which was characteristic of the man.

'I am afraid we haven't left all sickness behind us, sir.'

'We haven't! What's the matter?'

He told me then that two of our men had been taken bad with fever in the night. One of them was burning and the other was shivering, but he thought that it was pretty much the same thing. I thought so too. I felt shocked by the news. 'One burning, the other shivering, you say? No. We haven't left the sickness behind. Do they look very ill?'

'Middling bad, sir.' Ransome's eyes gazed steadily into mine. We exchanged smiles. Ransome's a little wistful, as usual, mine no doubt grim enough, to correspond with my secret exasperation.

I asked:

'Was there any wind at all this morning?'

'Can hardly say that, sir. We've moved all the time though. The land ahead seems a little nearer.'

That was it. A little nearer. Whereas if we had only had a little more wind, only a very little more, we might, we should, have been abreast of Liant by this time and increasing our distance from that contaminated shore. And it was not only the distance. It seemed to me that a stronger breeze would have blown away the infection which clung to the ship. It obviously did cling to the ship. Two men. One burning, one shivering. I felt a distinct reluctance to go and look at them. What was the good? Poison is poison. Tropical fever is tropical fever. But that it should have stretched its claw after us over the sea seemed to me an extraordinary and unfair licence. I could hardly believe that it could be anything worse than the last desperate pluck of the evil from which we were escaping into the clean breath of the sea. If only that breath had been a little stronger. However, there was the quinine against the fever. I went into the spare cabin where the medicine chest was kept to prepare two doses. I opened it full of faith as a man opens a miraculous shrine. The upper part was inhabited by a collection of bottles, all square-shouldered and as like each other as peas. Under that orderly array there were two drawers, stuffed as full of things as one could imagine – paper packages, bandages, cardboard boxes officially labelled. The lower of the two, in one of its compartments, contained our provision of quinine.

There were five bottles, all round and all of a size. One was about a third full. The other four remained still wrapped up in paper and sealed. But I did not expect to see an envelope lying on top of them. A square envelope, belonging, in fact, to the ship's stationery.

It lay so that I could see it was not closed down, and on picking it up and turning it over I perceived that it was addressed to myself. It contained a half-sheet of notepaper, which I unfolded with a queer sense of dealing with the uncanny, but without any excitement as people meet and do extraordinary things in a dream.

'My dear Captain,' it began,[58] but I ran to the signature. The writer was the doctor. The date was that of the day on which,

173

returning from my visit to Mr Burns in the hospital, I had found the excellent doctor waiting for me in the cabin; and when he told me that he had been putting in time inspecting the medicine chest for me. How bizarre! While expecting me to come in at any moment he had been amusing himself by writing me a letter, and then as I came in had hastened to stuff it into the medicine chest drawer. A rather incredible proceeding. I turned to the text in wonder.

In a large, hurried, but legible hand the good, sympathetic man for some reason, either of kindness or more likely impelled by the irresistible desire to express his opinion, with which he didn't want to damp my hopes before, was warning me not to put my trust in the beneficial effects of a change from land to sea. 'I didn't want to add to your worries by discouraging your hopes,' he wrote. 'I am afraid that, medically speaking, the end of your troubles is not yet.' In short, he expected me to have to fight a probable return of tropical illness. Fortunately I had a good provision of quinine. I should put my trust in that, and administer it steadily, when the ship's health would certainly improve.

I crumpled up the letter and rammed it into my pocket. Ransome carried off two big doses to the men forward. As to myself, I did not go on deck as yet. I went instead to the door of Mr Burns' room, and gave him that news too.

It was impossible to say the effect it had on him. At first I thought that he was speechless. His head lay sunk in the pillow. He moved his lips enough, however, to assure me that he was getting much stronger; a statement shockingly untrue on the face of it.

That afternoon I took my watch as a matter of course. A great over-heated stillness enveloped the ship and seemed to hold her motionless in a flaming ambience composed in two shades of blue. Faint, hot puffs eddied nervelessly from her sails. And yet she moved. She must have. For, as the sun was setting, we had drawn abreast of Cape Liant and dropped it behind us: an ominous retreating shadow in the last gleams of twilight.

In the evening, under the crude glare of his lamp, Mr Burns seemed to have come more to the surface of his bedding. It was as if a depressing hand had been lifted off him. He answered my few words by a comparatively long, connected speech. He asserted himself strongly. If he escaped being smothered by this stagnant heat, he said, he was confident that in a very few days he would be able to come up on deck and help me.

While he was speaking I trembled lest this effort of energy should leave him lifeless before my eyes. But I cannot deny that there was something comforting in his willingness. I made a suitable reply, but pointed out to him that the only thing that could really help us was wind – a fair wind.

He rolled his head impatiently on the pillow. And it was not comforting in the least to hear him begin to mutter crazily about the late captain, that old man buried in latitude 8° 20′ , right in our way – ambushed at the entrance of the Gulf.

'Are you still thinking of your late captain, Mr Burns?' I said. 'I imagine the dead feel no animosity against the living. They care nothing for them.'

'You don't know that one,' he breathed out feebly.

'No. I didn't know him, and he didn't know me. And so he can't have any grievance against me, anyway.'

'Yes. But there's all the rest of us on board,' he insisted.

I felt the inexpugnable strength of common sense being insidiously menaced by this gruesome, by this insane delusion. And I said:

'You musn't talk so much. You will tire yourself.'

'And there is the ship herself,' he persisted in a whisper.

'Now, not a word more,' I said, stepping in and laying my hand on his cool forehead. It proved to me that this atrocious absurdity was rooted in the man himself and not in the disease, which, apparently, had emptied him of every power, mental and physical, except that one fixed idea.

I avoided giving Mr Burns any opening for conversation for the next few days. I merely used to throw him a hasty, cheery word when passing his door. I believe that if he had had the strength he would have called out after me more than once. But he hadn't the strength. Ransome, however, observed to me one afternoon that the mate 'seemed to be picking up wonderfully'.

'Did he talk any nonsense to you of late?' I asked casually.

'No, sir.' Ransome was startled by the direct question; but, after a pause, he added equably: 'He told me this morning, sir, that he was sorry he had to bury our late captain right in the ship's way, as one may say, out of the Gulf.'

'Isn't this nonsense enough for you?' I asked, looking confidently at the intelligent, quiet face on which the secret uneasiness in the man's breast had thrown a transparent veil of care.

Ransome didn't know. He had not given a thought to the matter. And with a faint smile he flitted away from me on his never-ending duties, with his usual guarded activity.

Two more days passed. We had advanced a little way – a very little way – into the larger space of the Gulf of Siam. Seizing eagerly upon the elation of the first command thrown into my lap, by the agency of Captain Giles, I had yet an uneasy feeling that such luck as this has got perhaps to be paid for in some way. I had held, professionally, a review of my chances. I was competent enough for that. At least, I thought so. I had a general sense of my preparedness which only a man pursuing a calling he loves can know. That feeling seemed to me the most natural thing in the world. As natural as breathing. I imagined I could not have lived without it.

I don't know what I expected. Perhaps nothing else than that special intensity of existence which is the quintessence of youthful aspirations. Whatever I expected I did not expect to be beset by hurricanes. I knew better than that. In the Gulf of Siam there are no hurricanes. But neither did I expect to find myself bound hand and foot to the hopeless extent which was revealed to me as the days went on.

Not that the evil spell held us always motionless. Mysterious currents drifted us here and there, with a stealthy power made manifest by the changing vistas of the islands fringing the east shore of the Gulf. And there were winds too, fitful and deceitful. They raised hopes only to dash them into the bitterest disappointment, promises of advance ending in lost ground, expiring in sighs, dying into dumb stillness in which the currents had it all their own way – their own inimical way.

The Island of Koh-ring, a great, black, upheaved ridge amongst a lot of tiny islets, lying upon the glassy water like a triton amongst minnows, seemed to be the centre of the fatal circle.[59] It seemed impossible to get away from it. Day after day it remained in sight.

More than once, in a favourable breeze, I would take its bearing in the fast ebbing twilight, thinking that it was for the last time. Vain hope. A night of fitful airs would undo the gains of temporary favour, and the rising sun would throw out the black relief of Kohring, looking more barren, inhospitable, and grim than ever.

'It's like being bewitched, upon my word,' I said once to Mr Burns, from my usual position in the doorway.

He was sitting up in his bed-place. He was progressing towards the world of living men; if he could hardly have been said to have rejoined it yet. He nodded to me his frail and bony head in a wisely mysterious assent.

'Oh, yes, I know what you mean,' I said. 'But you cannot expect me to believe that a dead man has the power to put out of joint the meteorology of this part of the world. Though indeed it seems to have gone utterly wrong. The land and sea breezes have got broken up into small pieces. We cannot depend upon them for five minutes together.'

'It won't be very long now before I can come up on deck,' muttered Mr Burns, 'and then we shall see.'

Whether he meant this for a promise to grapple with supernatural evil I couldn't tell. At any rate, it wasn't the kind of assistance I needed. On the other hand, I had been living on deck practically night and day so as to take advantage of every chance to get my ship a little more to the southward. The mate, I could see, was extremely weak yet, and not quite rid of his delusion, which to me appeared but a symptom of his disease. At all events, the hopefulness of an invalid was not to be discouraged. I said:

'You will be most welcome there, I am sure, Mr Burns. If you go on improving at this rate you'll be presently one of the healthiest men in the ship.'

This pleased him, but his extreme emaciation converted his self-satisfied smile into a ghastly exhibition of long teeth under the red moustache.

'Aren't the fellows improving, sir?' he asked soberly, with an extremely sensible expression of anxiety on his face.

I answered him only with a vague gesture and went away from the door. The fact was that disease played with us capriciously very much as the winds did. It would go from one man to another with a lighter or heavier touch, which always left its mark behind, staggering some, knocking others over for a time, leaving this one, returning to another, so that all of them had now an invalidish aspect and a hunted, apprehensive look in their eyes; while Ransome and I, the only two completely untouched, went amongst them assiduously distributing quinine. It was a double fight. The adverse weather held us in front and the disease pressed on our rear. I must say that the men were very good. The constant toil of trimming the yards they faced willingly. But all spring was out of their limbs, and as I looked at them from the poop I could not keep from my mind the dreadful impression that they were moving in poisoned air.

Down below, in his cabin, Mr Burns had advanced so far as not only to be able to sit up, but even to draw up his legs. Clasping them with bony arms, like an animated skeleton, he emitted deep, impatient sighs.

'The great thing to do, sir,' he would tell me on every occasion, when I gave him the chance, 'the great thing is to get the ship past 8° 20' of latitude. Once she's past that we're all right.'

At first I used only to smile at him, though, God knows, I had not much heart left for smiles. But at last I lost my patience.

'Oh, yes. The latitude 8° 20' . That's where you buried your late captain, isn't it?' Then with severity: 'Don't you think, Mr Burns, it's about time you dropped all that nonsense?'

He rolled at me his deep-sunken eyes in a glance of invincible obstinacy. But for the rest, he only muttered, just loud enough for me to hear, something about 'Not surprised . . . find . . . play us some beastly trick yet. . . .'

Such passages as this were not exactly wholesome for my resolution. The stress of adversity was beginning to tell on me. At the same time I felt a contempt for that obscure weakness of my soul. I said to myself disdainfully that it should take much more than that to affect in the smallest degree my fortitude.

I didn't know then how soon and from what unexpected direction it would be attacked.

It was the very next day. The sun had risen clear of the southern shoulder of Koh-ring, which still hung, like an evil attendant, on our port quarter. It was intensely hateful to my sight. During the night we had been heading all round the compass, trimming the yards again and again, to what I fear must have been for the most part imaginary puffs of air. Then just about sunrise we got for an hour an inexplicable, steady breeze, right in our teeth. There was no sense in it. It fitted neither with the season of the year, nor with the secular experience of seamen as recorded in books, nor with the aspect of the sky. Only purposeful malevolence could account for it. It sent us travelling at a great pace away from our proper course; and if we had been out on pleasure sailing bent it would have been a delightful breeze, with the awakened sparkle of the sea, with the sense of motion and a feeling of unwonted freshness. Then all at once, as if disdaining to carry farther the sorry jest, it dropped and died out completely in less than five minutes. The ship's head swung where it listed; the stilled sea took on the polish of a steel plate in the calm.

I went below, not because I meant to take some rest, but simply because I couldn't bear to look at it just then. The indefatigable Ransome was busy in the saloon. It had become a regular practice with him to give me an informal health report in the morning. He turned away from the sideboard with his usual pleasant, quiet gaze. No shadow rested on his intelligent forehead.

'There are a good many of them middling bad this morning, sir,' he said in a calm tone.

'What? All knocked out?'

'Only two actually in their bunks, sir, but. . . .'

'It's the last night that has done for them. We have had to pull and haul all the blessed time.'

'I heard, sir. I had a mind to come out and help only, you know. . . .'

'Certainly not. You mustn't. . . . The fellows lie at night about the decks, too. It isn't good for them.'

Ransome assented. But men couldn't be looked after like children. Moreover, one could hardly blame them for trying for such coolness and such air as there was to be found on deck. He himself, of course, knew better.

He was, indeed, a reasonable man. Yet it would have been hard to say that the others were not. The last few days had been for us like the ordeal of the fiery furnace. One really couldn't quarrel with their common, imprudent humanity making the best of the moments of relief, when the night brought in the illusion of coolness and the starlight twinkled through the heavy, dew-laden air. Moreover, most of them were so weakened that hardly anything could be done without everybody that could totter mustering on the braces. No, it was no use remonstrating with them. But I fully believed that quinine was of very great use indeed.

I believed in it. I pinned my faith to it. It would save the men, the ship, break the spell by its medicinal virtue, make time of no account, the weather but a passing worry, and, like a magic powder working against mysterious malefices, secure the first passage of my first command against the evil powers of calms and pestilence. I looked upon it as more precious than gold, and unlike gold, of which there ever hardly seems to be enough anywhere, the ship had a sufficient store of it. I went in to get it with the purpose of weighing out doses. I stretched my hand with the feeling of a man reaching for an unfailing panacea, took up a fresh bottle and unrolled the wrapper, noticing as I did so that the ends, both top and bottom, had come unsealed. . . .

But why record all the swift steps of the appalling discovery. You have guessed the truth already. There was the wrapper, the bottle, and the white powder inside, some sort of powder! But it wasn't quinine. One look at it was quite enough. I remember that at the very moment of picking up the bottle, before I even dealt with the wrapper, the weight of the object I had in my hand gave me an instant of premonition. Quinine is as light as feathers; and my nerves must have been exasperated into an extraordinary sensibility. I let the bottle smash itself on the floor. The stuff, whatever it was, felt gritty under the sole of my shoe. I snatched up the next bottle and then the next. The weight alone told the tale. One after another they fell, breaking at my feet, not because I threw them down in my dismay, but slipping through my fingers as if this disclosure were too much for my strength.

It is a fact that the very greatness of a mental shock helps one to bear up against it, by producing a sort of temporary insensibility. I came out of the state-room stunned, as if something heavy had dropped on my head. From the other side of the saloon, across the table, Ransome, with a duster in his hand, stared open-mouthed. I don't think that I looked wild. It is quite possible that I appeared to be in a hurry because I was instinctively hastening up on deck. An example this of training become instinct. The difficulties, the dangers, the problems of a ship at sea must be met on deck.

To this fact, as it were of nature, I responded instinctively; which may be taken as a proof that for a moment I must have been robbed of my reason.

I was certainly off my balance, a prey to impulse, for at the bottom of the stairs I turned and flung myself at the doorway of Mr Burns' cabin. The wildness of his aspect checked my mental disorder. He was sitting up in his bunk, his body looking immensely long, his head drooping a little sideways, with affected complacency. He flourished, in his trembling hand, on the end of a fore-arm no thicker than a stout walking-stick, a shining pair of scissors which he tried before my very eyes to jab at his throat.

I was to a certain extent horrified; but it was rather a secondary sort of effect, not really strong enough to make me yell at him in some such manner as: 'Stop!' . . . 'Heavens!' . . . 'What are you doing?'

In reality he was simply overtaxing his returning strength in a shaky attempt to clip off the thick growth of his red beard. A large towel was spread over his lap, and a shower of stiff hairs, like bits of copper wire, was descending on it at every snip of the scissors.

He turned to me his face grotesque beyond the fantasies of mad dreams, one cheek all bushy as if with a swollen flame, the other denuded and sunken, with the untouched long moustache on that side asserting itself, lonely and fierce. And while he stared thunder-struck, with the gaping scissors on his fingers, I shouted my dis-covery at him fiendishly, in six words, without comment.

5

I heard the clatter of the scissors escaping from his hand, noted the perilous heave of his whole person over the edge of the bunk after them, and then, returning to my first purpose, pursued my course on to the deck. The sparkle of the sea filled my eyes. It was gorgeous and barren, monotonous and without hope under the empty curve of the sky. The sails hung motionless and slack, the very folds of their sagging surfaces moved no more than carved granite. The impetuosity of my advent made the man at the helm start slightly. A block aloft squeaked incomprehensibly, for what on earth could have made it do so? It was a whistling note like a bird's. For a long, long time I faced an empty world, steeped in an infinity of silence, through which the sunshine poured and flowed for some mysterious purpose. Then I heard Ransome's voice at my elbow.

'I have put Mr Burns back to bed, sir.'

'You have.'

'Well, sir, he got out, all of a sudden, but when he let go of the edge of his bunk he fell down. He isn't light-headed, though, it seems to me.'

'No,' I said dully, without looking at Ransome. He waited for a moment, then, cautiously as if not to give offence: 'I don't think we need lose much of that stuff, sir,' he said, 'I can sweep it up, every bit of it almost, and then we could sift the glass out. I will go about it at once. It will not make the breakfast late, not ten minutes.'

'Oh, yes,' I said bitterly. 'Let the breakfast wait, sweep up every bit of it, and then throw the damned lot overboard!'

The profound silence returned, and when I looked over my shoulder Ransome – the intelligent, serene Ransome – had vanished from my side. The intense loneliness of the sea acted like poison on my brain. When I turned my eyes to the ship, I had a morbid vision of her as a floating grave. Who hasn't heard of ships found drifting, haphazard, with their crews all dead?[60] I looked at the seaman at the helm, I had an impulse to speak to him, and, indeed, his face took on an expectant cast as if he had guessed my intention. But in the end I went below, thinking I would be alone with the greatness of my trouble for a little while. But through his open door Mr Burns saw me come down, and addressed me grumpily: 'Well, sir?'

I went in. 'It isn't well at all,' I said.

Mr Burns, re-established in his bed-place, was concealing his hirsute cheek in the palm of his hand.

'That confounded fellow has taken away the scissors from me,' were the next words he said.

The tension I was suffering from was so great that it was perhaps just as well that Mr Burns had started on this grievance. He seemed very sore about it and grumbled, 'Does he think I am mad, or what?'

'I don't think so, Mr Burns,' I said. I looked upon him at that moment as a model of self-possession. I even conceived on that account a sort of admiration for that man, who had (apart from the intense materiality of what was left of his beard) come as near to being a disembodied spirit as any man can do and live. I noticed the preternatural sharpness of the ridge of his nose, the deep cavities of his temples, and I envied him. He was so reduced that he would probably die very soon. Enviable man! So near extinction – while I had to bear within me a tumult of suffering vitality, doubt, confusion, self-reproach, and an indefinite reluctance to meet the horrid logic of the situation. I could not help muttering: 'I feel as if I were going mad myself.'

Mr Burns glared spectrally, but otherwise wonderfully composed.

'I always thought he would play us some deadly trick,' he said, with a peculiar emphasis on the *he*.

It gave me a mental shock, but I had neither the mind, nor the heart, nor the spirit to argue with him. My form of sickness was indifference. The creeping paralysis of a hopeless outlook. So I only gazed at him. Mr Burns broke into further speech.

'Eh? What? No! You won't believe it? Well, how do you account for this? How do you think it could have happened?'

'Happened?' I repeated dully. 'Why, yes, how in the name of the infernal powers did this thing happen?'

Indeed, on thinking it out, it seemed incomprehensible that it should just be like this: the bottles emptied, refilled, rewrapped, and replaced. A sort of plot, a sinister attempt to deceive, a thing resembling sly vengeance – but for what? – or else a fiendish joke. But Mr Burns was in possession of a theory. It was simple, and he uttered it solemnly in a hollow voice.

'I suppose they have given him about fifteen pounds in Haiphong for that little lot.'

'Mr Burns!' I cried.

He nodded grotesquely over his raised legs, like two broomsticks in the pyjamas, with enormous bare feet at the end.

'Why not? The stuff is pretty expensive in this part of the world, and they were very short of it in Tonkin. And what did he care? You have not known him. I have, and I have defied him. He feared neither God, nor devil, nor man, nor wind, nor sea, nor his own conscience. And I believe he hated everybody and everything. But I think he was afraid to die. I believe I am the only man who ever stood up to him. I faced him in that cabin where you live now, when he was sick, and I cowed him then. He thought I was going to twist his neck for him. If he had had his way we would have been beating up against the North-East monsoon, as long as he lived and afterwards too, for ages and ages. Acting the Flying Dutchman in the China Sea! Ha! Ha!'

'But why should he replace the bottles like this?' . . . I began.

'Why shouldn't he? Why should he want to throw the bottles away? They fit the drawer. They belong to the medicine chest.'

'And they were wrapped up,' I cried.

'Well, the wrappers were there. Did it from habit, I suppose, and as to refilling, there is always a lot of stuff they send in paper parcels that burst after a time. And then, who can tell? I suppose you didn't taste it, sir? But, of course, you are sure. . . .'

'No,' I said. 'I didn't taste it. It is all overboard now.'

Behind me, a soft, cultivated voice said: 'I have tasted it. It seemed a mixture of all sorts, sweetish, saltish, very horrible.'

Ransome, stepping out of the pantry, had been listening for some time, as it was very excusable in him to do.

'A dirty trick,' said Mr Burns. 'I always said he would.'

The magnitude of my indignation was unbounded. And the kind, sympathetic doctor too. The only sympathetic man I ever knew . . . instead of writing that warning letter, the very refinement of sympathy, why didn't the man make a proper inspection? But, as a matter of fact, it was hardly fair to blame the doctor. The fittings were in order and the medicine chest is an officially arranged affair. There was nothing really to arouse the slightest suspicion. The person I could never forgive was myself. Nothing should ever be taken for granted. The seed of everlasting remorse was sown in my breast.

'I feel it's all my fault,' I exclaimed, 'mine, and nobody else's. That's how I feel. I shall never forgive myself.'

'That's very foolish, sir,' said Mr Burns fiercely.

And after this effort he fell back exhausted on his bed. He closed his eyes, he panted; this affair, this abominable surprise had shaken him up too. As I turned away I perceived Ransome looking at me blankly. He appreciated what it meant, but he managed to produce his pleasant, wistful smile. Then he stepped back into his pantry, and I rushed up on deck again to see whether there was any wind, any breath under the sky, any stir of the air, any sign of hope. The deadly stillness met me again. Nothing was changed except that there was a different man at the wheel. He looked ill. His whole figure drooped, and he seemed rather to cling to the spokes than hold them with a controlling grip. I said to him:

'You are not fit to be here.'

'I can manage, sir,' he said feebly.

As a matter of fact, there was nothing for him to do. The ship had no steerage way. She lay with her head to the westward, the ever-lasting Koh-ring visible over the stern, with a few small islets, black spots in the great blaze, swimming before my troubled eyes. And but for those bits of land there was no speck on the sky, no speck on the water, no shape of vapour, no wisp of smoke, no sail, no boat, no stir of humanity, no sign of life, nothing!

The first question was, what to do? What could one do? The first thing to do obviously was to tell the men. I did it that very day. I wasn't going to let the knowledge simply get about. I would face them. They were assembled on the quarter-deck for the purpose. Just before I stepped out to speak to them I discovered that life could hold terrible moments. No confessed criminal had ever been so oppressed by his sense of guilt. This is why, perhaps, my face was set hard and my voice curt and unemotional while I made my declaration that I could do nothing more for the sick, in the way of drugs. As to such care as could be given them they knew they had had it.

I would have held them justified in tearing me limb from limb. The silence which followed upon my words was almost harder to bear than the angriest uproar. I was crushed by the infinite depth of its reproach. But, as a matter of fact, I was mistaken. In a voice which I had great difficulty in keeping firm, I went on: 'I suppose, men, you have understood what I said, and you know what it means.'

A voice or two were heard: 'Yes, sir. . . . We understand.'

They had kept silent simply because they thought that they were not called to say anything; and when I told them that I intended to run into Singapore and that the best chance for the ship and the men was in the efforts all of us, sick and well, must make to get her along out of this, I received the encouragement of a low assenting murmur and of a louder voice exclaiming: 'Surely there is a way out of this blamed hole.'

*

Here is an extract from the notes I wrote at the time:[61]

We have lost Koh-ring at last. For many days now I don't think I have been two hours below altogether. I remain on deck, of course, night and day, and the nights and the days wheel over us in succession, whether long or short, who can say? All sense of time is lost in the monotony of expectation, of hope, and of desire – which is only one: Get the ship to the southward! Get the ship to the southward! The effect is curiously mechanical; the sun climbs and descends, the night swings over our heads as if somebody below the horizon were turning a crank. It is the pettiest, the most aimless![62] . . . and all through that miserable performance I go on, tramping, tramping the deck. How many miles have I walked on the poop of that ship! A stubborn pilgrimage of sheer restlessness, diversified by short excursions below to look upon Mr Burns. I don't know whether it is an illusion, but he seems to become more substantial from day to day. He doesn't say much, for, indeed, the situation doesn't lend itself to idle remarks. I notice this even with the men as I watch them moving or sitting about the decks. They don't talk to each other. It strikes me that if there exist an invisible ear catching the whispers of the earth, it will find this ship the most silent spot on it. . . .

No, Mr Burns has not much to say to me. He sits in his bunk with his beard gone, his moustache flaming, and with an air of silent determination on his chalky physiognomy. Ransome tells me he devours all the food that is given him to the last scrap, but that, apparently, he sleeps very little. Even at night, when I go below to fill my pipe, I notice that, though dozing flat on his back, he still looks very determined. From the side glance he gives me when awake it seems as though he were annoyed at being interrupted in some arduous mental operation; and as I emerge on deck the ordered arrangement of the stars meets my eye, unclouded, infinitely wearisome. There they are: stars, sun, sea, light, darkness, space, great waters; the formidable Work of the Seven Days, into which mankind seems to have blundered unbidden. Or else decoyed. Even as I have been decoyed into this awful, this death-haunted command. . . .

*

The only spot of light in the ship at night was that of the compasslamps, lighting up the faces of the succeeding helmsmen; for the rest we were lost in the darkness, I walking the poop and the men lying about the decks. They were all so reduced by sickness that no watches could be kept. Those who were able to walk remained all the time on duty, lying about in the shadows of the main deck, till my voice raised for an order would bring them to their enfeebled feet, a tottering little group, moving patiently about the ship, with hardly a murmur, a whisper amongst them all. And every time I had to raise my voice it was with a pang of remorse and pity.

Then about four o'clock in the morning a light would gleam forward in the galley. The unfailing Ransome with the uneasy heart, immune, serene, and active, was getting ready the early coffee for the men. Presently he would bring me a cup on the poop, and it was then that I allowed myself to drop into my deck chair for a couple of hours of real sleep. No doubt I must have been snatching short dozes when leaning against the rail for a moment in sheer exhaustion; but, honestly, I was not aware of them, except in the painful form of convulsive starts that seemed to come on me even while I walked. From about five, however, until after seven I would sleep openly under the fading stars.

I would say to the helmsman: 'Call me at need,' and drop into that chair and close my eyes, feeling that there was no more sleep for me on earth. And then I would know nothing till, some time between seven and eight, I would feel a touch on my shoulder and look up at Ransome's face, with its faint, wistful smile and friendly, grey eyes, as though he were tenderly amused at my slumbers. Occasionally the second mate would come up and relieve me at early coffee time. But it didn't really matter. Generally it was a dead calm, or else faint airs so changing and fugitive that it really wasn't worth while to touch a brace for them. If the air steadied at all the seaman at the helm could be trusted for a warning shout: 'Ship's all aback, sir!' which like a trumpet-call would make me spring a foot above the deck. Those were the words which it seemed to me would have made me spring up from eternal sleep. But this was not often. I have never met since such breathless sunrises. And if the second mate happened to be there (he had generally one day in three free of fever) I would find him sitting on the skylight half-senseless, as it were, and with an idiotic gaze fastened on some object near by – a rope, a cleat, a belaying pin, a ringbolt.

That young man was rather troublesome. He remained cubbish in his sufferings. He seemed to have become completely imbecile; and when the return of fever drove him to his cabin below the next thing would be that we would miss him from there. The first time it happened Ransome and I were very much alarmed. We started a quiet search and ultimately Ransome discovered him curled up in the sail-locker, which opened into the lobby by a sliding-door. When remonstrated with, he muttered sulkily, 'It's cool in there.' That wasn't true. It was only dark there.

The fundamental defects of his face were not improved by its uniform livid hue. It was not so with many of the men. The wastage of ill-health seemed to idealize the general character of the features, bringing out the unsuspected nobility of some, the strength of others, and in one case revealing an essentially comic aspect. He was a short, gingery, active man with a nose and chin of the Punch type,[63] and whom his ship-mates called 'Frenchy'. I don't know why. He may have been a Frenchman, but I have never heard him utter a single word in French.

To see him coming aft to the wheel comforted one. The blue dungaree trousers turned up the calf, one leg a little higher than the other, the clean check shirt, the white canvas cap, evidently made by himself, made up a whole of peculiar smartness, and the persistent jauntiness of his gait, even, poor fellow, when he couldn't help tottering, told of his invincible spirit. There was also a man called Gambril. He was the only grizzled person in the ship. His face was of an austere type. But if I remember all their faces, wasting tragically before my eyes, most of their names have vanished from my memory.

The words that passed between us were few and puerile in regard of the situation. I had to force myself to look them in the face. I expected to meet reproachful glances. There were none. The expression of suffering in their eyes was indeed hard enough to bear. But that they couldn't help. For the rest, I ask myself whether it was the temper of their souls or the sympathy of their imagination that made them so wonderful, so worthy of my undying regard.[64]

For myself, neither my soul was highly tempered, nor my imagination properly under control. There were moments when I felt, not only that I would go mad, but that I had gone mad already; so that I dared not open my lips for fear of betraying myself by some insane shriek. Luckily I had only orders to give, and an order has a steadying influence upon him who has to give it. Moreover, the seaman, the officer of the watch, in me was sufficiently sane. I was like a mad carpenter making a box. Were he ever so convinced that he was King of Jerusalem,[65] the box he would make would be a sane box. What I feared was a shrill note escaping me involuntarily and upsetting my balance. Luckily, again, there was no necessity to raise one's voice. The brooding stillness of the world seemed sensitive to the slightest sound like a whispering gallery. The conversational tone would almost carry a word from one end of the ship to the other. The terrible thing was that the only voice that I ever heard was my own. At night especially it reverberated very lonely amongst the planes of the unstirring sails.

Mr Burns, still keeping to his bed with that air of secret determination, was moved to grumble at many things. Our interviews were short five-minute affairs, but fairly frequent. I was everlastingly diving down below to get a light, though I did not consume much tobacco at that time. The pipe was always going out; for in truth my mind was not composed enough to enable me to get a decent smoke. Likewise, for most of the time during the twenty-four hours I could have struck matches on deck and held them aloft till the flame burnt my fingers. But I always used to run below. It was a change. It was the only break in the incessant strain; and, of course, Mr Burns through the open door could see me come in and go out every time.

With his knees gathered up under his chin and staring with his greenish eyes over them, he was a weird figure, and with my knowledge of the crazy notion in his head, not a very attractive one for me. Still, I had to speak to him now and then, and one day he complained that the ship was very silent. For hours and hours, he said, he was lying there, not hearing a sound, till he did not know what to do with himself.

'When Ransome happens to be forward in his galley everything's so still that one might think everybody in the ship was dead,' he grumbled. 'The only voice I do hear sometimes is yours, sir, and that isn't enough to cheer me up. What's the matter with the men? Isn't there one left that can sing out at the ropes?'

'Not one, Mr Burns,' I said. 'There is no breath to spare on board this ship for that. Are you aware that there are times when I can't muster more than three hands to do anything?'

He asked swiftly but fearfully:

'Nobody dead yet, sir?'

'No.'

'It wouldn't do,' Mr Burns declared forcibly. 'Mustn't let him. If he gets hold of one he will get them all.'

I cried out angrily at this. I believe I even swore at the disturbing effect of these words. They attacked all the self-possession that was left to me. In my endless vigil in the face of the enemy I had been haunted by gruesome images enough. I had had visions of a ship drifting in calms and swinging in light airs, with all her crew dying slowly about her decks. Such things had been known to happen.[66]

Mr Burns met my outburst by a mysterious silence.

'Look here,' I said. 'You don't believe yourself what you say. You can't. It's impossible. It isn't the sort of thing I have a right to expect from you. My position's bad enough without being worried with your silly fancies.'

He remained unmoved. On account of the way in which the light fell on his head I could not be sure whether he had smiled faintly or not. I changed my tone.

'Listen,' I said. 'It's getting so desperate that I had thought for a moment, since we can't make our way south, whether I wouldn't try to steer west and make an attempt to reach the mail-boat track. We could always get some quinine from her, at least. What do you think?'

He cried out: 'No, no, no. Don't do that, sir. You mustn't for a moment give up facing that old ruffian. If you do he will get the upper hand of us.'

I left him. He was impossible. It was like a case of possession. His protest, however, was essentially quite sound. As a matter of fact, my notion of heading out west on the chance of sighting a problematical steamer could not bear calm examination. On the side where we were we had enough wind, at least from time to time, to struggle on towards the south. Enough, at least, to keep hope alive. But suppose that I had used those capricious gusts of wind to sail away to the westward, into some region where there was not a breath of air for days on end, what then? Perhaps my appalling vision of a ship floating with a dead crew would become a reality for the discovery weeks afterwards by some horror-stricken mariners.

That afternoon Ransome brought me up a cup of tea, and while waiting there, tray in hand, he remarked in the exactly right tone of sympathy:

'You are holding out well, sir.'

'Yes,' I said. 'You and I seem to have been forgotten.'

'Forgotten, sir?'

'Yes, by the fever-devil who has got on board this ship,' I said.

Ransome gave me one of his attractive, intelligent, quick glances and went away with the tray. It occurred to me that I had been talking somewhat in Mr Burns' manner. It annoyed me. Yet often in darker moments I forgot myself into an attitude towards our troubles more fit for a contest against a living enemy.

Yes. The fever-devil had not laid his hand yet either on Ransome or on me. But he might at any time. It was one of those thoughts one had to fight down, keep at arm's length at any cost. It was unbearable to contemplate the possibility of Ransome, the housekeeper of the ship, being laid low. And what would happen to my command if I got knocked over, with Mr Burns too weak to stand without holding on to his bed-place and the second mate reduced to a state of permanent imbecility? It was impossible to imagine, or, rather, it was only too easy to imagine.

I was alone on the poop. The ship having no steerage way, I had sent the helmsman away to sit down or lie down somewhere in the shade. The men's strength was so reduced that all unnecessary calls on it had to be avoided. It was the austere Gambril with the grizzly beard. He went away readily enough, but he was so weakened by repeated bouts of fever, poor fellow, that in order to get down the poop ladder he had to turn sideways and hang on with both hands to the brass rail. It was just simply heart-breaking to watch. Yet he was neither very much worse nor much better than most of the half-dozen miserable victims I could muster up on deck.

It was a terribly lifeless afternoon. For several days in succession low clouds had appeared in the distance, white masses with dark convolutions resting on the water, motionless, almost solid, and yet all the time changing their aspects subtly. Towards evening they vanished as a rule. But this day they awaited the setting sun, which glowed and smouldered sulkily amongst them before it sank down. The punctual and wearisome stars reappeared over our mast-heads, but the air remained stagnant and oppressive.

The unfailing Ransome lighted the binnacle lamps and glided, all shadowy, up to me.

'Will you go down and try to eat something, sir?' he suggested.

His low voice startled me. I had been standing looking out over the rail, saying nothing, feeling nothing, not even the weariness of my limbs, overcome by the evil spell.

'Ransome,' I asked abruptly, 'how long have I been on deck? I am losing the notion of time.'

'Fourteen days, sir,' he said. 'It was a fortnight last Monday since we left the anchorage.'

His equable voice sounded mournful somehow. He waited a bit, then added: 'It's the first time that it looks as if we were to have some rain.'

I noticed then the broad shadow on the horizon extinguishing the low stars completely, while those overhead, when I looked up, seemed to shine down on us through a veil of smoke.

How it got there, how it had crept up so high, I couldn't say. It had an ominous appearance. The air did not stir. At a renewed invitation from Ransome I did go down into the cabin to – in his words – 'try and eat something'. I don't know that the trial was very successful. I suppose at that period I did exist on food in the usual way; but the memory is now that in those days life was sustained on invincible anguish, as a sort of infernal stimulant exciting and consuming at the same time.

It's the only period of my life in which I attempted to keep a diary. No, not the only one. Years later, in conditions of moral isolation, I did put down on paper the thoughts and events of a score of days. But this was the first time. I don't remember how it came about or how the pocket-book and the pencil came into my hands. It's inconceivable that I should have looked for them on purpose. I suppose they saved me from the crazy trick of talking to myself.

Strangely enough, in both cases I took to that sort of thing in circumstances in which I did not expect, in colloquial phrase, 'to come out of it'. Neither could I expect the record to outlast me. This shows that it was purely a personal need for intimate relief and not a call of egotism.

Here I must give another sample of it, a few detached lines, now looking very ghostly to my own eyes, out of the part scribbled that very evening:

*

There is something going on in the sky like a decomposition, like a corruption of the air, which remains as still as ever. After all, mere clouds, which may or may not hold wind or rain. Strange that it should trouble me so. I feel as if all my sins had found me out. But I suppose the trouble is that the ship is still lying motionless, not

193

under command; and that I have nothing to do to keep my imagination from running wild amongst the disastrous images of the worst that may befall us. What's going to happen? Probably nothing. Or anything. It may be a furious squall coming, butt-end foremost. And on deck there are five men with the vitality and the strength of, say, two. We may have all our sails blown away. Every stitch of canvas has been on her since we broke ground at the mouth of the Mei-nam, fifteen days ago . . . or fifteen centuries.[67] It seems to me that all my life before that momentous day is infinitely remote, a fading memory of light-hearted youth, something on the other side of a shadow. Yes, sails may very well be blown away. And that would be like a death sentence on the men. We haven't strength enough on board to bend another suit; incredible thought, but it is true. Or we may even get dismasted. Ships have been dismasted in squalls simply because they weren't handled quick enough, and we have no power to whirl the yards around. It's like being bound hand and foot preparatory to having one's throat cut. And what appals me most of all is that I shrink from going on deck to face it. It's due to the ship, it's due to the men who are there on deck – some of them, ready to put out the last remnant of their strength at a word from me. And I am shrinking from it. From the mere vision. My first command. Now I understand that strange sense of insecurity in my past. I always suspected that I might be no good. And here is proof positive, I am shirking it, I am no good.

*

At that moment, or, perhaps, the moment after, I became aware of Ransome standing in the cabin. Something in his expression startled me. It had a meaning which I could not make out. I exclaimed:

'Somebody's dead.'

It was his turn then to look startled.

'Dead? Not that I know of, sir. I have been in the forecastle only ten minutes ago and there was no dead man there then.'

'You did give me a scare,' I said.

His voice was extremely pleasant to listen to. He explained that he had come down below to close Mr Burns' port in case it should come on to rain. He did not know that I was in the cabin, he added.

'How does it look outside?' I asked him.

'Very black indeed, sir. There is something in it for certain.'

'In what quarter?'

'All round, sir.'

I repeated idly: 'All round. For certain,' with my elbows on the table.

Ransome lingered in the cabin as if he had something to do there, but hesitated about doing it. I said suddenly:

'You think I ought to be on deck?'

He answered at once but without any particular emphasis or accent: 'I do, sir.'

I got to my feet briskly, and he made way for me to go out. As I passed through the lobby I heard Mr Burns' voice saying:

'Shut the door of my room, will you, steward?' And Ransome's rather surprised: 'Certainly, sir.'

I thought that all my feelings had been dulled into complete indifference. But I found it as trying as ever to be on deck. The impenetrable blackness beset the ship so close that it seemed that by thrusting one's hand over the side one could touch some unearthly substance. There was in it an effect of inconceivable terror and of inexpressible mystery. The few stars overhead shed a dim light upon the ship alone, with no gleams of any kind upon the water, in detached shafts piercing an atmosphere which had turned to soot. It was something I had never seen before, giving no hint of the direction from which any change would come, the closing in of a menace from all sides.

There was still no man at the helm. The immobility of all things was perfect. If the air had turned black, the sea, for all I knew, might have turned solid. It was no good looking in any direction, watching for any signs, speculating upon the nearness of the moment. When the time came the blackness would overwhelm silently the bit of starlight falling upon the ship, and the end of all things would come without a sigh, stir, or murmur of any kind, and all our hearts would cease to beat like run-down clocks.

It was impossible to shake off that sense of finality. The quietness that came over me was like a foretaste of annihilation. It gave me a sort of comfort, as though my soul had become suddenly reconciled to an eternity of blind stillness.

The seaman's instinct alone survived whole in my moral dissolution. I descended the ladder to the quarter-deck. The starlight seemed to die out before reaching that spot, but when I asked quietly: 'Are you there, men?' my eyes made out shadowy forms starting up around me, very few, very indistinct; and a voice spoke: 'All here, sir.' Another amended anxiously:

'All that are any good for anything, sir.'

Both voices were very quiet and unringing; without any special character of readiness or discouragement. Very matter-of-fact voices.

'We must try to haul this mainsail close up,' I said.

The shadows swayed away from me without a word. Those men were the ghosts of themselves, and their weight on a rope could be no more than the weight of a bunch of ghosts.[68] Indeed, if ever a sail was hauled up by sheer spiritual strength it must have been that sail, for, properly speaking, there was not muscle enough for the task in the whole ship, let alone the miserable lot of us on deck. Of course, I took the lead in the work myself. They wandered feebly after me from rope to rope, stumbling and panting. They toiled like Titans.[69] We were an hour at it at least, and all the time the black universe made no sound. When the last leech-line was made fast, my eyes, accustomed to the darkness, made out the shapes of exhausted men drooping over the rails, collapsed on hatches. One hung over the after-capstan, sobbing for breath; and I stood amongst them like a tower of strength, impervious to disease and feeling only the sickness of my soul. I waited for some time fighting against the weight of my sins, against my sense of unworthiness, and then I said:

'Now, men, we'll go aft and square the mainyard. That's about all we can do for the ship; and for the rest she must take her chance.'

6

As we all went up it occurred to me that there ought to be a man at the helm. I raised my voice not much above a whisper, and, noiselessly, an uncomplaining spirit in a fever-wasted body appeared in the light aft, the head with hollow eyes illuminated against the blackness which had swallowed up our world – and the universe. The bare fore-arm extended over the upper spokes seemed to shine with a light of its own. I murmured to that luminous appearance:

'Keep the helm right amidships.'

It answered in a tone of patient suffering:

'Right amidships, sir.'

Then I descended to the quarter-deck. It was impossible to tell whence the blow would come. To look round the ship was to look into a bottomless, black pit. The eye lost itself in inconceivable depths. I wanted to ascertain whether the ropes had been picked up off the deck. One could only do that by feeling with one's feet. In my cautious progress I came against a man in whom I recognized Ransome. He possessed an unimpaired physical solidity which was manifest to me at the contact. He was leaning against the quarter-deck capstan and kept silent. It was like a revelation. He was the collapsed figure sobbing for breath I had noticed before we went on the poop.

'You have been helping with the mainsail!' I exclaimed in a low tone.

'Yes, sir,' sounded his quiet voice.

'Man! What were you thinking of? You mustn't do that sort of thing.'

After a pause he assented. 'I suppose I mustn't.' Then after another short silence he added: 'I am all right now,' quickly, between the tell-tale gasps.

I could neither hear nor see anything else; but when I spoke up, answering sad murmurs filled the quarter-deck, and its shadows seemed to shift here and there. I ordered all the halyards laid down on deck clear for running.

'I'll see to that, sir,' volunteered Ransome in his natural, pleasant tone, which comforted one and aroused one's compassion too, somehow.

That man ought to have been in his bed, resting, and my plain duty was to send him there. But perhaps he would not have obeyed me. I had not the strength of mind to try. All I said was:

'Go about it quietly, Ransome.'

Returning on the poop I approached Gambril. His face, set with hollow shadows in the light, looked awful, finally silenced. I asked him how he felt, but hardly expected an answer. Therefore I was astonished at his comparative loquacity.

'Them shakes leaves me as weak as a kitten, sir,' he said, preserving finely that air of unconsciousness as to anything but his business a helmsman should never lose. 'And before I can pick up my strength that there hot fit comes along and knocks me over again.'

He sighed. There was no complaint in his tone, but the bare words were enough to give me a horrible pang of self-reproach. It held me dumb for a time. When the tormenting sensation had passed off I asked:

'Do you feel strong enough to prevent the rudder taking charge if she gets sternway on her? It wouldn't do to get something smashed about the steering-gear now. We've enough difficulties to cope with as it is.'

He answered with just a shade of weariness that he was strong enough to hang on. He could promise me that she shouldn't take the wheel out of his hands. More he couldn't say.

At that moment Ransome appeared quite close to me, stepping out of the darkness into visibility suddenly, as if just created with his composed face and pleasant voice.

Every rope on deck, he said, was laid down clear for running, as far as one could make certain by feeling. It was impossible to see anything. Frenchy had stationed himself forward. He said he had a jump or two left in him yet.

Here a faint smile altered for an instant the clear, firm design of Ransome's lips. With his serious, clear, grey eyes, his serene temperament, he was a priceless man altogether. Soul as firm as the muscles of his body.

He was the only man on board (except me, but I had to preserve my liberty of movement) who had a sufficiency of muscular strength to trust to. For a moment I thought I had better ask him to take the wheel. But the dreadful knowledge of the enemy he had to carry about him made me hesitate. In my ignorance of physiology it occurred to me that he might die suddenly, from excitement, at a critical moment.

While this gruesome fear restrained the ready words on the tip of my tongue, Ransome stepped back two paces and vanished from my sight.

At once an uneasiness possessed me, as if some support had been withdrawn. I moved forward too, outside the circle of light, into the darkness that stood in front of me like a wall. In one stride I penetrated it. Such must have been the darkness before creation.[70] It had closed behind me. I knew I was invisible to the man at the helm. Neither could I see anything. He was alone, I was alone, every man was alone where he stood. And every form was gone, too, spar, sail, fittings, rails; everything was blotted out in the dreadful smoothness of that absolute night.

A flash of lightning would have been a relief – I mean physically. I would have prayed for it if it hadn't been for my shrinking apprehension of the thunder. In the tension of silence I was suffering from it seemed to me that the first crash must turn me into dust.

And thunder was, most likely, what would happen next. Stiff all over and hardly breathing, I waited with a horribly strained expectation. Nothing happened. It was maddening. But a dull, growing ache in the lower part of my face made me aware that I had been grinding my teeth madly enough, for God knows how long.

It's extraordinary I should not have heard myself doing it; but I hadn't. By an effort which absorbed all my faculties I managed to keep my jaw still. It required much attention, and while thus engaged I became bothered by curious, irregular sounds of faint tapping on the deck. They could be heard single, in pairs, in groups. While I wondered at this mysterious devilry, I received a slight blow under the left eye and felt an enormous tear run down my cheek. Raindrops. Enormous. Forerunners of something. Tap. Tap. Tap. . . .

I turned about, and, addressing Gambril earnestly, entreated him to 'hang on to the wheel'. But I could hardly speak from emotion. The fatal moment had come. I held my breath. The tapping had stopped as unexpectedly as it had begun, and there was a renewed moment of intolerable suspense; something like an additional turn of the racking screw. I don't suppose I would have ever screamed, but I remember my conviction that there was nothing else for it but to scream.

Suddenly – how am I to convey it? Well, suddenly the darkness turned into water. This is the only suitable figure. A heavy shower, a downpour, comes along, making a noise. You hear its approach on the sea, in the air too, I verily believe. But this was different. With no preliminary whisper or rustle, without a splash, and even without the ghost of impact, I became instantaneously soaked to the skin. Not a very difficult matter, since I was wearing only my sleeping suit. My hair got full of water in an instant, water streamed on my skin, it filled my nose, my ears, my eyes. In a fraction of a second I swallowed quite a lot of it.

As to Gambril, he was fairly choked. He coughed pitifully, the broken cough of a sick man; and I beheld him as one sees a fish in an aquarium by the light of an electric bulb, an elusive, phosphorescent shape. Only he did not glide away. But something else happened. Both binnacle lamps went out. I suppose the water forced itself into them, though I wouldn't have thought that possible, for they fitted into the cowl perfectly.

The last gleam of light in the universe had gone, pursued by a low exclamation of dismay from Gambril. I groped for him and seized his arm. How startlingly wasted it was.

'Never mind,' I said. 'You don't want the light. All you need to do is to keep the wind, when it comes, at the back of your head. You understand?'

'Aye, aye, sir. . . . But I should like to have a light,' he added nervously.

All that time the ship lay as steady as a rock. The noise of the water pouring off the sails and spars, flowing over the break of the poop, had stopped short. The poop scuppers gurgled and sobbed for a little while longer, and then perfect silence, joined to perfect immobility, proclaimed the yet unbroken spell of our helplessness, poised on the edge of some violent issue, lurking in the dark.

I started forward restlessly. I did not need my sight to pace the poop of my ill-starred first command with perfect assurance. Every square foot of her decks was impressed indelibly on my brain, to the very grain and knots of the planks. Yet, all of a sudden, I fell clean over something, landing full length on my hands and face.

It was something big and alive. Not a dog – more like a sheep, rather. But there were no animals in the ship. How could an animal. . . . It was an added and fantastic horror which I could not resist. The hair of my head stirred even as I picked myself up, awfully scared; not as a man is scared while his judgement, his reason still try to resist, but completely, boundlessly, and, as it were, innocently scared – like a little child.

I could see It – that Thing! The darkness, of which so much had just turned into water, had thinned down a little. There It was! But I did not hit upon the notion of Mr Burns issuing out of the companion on all fours till he attempted to stand up, and even then the idea of a bear crossed my mind first.[71]

He growled like one when I seized him round the body. He had buttoned himself up into an enormous winter overcoat of some woolly material, the weight of which was too much for his reduced state. I could hardly feel the incredibly thin lath of his body, lost within the thick stuff, but his growl had depth and substance: Confounded dumb ship with a craven, tip-toeing crowd. Why couldn't they stamp and go with a brace? Wasn't there one God-forsaken lubber in the lot fit to raise a yell on a rope?

'Skulking's no good, sir,' he attacked me directly. 'You can't slink past the old murderous ruffian. It isn't the way. You must go for him boldly – as I did. Boldness is what you want. Show him that you don't care for any of his damned tricks. Kick up a jolly old row.'

'Good God, Mr Burns,' I said angrily. 'What on earth are you up to? What do you mean by coming up on deck in this state?'

'Just that! Boldness. The only way to scare the old bullying rascal.'

I pushed him, still growling, against the rail. 'Hold on to it,' I said roughly. I did not know what to do with him. I left him in a hurry, to go to Gambril, who had called faintly that he believed there was some wind aloft. Indeed, my own ears had caught a feeble flutter of wet canvas, high up overhead, the jingle of a slack chain sheet. . . .

These were eerie, disturbing, alarming sounds in the dead stillness of the air around me. All the instances I had heard of topmasts being whipped out of a ship while there was not wind enough on her deck to blow out a match rushed into my memory.

'I can't see the upper sails, sir,' declared Gambril shakily.

'Don't move the helm. You'll be all right,' I said confidently.

The poor man's nerve was gone. I was not in much better case. It was the moment of breaking strain and was relieved by the abrupt sensation of the ship moving forward as if of herself under my feet.[72] I heard plainly the soughing of the wind aloft, the low cracks of the upper spars taking the strain, long before I could feel the least draught on my face turned aft, anxious and sightless like the face of a blind man.

Suddenly a louder sounding note filled our ears, the darkness started streaming against our bodies, chilling them exceedingly. Both of us, Gambril and I, shivered violently in our clinging, soaked garments of thin cotton. I said to him:

'You are all right now, my man. All you've got to do is to keep the wind at the back of your head. Surely you are up to that. A child could steer this ship in smooth water.'

He muttered: 'Aye! A healthy child.' And I felt ashamed of having been passed over by the fever which had been preying on every man's strength but mine, in order that my remorse might be the more bitter, the feeling of unworthiness more poignant, and the sense of responsibility heavier to bear.

The ship had gathered great way on her almost at once on the calm water. I felt her slipping through it with no other noise but a mysterious rustle alongside. Otherwise she had no motion at all, neither lift nor roll. It was a disheartening steadiness which had lasted for eighteen days now; for never, never had we had wind enough in that time to raise the slightest run of the sea. The breeze freshened suddenly. I thought it was high time to get Mr Burns off the deck. He worried me. I looked upon him as a lunatic who would be very likely to start roaming over the ship and break a limb or fall overboard.

I was truly glad to find he had remained holding on where I had left him, sensibly enough. He was, however, muttering to himself ominously.

This was discouraging. I remarked in a matter-of-fact tone:

'We have never had so much wind as this since we left the roads.'

'There's some heart in it too,' he growled judiciously. It was a remark of a perfectly sane seaman. But he added immediately: 'It was about time I should come on deck. I've been nursing my strength for this – just for this. Do you see it, sir?'

I said I did, and proceeded to hint that it would be advisable for him to go below now and take a rest.

His answer was an indignant: 'Go below! Not if I know it, sir.'

Very cheerful! He was a horrible nuisance. And all at once he started to argue. I could feel his crazy excitement in the dark.

'You don't know how to go about it, sir. How could you? All this whispering and tip-toeing is no good. You can't hope to slink past a cunning, wide-awake, evil brute like he was. You never heard him talk. Enough to make your hair stand on end. No! No! He wasn't mad. He was no more mad than I am. He was just downright wicked. Wicked so as to frighten most people. I will tell you what he was. He was nothing less than a thief and a murderer at heart. And do you think he's any different now because he's dead? Not he! His carcass lies a hundred fathom under, but he's just the same . . . in latitude 8° 20′ North.'

He snorted defiantly. I noted with weary resignation that the breeze had got lighter while he raved. He was at it again.

'I ought to have thrown the beggar out of the ship over the rail like a dog. It was only on account of the men. . . . Fancy having to read the Burial Service over a brute like that! . . . ''Our departed brother''. . . . I could have laughed. That was what he couldn't bear. I suppose I am the only man that ever stood up to laugh at him. When he got sick it used to scare that . . . brother . . . Brother . . . Departed. . . . Sooner call a shark brother.'

The breeze had let go so suddenly that the way of the ship brought the wet sails heavily against the mast. The spell of deadly stillness had caught us up again. There seemed to be no escape.

'Hallo!' exclaimed Mr Burns in a startled voice. 'Calm again!'

I addressed him as though he had been sane.

'This is the sort of thing we've been having for seventeen days, Mr Burns,' I said with intense bitterness. 'A puff, then a calm, and in a moment, you'll see, she'll be swinging on her heel with her head away from her course to the devil somewhere.'

He caught at the word. 'The old dodging Devil,' he screamed piercingly, and burst into such a loud laugh as I had never heard before. It was a provoking, mocking peal, with a hair-raising, screeching over-note of defiance. I stepped back utterly confounded.

Instantly there was a stir on the quarter-deck, murmurs of dismay. A distressed voice cried out in the dark below us: 'Who's that gone crazy, now?'

Perhaps they thought it was their captain! Rush is not the word that could be applied to the utmost speed the poor fellows were up to; but in an amazing short time every man in the ship able to walk upright had found his way on to that poop.

I shouted to them: 'It's the mate. Lay hold of him a couple of you. . . .'

I expected this performance to end in a ghastly sort of fight. But Mr Burns cut his derisive screeching dead short and turned upon them fiercely, yelling:

'Aha! Dog-gone ye! You've found your tongues – have ye? I thought you were dumb. Well, then – laugh! Laugh – I tell you. Now then – all together. One, two, three – laugh!'

A moment of silence ensued, of silence so profound that you could have heard a pin drop on the deck. Then Ransome's unperturbed voice uttered pleasantly the words:

'I think he has fainted, sir—' The little motionless knot of men stirred, with low murmurs of relief. 'I've got him under the arms. Get hold of his legs, someone.'

Yes. It was a relief. He was silenced for a time – for a time. I could not have stood another peal of that insane screeching. I was sure of it; and just then Gambril, the austere Gambril, treated us to another vocal performance. He began to sing out for relief. His voice wailed pitifully in the darkness: 'Come aft, somebody! I can't stand this. Here she'll be off again directly and I can't. . . .'

I dashed aft myself meeting on my way a hard gust of wind whose approach Gambril's ear had detected from afar and which filled the sails on the main in a series of muffled reports mingled with the low plaint of the spars. I was just in time to seize the wheel while Frenchy, who had followed me, caught up the collapsing Gambril. He hauled him out of the way, admonished him to lie still where he was, and then stepped up to relieve me, asking calmly:

'How am I to steer her, sir?'

'Dead before it, for the present. I'll get you a light in a moment.'

But going forward I met Ransome bringing up the spare binnacle lamp. That man noticed everything, attended to everything, shed comfort around him as he moved. As he passed me he remarked in a soothing tone that the stars were coming out. They were. The breeze was sweeping clear the sooty sky, breaking through the indolent silence of the sea.

The barrier of awful stillness which had encompassed us for so many days as though we had been accursed was broken. I felt that. I let myself fall on to the skylight seat. A faint white ridge of foam, thin, very thin, broke alongside. The first for ages – for ages. I could have cheered, if it hadn't been for the sense of guilt which clung to all my thoughts secretly. Ransome stood before me.

'What about the mate,' I asked anxiously. 'Still unconscious?'

'Well, sir – it's funny.' Ransome was evidently puzzled. 'He hasn't spoken a word, and his eyes are shut. But it looks to me more like sound sleep than anything else.'

I accepted this view as the least troublesome of any, or at any rate, least disturbing. Dead faint or deep slumber, Mr Burns had to be left to himself for the present. Ransome remarked suddenly:

'I believe you want a coat, sir.'

'I believe I do,' I sighed out.

But I did not move. What I felt I wanted were new limbs. My arms and legs seemed utterly useless, fairly worn out. They didn't even ache. But I stood up all the same to put on the coat when Ransome brought it up. And when he suggested that he had better now 'take Gambril forward', I said:

'All right. I'll help you to get him down on the main deck.'

I found that I was quite able to help, too. We raised Gambril up between us. He tried to help himself along like a man, but all the time he was inquiring piteously:

'You won't let me go when we come to the ladder? You won't let me go when we come to the ladder?'

The breeze kept on freshening and blew true, true to a hair. At daylight by careful manipulation of the helm we got the foreyards to run square by themselves (the water keeping smooth) and then went about hauling the ropes tight. Of the four men I had with me at night, I could see now only two. I didn't inquire as to the others. They had given in. For a time only I hoped.

Our various tasks forward occupied us for hours, the two men with me moved so slowly and had to rest so often. One of them remarked that 'every blamed thing in the ship felt about a hundred times heavier than its proper weight'. This was the only complaint uttered. I don't know what we should have done without Ransome. He worked with us, silent too, with a little smile frozen on his lips. From time to time I murmured to him: 'Go steady' – 'Take it easy, Ransome' – and received a quick glance in reply.

When we had done all we could do to make things safe, he disappeared into his galley. Some time afterwards, going forward for a look round, I caught sight of him through the open door. He sat upright on the locker in front of the stove, with his head leaning back against the bulkhead. His eyes were closed; his capable hands held open the front of his thin cotton shirt baring tragically his powerful chest, which heaved in painful and laboured gasps. He didn't hear me.

I retreated quietly and went straight on to the poop to relieve Frenchy, who by that time was beginning to look very sick. He gave me the course with great formality and tried to go off with a jaunty step, but reeled widely twice before getting out of my sight.

And then I remained all alone aft, steering my ship, which ran before the wind with a buoyant lift now and then, and even rolling a little. Presently Ransome appeared before me with a tray. The sight of food made me ravenous all at once. He took the wheel while I sat down on the after grating to eat my breakfast.

'This breeze seems to have done for our crowd,' he murmured. 'It just laid them low – all hands.'

'Yes,' I said. 'I suppose you and I are the only two fit men in the ship.'

'Frenchy says there's still a jump left in him. I don't know. It can't be much,' continued Ransome with his wistful smile. 'Good little man that. But suppose, sir, that this wind flies round when we are close to the land – what are we going to do with her?'

'If the wind shifts round heavily after we close in with the land she will either run ashore or get dismasted or both. We won't be able to do anything with her. She's running away with us now. All we can do is to steer her. She's a ship without a crew.'[73]

'Yes. All laid low,' repeated Ransome quietly. 'I do give them a look-in forward every now and then, but it's precious little I can do for them.'

'I, and the ship, and everyone on board of her, are very much indebted to you, Ransome,' I said warmly.

He made as though he had not heard me, and steered in silence till I was ready to relieve him. He surrendered the wheel, picked up the tray, and for a parting shot informed me that Mr Burns was awake and seemed to have a mind to come up on deck.

'I don't know how to prevent him, sir. I can't very well stop down below all the time.'

It was clear that he couldn't. And sure enough Mr Burns came on deck dragging himself painfully aft in his enormous overcoat. I beheld him with a natural dread. To have him around and raving about the wiles of a dead man while I had to steer a wildly rushing ship full of dying men was a rather dreadful prospect.

But his first remarks were quite sensible in meaning and tone. Apparently he had no recollection of the night scene. And if he had he didn't betray himself once. Neither did he talk very much. He sat on the skylight looking desperately ill at first, but that strong breeze, before which the last remnant of my crew had wilted down, seemed to blow a fresh stock of vigour into his frame with every gust. One could almost see the process.

By way of sanity test I alluded on purpose to the late captain. I was delighted to find that Mr Burns did not display undue interest in the subject. He ran over the old tale of that savage ruffian's iniquities with a certain vindictive gusto and then concluded unexpectedly:

'I do believe, sir, that his brain began to go a year or more before he died.'

A wonderful recovery. I could hardly spare it as much admiration as it deserved, for I had to give all my mind to the steering.

In comparison with the hopeless languor of the preceding days this was dizzy speed. Two ridges of foam streamed from the ship's bows;

the wind sang in a strenuous note which under other circumstances would have expressed to me all the joy of life. Whenever the hauled-up mainsail started trying to slat and bang itself to pieces in its gear, Mr Burns would look at me apprehensively.

'What would you have me do, Mr Burns? We can neither furl it nor set it. I only wish the old thing would thrash itself to pieces and be done with it. This beastly racket confuses me.'

Mr Burns wrung his hands, and cried out suddenly:

'How will you get the ship into harbour, sir, without men to handle her?'

And I couldn't tell him.

Well – it did get done about forty hours afterwards. By the exorcising virtue of Mr Burns' awful laugh, the malicious spectre had been laid, the evil spell broken, the curse removed. We were now in the hands of a kind and energetic Providence. It was rushing us on. . . .

I shall never forget the last night, dark, windy, and starry. I steered. Mr Burns, after having obtained from me a solemn promise to give him a kick if anything happened, went frankly to sleep on the deck close to the binnacle. Convalescents need sleep. Ransome, his back propped against the mizzenmast and a blanket over his legs, remained perfectly still, but I don't suppose he closed his eyes for a moment. That embodiment of jauntiness, Frenchy, still under the delusion that there was 'a jump' left in him, had insisted on joining us; but mindful of discipline, had laid himself down as far on the forepart of the poop as he could get, alongside the bucket-rack.

And I steered, too tired for anxiety, too tired for connected thought. I had moments of grim exultation and then my heart would sink awfully at the thought of that forecastle at the other end of the dark deck, full of fever-stricken men – some of them dying. By my fault. But never mind. Remorse must wait. I had to steer.

In the small hours the breeze weakened, then failed altogether. About five it returned, gentle enough, enabling us to head for the roadstead. Daybreak found Mr Burns sitting wedged up with coils of rope on the stern-grating, and from the depths of his overcoat steering the ship with very white bony hands; while Ransome and I rushed along the decks letting go all the sheets and halliards by the run.

We dashed next up on to the forecastle head. The perspiration of labour and sheer nervousness simply poured off our heads as we toiled to get the anchors cock-billed. I dared not look at Ransome as we worked side by side. We exchanged curt words; I could hear him panting close to me and I avoided turning my eyes his way for fear of seeing him fall down and expire in the act of putting out his strength – for what? Indeed for some distinct ideal.

The consummate seaman in him was aroused. He needed no directions. He knew what to do. Every effort, every movement was an act of consistent heroism. It was not for me to look at a man thus inspired.

At last all was ready, and I heard him say, 'Hadn't I better go down and open the compressors now, sir?'

'Yes. Do,' I said. And even then I did not glance his way. After a time his voice came up from the main deck:

'When you like, sir. All clear on the windlass here.'

I made a sign to Mr Burns to put the helm down and then I let both anchors go one after another, leaving the ship to take as much cable as she wanted. She took the best part of them both before she brought up. The loose sails coming aback ceased their maddening racket above my head. A perfect stillness reigned in the ship. And while I stood forward feeling a little giddy in that sudden peace, I caught faintly a moan or two and the incoherent mutterings of the sick in the forecastle.

As we had a signal for medical assistance flying on the mizzen it is a fact that before the ship was fairly at rest three steam-launches from various men-of-war arrived alongside; and at least five naval surgeons clambered on board. They stood in a knot gazing up and down the empty main deck, then looked aloft – where not a man could be seen either.

I went towards them – a solitary figure in a blue and grey striped sleeping suit and a pipe-clayed cork helmet on its head. Their disgust was extreme. They had expected surgical cases. Each one had brought his carving tools with him. But they soon got over their little disappointment. In less than five minutes one of the steam-launches was rushing shorewards to order a big boat and some hospital people for the removal of the crew. The big steam-pinnace went off to her ship to bring over a few bluejackets to furl my sails for me.

One of the surgeons had remained on board. He came out of the forecastle looking impenetrable, and noticed my inquiring gaze.

'There's nobody dead in there, if that's what you want to know,' he said deliberately. Then added in a tone of wonder: 'The whole crew!'

'And very bad?'

'And very bad,' he repeated. His eyes were roaming all over the ship. 'Heavens! What's that?'

'That,' I said, glancing aft, 'is Mr Burns, my chief officer.'

Mr Burns with his moribund head nodding on the stalk of his lean neck was a sight for any one to exclaim at. The surgeon asked:

'Is he going to the hospital too?'

'Oh, no,' I said jocosely. 'Mr Burns can't go on shore till the mainmast goes. I am very proud of him. He's my only convalescent.'

'You look . . .' began the doctor staring at me. But I interrupted him angrily:

'I am not ill.'

'No. . . . You look queer.'

'Well, you see, I have been seventeen days on deck.'

'Seventeen! . . . But you must have slept.'

'I suppose I must have. I don't know. But I'm certain that I didn't sleep for the last forty hours.'

'Phew! . . . You will be going ashore presently, I suppose?'

'As soon as ever I can. There's no end of business waiting for me there.'

The surgeon released my hand, which he had taken while we talked, pulled out his pocket-book, wrote in it rapidly, tore out the page, and offered it to me.

'I strongly advise you to get this prescription made up for yourself ashore. Unless I am much mistaken you will need it this evening.'

'What is it then?' I asked with suspicion.

'Sleeping draught,' answered the surgeon curtly; and moving with an air of interest towards Mr Burns he engaged him in conversation.

As I went below to dress to go ashore, Ransome followed me. He begged my pardon; he wished, too, to be sent ashore and paid off.

I looked at him in surprise. He was waiting for my answer with an air of anxiety.

'You don't mean to leave the ship!' I cried out.

'I do really, sir. I want to go and be quiet somewhere. Anywhere. The hospital will do.'

'But, Ransome,' I said, 'I hate the idea of parting with you.'

'I must go,' he broke in. 'I have a right!' He gasped and a look of almost savage determination passed over his face. For an instant he was another being. And I saw under the worth and the comeliness of the man the humble reality of things. Life was a boon to him – this precarious hard life – and he was thoroughly alarmed about himself.

'Of course I shall pay you off if you wish it,' I hastened to say. 'Only I must ask you to remain on board till this afternoon. I can't leave Mr Burns absolutely by himself in the ship for hours.'

He softened at once and assured me with a smile and in his natural pleasant voice that he understood that very well.

When I returned on deck everything was ready for the removal of the men. It was the last ordeal of that episode which had been maturing and tempering my character – though I did not know it.

It was awful. They passed under my eyes one after another – each of them an embodied reproach of the bitterest kind, till I felt a sort of revolt wake up in me. Poor Frenchy had gone suddenly under. He was carried past me insensible, his comic face horribly flushed and as if swollen, breathing stertorously. He looked more like Mr Punch than ever; a disgracefully intoxicated Mr Punch.

The austere Gambril, on the contrary, had improved temporarily. He insisted on walking on his own feet to the rail – of course with assistance on each side of him. But he gave way to a sudden panic at the moment of being swung over the side and began to wail pitifully:

'Don't let them drop me, sir. Don't let them drop me, sir!' While I kept on shouting to him in most soothing accents: 'All right, Gambril. They won't! They won't!'

It was no doubt very ridiculous. The bluejackets on our deck were grinning quietly, while even Ransome himself (much to the fore in lending a hand) had to enlarge his wistful smile for a fleeting moment.

I left for the shore in the steam-pinnace, and on looking back beheld Mr Burns actually standing up by the taffrail, still in his enormous woolly overcoat. The bright sunlight brought out his weirdness amazingly. He looked like a frightful and elaborate scarecrow set up on the poop of a death-stricken ship, to keep the seabirds from the corpses.

Our story had got about already in town and everybody on shore was most kind. The marine office let me off the port dues, and as there happened to be a shipwrecked crew staying in the Home I had no difficulty in obtaining as many men as I wanted. But when I inquired if I could see Captain Ellis for a moment I was told in accents of pity for my ignorance that our deputy-Neptune had retired and gone home on a pension about three weeks after I left the port. So I suppose that my appointment was the last act, outside the daily routine, of his official life.

It is strange how on coming ashore I was struck by the springy step, the lively eyes, the strong vitality of everyone I met. It impressed me enormously. And amongst those I met there was Captain Giles of course. It would have been very extraordinary if I had not met him. A prolonged stroll in the business part of the town was the regular employment of all his mornings when he was ashore.

I caught the glitter of the gold watch-chain across his chest ever so far away. He radiated benevolence.

'What is it I hear?' he queried with a 'kind uncle' smile, after shaking hands. 'Twenty-one days from Bankok?'

'Is this all you've heard?' I said. 'You must come to tiffin with me. I want you to know exactly what you have let me in for.'

He hesitated for almost a minute.

'Well – I will,' he decided condescendingly at last.

We turned into the hotel. I found to my surprise that I could eat quite a lot. Then over the cleared table-cloth I unfolded to Captain Giles all the story since I took command in all its professional and emotional aspects, while he smoked patiently the big cigar I had given him.

Then he observed sagely:

'You must feel jolly well tired by this time.'

'No,' I said. 'Not tired. But I'll tell you, Captain Giles, how I feel. I feel old. And I must be. All of you on shore look to me just a lot of skittish youngsters that have never known a care in the world.'

He didn't smile. He looked insufferably exemplary. He declared:

'That will pass. But you do look older – it's a fact.'

'Aha!' I said.

'No! No! The truth is that one must not make too much of anything in life, good or bad.'

'Live at half-speed,' I murmured perversely. 'Not everybody can do that.'

'You'll be glad enough presently if you can keep going even at that rate,' he retorted with his air of conscious virtue. 'And there's another thing: a man should stand up to his bad luck, to his mistakes, to his conscience, and all that sort of thing. Why – what else would you have to fight against?'

I kept silent. I don't know what he saw in my face, but he asked abruptly:

'Why – you aren't faint-hearted?'

'God only knows, Captain Giles,' was my sincere answer.

'That's all right,' he said calmly. 'You will learn soon how not to be faint-hearted. A man has got to learn everything – and that's what so many of those youngsters don't understand.'

'Well I am no longer a youngster.'

'No,' he conceded. 'Are you leaving soon?'

'I am going on board directly,' I said. 'I shall pick up one of my anchors and heave in to half-cable on the other as soon as my new crew comes on board and I shall be off at daylight to-morrow.'

'You will?' grunted Captain Giles approvingly. 'That's the way. You'll do.'

'What did you expect? That I would want to take a week ashore for a rest?' I said, irritated by his tone. 'There's no rest for me till she's out in the Indian Ocean and not much of it even then.'

He puffed at the cigar moodily, as if transformed.

'Yes, that's what it amounts to,' he said in a musing tone. It was as if a ponderous curtain had rolled up disclosing an unexpected Captain Giles. But it was only for a moment, merely the time to let him add: 'Precious little rest in life for anybody. Better not think of it.'

We rose, left the hotel, and parted from each other in the street with a warm handshake, just as he began to interest me for the first time in our intercourse.

The first thing I saw when I got back to the ship was Ransome on the quarter-deck sitting quietly on his neatly lashed sea-chest.

I beckoned him to follow me into the saloon where I sat down to write a letter of recommendation for him to a man I knew on shore.

When finished I pushed it across the table. 'It may be of some good to you when you leave the hospital.'

He took it, put it in his pocket. His eyes were looking away from me – nowhere. His face was anxiously set.

'How are you feeling now?' I asked.

'I don't feel bad now, sir,' he answered stiffly. 'But I am afraid of its coming on. . . .' The wistful smile came back on his lips for a moment. 'I – I am in a blue funk about my heart, sir.'

I approached him with extended hand. His eyes, not looking at me, had a strained expression. He was like a man listening for a warning call.

'Won't you shake hands, Ransome?' I said gently.

He exclaimed, flushed up dusky red, gave my hand a hard wrench – and next moment, left alone in the cabin, I listened to him going up the companion stairs cautiously, step by step, in mortal fear of starting into sudden anger our common enemy it was his hard fate to carry consciously within his faithful breast.[74]

THE END

214

Critical commentary

Conrad's view of the function of criticism, and also of the motives that he feared might inspire the work of critics, is trenchantly expressed in a letter to William Blackwood (item 22). 'Criticism', he says, 'is poor work, and to expose the weaknesses of humanity as exhibited in literary work is a thankless and futile task.' Where the critic is point-ing out 'beauties not manifest to the common eye' or even 'generous failings', then the 'toil' is not unworthy. But, he goes on, 'the blind distribution of praise or blame, done with a light heart and an empty mind, which is of the very essence of "periodical" criticism seems to me to be a work less useful than skirt-dancing and not quite as honourable as pocket-picking'.

Conrad himself wrote little periodical criticism and what he did undertake was often by special invitation because of the nature of the subject or his relationship with the author. One reason for this is that for the bulk of his writing life Conrad was engaged in writing fiction. He was in debt to his agent, J. B. Pinker, and Pinker wanted copy. However, Conrad also believed that the act of criticism was a serious responsibility, a matter of honest engagement with the writer's rendering of truth as he saw it. As he says in a letter written late in his life to Barrett H. Clark (item 45), 'I have given there all the truth that is in me; and all that the critics may say can make my honesty neither more nor less. . . . It is the critic's affair to bring to

215

its contemplation his own honesty, his sensibility and intelligence.' Not only does this place a duty of honesty upon the critic second only in seriousness to the honesty of the artist himself; it also lifts the critical act from the detached discovery of 'beauties' and 'failings' to the level of a relationship, almost, of mutual respect and sympathetic understanding between critic and author. The critic should discard 'petty scruples' and 'superficial formulas' if his judgement is not to be 'superficial and petty'. He should take the writer's 'truth' in good faith, and Conrad feels, as an artist himself, that he 'has no right to quarrel with the inspirations, either lofty or base, of another soul' (item 45).

Here we have another reason, then, why Conrad's critical pieces are to be found predominantly in letters to friends and in articles that are really, like his reviews of Galsworthy and Henry James, extensions of friendship. True criticism is too serious to be carried in the 'empty' and light-hearted periodicals: it is either a communication between like minds held in mutual respect, artist and more than usually sensitive reader, or it had better not be undertaken at all. It is on these grounds that Conrad declines to give Blackwood his full opinion of John Buchan (item 22).

The criticism Conrad writes can be divided, roughly, into three kinds: criticism of writers whom he admires but with whom he has little in common; criticism of writers whom he admires and with whom he recognizes that he shares a great deal; and, broadly speaking, self-criticism, especially that dealing with what he was trying to achieve as a writer. (When he writes of how successfully or otherwise he has carried out his intentions he is less trustworthy because instinctively evasive or self-deprecatory.) To these categories we should add Conrad's letters of advice to beginners such as Edward Noble and Helen Sanderson, or to 'amateur' creative talents like Sir Hugh Clifford and even, in Conrad's opinion, his friend Garnett. These letters are frequently remarkable in their ability to combine Conrad's genuine understanding of the intention of the writer with suggestions for different techniques in treatment which we can see arising from his sense of what was important in his own work. His advice to Clifford, for example (item 21), in which he strips down a passage from Clifford's book and brings out the distinction between

216

'truth effectively stated' and 'the sort of thing that writes itself', both enables the original passage to be what it apparently set out to be, and, at the same time, provides a fascinating insight into the artistic mind at its habitual work, the 'mere craftsman' of words. As he acknowledges to Clifford of one phrase, 'it is the sort of thing I write twenty times a day and . . . spend half my nights in taking out of my work'. And, as a measure of Conrad's modernism, what he does to the Clifford passage in 1899, and what he does, we may conclude, in his own work, is very much the kind of paring down that James Joyce performed on a far larger scale in rendering *Stephen Hero* into *A Portrait of the Artist as a Young Man* some ten years later.

The writers we find in the first category of criticism include, rather surprisingly for a man who made so many literary friendships, most of Conrad's major contemporaries and many of his acquaintances: Henry James, H. G. Wells, Arnold Bennett, Kipling, his close friend John Galsworthy, and Proust. Their works are praised for the qualities they have, but they are not qualities Conrad would wish to have himself. Kipling's work, for example, can be 'of impeccable form and because of that little thing, he shall sojourn in Hell only a very short while. He squints with the rest of his excellent sort' (item 8). Conrad always addressed Henry James in correspondence as 'Très Cher Maître'. His praise of James's work, however, contained in a letter to Galsworthy, is less unambiguous. He ostensibly intends to defend James against the charge of lifelessness in his characters, but we gradually sense that Conrad is beginning to protest just a little too much in his finding synonyms for James's virtues, until finally he slips in the hesitated reservation we were almost expecting.

The outlines are so clear, the figures so finished, chiselled, carved and brought out that we exclaim, – we, used to the shades of the contemporary fiction, to the more or less malformed shades, – we exclaim, – stone! Not at all. I say flesh and blood, – very perfectly presented, – perhaps with too much perfection of *method*.

(item 20)

Needless to say, if Conrad's own characters are rarely dismissed as 'shades', they are even less often described as 'carved' or 'chiselled'. Conrad's admiration for James was certainly genuine, and *Chance* is usually regarded as the most Jamesian of his works. But *Chance* has not weathered criticism well, and even James himself made of *Chance* the comment that it 'places Mr Conrad absolutely alone as a votary of the way to do a thing that shall make it undergo most doing'; it is an example of objectivity 'not only menaced but definitely compromised' (James, 1914, pp. 379, 382).

More significant, in terms of writing about those qualities which are characteristic of Conrad's own fiction, is his obviously sympathetic admiration for Flaubert, Turgenev and Maupassant. About these writers he expresses himself with a warmth quite different from the careful precision with which he praises work by Bennett or Proust; notice, for example, in his letter to Scott Moncrieff (item 54), the distinct change of tone between his remarks on Proust's prose, which is 'so full of life' yet with 'no reverie, no emotion, no marked irony, no warmth of conviction, not even a marked rhythm to charm our fancy', and his immediately succeeding comment that this is 'more or less what I think, or imagine that I think'. As soon as we turn to his essay on Turgenev (item 43) – based on a letter to Garnett, as his Proust letter was intended as a contribution to Scott Moncrieff's commemorative volume – the warmth of appreciation for a like-minded artist is apparent. Turgenev is praised for 'his essential humanity', and how frequently in his letters and author's notes is Conrad anxious to testify to his own humane sympathy, even to the extent of denying of *The Secret Agent* that he had 'intended to commit a gratuitous outrage on the feelings of mankind' (item 50). Turgenev's characters, like so many of Conrad's own, 'are human beings, fit to live, fit to suffer, fit to struggle, fit to win, fit to lose, in the endless and inspiring game of pursuing from day to day the ever-receding future'. Flaubert, too, is praised for the power of his 'imagination': 'One never questions for a moment either his characters or his incidents; one would rather doubt one's own existence' (Karl and Davies, 1983, p. 111). This is a revealing comment, even in 1892, when this letter was written, an intriguing glimpse of the response to created characters by a man who would lie in his bed and converse with his own characters during the breakdown that followed *Under Western Eyes*.

It is in his essay on Maupassant (item 28), however, that Conrad is most explicit about what he values most highly in a writer: simplicity and fidelity, simplicity in looking directly at the things that he sees and describing them as he sees them, and fidelity in not being led away from his most deeply held convictions, whatever they may happen to be. Maupassant's 'singleness of purpose is in itself an admirable lesson in the power of artistic honesty', his 'point of view' is 'consistently preserved and never obtruded for the end of personal gratification'. In particular, Maupassant is praised for one notably Conradian feature, that 'all his high qualities appear inherent in the very things of which he speaks, as if they had been altogether independent of his presentation'. This means, above all, that he deals with what is real, he has paid 'prolonged and devoted attention to the aspects of the visible world', to the 'universe of vain appearances wherein we men have found everything to make us proud, sorry, exalted, and humble'. This listing of apparently contradictory qualities that are to be held together without opposition is a frequent stylistic device, here as in his remarks on Turgenev's characters, when Conrad is reaching out to describe a properly compassionate attitude towards mankind. Maupassant's 'attention' has given him 'the right words as if miraculously impressed for him upon the face of things and events'. He is a demanding writer because, like a true artist, he deals not with 'empty phrases requiring no effort' but so renders his 'facts' that 'like the actualities of life itself, they demand from the reader the faculty of observation which is rare'. He has the intention, in other words, like Conrad himself, of making us 'see' (item 7). And yet he makes us see ultimately, again as Conrad himself would wish to do, with a compassionate eye, for Maupassant, says Conrad, 'wrote from the fulness of a compassionate heart'. He 'looks with an eye of profound pity upon' the 'troubles, deceptions and misery' of mankind: 'But he looks at them all. He sees – and does not turn away his head.'

It is perhaps a little surprising to find Maupassant described in such terms, and indeed Conrad does acknowledge that there is another side to his writing: he 'forgets to strew paper roses over the tombs', and disregarding 'these common decencies lays him open to the charges of cruelty, cynicism, hardness'. But Conrad also believes that Maupassant 'is not always properly understood', another claim he frequently makes of his own work. Beneath the cruelty, the disregard of 'decencies', Conrad finds not only the artist, but an artist in whom he clearly recognizes a reflection of his own most serious artistic efforts and intentions. Whether the judgement of Maupassant is just or not is not the issue. What is valuable in the essay is the extent to which we can clearly see Conrad himself in the features he chooses to emphasize in Maupassant.

ART AND THE ARTIST

At the end of his essay 'Books', Conrad summarizes his sense of how the writer should prepare himself for his task. 'Let him', he says, 'mature the strength of his imagination amongst the things of this earth, which it is his business to cherish and know, and refrain from calling down his inspiration ready-made from some heaven of perfections of which he knows nothing' (item 31). The emphasis on the real, the 'things of this earth', and on the effort that the cherishing and knowing will entail, as against the temptation to seek 'ready-made' inspiration from an unknowable sphere, is one that underlies Conrad's attitude towards art over the whole of his writing career. It is expressed in the Author's note to *Almayer's Folly*, where he speaks of those fictional characters that are only 'charming and graceful phantoms', 'softly luminous with the radiance of all our virtues; that are possessed of all refinements . . . but, being only phantoms, possess no heart'. Conrad himself, on the other hand, is 'content to sympathize with common mortals, no matter where they live' (item 1). We find it, too, in his remarks on John Galsworthy, who has 'the individual vision of a novelist seeking his inspiration amongst the realities of this earth' (item 32). Most notably, it is the article of artistic belief that directs the argument of Conrad's fullest and best-known piece of critical writing, the Preface to *The Nigger of the 'Narcissus'*.

Art, for Conrad, as defined at the beginning of the *Nigger* Preface, is 'a single-minded attempt to render the highest kind of justice to the visible universe, by bringing to light the truth, manifold and one, underlying its every aspect' (item 7). In this attempt, artistic 'isms', like 'Realism, Romanticism, Naturalism', can be only 'temporary formulas' the conventions of which soon limit the creative imagination. At their worst, as he says in 'Books', these 'fettering dogmas' are adopted as 'the cunning device of those who, uncertain of their talent, would seek to add lustre to it by the authority of a school' (item 31). For the true artist, and for the novelist specifically, the 'most precious possession' should be 'Liberty of imagination' (item 31). Rendering 'the highest kind of justice to the visible universe' binds the artist's imagination to two primary responsibilities: his responsibility to those 'aspects of matter' and 'facts of life' that are taken to constitute the 'visible universe', and his responsibility to the readers who are to be brought to apprehend 'the very truth' of these constituent facts, who will acknowledge that 'the highest kind of justice' has been done. The writer whose words will make his readers 'hear', 'feel' and, 'before all', make them '*see*', can only do so by responding, like Maupassant, with honesty to the 'aspects of the visible world' (item 28).

But the 'written word' will gain its 'power' (item 7) not only by its fidelity to the 'visible world' of facts and events but by the writer's unflinching honesty in rendering the response of the temperament that has 'seen' and experienced the 'visible world': as Michael Levenson points out, the 'central notion' of Conrad's claim is 'that of temperament ''endowing'' events with their ''true meaning''' (1984, p. 2). And when Conrad speaks of fiction's appeal as 'the appeal of one temperament to all the other innumerable temperaments' (item 7), this, says Levenson,

> by no means marks a retreat from the programme of rendering 'the highest kind of justice to the visible universe'; indeed it constitutes that justice. The 'subtlety' of human consciousness is the source of meaning and artistic 'justice'; against the evanescent flux of the phenomenal world, it provides permanence, pattern and significance.   (1984, p. 2)

Here we have some suggestion of just what Conrad means by 'truth': when a reader has been brought to acknowledge the authenticity of the writer's vision, when 'meaning' has been conveyed about those 'aspects of matter' of which the writer treats, be it a death, the leaving of a ship, the telling of a lie to a young woman, as at the end of *Heart of Darkness*, or the cutting off, as Nostromo does, of a set of silver buttons, then some degree of artistic truth has been achieved. This truth is found not in the acknowledgement that such a fact or event actually existed or took place, for frequently it did not, but rather in the recognition that such a piece of fiction had the significance with which it has been invested. Clearly, if this is to be the case, then, as Conrad tells Sir Hugh Clifford, 'the *whole* of the truth' must lie 'in the presentation' (item 21). It is D. H. Lawrence who describes as artistic 'immorality' the occasions when 'the novelist puts his thumb in the scale, to pull down the balance to his own predilection' (1925, p. 177). Significance, in other words, should not be found in the assertions of the writer, but should rather, as Conrad says of Maupassant, 'appear inherent in the very things of which he speaks' (item 28). This, for example, is what Conrad intended as the impression of his treatment of Alvan Hervey in his story 'The return': 'I wanted the reader to *see him think* and then to hear him speak – and shudder' (item 10). The reader's shudder would be for Conrad the guarantee of a moment of artistic truth, of the morality of the novelist's dealing with one of the 'facts of life' he has chosen for presentation.

But there is another, broader kind of truth to which we have access through Conrad's work. In the *Nigger* Preface, it is the 'subtle and resistless power' of the appeal made by fiction that 'endows passing events with their true meaning' (item 7). This implied contrast between the 'true' and the 'passing' is what Levenson picks up when he sets 'permanence, pattern and significance' against 'the evanescent flux of the phenomenal world'. When the captain–narrator of *The Shadow-Line* says of his months as mate aboard the trading steamship 'that there was no truth to be got out of them', he, too, acknowledges the contrast, for what he means by 'truth' is something other than the 'dreary, prosaic waste of days' (p. 118) of his experience. The 'passing events' of his last eighteen months have, apparently, no 'true meaning' to yield; they are part of the 'flux', and no more. One feature of the story is the emerging consciousness of the captain, the developing sensitivity that will enable him to read 'meaning' and 'truth' in 'the passing events' of his own life. But what will be the nature of this 'truth'? In one sense it will be the very ability to perceive those patterns of personal development that are actually recorded in *The Shadow-Line*, that are responsible for its existence as a story. The captain–narrator has been created in order to render justice to the process that created him. He is a narrative device through which Conrad is able to explain a series of influences that were important in the shaping of his own individuality. The events and emotions of his period as captain of the *Otago* have 'truth to be got out of them', personal truth, a 'meaning' that can be read and communicated by the person they helped to form.

There is, though, one further sense of truth beyond the drawing out of patterns of personal development from the 'evanescent flux of the phenomenal world', and it is one of which Conrad is acutely aware. In the earliest of his Author's notes, that to *Almayer's Folly*, his avowal of sympathy 'with common mortals, no matter where they live' is followed by an explanation of the impulsion towards sympathy. It lies in the awareness of common humanity: 'Their hearts – like ours – must endure the load of the gifts from Heaven: the curse of facts and the blessing of illusions, the bitterness of our wisdom and the deceptive consolation of our folly' (item 1). The artist, says Conrad in the *Nigger* Preface, confronted by the 'enigmatical spectacle' of the world, 'descends within himself, and in that lonely region of stress and strife, if he be deserving and fortunate, he finds the terms of his appeal' (item 7). The descent may be to a 'lonely region', but the 'appeal' made by the artist is to our common humanity, 'to our sense of pity, and beauty, and pain; to the latent feeling of fellowship with all creation'. And the ultimate intention of the artist should be to 'awaken in the hearts of the beholders that feeling of unavoidable solidarity; of the solidarity in mysterious origin, in toil, in joy, in hope, in uncertain fate, which binds men to each other and all mankind to the visible world' (item 7). Here is 'pattern' to be drawn from 'evanescent flux'. Art may not help us to understand 'passing events' or reconcile us to their remorseless passing, but it can bring us to know and feel the common lot of mankind, as the captain–narrator of *The Shadow-Line* ends his tale not with what is unique in his experience, but with the reminder of death that is 'our common enemy' (p. 214).

It is entirely appropriate, then, that Conrad should define art in terms of 'truth', for truth is properly the only concern of art. What his works reveal is the truth to be 'got out of' their individual experiences by his narrators and protagonists, but what makes those truths more than just stages in private stories is the awareness that is also revealed of the place of the individual in relation to common human experience. Conrad's art deals with truth not only in so far as Marlow, or the captain–narrator, learns something about himself, but because something is learnt, of honour, or fidelity, or mortality, that is 'seen' as a source of the 'solidarity' we should feel between ourselves and 'all mankind'. And feelings, as Conrad observes to Garnett, '*are*, and in submitting to them we can avoid neither death nor suffering which are our common lot, but we can bear them in peace' (Garnett, 1928, pp. 282–3).

THE ART OF NARRATIVE

Conrad adopts many devices, structural as well as stylistic, in order to achieve objective rendering of his own feelings, his own way of seeing. His multiple viewpoints, his dislocations of time, his adoption of 'placed' narrators like Marlow and the captains of 'The secret sharer' and *The Shadow-Line*, are all rooted in his clear critical understanding of the overriding necessity that the artist remain true to yet detached from the simplicity of his perceptions. At one level this means, as Conrad says in the *Nigger* Preface, that the writer should maintain 'an unremitting never-discouraged care for the shape and ring of sentences' (item 7). This is clear, too, from his extensive comments on Clifford's work. But it also means, for Conrad, the careful manipulation of what he at different times calls his groupings, his episodes and his perspective. To his friend Meldrum, for example, he writes that 'Upon the episodes, after all, the effect of reality depends and as to me I depend upon the reader *looking back* upon my story as a whole' (Blackburn, 1958, p. 170). Making you see, for Conrad, takes time. Tom Lingard is to have 'all the first part' of *The Rescue* 'given up to the presentation of his personality' with the aim of 'stimulating vision in the reader' (item 9). While 'the shape and ring of sentences', however, will make for a certain kind of seeing, an equally crucial kind is achieved only through 'the reader *looking back*', a looking back which should take in the full impact of details and ironies which were not apparent at the time of first reading. So, with *The Rescue*, the reader will achieve proper seeing at the same moment as Lingard, who is 'perfectly enlightened' 'only at the very last . . . when the work of rescue and destruction is ended and nothing is left to him but to try and pick up as best he may the broken thread of his life' (item 9). At its most complex, such perspective involves the groupings, time-shifts and multiple narrative viewpoints of *Nostromo*, of which the lighthouse of the final part, the 'whole refracting apparatus' with its 'rings of prisms' that 'glittered and sparkled like a dome-shaped shrine of diamonds' (1904, p. 552), is such a compelling image. It is also an image to which Conrad returns, for example in a letter written towards the end of his life to Richard Curle (item 56). His 'art', he says, 'is fluid, depending on grouping (sequence) which shifts, and on the changing lights giving varied effects of perspective' – light and dark, too, of course, comprising one of the major patterns of suggestiveness of Conrad's fiction, with *Nostromo*, again, as a prominent example.

More simply than in *Nostromo*, *The Shadow-Line* presents us with the shifting meanings of the shadow-line itself, both in the mind of the captain–narrator and in what Conrad makes his readers see are other valid readings of the image. Most immediately, it is, as we are told at the beginning, 'a shadow-line warning one that the region of early youth, too, must be left behind' (p. 116), appropriate enough, of course, for a story that is to involve the understanding of maturity. But the shadow-line is also to be looked at in ways that are much more disturbing. When the new captain, at the beginning of part 3, sits alone in his saloon he is struck by the not unflattering thought that 'A succession of men had sat in that chair.' It is 'as if a sort of composite soul, the soul of command, had whispered suddenly to mine of long days at sea and of anxious moments'. He catches sight of his own face 'Deep within the tarnished ormolu frame' and continues, bringing out more emphatically the shadow-line image:

It struck me that this quietly staring man whom I was watching, both as if he were myself and somebody else, was not exactly a lonely figure. He had his place in a line of men whom he did not know, of whom he had never heard; but who were fashioned by the same influences, whose souls in relation to their humble life's work had no secrets for him. (pp. 153–4)

Having established this self-gratifying reading of the shadow-line, Conrad has Mr Burns relating the story of the late captain, the immediate predecessor – 'fashioned by the same influences', whose 'humble life's work had no secrets' and whose end has, the captain–narrator concludes, disgraced the line of heredity: 'And like a member of a dynasty, feeling a semi-mystical bond with the dead, I was profoundly shocked by my immediate predecessor.' The lesson is not lost:

> That man had been in all essentials but his age just such another man as myself. Yet the end of his life was a complete act of treason, the betrayal of a tradition which seemed to me as imperative as any guide on earth could be. (pp. 160–1)

While the captain ascribes the moral dissolution to 'evil spirits', however, and to 'unknown powers that shape our destinies', the reader should be more alert to the self-satisfaction that has been shaken, and to the captain's sentimentally self-pleasing identification with a shadow-line that existed only in his own mind. The association of that self-gratification with mirrors – even the mahogany table is rendered as a kind of foreboding mirror, shining 'in the twilight like a dark pool of water' (p. 153) – also sends us back to the tale's epigraph, the disturbing 'grand miroir/De mon désespoir', and forward to that other implement of self-reflection, the captain's diary, where we find such despairing comments of self-recognition as 'I feel as if all my sins had found me out' (p. 193) and, at the very nadir of his mental journey, 'I always suspected that I might be no good. And here is proof positive, I am shirking it, I am no good' (p. 194).

There are other associations picked up by the image of the shadow-line, but this particular part of the pattern is enough to demonstrate Conrad's skill in 'varied effects of perspective'. Moreover, Conrad is able to elicit two important levels of reading through his handling of this thread in the narrative. First of all, in so far as we experience the events and the emotions of the captain as the story proceeds chronologically, we are reading with the same limited understanding as the protagonist who is supposed to have lived those events. This is the most basic kind of involvement that any story must achieve if the reader's interest is to be held until the final page. Conrad's objection to the work of many of his contemporaries was that this was the only kind of reading demanded. The subtler aspects of Conrad's treatment of the shadow-line and its associations, however, gradually develop our capacity for '*looking back*', and so produce our recognition both of the state of mind of the captain at the time and of the significance of the episode in the saloon to the overall organization of the narrative. Here we are reading at the level not of the man who lived the events but of the man who, having been changed by those events, is now engaged in recalling them. We are being provided, in other words, with a double focus on experience, one in which the narrator's fidelity is to the truth of events and a state of mind lived and felt at the time, and another, broader focus in which fidelity is demanded to a truth perceived only afterwards, when 'meaning' has been drawn from 'evanescent flux'.

THE SHADOW-LINE: SHAPING THE NARRATIVE

If the material for *The Shadow-Line* was from Conrad's experience on the *Otago*, the form that material finally took depended upon decisions made by the man who sat down to write a work of fiction nearly thirty years later. And one significant factor in the shaping of the narrative was his choice of a first-person narrator, or rather *the* first-person narrator whose ship, as Cedric Watts puts it, 'resembles Conrad's *Otago*' (1984, p. 149) and who also apparently narrates 'Falk', 'The secret sharer' and 'A smile of fortune'. A consequence of this choice is its effects on characterization. A narrator–protagonist does enable a writer to achieve free access to the thoughts and feelings of a single character. Sometimes, as in *Lord Jim*, when the narrator is a participant in the action though not central to it, the first-person voice will nevertheless have the crucial functions both of interpreting the actions and personality of the protagonist through comment and reflection, and of authenticating the value to be attached, for example to Jim himself, through emotional involvement. In such works as *Heart of Darkness*, 'The secret sharer' and

The Shadow-Line, the narrator is also the protagonist, though in *Heart of Darkness* this is disguised by the device of having the search for Kurtz as the impetus for the action. In such cases, access to one character has to be set against loss of access to all the others. We see what they say and do, but only through the eyes of the narrator–protagonist. We have no more access to their inner selves than the narrator, who interprets for us, according to the evidence available to him, with the colouring of his own personality. One way of disguising this limitation is to make, as Conrad does in *The Shadow-Line*, the inaccessibility of those other characters a main feature of their personalities. Mr Burns is temporarily insane. Captain Giles is not only something of an eccentric, but is also possessed of a wisdom, about reefs, about the offered command, about the nature of experience, which is fully available neither to the protagonist nor to the reader. Ransome, too, is removed by his inner grace, and by his permanent closeness to death.

But this inaccessibility also has advantages. In particular, in a narrative that is primarily concerned with personal changes, the intensity of the experience of one character, seen through his own eyes, is sharpened for us by denying the distraction of seeing and feeling equally intense experiences from other points of view. The madness of Mr Burns, for example, which could, differently treated, have given revealing access to his character, is used rather as a reflection upon the captain's state of mind. His loneliness is intensified by the inaccessibility of his first mate, just as his own derangement, into which we are fully taken, is fed by and highlighted by the insanity of Burns. In this respect, then, other characters are present in the story not because they actually existed (though many of them did) but because they are necessary to develop in some way the state of mind of the protagonist.

A second feature of Conrad's treatment of the experience he was reworking from memory is his use of purely literary models to point and give significance to mood and event. Two works are particularly heavily drawn on, *Hamlet* and Coleridge's poem *The Ancient Mariner*. The similarity of the captain's situation with that of the mariner is at first glance more apparent than what he shares with Hamlet. There is a mysterious and hazardous sea journey during which the protagonist is afflicted by physical suffering and by loneliness. Moreover, some crime or shortcoming of the protagonist causes even more physical suffering to descend upon the crew, so that the journey becomes a period of trial at the end of which some degree of redemption is achieved. Each protagonist is later able to, or constrained to, narrate the story and significance of his own experience. The allusions to *Hamlet*, though, are on the grounds not so much of similarity in events but rather of the topics the two works have in common, even though arising from treatment of quite different events: despair, inactivity, an obsessive concern with madness and death. Several of the echoes of *Hamlet*, for example, point to a single soliloquy, Hamlet's 'To be, or not to be', in which he speculates on death, suicide, the lot of suffering humanity, fear of divine punishment, and the implications such fears have for human enterprise and activity. Several of them, too, raise the prospect of a shaping providence ruling over human affairs, like Hamlet's 'There's a divinity that shapes our ends,/Rough-hew them how we will' (V. ii. 10–11).

It is here that the three works begin to come together. Coleridge, most firmly, posits a providential universe, with avenging or redeeming spirits, angelic troops and the figures of Death and Life-in-Death, all working, apparently, under the direction of a divine omnipotence. *Hamlet*, in spite of the assurance of the above lines, is a play rather of doubt and speculation in a world where nothing, not even death, can be taken as certain and where a shaping providence cannot be ruled out any more than it can be accepted. *The Shadow-Line*, in what Watts calls 'the supernatural plot' (1984, p. 90), allows, like *Hamlet*, the possibility of a divinely ordained universe and all that that implies, a curse from the dead, an act of exorcism, evil spirits and bad luck, everything that is apparently accepted in *The Ancient Mariner*, yet also allows us to dismiss a belief in providence as the temporary expedient of a mind or minds for a while unhinged. Conrad, after all, in his Author's note, denies any intention to write a tale of the 'Supernatural', declaring instead his interest in 'the effect of a mental or moral shock on a common mind' (p. 111). A voyage afflicted by disease and becalming takes its toll, but is eventually successfully completed. Everything else is in the mind, or could be.

One reason for a writer's choosing to shape his work through use of literary models is in order to broaden the applicability of his material. A single sea journey becomes the journey from curse to exorcism, from innocence through guilt to redemption. One man's derangement becomes the dilemma of suffering humanity caught in an uncertain world where to do nothing is the only logical conclusion, and yet where action is required. Individual experience, then, is made to yield meaning, not only for the individual concerned but for mankind, for readers who have never captained a ship, or dealt with a mad first mate, or mistaken common salt for quinine. Conrad's handling of providence, drawing as it does upon his use of *Hamlet* and *The Ancient Mariner*, similarly broadens the significance of his story, making it more recognizable as a version of the doubts and dilemmas under which thinking humanity has always laboured. We are given access to a world of faith and doubt, of good and evil, of pattern and significance, that is not only beyond the bare events of the experience but beyond the grasp of the man who was then living them. Or, as Conrad puts it in the Author's note, 'when we begin to meditate on the meaning of our own past it seems to fill all the world in its profundity and its magnitude' (p. 112).

NARRATIVE STRUCTURE IN THE SHADOW-LINE: 'SEEING' THE CAPTAIN

Albert Guerard, in an illuminating misreading, finds *The Shadow-Line* 'distinctly less perfect' than 'The secret sharer' in so far as it 'gets underway very slowly and uncertainly', and he suggests that to 'cut out the first two chapters' would 'make the two stories truly analogous'. Guerard asks for 'a naive and buoyant confidence' from the captain–narrator at the story's opening, which should be evaporated by the events of the journey (1958, p. 30), a view that was quickly challenged by Ian Watt in his closely argued article 'Story and idea in Conrad's *The Shadow-Line*' (1960). In Guerard's reading of the two stories, and of *Heart of Darkness*, as 'symbolist masterpieces', the 'sea voyages and the one great Congo journey are unmistakably journeys within', journeys through a darkness and into the unconscious, without which 'integration of the personality is impossible' (1958, p. 15).

While it is undeniable that this is a significant dimension of the story, as it is of Conrad's view of art, Guerard's emphasis loses sight of Conrad's abiding insistence upon the *real*, 'the visible universe' with which art should concern itself. In the opening sections of *The Shadow-Line*, as in the opening pages of *Heart of Darkness* and 'The secret sharer', Conrad is establishing what is real, both in the world in which his protagonists are moving and in the sensations and motives – or lack of them – that they exhibit in their thoughts and behaviour. In each story there are important features to be drawn out of the protagonist's relationship to the world about him, and to himself as he apparently sees himself, before the journey can begin to the heart of darkness, or to the heart of the experience of *The Shadow-Line*.

Marlow's narrative in *Heart of Darkness* begins by showing us something of the younger Marlow before his Congo experience, a man secure in his conviction of certain fixed values, such as the value of work, and of truthfulness, and yet one who is entering the 'whited sepulchre' of Brussels, having used, for the first and only time, the intervention of a relative to gain a professional position. These features, almost incidental in comparison with the horrors of the Congo itself, nevertheless assist our 'looking back' from various points in the narrative, for they give us something to look back to as we encounter Marlow's experience of futility, corruption, death and dishonesty. 'The secret sharer', even more than *The Shadow-Line*, is one long process of 'looking back' that is achieved through the suggestion of mirrors which reflect upon the protagonist as he was and as he is becoming. This is underlined for us at the very beginning of the tale, when the narrator speaks of himself and his new command as seeming to be engaged in 'measuring our fitness for a long and arduous enterprise'. He himself, he acknowledges, is 'untried as yet by a position of the fullest responsibility', and has leisure to wonder 'how far I should turn out faithful to that ideal conception of one's own personality every man sets up for himself secretly' (1912b, pp. 92, 94). Unlike the captain–narrator of *The Shadow-Line*, this captain's self-doubts are all present to him from the outset of his narrative, and it is a confident, active, and therefore attractively dangerous, self that appears to him from 'the face of that silent, darkened tropical sea' and whom he straight away recognizes as his 'double'. 'It was, in the night, as though I had been faced by my own reflection in the depths of a sombre and immense mirror' (1912b, p. 101). As this self is hidden and nurtured in the captain's cabin, 'secretly', we measure his willingness to take increasingly out-rageous risks, to become increasingly isolated from his officers and crew, against the introverted man of doubts of the first pages of the narrative. Our tension in the presence of this narrator is held almost until the end of the story; will he prove capable of being 'faithful to that ideal conception', or will the crew's growing conviction of his instability be justified by physical or mental disaster? It is only when the slim chance of success from the final, ultimate risk to the ship itself is realized that we can look back with assurance to the secret 'ideal conception' and acknowledge, as we do so, the narrator's right to the swelling tones of exultation with which he draws his narration to a close:

> Already the ship was drawing ahead. And I was alone with her. Nothing! no one in the world should stand now between us, throwing a shadow on the way of silent knowledge and mute affection, the perfect communion of a seaman with his first com-mand.   (1912b, p. 143)

The Shadow-Line does take considerably longer to 'get underway'. This is due, however, to the greater complexity of what is to be established before this 'subtlest' of adventure stories can begin. The captain–narrator does not share the self-doubts of 'The secret sharer' captain, but nor is he a man fixed in certainty. He has neither an 'ideal conception' of himself nor the firmly held convictions of a Marlow. Rather, he is quite without convictions, without any firm sense of self as much as he is without any *lack* of a firm sense of self. He could be anything and anybody, and he could as easily not be! It is to the placing of this subtle state of mind that the opening sections of *The Shadow-Line* are necessarily devoted: we are to have established for us the terms within which this captain–narrator is to be 'seen'. It is for this reason that almost every character, even if minor, has some expressed or implied opinion of the captain-to-be, for Conrad is deal-ing with his capacities, with what he could become, as much as with any clearly focused present attainment. So, to Captain Kent, who has also 'been young at one time' (p. 117), he appears as a version of himself and his wish that the protagonist 'would find what I was so anxious to go and look for' (p. 118) is an acknowledgement both of the range of possibilities open to him and of the uncertainty of a search for something that cannot be specified. To John Nieven, the second engineer, it is a friendship 'turned to ashes' (p. 118) in favour, as he sees it, of the role of a married man, while the chief engineer explains the desire to quit – the only unprompted decision the captain–narrator takes until he determines against all advice to have the sick Burns back on the ship – as the first signs of the life of a 'confirmed dyspeptic' (p. 118). Such views, while reflecting the confirmed limitations of those who hold them, nevertheless are also indicative of the kinds and seriousness of the roles into which this character's uncertainty might eventually resolve. Even the 'sorrowful expression' (p. 119) of the harbour official contributes to this range of possibilities. Hamilton's judgement, too, of the 'rank outsider' (p. 122), is neither right nor wrong, but possible, especially as we look back from the captain's harsh judgements on himself at the lowest point of his voyage: 'I am shirking it, I am no good' (p. 194).

Conrad does not rely only on the opinions of other characters, however. The examples those characters present, as well as the attitudes of the protagonist himself in response to them, play an important part in establishing the reality that we see at the beginning of the story. The work-shy loafer Hamilton represents one pattern into which the unfixed narrator could drift, as does the Steward's 'Drug habit or solitary tippling' (p. 133). That he will not drift in these directions is due to the active influence of Captain Giles; and yet the narrator's attitude to Giles, from whom he receives the impression of 'mild, dreary lunacy' as he realizes that 'high professional reputation was not necessarily a guarantee of sound mind' (p. 129), is a measure of his own aggressive uncertainty in judgement. This uncertainty attempts to fix itself in finding everyone else either mad or insulting, at the same time as it is a prefiguration of the trials to come; as he says of the Steward's behaviour, 'In that twilight region between youth and maturity, in which I had my being then, one is peculiarly sensitive to that kind of insult' (p. 133). It is Giles, too, whose humanity makes him put the Steward out of *his* misery of suspense while the captain, regarding him as not 'very fit to live, anyhow' (p. 143), would have happily 'Let the beggar suffer' (p. 142), a marked contrast to his later judgement that his own 'sternness seemed criminal' (p. 167) in not telling Burns at once that he would, after all, take him back on board.

This process of providing the terms in which we are to 'see' the captain–narrator continues even after he has experienced the 'enchantment' (p. 144) of being given his first command. 'Enchantment' brings in a new phase of the narrative for 'command' casts on the stale realities of the captain's existence a fresh and 'magic' (p. 135) light. The insistence in the trip to the Harbour Office on the 'miraculous', the 'deputy-Neptune', and on 'floating' on air (pp. 140, 136), is responsible for the introduction of this strand in the narrative pattern. But 'enchantment' also prepares the way for other features of the story, and in particular for the serious doubts that are to be raised concerning the captain's capacity for self-reliance. His readiness to accept, albeit whimsically, that events may be due to the influence of magic will become his readiness to succumb to feelings of guilt, and eventually to despair and madness. We have already seen the puncturing of the newly arrived captain's complacency by the story of his predecessor. That he also immediately recognizes the second mate as 'rather a cub' (p. 154) should remind us of his own recent cubbish possibilities, and warns us, too, that the touch of the wand of command does not necessarily confer the maturity and self-reliance that the ring of the captain's words to Mr Burns suggests: 'I am here to take the ship home first of all, and you may be sure that I shall see to it that every one of you on board here does his duty to that end. This is all I have to say – for the present' (p. 161). These are words which, in the light of the crew's immense loyalty, '*Worthy of my undying regard*', and of the captain's growing sense of personal worthlessness, come to take on a harsh irony, for they are a measure of how far the newly enchanted captain still has to travel.

The emphasis on magic, though, is not confined to the captain's attitude towards his command, for we slowly realize, from his thoughts and conversations, that many of his most fundamental assumptions, even before the 'death-haunted' (p. 187) voyage begins, are rooted in a superstition not far removed from the magic with which he decorates his account of the getting of his captaincy. His first reaction to the old captain is to assume that he was 'unlucky' (p. 156), and after hearing the full story he puts him down not as mad, but as 'the victim of evil spirits' (p. 161). The same 'luck', or lack of it, is held responsible for their slow progress during the first part of the journey, a luck which has already been identified with the 'first breeze' which will not only move the ship away from the town, 'Oriental and squalid', but will blow away the 'languor' of shore habits and the fever picked up there, all that has been associated with 'the mortal coil of shore affairs' (pp. 168–9). This allusion to Hamlet's 'To be, or not to be' soliloquy suggests the crossing of quite a different kind of 'shadow-line' between life and death. The 'bar' that has just been crossed, at the mouth of the Meinam river, provides a physical reinforcement of the captain's inclination to see such a 'shadow-line'. The increasing faith in 'the clean breath of the sea' (p. 173), moreover, is matched, more disastrously, by the faith in quinine, and it is the terms in which this faith is expressed that focus for us several of the captain's major points of vulnerability.

> I believed in it. I pinned my faith to it. It would save the men, the ship, break the spell by its medicinal virtue, make time of no account, the weather but a passing worry, and, like a magic powder working against mysterious malefices, secure the first passage of my first command against the evil powers of calms and pestilence. (p. 180)

Here we have the summation of the captain's belief in a magical faith which would ward off the powers of evil. But here too is the naivety that can imagine any human endeavour as absolutely 'secure'. He takes refuge in the comforting assumption of a new era being established in his life, implied by the phrasing: 'first passage of my first command'. He thinks that 'time' in human affairs can be 'of no account'. Such beliefs are characteristic of the 'enchanted garden', the 'twilight region', in which the captain continues to have his being. He appears to believe that the disasters will be none of his making. The obtaining of the captaincy was brought about virtually on his behalf when Captain Ellis brought the command 'out of a drawer almost as unexpectedly as in a fairy tale' (p. 144). The quinine, or a good breeze, will solve all his problems for him. This is not self-responsibility, but rather a measure of the maturity he has yet to gain.

His reaction, though, to the discovery of the missing quinine, sold by his predecessor who was 'in all essentials . . . just such another man as myself' (pp. 160–1), is no more indicative of maturity than his unreasonable faith in it. He is at first 'a prey to impulse'. His 'mental disorder' is 'checked' only by catching sight of the 'wildness' of Mr Burns (p. 181). He has a 'morbid vision' of his ship 'as a floating grave' (p. 182). What he identifies as 'the creeping paralysis of a hopeless outlook' (p. 183) is as much an extreme superstition as his utter trust in the quinine, two mental extremes to match the extreme and conflicting symptoms of the fever itself: 'two of our men had been taken bad with fever in the night. One of them was burning and the other was shivering, but he thought that it was pretty much the same thing' (p. 172).

The discovery of the lost quinine is one of the major turning-points of the tale, but, far from forcing on the captain a just sense of his self-responsibility, it produces in him a mental state that can only be described as a species of madness, the very condition that he had refrained from attributing to his predecessor, but to which he had happily consigned Captain Giles. The tendency towards madness has already been established in the narrative in a number of ways. The 'claw' of the tropical fever, for example, which is seen as 'stretched . . . after us over the sea' (p. 173), should have made us pause and reflect upon the kind of visualization the captain is employing as he considers his unseen antagonist. In particular, 'claw' should remind us of Mr Burns, lying in hospital, presenting 'his case' to be taken on board 'with a sort of crazy vigour', and clasping 'his fleshless claws' (p. 166). That Mr Burns is for much of the story in the grip of a madness is not in doubt. That the captain should be seen thinking in terms which ally him with Burns must begin, even before the quinine discovery, to cast serious doubts upon his own sanity. Significantly, it is at the hospital that captain and mate are drawn closer together, for Burns's argument that 'You and I are sailors' (p. 166) is crucial in the decision to let him sail. Moreover, what Burns says is not the only persuasive factor. There is, apparently, a fascination in his very 'craziness': 'That prostrated man, with hardly strength enough to breathe and ravaged by a passion of fear, was irresistible' (p. 167). From this point, the captain and Mr Burns are increasingly frequently rendered as cases of parallel obsessions, by the juxtaposing of their respective conditions: 'his hold on life was as slender as his hold on sanity. I was oppressed by my lonely responsibilities' (p. 170). Also Burns's language begins to infect more and more the thought patterns of the narrator. And when we are brought at last to the nub of the captain's madness – ' "I feel it's all my fault," I exclaimed, "mine, and nobody else's. That's how I feel. I shall never forgive myself." ' – it is Mr Burns who instantly recognizes the delirium: ' "That's very foolish, sir," said Mr Burns fiercely' (p. 185). The complementarity of the two characters extends to their ability to see through each other's obsession while remaining convinced of the validity of their own. The one regards himself as being utterly worthless, while the other believes that the old captain is lying in wait at latitude 8° 20', another 'shadow-line', and one which picks up the tendencies to superstition and obsession in the story, and therefore suggests the shadow-line in the human mind between sanity and madness, the captain's quite as much as Mr Burns's.

That the captain is by now an irresponsibly obsessed man is stressed again and again as Conrad distinguishes the several aspects of his insanity. His repeated self-condemnation is matched by an envy of Burns, 'So near extinction – while I had to bear within me a tumult of suffering vitality, doubt, confusion, self-reproach' (p. 183), and by an idealization of the crew whom, like his prototype, the Ancient Mariner, the captain has endangered through his own lack of responsibility:

> The wastage of ill-health seemed to idealize the general character of the features, bringing out the unsuspected nobility of some, the strength of others. . . . I ask myself whether it was the temper of their souls or the sympathy of their imagination that made them so wonderful, so worthy of my undying regard.   (pp. 188–9)

As this implies, one feature of his madness is his increasing conviction of his own isolation, not, as with his predecessor, locked in his cabin with a violin, but in the midst of the comings and goings of the crew he once rashly doubted, and of whom he is now convinced he can never be worthy. And that isolation takes on, too, a more than human dimension.

The two extracts we are given from the captain's notes, or diary, are significant in that they are supposedly the words used at the time of the events rather than, like the bulk of the tale, those that have been chosen by the narrator with the benefit of hindsight. As such, they record two of the very lowest points of the journey. In one, as we have seen, the captain is brought to pass the harshest of all judgements upon himself, and one that embraces his past personality, re-interpreted in the light of a new understanding, as well as his present: 'Now I understand that strange sense of insecurity in my past' (p. 194). He is seeing himself as morally separated from the rest of his kind, and accepting as peculiar an 'insecurity' which in fact should bind him to man's common experience of youthfulness. In the other extract, however, the isolation is expressed in terms which suggest that his despair has reached literally cosmic proportions: 'The effect is curiously mechanical; the sun climbs and descends, the night swings over our heads as if somebody below the horizon were turning a crank. It is the pettiest, the most aimless! . . . and all through that miserable performance I go on' (p. 186). His sense of personal worthlessness has embraced the whole universe, the belief in life itself. Even the crew move about in silence, as if there is nothing worth saying. To the captain's obsessed vision, they are all walking reminders of his guilt. Only Mr Burns, fixed in the pattern of the madness on board, 'seems to become more substantial from day to day' (p. 186).

The one character, however, who remains fixed and strong enough to be set against the increasingly 'substantial' example of Burns, and who therefore has a crucial role of his own to play in the story, is Ransome. If the old captain is the devil for Mr Burns, Ransome, with his 'grace' (p. 169) and his selfless dedication to duty, is, for the captain–narrator, a redeeming Christ-figure. His very name recalls the 'ransom' paid by Christ for the sins of mankind

(*Matthew* 20: 28; *Mark* 10: 45). Burdened with the perpetual reminder of death in life, Ransome is peculiarly exempt from visitation either by fever or by madness. It is his presence that enables the captain to retain some hold on sanity, for he provides a focus of normality, an objective eye through which the captain can sometimes see: 'Ransome gave me one of his attractive, intelligent, quick glances. . . . It occurred to me that I had been talking somewhat in Mr Burns' manner. It annoyed me' (p. 191). When the captain begins to lose 'the notion of time', as if in punishment for having wished to disregard it, it is Ransome who can provide the prosaic information: 'It was a fortnight last Monday since we left the anchorage' (p. 192). And as the ship is beset by overwhelming blackness, when 'the end of all things would come without a sigh, stir, or murmur of any kind, and all our hearts would cease to beat like run-down clocks' (p. 195), as the captain puts it, it is Ransome who is looked to as the touchstone for responsible action: '"You think I ought to be on deck?" He answered at once, but without any particular emphasis or accent: "I do, sir"' (p. 195).

The events of this darkness, 'the darkness before creation' (p. 199), provide the final turning-point of the story. For the captain it is the darkness of the end of the world, of utter annihilation, of the universe finally running down, and as such befitting the despair in his soul, indeed the expectation gives him 'a sort of comfort' (p. 196). But, in terms of the captain's redemption, it is the 'darkness before creation' rather than the darkness of annihilation that is the significant association. While he is experiencing what he takes to be the end of all things he is in fact being brought to a new beginning, a kind of rebirth. As the darkness turns 'into water' (p. 200) and the binnacle lamps go out, the captain falls over something in the dark:

> It was an added and fantastic horror which I could not resist. The hair of my head stirred even as I picked myself up, awfully scared; not as a man is scared while his judgement, his reason still try to resist, but completely, boundlessly, and, as it were, innocently scared – like a little child.   (p. 201)

That he is able to speak of himself as an innocent, and compare himself with 'a little child' does not mean that his sense of sinfulness is past. He can still, close to the end of his narrative, speak of the 'fever-stricken men – some of them dying. By my fault.' But by then he can also declare, 'But never mind. Remorse must wait. I had to steer' (p. 208). He has gained, in other words, the perspective to know that while conscience and remorse, a sense of personal unworthiness, are appropriate concerns of a fully mature individual, nevertheless there are other equally appropriate responsibilities which are immediate and involve the action that remorse would deny. The 'seaman's instinct', in this case, that has 'survived whole in my moral dissolution' (p. 196) is able to assert itself, in strong contrast to the diary extract where he finds himself to be 'shirking it'.

At the heart of this darkness has been found a horror, not Kurtz's horror in the knowledge of the awfulness of existence, which is also a judgement, but the horror that judges or asserts nothing because it is beyond reason or language altogether. It is the spontaneous self-forgetfulness of sheer terror. Mr Burns, with a different but parallel obsession, also finds a spontaneous self-forgetfulness, but horror is replaced by laughter, equally beyond language or reason, and equally capable, here, of effecting a kind of rebirth from madness to normality. After Kurtz's horror there is no going on and even Marlow, the observer, can do so only after an 'unexciting contest' (1902, p. 150) with death. That horror is a knowledge from which there is no redemption. The captain, however, from his childlike state, has to piece together again his universe, make sense of what has happened and go on living, rather than indulging in some imagined 'comfort' from the impending 'annihilation'. We see the rebirth taking place before our eyes. He thinks of 'It', 'that Thing', 'the idea of a bear', 'the notion of Mr Burns', and only with Burns's outcry the enforced memory of the ship, the perilous situation, and the previous captain (p. 201). And as the captain remembers his responsibilities, having literally and metaphorically fallen over Mr Burns and his pattern of madness, he pushes the mate to one side ('Remorse must wait') while the breeze, the longed-for sign of hope in the universe, begins to catch at the sails.

By the end of the story, after the successful run into Singapore, the dispatching of the sick crew to hospital, and our final sight of the recovered but bizarre Mr Burns 'like a frightful and elaborate

240

scarecrow set up on the poop of a death-stricken ship, to keep the sea-birds from the corpses' (p. 212), we have been given the measure of the narrator's new maturity, the 'truth', in personal terms, that has been 'got out of' the experience. We have 'seen' him, in the words of Captain Giles, 'stand up to his bad luck, to his mistakes', and especially 'to his conscience'; he has earned the right to be drawn to Giles's side of the shadow-line:

> 'A man has got to learn everything – and that's what so many of these youngsters don't understand.'
> 'Well I am no longer a youngster.'
> 'No,' he conceded.   (p. 213)

'OUR COMMON ENEMY'

There is, however, one last lesson Conrad has to draw, one final piece of 'truth', before he can close the story. It is the parting with Ransome which points most sharply the relationship between life and death, the living and the dead, that has been an important dimension of the narrative, not least in the allusions to *Hamlet* and *The Ancient Mariner*. In the Author's note Conrad speaks of 'the intimate delicacies of our relation to the dead and to the living, in their countless multitudes' (p. 111). If Ransome is an example of a man allowing to himself what is his due, his necessity, he is also the exemplification, for the captain as for the reader, of an intimately delicate relation between life and death. Ransome's 'hard fate' may be his bad heart, and this makes him unique in the story, but what he carries 'consciously' is not a particular bit of 'bad luck' or any evil power. Rather, it is 'our common enemy' (p. 214), of which Ransome is perpetually conscious, aware that he must cope always with the presence of death in his life. In that, and in the respect and sympathy the captain feels for him, he is perhaps Conrad's most clearly defined representative of the 'solidarity' of all humanity, all those who have died, and all those who will die and who have been brought to know it.

Writing as a young man in the Preface to *The Nigger of the 'Narcissus'*, Conrad had required that the artist's 'appeal' be made 'to our sense of pity, and beauty, and pain; to the latent feeling of fellowship with all creation' (item 7). For a long while, during the first decade of the century, Conrad was at the forefront of literary modernism. With *Heart of Darkness*, *Lord Jim*, *Nostromo*, *The Secret Agent*, he was breaking new ground, and was recognized as doing so. The only other major modernist working in the novel in England was Henry James. In 1916 James died, and Conrad began to publish *The Shadow-Line*. By then, however, though Conrad's more conventional contemporaries, Galsworthy, Bennett, Wells, continued to publish with considerable popular success, the thrust of literary modernism was coming from other figures. *Sons and Lovers* had been published in 1913, *Dubliners* in 1914 and *The Rainbow* a year later. *The Shadow-Line* was preceded earlier in 1916 by *A Portrait of the Artist as a Young Man*. Opinions had changed both as to what constituted the 'visible universe' and to how one could 'see' it. The temper of the novel, too, was changing dramatically, a tone caught by Virginia Woolf when she reviewed *The Rescue* in 1920.

> When the new book comes late in the list of its author's works we must be ready to grasp some new development wrought out of the stuff of his old achievement. The worst compliment we could pay Mr. Conrad would be to talk of *The Rescue* as if it were an attempt to rewrite *Lord Jim* twenty years later. But in what direction can we expect Mr. Conrad to develop?   (Sherry, 1973, p. 332)

The question is one that has sooner or later to be asked of any great writer, and only if the writer happens to be Shakespeare – or Yeats – will there be an answer. By 1916, Conrad's time was passing. One of the achievements of *The Shadow-Line*, however, is that the 'latent' feelings 'of fellowship with all creation' are finally brought out in the full knowledge of death, not the death that faces a man when he undertakes a life of unknown dangers on the seas of the globe, or even when he looks for a shadowy enemy across the lines of trenches, but the death he knows because he is ill, or because he is getting old, is 'no longer a youngster'. *The Shadow-Line* is an act of memory in so far as Conrad is recalling events long past, and the protagonist he presents is in most respects a young man going through a young man's experience. But it is an experience and a state of mind that, he confesses, looks, like the captain's diary, 'very ghostly to my own eyes' (p. 193). In one sense the story is itself 'like . . . a scarecrow . . . to keep the seabirds from the corpses', for it preserves a piece of the past with lifelike clarity. It is also, though, the past rendered through a veil of maturity, and that maturity involves knowing that the past, and all who made it, have gone for ever. If that makes *The Shadow-Line* an old man's story, it also makes for a greater sense of 'solidarity' in the face of the fragility of 'pity, and beauty, and pain', just as it renders more poignant the tribute of 'undying regard' which the tenor of the narrative puts into a context of human transitoriness.

References

Baines, Jocelyn (1960) *Joseph Conrad: A Critical Biography*, London, Weidenfeld & Nicolson.

Blackburn, William (ed.) (1958) *Joseph Conrad: Letters to William Blackwood and David S. Meldrum*, Durham, North Carolina, Duke University Press.

Conrad, Jessie (1935) *Joseph Conrad and His Circle*, New York, Dutton.

Conrad, Joseph (1896) *An Outcast of the Islands*, London, T. Fisher Unwin (reissued in Dent's Collected Edition, 1949).

—— (1900) *Lord Jim*, Edinburgh and London, William Blackwood (reissued in Dent's Collected Edition, 1946).

—— (1902) *Youth: A Narrative and Two Other Stories*, Edinburgh and London, William Blackwood (reissued in Dent's Collected Edition, 1946).

—— (1904) *Nostromo: A Tale of the Seaboard*, London, Harper (reissued in Dent's Collected Edition, 1947).

—— (1906) *The Mirror of the Sea*, London, Methuen (reissued in Dent's Collected Edition, 1946).

—— (1912a) *A Personal Record*, New York, Harper (reissued in Dent's Collected Edition, 1946).

—— (1912b) *'Twixt Land and Sea: Tales*, London, J. M. Dent (reissued in Dent's Collected Edition, 1947).

Eliot, T. S. (1920) *The Sacred Wood*, London, Methuen.

Ford, Ford Madox (1924) *Joseph Conrad: A Personal Remembrance*, London, Duckworth.

Forster, E. M. (1936) *Abinger Harvest*, London, Edward Arnold (Penguin edn, 1967).

Garnett, Edward (ed.) (1928) *Letters from Conrad, 1895–1924*, London, Nonesuch.

Gee, J. A. and Sturm, P. J. (eds) (1940) *Letters of Joseph Conrad to Marguerite Poradowska, 1890–1920*, New Haven, Yale University Press.

Graver, Lawrence (1969) *Conrad's Short Fiction*, Berkeley, University of California Press.

Guerard, Albert J. (1958) *Conrad the Novelist*, Cambridge, Mass., Harvard University Press.

Hawthorn, Jeremy (ed.) (1985) *The Shadow-Line*, Oxford, Oxford University Press.

James, Henry (1884) 'The art of fiction', *Longman's Magazine*, IV (Sept.), pp. 502–21 (Penguin edn, 1968).

—— (1914) 'The new novel', *Times Literary Supplement*, no. 635 (10 March), pp. 133–4; no. 637 (2 April), pp. 157–8; revised, *Notes on Novelists*, 1914 (Penguin edn, 1968).

Jean-Aubry, G. (ed.) (1927) *Joseph Conrad: Life and Letters*, 2 vols, London, Heinemann.

Karl, Frederick R. (1979) *Joseph Conrad: The Three Lives*, London, Faber & Faber.

Karl, Frederick R. and Davies, Laurence (eds) (1983) *The Collected Letters of Joseph Conrad: Volume I, 1861–1897*, Cambridge, Cambridge University Press.

Lawrence, D. H. (1925) 'Morality and the novel', *Calendar of Modern Letters* (Dec.) (Penguin edn, 1971).

Leavis, F. R. (1948) *The Great Tradition*, London, Chatto & Windus (Penguin edn, 1962).

Levenson, Michael H. (1984) *A Genealogy of Modernism*, Cambridge, Cambridge University Press.

Meyer, Bernard (1967) *Joseph Conrad: A Psychoanalytic Biography*, Princeton, NJ, Princeton University Press.

Said, Edward W. (1966) *Joseph Conrad and the Fiction of Autobiography*, Cambridge, Mass., Harvard University Press.

Schwarz, Daniel R. (1982) *Conrad: The Later Fiction*, London, Macmillan.

Sherry, Norman (1966) *Conrad's Eastern World*, Cambridge, Cambridge University Press.

—— (ed.) (1973) *Conrad: The Critical Heritage*, London, Routledge & Kegan Paul.

Thorburn, David (1974) *Conrad's Romanticism*, New Haven, Yale University Press.

Watt, Ian (1960) 'Story and idea in Conrad's *The Shadow-Line*', *Critical Quarterly*, 2 (Summer), pp. 133–48; reprinted in Schorer, Mark (ed.) (1961) *Modern British Fiction: Essays in Criticism*, New York, Oxford University Press.

Watts, Cedric (1982) *A Preface to Conrad*, London, Longman.

—— (1984) *The Deceptive Text*, Brighton, Harvester Press.

Wells, H. G., Huxley, Julian and Wells, G. P. (1931) *The Science of Life*, London, Cassell (1946 edn).

Reading list

The following works, a small selection from the enormous number published, are recommended not only for their quality but because they represent a variety of approaches, biographical as well as critical, to the reading of Conrad.

BIOGRAPHY AND BACKGROUND

Karl, Frederick R. (1979) *Joseph Conrad: The Three Lives*, London, Faber & Faber. Probably now the standard biography, full and detailed presentation of a particular view of Conrad's life.

Najder, Zdzislaw (1983) *Joseph Conrad: A Chronicle*, transl. Halina Carroll Najder, Cambridge, Cambridge University Press. An unassuming and meticulously researched account with perceptive criticism of the novels.

Sherry, Norman (1972) *Conrad and his World*, London, Thames & Hudson. The best brief biography, factual, highly readable, and with over 100 illustrations.

—— (1966) *Conrad's Eastern World*, Cambridge, Cambridge University Press. Fascinating explorations into the biographical background to Conrad's fiction of the East, including *The Shadow-Line*; companion volume to *Conrad's Western World*, Cambridge, Cambridge University Press, 1971, which does the same for Africa, South America and London.

249

Watts, Cedric (1982) *A Preface to Conrad*, London, Longman. An interestingly different approach dealing with biographical and cultural background against which selected aspects of works (including *The Shadow-Line*) are examined; the best introduction available.

The Shadow-Line

Leavis, F. R. (1967) 'The Shadow-Line', in *Anna Karenina and Other Essays*, London, Chatto & Windus. Originally a lecture; argues that the story is 'central to Conrad's genius'.

Watt, Ian (1960) 'Story and idea in Conrad's *The Shadow-Line*', *Critical Quarterly*, 2 (Summer), 133–48; reprinted in Schorer, Mark (ed.) (1961) *Modern British Fiction: Essays in Criticism*, New York, Oxford University Press. A lucid and convincing exposition, the single most important item on *The Shadow-Line*.

General

Gordan, John Dozier (1941) *Joseph Conrad: The Making of a Novelist*, Cambridge, Mass., Harvard University Press; reissued 1963, New York, Russell & Russell. A significant pioneering work on Conrad dealing especially with the act and art of writing.

Graver, Lawrence (1969) *Conrad's Short Fiction*, Berkeley, University of California Press. A useful book for study of the short stories, especially in relation to Conrad's critical principles.

Guerard, Albert J. (1958) *Conrad the Novelist*, Cambridge, Mass., Harvard University Press. One of the first and still one of the most important critical works dealing with all the major fiction.

Hewitt, Douglas (1968) *Conrad: A Reassessment*, 2nd edn, London, Bowes & Bowes. Another significant and influential early work, clearly written, and dealing with the decline in Conrad's later fiction.

Leavis, F. R. (1948) *The Great Tradition*, London, Chatto & Windus; reissued 1962, Harmondsworth, Penguin. Leavis's major examination of Conrad's works alongside those of George Eliot and Henry James.

Said, Edward W. (1966) *Joseph Conrad and the Fiction of Autobiography*, Cambridge, Mass., Harvard University Press. One of the only books to deal substantially with Conrad's shorter fiction in the light of his letters over the whole range of his writing career.

Thorburn, David (1974) *Conrad's Romanticism*, New Haven, Yale University Press. Examines Conrad's major works in terms of the autobiographies, and of Romantic modes of story-telling; a positive and original book.

Notes

1 Conrad was working on *Almayer's Folly* from 1889 to 1894. He was often rather casual over dates, although here he may have in mind the period of continuous attention to the manuscript, from late 1891.

2 Conrad had sent to James a copy of *An Outcast of the Islands* in October 1896 with a long, deferential inscription. James wrote, more briefly: 'Joseph Conrad, in dreadfully delayed but very grateful acknowledgement of an offering singularly generous and beautiful.' (See also Karl, 1979, p. 382.)

3 'An outpost of progress' was in fact dropped from the April–May issue of *Cosmopolis* in order to allow the inclusion of 'Slaves of the lamp', appearing instead in the June–July number.

4 Stephen Crane (1871–1900) was a talented American novelist, poet and journalist. His best-known work, for which Conrad wrote a preface in 1923, is *The Red Badge of Courage* (1895), a novel about the American Civil War. His other works include *Maggie: A Girl of the Streets* (1893) and, referred to here, the short story 'The open boat'.

5 This essay was first published in *Outlook*, 4 June 1898, under the title 'Views and reviews. Tales of the sea'. It was published separately in 1919 in a limited edition, and included in *Notes on Life and Letters* in 1921. Captain Frederick Marryat RN (1792–1848)

produced a series of sea novels, including *Peter Simple* (1834) and *Mr. Midshipman Easy* (1836). James Fenimore Cooper (1789–1851) is probably best known for his *Leatherstocking Tales*, a series of four novels, including *The Last of the Mohicans* (1826) and *The Deerslayer* (1841), which deal with Indian and pioneer life and with the adventures of Natty Bumppo – or Hawkeye. *The Pilot* (1824) and *The Red Rover* (1828), however, are both adventure novels of the sea.

6 The original of this letter is in Polish. Aniela's translations of Conrad include *Almayer's Folly*, *An Outcast of the Islands*, *Heart of Darkness*, *Lord Jim* and *The Secret Agent*.

7 Henry James's *The Real Thing and Other Tales* was published in 1893, *The Lesson of the Master* in 1892 and *Terminations* in 1895. See also items 29 on James and 43 on Turgenev.

8 As Blackburn (1958, pp. 72–3n.) points out, there are some similarities between Buchan's story and Kipling's 'The finest story in the world', including the conflict 'between dream and reality' and the protagonists' dreams of boat travel, but these hardly justify the charges of flagrant plagiarism that Conrad makes.

9 This essay was first published as 'The enterprise of writing a book' and 'Joseph Conrad as critic' in 1925 in different journals, although it was written much earlier, in March 1904. It was included in *Last Essays* under the present title in 1926. The two books in question are Galsworthy's *The Island Pharisees* and W. H. Hudson's *Green Mansions* (both 1904).

10 This essay first appeared as a preface to *Yvette and Other Stories* (1904), translated by Ada Galsworthy, John's wife. It was privately published in 1919 and finally included in *Notes on Life and Letters*. Guy de Maupassant (1850–93) was a follower of Flaubert and is best known for his short stories. Much of his work is marked by a rather bitter irony.

11 This essay was composed by October 1904 and first published in the *North American Review*, January 1905. Like many other essays it was privately printed in a limited edition in 1919, and later included in *Notes on Life and Letters*.

12 'Books' was first published in the *Speaker*, July 1905, privately printed in 1920, and included in *Notes on Life and Letters*.

13 This review of Galsworthy's *The Man of Property* (1906) was published as 'A middle class family' in *Outlook*, March 1906, and privately printed in 1922 under the title 'John Galsworthy. An appreciation'. Conrad wrote to Galsworthy in June 1921, after the publication of *Notes on Life and Letters*, in which the essay did not appear: 'You can't imagine my disgust with myself and my consternation when I discovered that the article I wrote on you (on the occasion of *M. of P.*) has got left out of the *Life and Letters* vol. What indeed can I do but confess that I had forgotten all about it? Indeed I had forgotten the "Henry James," "Books" and a lot of others' (Jean-Aubry, 1927, II, p. 259). He promised that the article would appear in the collected edition, but while the James piece and 'Books' were inserted, 'John Galsworthy' had to wait until *Last Essays*.

14 Garnett had written: 'we may mention that the real heroine of the story is concealed in the trivial figure of Mr. Verloc's mother-in-law, whose effacement of self for the sake of her son, Stevie, is the cause contributory to his own and her daughter's ruin'; and: 'While the psychological analysis of the characters' motives is as full of acumen as is the author's philosophical penetration into life, it is right to add that Mr. Verloc and his wife are less convincing in their actions than in their meditations. There is a hidden weakness in the springs of impulse of both these figures, and at certain moments they become automata. But such defects are few' (Sherry, 1973, p. 193).

15 This, at least, is how Karl (1979, pp. 703–4 and n.) explains the letter, pointing to sentences from the review – 'It is, however, in the suggestiveness of the national background of the illusions of frustrated and blighted generations, stretching ominously like a gloomy curtain behind the figures in the drama, that the author's special triumph lies' – to account for Conrad's reaction. Sherry, however (1973, pp. 24–5, 236), finding 'no evidence of a serious charge against Conrad' in the review itself – indeed, it is for the most part highly complimentary, and concludes by comparing Conrad to Turgenev and Dostoevsky (most of it is reprinted in Sherry, 1973, pp. 237–9) – suggests that Conrad's response is to 'a letter to Conrad which has not survived' in which 'Garnett

attacked him on the grounds of putting "hatred" into the novel'.

16 The events took place in January–March 1888, not March–April 1887 (Sherry, 1966, p. 211). Bangkok and Singapore are both named (see Sherry, 1966, pp. 173–4).

17 This essay was originally a preface to Garnett's *Turgenev: A Study* (1917) and reproduced a great deal from a letter to Garnett of 2 May 1917 (Garnett, 1928, pp. 268–71). It was later included in *Notes on Life and Letters* with the present title.

18 Conrad had written to his aunt, Marguerite Poradowska, on 6 April 1892: 'you remind me a little of Flaubert, whose *Madame Bovary* I have just reread with respectful admiration' (Karl and Davies, 1983, p. 111; original in French). *Almayer's Folly* was finished on 24 April 1894.

19 Conrad's remarks, of course, are made in the light of the Russian Revolution of 1917, six years after the publication of the novel. (See especially Karl, 1979, pp. 794–5 and n. for Conrad's attitude to the Russian Revolution.)

20 F. R. Leavis (1948, p. 209) notes 'that Conrad can write shockingly bad magazine stuff – see the solemnly dedicated collection called *Within the Tides*'. The actual dedication is 'To Mr. and Mrs. Ralph Wedgwood This Sheaf of Care-Free Ante-Bellum Pages in Gratitude for their Charming Hospitality in the Last Month of Peace'. The collection contains some of Conrad's least distinguished pieces.

21 Jack London (1876–1916, real name John Griffith London) was an American writer from a poor background whose work showed the influence of Marx and Nietzsche. His active life led to novels of adventure from Alaska to the South Seas. His best-known works include *The Call of the Wild* (1903), *The Sea-Wolf* (1904) and *Martin Eden* (1909). He committed suicide in 1916.

THE SHADOW-LINE

For nautical and eastern terms, see the Glossary on pp. 271–3.

1 The letter, sent by Henry Simpson and Co., on 2 April 1889, is reprinted by Jean-Aubry (1927, I, p. 116).

2 The story was originally to be called 'First Command'. Jessie Conrad objected to the new title's suggestion of the 'valley of the shadow of death' (1935, pp. 193–4), though for Conrad, no doubt, this would have been one of its attractions.

3 Borys was born on 15 January 1898. His name, as Karl points out (1979, pp. 416–17), shows the strength of Conrad's feelings for his own Polish heritage. The Conrads' second child, born on 2 August 1906, was named John after John Galsworthy. Borys entered the British Army in September 1915 as a second lieutenant in a Mechanical Transport Corps and served at the Flanders front, with very little break, until sent home in October 1918 to recover from gassing and shellshock. Conrad had written to J. B. Pinker early in 1917 of his intention to 'cancel the dedication as I don't want the boy's name to be connected with a work of which some imbecile is likely to say: that it is a "good enough" sort of story in the Conrad manner but not a work to be put out by itself with all that pomp, etc., etc. and to be charged such a price for' (Jean-Aubry, 1927, II, p. 182).

4 As Ian Watt points out (1960, p. 141), 'The calm, of course, has its psychological parallel in the narrator's prolonged inward lethargy, a parallel to which Conrad draws attention in the epigraph; in Baudelaire's sonnet "La musique" the poet's quest for "ma pâle étoile" is most deeply menaced, not by tempests but by the "calme plat" which is the "great mirror of his despair".'

5 This is the first of the allusions to *Hamlet* in *The Shadow-Line*, indicative of the several topics the two works have in common (see the Critical commentary, pp. 228–30). Here the reference is to Hamlet's 'To be, or not to be' soliloquy, in which death is 'The undiscover'd country, from whose bourn/No traveller returns' (III. i. 79–80).

6 The superiority of sail over steam is an abiding feature of Conrad's work, and is dealt with most feelingly in *The Mirror of the Sea*. Conrad there describes himself as 'the man of the masts and sails' and goes on to contrast a journey by sail with one by steam:

> The length of passages, the growing sense of solitude, the close dependence upon the very forces that, friendly today,

257

without changing their nature, by the mere putting forth of their might, become dangerous tomorrow, make for that sense of fellowship which modern seamen, good men as they are, cannot hope to know. And, besides, your modern ship which is a steamship makes her passage on other principles than yielding to the weather and humouring the sea. She receives smashing blows, but she advances; it is a slogging fight, and not a scientific campaign. The machinery, the steel, the fire, the steam have stepped in between the man and the sea. A modern fleet of ships does not so much make use of the sea as exploit a highway. The modern ship is not the sport of the waves. Let us say that each of her voyages is a triumphant progress; and yet it is a question whether it is not a more subtle and more human triumph to be the sport of the waves and yet survive, achieving your end. (1906, pp. 71–2)

7 The British Empire at this time stretched from Canada, through substantial parts of Africa to India, Australia and New Zealand. Apart from India, Britain's possessions east of Suez included Aden, Ceylon, Burma, Malaya, North Borneo and Hong Kong. Sarawak was added in 1888, the year in which the events of *The Shadow-Line* took place. The Empire remained virtually intact until the independence movements that began after the Second World War.

8 The Suez Canal, connecting the Mediterranean to the Red Sea, had been open since 1869. The British Government had a substantial shareholding in the Egyptian-based company that ran the canal.

9 Norman Sherry (1966, pp. 205–7) identifies the *Vidar*'s owner as Syed Mohsin Bin Salleh Al Jooffree, a member of one of the largest trading families of the region. Sherry comments, 'as a Syed, or male descendant of Fatimah, daughter of Mohammed', he 'would be held in reverence and considered by the Malays to have occult powers'. His obituary notice from the *Singapore Free Press* of 22 May 1894 (printed by Sherry) confirms his failing eyesight.

10 Captain James Craig had taken command of the *Vidar* in May 1886, and first met Conrad in August 1887. The second engineer

was John Niven, and the chief engineer James Allen (Sherry, 1966, pp. 29, 31). Lawrence Graver (1969, p. 180) quotes a letter to Conrad, written in 1923, from Niven and on behalf of Craig and Allen, wishing him 'our sincere congratulations on your great accomplishments'.

11 It is not known whether John Niven was a 'fierce mysogynist [sic]'. Conrad's own attitude towards women, however, sometimes seems to have a misogynistic side, either directly, as in item 39 above, or through a narrator such as Marlow, who resents having to rely on the influence of a female relative for the securing of his post in *Heart of Darkness*, and whose tone, in *Chance* especially, is of a generally anti-feminine nature. Against this, though, we should remember Conrad's long and open correspondence with his aunt, Marguerite Poradowska, the attitudes of female friends such as Helen Sanderson, who clearly liked and trusted him, and, of course, his own marriage which survived in relative security from 1896 until his death.

12 The engineer's preoccupation has always been a particularly common explanation of physical and temperamental disorders. H. G. Wells, however, comments in *The Science of Life*:

> Nevertheless, the liver does not deserve most of the abuse that is showered upon it. It is imagined as a capricious, temperamental gland, the most delicate part of our bodies. But, in fact, most of the headaches and furred tongues and losses of appetite that we call 'bilious attacks' or 'touches of liver' have nothing to do with that organ at all; they are disorders of the stomach due to errors in eating and drinking. . . . Wherefore, if the reader is in the habit of maligning his liver we appeal to him to revise his estimate. It is an ingenious, busy organ, doing responsible work in a very exposed situation, and any irregularity in its function is far more likely to be due to the way he treats it, or has treated it in the past, than to any inherent frailty in its own constitution.   (Wells *et al.*, 1931, p. 70)

Many traditional liver pills and salts were not only habit-forming but also produced drastic purgative effects.

13 See the Critical commentary, pp. 220–4 for discussion of Conrad's views of 'truth' in art.

14 Hades is the underworld of Greek mythology. The souls of the dead were ferried across the River Styx by the boatman Charon. (In Dante's *Inferno* the river is Acheron.) In *The Mirror of the Sea* Conrad speaks of a retired sea captain's attitude towards his approaching death in terms of a journey to another world, and makes, too, the same allusion to *Hamlet* identified above: 'Was he looking out for a strange Landfall, or taking with an untroubled mind the bearings for his last Departure? It is hard to say; for in that voyage from which no man returns Landfall and Departure are instantaneous, merging together into one moment of supreme and final attention' (1906, p. 12).

15 This would no doubt be the Hotel de l'Europe, which is referred to again in *Lord Jim*. The Sailors' Home in Singapore 'was pulled down in 1922 to make room for the cinema' (Sherry, 1966, p. 20).

16 The Chief Steward was C. Phillips, a man apparently prominent in temperance work in Singapore. Conrad wrote of him to W. G. St. Clair in 1917: 'He was a meagre wizened creature, always bemoaning his fate, and did try to do me an unfriendly turn for some reason or other' (Sherry, 1966, pp. 183, 317). For Hamilton, see n. 35 below.

17 Conrad wrote to St. Clair: 'My Captain Giles was a man called Patterson, a dear, thick, dreary creature with an enormous reputation for knowledge of the Sulu Sea' (Sherry, 1966, p. 317). The Solo – or Sulu – Sea lies between the Philippine Islands and North Borneo. It takes its name from the Sulu archipelago. The figure of the pilot, as at the beginning of *Heart of Darkness*, is one normally associated with reliability in Conrad's fiction.

18 'Tiffin' apparently originated in English colloquial use of 'tiffing' from the verb 'to tiff', meaning to sip or take a little drink. It then became specialized in Anglo-Indian usage to mean a light meal taken at around midday, luncheon (*OED*).

19 See the Critical commentary, pp. 229–30, for discussion of the use made of providence in *The Shadow-Line*.

20 This description of Captain Giles is one way of conveying an impression of his impenetrable wisdom: his 'big shiny head' (p. 123)

holds more than any other living man could grasp. But Giles's knowledge of these physical features of navigation also implies an equally impenetrable wisdom concerning the intricacies of human nature and experience. (See also the Critical commentary, p. 228.)

21 Palawan is a long island stretching between the Philippines and North Borneo. It separates the Solo Sea from the China Sea.

22 Queen Victoria's first jubilee celebrations took place in 1887.

23 Captain Henry Ellis, Master-Attendant at Singapore, also appears in *Lord Jim*, 'Falk' and 'The end of the tether' under the name of Eliott. It was he who had given Conrad the command of the *Otago* shortly before his own retirement. He apparently made a strong impression on Conrad, and was well known as a port 'character'. (See also Sherry, 1966, pp. 195–201.)

24 The Steward's behaviour here with its 'animal manner' is a foretaste of the loss of human dignity in the mind of the captain and, especially, in the behaviour of Mr Burns. For Burns's own depiction in animal terms, see pp. 166 and 201. Biblically, the Philistines inhabited southwest Palestine and were the enemies of the Israelites. Popularly, and especially since Matthew Arnold used the term in *Culture and Anarchy* in 1869, a Philistine is someone indifferent or hostile to cultural pursuits.

25 Another echo of *Hamlet*, here of Hamlet's lines, 'There's a divinity that shapes our ends,/Rough-hew them how we will' (V. ii. 10–11).

26 The expression 'surveying . . . his own handiwork' suggests a resemblance between Giles and the God who created and 'saw that it was good' (*Genesis* 1: 10), as if Giles is himself an agent of providence in the captain's life. Giles's 'big, paternal fist' of a few lines later would seem to reinforce this resemblance.

27 The allusion is to Hamlet's lines, 'How weary, stale, flat, and unprofitable/Seem to me all the uses of this world!' (I. ii. 133–4).

28 'Magic' forms a strong thread in this story, from the 'enchanted garden' of the opening (p. 116), though employed more for the psychological insights it reveals into the captain than for any real belief on Conrad's part in such powers. See the Critical commentary, p. 234 ff. for further discussion. In this connection,

see also what Conrad has to say about fairy stories in item 32 above.

29 The head shipping-master is treated more fully in *Lord Jim*, where he is described as 'so sympathetic and easily upset', and is also named: 'Archie Ruthvel had just come in, and, as his story goes, was about to begin his arduous day by giving a dressing-down to his chief clerk' (1900, pp. 37–8).

30 Neptune was the Roman god of the seas. Like most of the gods he was traditionally depicted as bearded. Neptune, however, was particularly distinguished by his trident (see p. 137).

31 Conrad's image is, of course, appropriate for the sailing ship, whose sails would be furled while in port.

32 An 'aureole' is a halo, bestowed upon the blessed once they have entered into heaven. It also has the meaning of an extra degree of blessedness granted to the souls of martyrs and virgins, and there-fore denotes a second circle to their halos.

33 Captain Giles is again suggested as being an agent of providence, if not God himself, in so far as he is 'looking after' part of the world, not merely the part he carries in his head, consisting of reefs, headlands and coasts (p. 122), but also in the disposing of rewards among the morally deserving. It is a measure of Giles's importance as a pattern of humane sympathy that he relieves the Steward from his agony, and of the cap-tain's immaturity that his tone here is one of mockery. He, of course, has just described his own surprise and indignation as being characteristic of his youthful side of the shadow-line (p. 142).

34 The shaping power of myth and of tales of magic is particularly evident here. The captain, blessed with unexpected good luck, seizes upon the rags-to-riches pattern of Cinderella, in which the heroine's true deserts are rewarded by an all-knowing and benevolent providence-figure without the necessity for action of any kind by Cinderella other than being herself. Life, for a while, seems simple and ordered, though full of surprises. Having achieved his command, the fairy-tale captain should 'live happily ever after'. See also the Critical commentary, pp. 234–6.

35 In the version of these events that appears in 'The end of the tether', Hamilton is actually offered the job first but turns it down. Sherry (1966, p. 214) argues:

> there was a C. Hamilton in the East who is mentioned in the *Singapore and Straits Directory*, 1883, the year of Conrad's first visit to Singapore. In 1883 Hamilton was first mate of the S.S. *Martaban*. There is no way of determining, since most marine records have been destroyed, whether this was the Hamilton of Conrad's novels, but First Officer Hamilton would know the sea route from Singapore to Bangkok very well, for the regular run of the *Martaban* was from Singapore to Bangkok. Therefore, if Hamilton had left the *Martaban* by 1887 the Master-Attendant would probably have offered him the command of the *Otago* first. This must remain speculation, but certainly the grounds on which the command is refused in 'The end of the tether' might have been considered valid ones by a sailor accustomed to a steamship. The Master-Attendant's outburst: 'Afraid of the sails. Afraid of a white crew. Too much trouble. Too much work', could be applied to the *Otago*, which was a sailing ship and which carried a white crew.

36 For the first time it is seriously suggested that the captain has some tendency to madness. That the suggestion comes from the reliable Captain Kent, rather than from Giles, whose sanity the captain has himself doubted (p. 129), gives the idea more force and startles him into attentiveness. He is being forced to see for a moment his new, fairy-tale life in terms of his personality and behaviour in the old.

37 Conrad did travel to Bangkok aboard the *Melita*, leaving Singapore late on 19 January 1888 and arriving on 24 January. The captain's name was Morck, according to the *Singapore Free Press*, and Moretz in the *Bangkok Times* (see Sherry, 1966, pp. 216–17).

38 Bangkok, the capital of Siam, is situated near the mouth of the Mei-nam – or Menam – river. The 'bar' is the bar of sand which runs across the mouth of the river. Unlike Singapore, which had been part of the British Empire since 1819, Bangkok was capital

of an independent country. It is described in some detail at the beginning of 'The secret sharer'.

39 The *Otago* 'was built in Glasgow in 1869 by A. Stephen and Sons, her tonnage was 367 tons gross and 346 tons nett; and her measurements were 147 ft. by 26 ft. by 14 ft.' (Sherry, 1966, p. 321). Conrad also pays tribute to his only command, and to his first mate 'Mr. B——', in *The Mirror of the Sea* (1906, pp. 18–20). As described here, the *Otago* is made to stand for that sense of harmony and of mastery over time that is found to be absent from human affairs.

40 Another Shakespearian echo, though one that is also common usage, this time of *The Tempest* (IV. i. 155, 156–7). For a moment, 'deep physical satisfaction' (p. 152) is found to coincide with the captain's dream world. Prospero's 'insubstantial pageant' and 'We are such stuff/As dreams are made on' are appropriately suggested at the beginning of the experience which is to bring the captain to question the reality of the world around him and the validity of his own perceptions. The same allusion is found on page 138.

41 The suggestion is that there is a soul made up of all those who have commanded ships, from which inspiration descends upon the initiate. The captain, who of course has no real sense of the actual 'long days' and 'anxious moments' ahead of him, will presumably himself expect to add to the 'composite soul' by his anticipated fulfilment of the role of commander.

42 'Dynasty' implies not only a line of succession but a sacred tradition in which divine approval is passed from one incumbent to the next. This sense is picked up in 'blessed simplicity' later in the sentence, and in the captain's remarks about hereditary kingship and 'the Grace of God' on p. 160.

43 For Conrad's relations with Charles Born, the original for Mr Burns, see the introduction, p. 17. Apart from *Lord Jim*, Born also appears in 'Falk', 'A smile of fortune' and, in a rather extreme vein, in 'The secret sharer'.

44 The account of Captain John Snadden given here is similar to that found in 'Falk'. As Sherry shows (1966, pp. 218–27), Snadden did become ill at sea, dying, on 8 December 1887, of

heart disease (a condition which Conrad preserves in *The Shadow-Line*, but significantly transfers to the living man Ransome). Snadden was also buried at sea, though probably not at the mouth of the Gulf of Siam. Moreover, Snadden and Born seem to have been on good terms and Snadden, by all accounts, seems to have been a competent and conscientious captain. However, in Sherry's words, 'the story Conrad gives of the previous captain's character and last days is more effective than the true one in that the contrast between the old master and the new is more striking. It also serves to complicate the predicament of the new master in taking over his first command' (1966, p. 227).

45 Haiphong is in what used to be North Vietnam, a sea port in the Gulf of Tongking.

46 That the 'female' is seen as resembling a medium or fortune-teller is appropriate to the captain's own sense of his good fortune. Indeed, that sense may well be directing his interpretation of her appearance. He, too, perhaps, would find himself attracted by such a woman, and concludes even from her photograph that 'she was striking'. This, of course, draws him unconsciously closer to his predecessor.

47 'Sortilege' is divination, here probably her magical powers over men as much as any actual powers of foretelling.

48 From Haiphong to Hong Kong is around 500 miles.

49 The growing madness of the old captain is the first real example of insanity in the story, although the topic has been alluded to several times. As such, it provides the pattern of breaking up which both Burns and the captain–narrator are to follow.

50 Pulo Condore is an island off the southern tip of Vietnam, then known as Cochin China. It is some 160 miles due south of Saigon.

51 Along with the Ancient Mariner, the legend of the Flying Dutchman is never very far from the surface in *The Shadow-Line*. Mr Burns's account of his late captain already shows the features of *his* character that gradually develop into an obsessive madness.

52 See n. 42.

53 John Carlson, the *Otago*'s cook and steward, did die in hospital in Bangkok, and of cholera, but eight days before Conrad arrived

(Sherry, 1966, pp. 230–2). It seems likely that Conrad took over some of the accounts of his condition and used them in describing the illness of Mr Burns, but the disease from which Burns and the rest of the crew suffer is apparently malaria, for which quinine was then the standard treatment.

54 There is no clear original for Ransome, though Sherry suggests Pat Conway, who left the *Otago* at Singapore too ill to sign the crew agreement. He apparently received more pay than normal, perhaps on account of undertaking extra duties (the *Otago* seems to have sailed from Bangkok without being able to obtain a replacement cook/steward after the death of Carlson). There is no evidence, however, of Conway's suffering from heart trouble. (See Sherry, 1966, p. 248.)

55 The 'mortal coil of shore affairs' echoes Hamlet's 'To be, or not to be': 'For in that sleep of death what dreams may come,/When we have shuffled off this mortal coil,/Must give us pause' (III. i. 66–8). The allusion brings together suggestions of different kinds of reality, different dimensions of existence. Shore life is associated with everyday reality and with mortality, but the freedom of the seas, including an apparent freedom from the constraints of man's mortality, also brings contact with and fear of the unknown.

56 At this point in the original manuscript is a long passage dealing with the captain's dream of the Bull of Bashan, roaring and striking with his hoof, and of the apparition of the late captain, which turns out to be the seaman who has come to wake him. (Hawthorn, 1985, pp. 139–40, includes the passage as a note; Graver, 1969, pp. 182–3, also prints it.)

57 Cape Liant is close to Bangkok. Like the island of Koh-ring, mentioned later (which is also a significant feature in 'The secret sharer'), Cape Liant is one of the fixed details against which the tantalizingly slow progress of the ship is measured as it edges closer to the line of madness, latitude 8° 20′ . It is also, perhaps, one of the 'headlands' which occupies the brain of the all-knowing Captain Giles.

58 The actual letter, from a William Willis, is now in the Keating Collection at Yale. As Graver points out (1969, p. 187), Conrad

has added an air of intimacy to the relationship with the doctor, for the original begins merely 'Dear Sir'.

59 For Koh-ring, see n. 57. Triton was the son of Poseidon (Roman Neptune), usually depicted with a dolphin's tail. He blows a conch, which creates the ocean's roar. Generally, the name is applied to the attendants of Poseidon. A triton amongst minnows is a giant amongst lesser creatures. The 'fatal circle' suggests a more deadly kind of magic than the benevolent fairies that brought the captain his command. It goes with Burns's seeing the old captain as a devil, lying in wait for the ship (for example, p. 203).

60 Both the Flying Dutchman and the Ancient Mariner are glanced at here, combining, as Karl points out (1979, p. 253), a curse on captain and ship with a curse on the entire crew.

61 The captain's diary as a literary device does serve to bring the narrator back to the 'reality', and especially to the psychological reality, of the events he is recalling after a gap of some years, but it is not known whether Conrad himself kept a diary at any time during his sea career. This and the later extract are unlikely to be authentic.

62 The captain's state of mind here recalls the attitudes expressed by Conrad in his 'knitting machine' letter to Cunninghame Graham (item 13 above), but also Coleridge's 'The Sun came up upon the left,/Out of the sea came he!/And he shone bright, and on the right/Went down into the sea' (*The Ancient Mariner*, Part I, stanza 7).

63 Punch, of the Punch and Judy shows, is of Roman or Italian origin. His characteristic features are his diminutive stature, hook nose and chin, hunchback and protruding stomach and breast.

64 Again, Conrad's words recall Coleridge's: 'The many men, so beautiful!/And they all dead did lie:/And a thousand thousand slimy things/Lived on; and so did I!' (*The Ancient Mariner*, Part IV, stanza 4).

65 The 'King' of Jerusalem was in fact King of all Israel. After the death of Solomon and the division of the kingdom in 938 BC, Jerusalem was under the King of Judah.

66 As indeed happens in Conrad's story 'Falk'.

67 The captain's state of mind makes the passing of time seem of no account, or rather, his memory, which would normally be the register of passing time, is unable to function. It is appropriately in the pages of the diary, rather than during the act of narrative recall, that this breakdown occurs.

68 Another echo of *The Ancient Mariner*: the corpses of the crew are moved by 'angelic spirits' to sail the becalmed ship:

> They groaned, they stirred, they all uprose,
> Nor spake, nor moved their eyes;
> It had been strange, even in a dream,
> To have seen those dead men rise.
>
> The helmsman steered, the ship moved on;
> Yet never a breeze up blew;
> The mariners all 'gan work the ropes,
> Where they were wont to do;
> They raised their limbs like lifeless tools –
> We were a ghastly crew.
>
> (Part V, stanzas 10–11)

69 Although the Titans were a race of Giants in Greek mythology, the children of Uranus (the sky) and Gaea (the earth), the allusion is appropriate in that they were overthrown by the next generation of gods, Zeus and the Olympians, and survived only as shadows of their former selves.

70 See the Critical commentary, pp. 239–41, for discussion of Conrad's use of this image.

71 The animal imagery, noted with reference to the Steward's 'lair' (n. 24), finds its fulfilment in the captain's momentary but real belief in the sudden presence of an actual animal on board his ship, or in his mind.

72 Coleridge, again, describes the sudden and unexpected moving forwards of the ship:

> The sun, right up above the mast,
> Had fixed her to the ocean:
> But in a minute she 'gan stir,

With a short uneasy motion –
Backwards and forwards half her length
With a short uneasy motion.

Then like a pawing horse let go,
She made a sudden bound:
It flung the blood into my head,
And I fell down in a swound.

(*The Ancient Mariner*, Part V,
stanzas 21–2)

73 The captain's fear, expressed on p. 190, has been brought about,
though not by the actual death of the crew.
74 See the Critical commentary, pp. 241–3, for discussion of the
ending of *The Shadow-Line*.

Glossary of nautical and eastern terms

all aback   To have the sails pressing against the masts with the wind from the front.

anchor-watch   The group that is on watch while the ship is at anchor.

Archipelago   Here the Malay Archipelago; generally a sea clustered with islands.

awning   Part of the deck of a ship that is covered over.

bar   A bank or shoal across the mouth of a harbour or river.

baulk   A squared timber beam.

belaying pin   A pin to which ropes would be made fast.

bells   A bell would be rung after each half-hour of a watch; thus 'seven bells' is three and a half hours into 'the forenoon watch'.

binnacle   The box in which the ship's compass is kept.

bluejackets   Sailors in the Navy, as opposed to the Merchant Service.

bows   The forepart of the ship.

braces   Ropes for squaring (making at right angles to the mast) the yards (beams on which the sails are spread) of the ship.

bulkheads   The partitions separating the interior parts of the ship.

capstan   A revolving machine turned by means of bars so that a cable may be wound in; the 'after-capstan' is that closer (more 'aft') to the stern (rear) of the ship.

chain sheet   A chain attached to a lower corner of a sail for changing its position.

cleat A wedge; pieces of wood attached to various parts of the ship for fastening ropes.

cock-billed Anchors that are cock-billed are suspended in preparation for dropping – ready to be 'Let go' (see Conrad, 1906, pp. 13–23).

companion-way The staircase from the deck to a cabin.

compressors Iron levers for checking or stopping the anchor chain-cable as it runs out.

coolies Properly, Indian or Chinese labourers under contract in a foreign country; also European name for hired native labourers in India or China.

coxswain A boat or ship's steersman.

forecastle Below deck at the forward part of the ship.

galley The ship's kitchen.

gharry A hired vehicle, rather like a bathing-machine drawn by a horse.

half-cable A cable-length is approximately 200 yards; to heave (or haul) in 'to half-cable' is thus to wind in half the length of the anchor cable.

halyards (also **halliards**) Ropes for raising or lowering a sail or yard (beam on which the sail is spread).

hatches Coverings to the hatchways leading below deck.

helm The ship's steering apparatus.

Kalashes Malay seamen.

leech-line The leech is the side edge of the sail, with lines (ropes) attached.

lobby A smaller apartment or antechamber to the main cabin.

mainyard The lower yard (beam) on the mainsail.

man-of-war A warship.

mizzenmast The mast nearest the stern (rear) of a three-masted sailing ship.

peon A native messenger.

poop A higher portion of the deck at the stern (rear) of the ship.

punkah A large fan, mechanically operated or pulled.

quarter-deck Part of the upper deck between the stern and after-mast usually restricted to officers.

Rajah A Malay chief or dignitary.

Red Ensign   Also known as the Red Duster, until 1864 the flag of one of the three squadrons of the British Navy (the Red, the White and the Blue); it then became the flag of the British Merchant Marine.

ringbolt   A bolt with a ring through a hole at one end.

roads (also **roadstead**)   A piece of water near the shore where ships may ride at anchor.

scuppers   Holes in a ship's sides to let water off from the deck.

sextant   An instrument for taking angular measurements (here the angle of the sun), based on a graduated arc of a sixth of a circle.

shore-fasts   Lines holding a ship to the quay.

spars   Generally all the masts, yards, etc., of the ship.

square   To make the yards (beams on which the sails are spread) at right angles to the mast.

steam-pinnace   A tender boat to a man-of-war.

stern-sheets   Originally the flooring boards at the aft of a boat, later referring to the seats provided there.

sternway   The backward motion of a ship.

stevedore   A man employed in the loading and unloading of ships.

taffrail   The rail around the ship's stern.

topmast   The second mast of a ship, fore of the mainmast.

trim   Make ready for sailing, adjust the inclination or balance of the sails.

trucks   Wooden blocks through which the ropes pass.

windlass   A machine employing wheel and axle and used for raising (or weighing) the anchor.

yards   Beams on which the sails are spread.

zenith   The highest point of the heavens, directly above the observer.